Universal Jungle: Dark Sentinels

M.Q. Abdullah

ISBN: 978-0-9988924-1-2
ISBN-13: 978-0-9988924-1-2

DEDICATION

I would like to dedicate this book to everyone that believed in me. Thank you for your support.

CONTENTS

ACKNOWLEDGMENTS

I would like to thank my lovely wife. Without her this would not be possible.

PLUS 0 HOURS
PROLOG
DEEP BLACK, NUBIAN SYSTEM
ARRIVAL

January 7, 2575 galactic standard date at 2:15 galactic standard time the Poveen entered the Nubian System with the use of an Einstein-Rosen bridge. That point of space time was only occupied by trace radiation leftover from the Big Bang. The simple particles were brushed aside from the force of the of the expanding passage. Moments later 14 Poveen capital cruisers entered the human controlled space 53.7 AU from the Nubian sun. An AU is short for Astronomical Unit and one AU represents the distance of the Earth from sun in the Sol System.

The standard cruiser measured ten kilometers in length and 2500 meters in height and width. A massive sphere began 5 thousand meters from the front of the spacecraft, continued for 3000 meters to the rear. The spherical section of the starship was the heart of the Poveen Cruiser and provided all means of propulsion and power with the use of a controlled singularity. It protruded outward from the triangular shaped hull creating the signature look of all Poveen craft. The front of the ship curved from the rigged triangular shape that dominated the hull to a point.

The Poveen were the second alien race humanity encountered during the Great Push Era and was the reason for the stoppage of the age of expansion. Humans and Poveen have engaged in regular combat. The Poveen, unlike the six other alien races humanity has contact with, in the same way as other species. They evolved from scavengers, if they see something unprotected or not well protected they tend to attack it and steal all that is valuable. In the mind of the Poveen they merely took something that you didn't want because its lack of protection denoted its lack of value.

The United Planets of Humanity Armed Forces regard them as the number one outside threat to human systems located near Poveen occupied space. The problem for humanity is that the Poveen are more advanced than humans and most military engagements concluded with defeat. They have technology and capabilities that humans could only dream to have. That advantage is the only reason why the UPHAF hasn't launched an all-out attack on the Poveen civilization.

The Poveen entry into the system did not go undetected. Ten thousand S-C100 sensor units, or S7s, littered the system in a comprehensive detection disc. The United Planets of Humanity Armed Forces deployed the Sentry 7 advanced detection grid in the Nubian System five years prior. The S7 units were autonomous installations equal distant from each other around the system. Each unit was 40 meters tip to tip vertically and horizontally. The unit took the appearance of two pyramids attached at each base. The design, carbon composite hull, and subspace dampening field made the units extremely hard to detect and destroy. With both passive and active sensor systems, the S7 units provided the ability to observe the entire system with minimal light lag providing an almost real time assessment.

Every S7 unit has a standard EM communications suite if necessary, but the true value of the S7 is the quantum entanglement communication technology. The S7s can communicate real time with Ogun Station. This breaks the reliance on speed of light detection systems and communications. The cost of this benefit is the corresponding sister units that need to be housed on the planet for each S7 unit needs and equally sized "sister" unit on Ogun Station for the system to work. The communication center of Ogun Station is extensive. Not only does it currently house 10 thousand sister units, 500 backup S7s and sister units, 25 space station units, and 100 ship units it also has room for 10,000 more. In total the communication units, corresponding power plant, and computer system capable of making sense of it all encompassed 6.5 million sq meters.

The massive investment in credits and material paid off. Without the grid the light from the ER bridge creation and reflected off the hulls of the Poveen Cruisers would take seven hours for the light to the reach the Combat Information Center, Ogun Station, on Nubia instead of the 12 minutes it would now take. Critical time that they needed to determine the intent of the Alien craft now in the system.

PLUS 15 MINUTES
COMMAND CORPS VICE COMMANDER
PRIYANKA KAHN
OGUN STATION, NUBIA
THE CALM

Vice Commander Priyanka Kahn reviewed her weekly assignments diligently executing what she could by herself before preparing intricate responses to the more in-depth problems before relaxing. Kahn, the System Vice Commander, was second in command of all joint military operations in the Nubian System. She was one of four Command Corps officers assigned to the system and it was her turn to serve her weekly duty at Ogun Station. The officers rotated this duty in one week cycles with an additional cycle when they all served together to solve major issues, plan future projects, and build on the system's progress.

The Vice Commander didn't mind the weekly assignments because it reminded her of her early deployments. She spent the first 28 of 35 years of service in the Astro Corps. It was the branch of the military tasked with assaulting or defending space stations, low gravity planets or moons, and breaching hostile solar systems. Lengthy readiness deployments on spacecraft and defensive engagements on or near space stations meant that an Astros were served almost exclusively in tight quarters. Rarely were you alone or even possessed the ability to be alone. The absence of that sometimes made her uneasy like she was lost or late for something.

Her command cabin was meters from the main combat information center. It was truly a home away from home. The living quarters had a large living upon entering and a dining area farther into the space along the left wall. On the right side, an open concept kitchen greeted toward the entrance while a bedroom with a master bathroom was deeper into the space. A far wall mimicked a window and showed the real-time view of Ogun City and the ocean. The living unit was roughly 1500 square feet. It provided a suitable place to sleep, eat, and work while off-duty.

After finishing the last of shift work Kahn ate a meal prepared by the artificial human chef and took a long hot relaxing shower. A white towel covered her head drying her hair while grey cotton sweat pants and a tank top completed her comfort agenda. Typically, the red couch would provide another hour of relaxation before she headed into her room for sleep. The days on Nubia were roughly 44 hours long and a week consisted of three days. During the weekly on site assignment command corps officers serve 11 shifts of 12 hours leaving her with another 11 hours before she was required to be on duty.

Kahn checked the personal correspondence waiting in queue via N-32 neural implant. During her shift two of her children and one grandchild sent her vids. Nothing is cuter than a 5-year-old rambling about her day at school or more prideful than your daughter being named the number one CEO on the planet Galileo. She responded to the messages with congratulations and a special song for her granddaughter. Like any proud mother that believed she had the best children in the universe. She filled her friend's newsfeeds and updates with vid articles on her daughter's success on all the popular social media networks in the Nubian system and universe even if she used that social media site wrong. A Kahn was number one and everyone was going to know about it.

Family time was replaced by play time once she felt her posts reached maximum saturation. While on duty she received messages from the 3 of her little boy toys. Each one different and exciting in their own way and she loved play and banter. The age difference didn't concern her because she wasn't trying to lock herself into another 50-year marriage commitment. This passed for fun and excitement while planet side. Fun she couldn't have if trapped for years once more on one of those damn spacecraft. At the age of 115 Kahn wasn't slowing down for anyone. If 150-year-old men could marry 25-year-old women without stigma she was going to date a 25-year-old too.

Kahn was married for 50 of the 52 years she taught on a college campus filled with young athletic and handsome men. It was a self-inflicted torture but she remained faithful the entire time because she valued commitment. After the 50-year marriage commitment concluded Kahn took full advantage of the body preserved by the life extension DNA augmentation provided by the United Planets of Humanity Armed Forces in return for her service at the age of 18. An unaugmented human had a natural life span between 135 and 150 years of age depending on the quality of nanobots they had. A DNA augmented human could live to 350 if they received the treatment early enough.

Kahn signed up at 18 years of age, the earliest you can sign up, but didn't start active duty until 80. Though the augmentation lengthened the life of humans it did not stop some of its functions. Women went into menopause between the age of 60 and 70. The overwhelming need to populate the planets terraformed in the Great Push was pounded into the social construct. Humanity needed continued growth and progress for protection against the larger and more advanced alien civilizations they encountered. Humanity responded to the challenge by doubling roughly every seven years. The population of the Human Sphere was now 817 Billion souls and was poised to reach 1 trillion in the next two or three years.

This occurred because women that signed up for United Planets of Humanity service had two options of service. The first commitment was to join the military and serve for 50 years after you went into menopause or your marriage commitment was concluded. The second form of service was that of a Surrogate Officers. Surrogate Officers were the technical term but everyone called them breeders. When the applicant gave birth to ten children provided to them by the United Planets of Humanity

Colonization Authority the commitment was considered fulfilled and service in the military would not be required. Kahn choose military service over insemination because she wanted children of her own.

Women could serve right away if they deserved but most of them choose delayed service. Men, on the other hand, had to serve the commitment upon signing. This made for distinct dynamic not present anywhere else in society. The bulk of the woman joined the service with a lifetime of experience, education, and refinement with a median age of 70 while the median age of men that joined the service was 27 though both groups looked almost the same age since most women signed at 18.

Before active duty Kahn had five children with her husband. She married the love of her life, a Reggae artist, at the age of 30. She taught students the lessons of the great push and the failures of early space warfare at Walker Military College at Light University on Nubia. At the age of 80 her marriage commitment concluded and she reported for duty. Her once husband, the term for a husband or wife that fulfilled the marriage commitment without resigning, started a 15-year tour with his band around the Human Sphere.

She moved quickly up the ranks of the Astro Corps. As Captain of the Dreadstar Fury Falcon she bravely led her starship into multiple engagements with pirates. Kahn hunted them without mercy. Slavers and human traffickers had no place in the human sphere and her crusade to destroy them was one of legend in the Astro Corps. The elite military record provided the reasoning for the Command Corps to offer her a commission. She seized on the opportunity and 8 years later Kahn was the second in command of the military forces in the Nubian system. The dynamic commander has fifteen years left on her commitment to the service and is poised to command a system of her own before she is finished.

After sending copious amounts of emoji's and sexually suggestive messages to her boy toys she still laid on the couch with her hands behind her head making an arm pillow. Carmel golden tanned feet rested on the arm of the couch as the French manicured toes wiggled to the beat of the reggae music created by her once husband. He sung about the most beautiful woman in the world, his world, which was her at the time. It always made her feel like the first time they met injecting life and emotion into her body like no one else could. Occasionally she would break into audible song or a violent head nod only to have one of her breast fall out of unsupportive tank top stopping the session. The volume of the music forced her nanobots into repair mode as her eardrums took damage from the volume but as Kahn always told visitors to her room, "if you don't fell the music, you don't have music".

The jam session ended when she received a ping from System Space Quasar Rodriguez, the highest-ranking officer on duty. A second later the automated yellow alert dominated HUD in her field of vision activated by her implant. All personal correspondence and links quickly shut down as the military network moved into combat mode.

The Vice Commander accepted access via the secure military network directly into her implant when all the other connections were confirmed closed. The System Quasar Rodriquez dominate her field of view. Rodriquez's face was stern and not at all apologetic. Kahn picked up on her body language and sat up. This wasn't a drill or an annoying interruption from a junior officer. The pink eyes of Rodriquez focused with intent as her purple skin crunched above her eyes.

"Sir, we have a Poveen incursion. We are tracking 14 Poveen Cruisers on 4…no make that 5 vectors. I am requesting your presence on the command deck," asked Rodriquez.

"Request accepted. I will be on deck momentarily. Prepare protocols," responded Kahn as she jumped from the couch and quickly ran to the door in excitement. Information from the various stations flooded her field of view. Quickly she realized that going to the command deck in a tank top that had two straps holding on for dear life and tight sweat pants would not be becoming of an officer of her rank. With tremendous speed, she moved to the small closet. In under a minute she was leaving the housing unit in the black uniform worn by all members of Command Corps.

The CIC was bustling with activity and movement as the officers of the deck dropped the daily maintenance and activity to ready the stations for any contingency. The ceiling and the south scenic wall slowly faded to black to highlight augmented reality readouts of the system. At the front of the room a 3-dimensional representation of the solar system dominated the wall. All the military assets of the system were highlighted in a blue color and the 14 enemy ships were highlighted by red triangles.

With confidence Vice Commander Kahn walked onto the deck of the CIC. She moved with grace and purpose to the rectangular station hub in the middle of the room to join Quasar Rodriquez and General Okafor. Before reaching the station, she stopped and spoke to the officers on duty. "This is why we prepare so hard people. Stay calm and work the problems. Use your training and you will be fine. Quasar Rodriquez, what is the situation?"

PLUS 18 MINUTES
SPACE COMMAND QUASAR
VALERIE RODRIGUEZ
OGUN STATION, NUBIA
DISCOVERY

Quasar Rodriguez stood in the command position of the rectangular station hub in the center of the CIC on the command deck. The table top black smart glass ringed the rectangular table. It could form 14 individual stations and provide visual information to complement the information received straight to the brain of the officer that used the station. Quasar Rodriguez used station at the head of the rectangular desk.

Rodriguez's lavender fingers plotted along the glassy surface organizing the starship deployment roster for the next month. Pink eyes scanned the reports providing the status of repairs on vessels that recently entered the system after an engagement and the status of the eight star carriers under construction at the Barca Staryards. Rodriguez was physically short with petite body structure but mentally she was a giant. Dark purple hair pushed the limits of length regulations so she pulled it behind her ears. It still touched the top of her dark grey Space Command uniform and she knew she would soon have to cut it.

Each branch of the United Planets of Humanity Armed Forces was represented in the CIC. The east wall had 14 work stations with 7 along the wall and 7 facing the center of the room. The Logistics Corps and Orbital

Guard branches both manned four of the stations while the remaining six where manned by Nubian Planetary Command.

The northern wall had 12 stations with six facing the wall and six facing the center of the room all manned by Space Command. The west wall also had 14 stations and was a mirror image of the other side. That wall was operated by the Meteor Corps, Comet Corps, and Astro Corps. The Meteor and Comet Corps both occupied 4 stations while the Astro Corps manned the final 6.

Two doors to the hallway bookended the 6 stations against the north while two doors lined the east and west wall after the 4th station along each wall respectfully. The middle of the room was dominated by a long rectangular workstation hub meant to be used by the command corps and the system commanders during combat situations. The East hallway led to a series of meeting rooms, areas, and advantaged communication centers. The west door led to the Sixteen onsite housing units used by the Command Corps and the systems generals and quasars.

Rodriguez fawned over the latest military starships that entered the system after a skirmish with Poveen forces 2 months prior. Three of the support stars were damaged in the conflict and they entire constellation bridged back for repairs. The UPHAF designated all military spacecraft stars. A collection of 1 to 20 stars are considered a constellation. A grouping of 1 to 5 constellations is considered a battle cluster. A super cluster consists of 3 to 5 Battle clusters. 1 to 3 battle clusters formed a numbered galaxy. Humanity was currently protected by 17 deep space numbered galaxies and 27 system galaxies.

She commanded the Nubian System Galaxy and was trying to find a good reason the travel to Barca Staryards to get a tour of the new starships. Memories of her first star commission, the Black Orca, filled her heart with warmth. It was a little spitfire of a craft. The starvette only had a crew of 8 but it was her crew and her starship. Her missions were mostly anti-piracy missions against thieves bent on stealing aquatic protein, the major export of her home system, Azteca. A small smile dawned her face until she realized that she was doing it, and then it faded.

Memory lane was cut short when the Logistics Command officer that monitored the Einstein-Rosen Gate control noticed a problem. The two largest ER gates controlled by the military shut down without warning. The dark-skinned man tried to re-open the gates with a test ER bridge and it failed. Quickly the officer performed a diagnostic when he noticed the 3rd, 4th, 5th….10th ER Gate failed in the system. It took thirty seconds for all ER Gates in the Nubian system to stop working. He rapidly passed the information to his commanding officer via the military network.

System General of the Logistics Corps Nakia Okafor received the information on her terminal. Rodriguez saw the change in her demeanor and watched closer. She was the only other senior officer on the deck and stood to Rodriguez's left along the side of the rectangular command station. Okafor was almost a foot taller than Rodriguez and sometimes she felt like a child standing next to her. The yellow uniform of the Logistics Corps seemed to make her chocolate skin glow even brighter.

General Okafor turned to the officer that sent her the information and said, "What in the hell could do this? I need answers."

"Unknown Sir. We haven't detected any subspace and gravimetric anomalies. I don't know how to describe it. The best interpretation of the readings that I am getting is that space has become heavy or dense. With full power, we cannot make even the smallest opening though space time. The gates are working because we can register that the gates are pushing against space. They just aren't getting through. All system techs and system scientist have been called to duty. Sir, it is almost as if space itself is fighting back against the ER gates and bridges," he said to his commander.

Supreme General Okafor responded, "We have a Sit 1. All stations priority. We have complete disruption of our ER gates and bridges. We need all ships capable of creating an ER bridge to attempt a jump. If jump is successful relay information to me. Any gravimetric or subspace anomalies that you detect please relay to the station. Repeat this is a Sit 1," said General Nakia Okafor.

Sit 1, short for a class 1 situation, demanded all personnel in the CIC to prioritize the command given. Without the order her request would be placed in a que and they didn't have time for that. The Nubian system was an exporter of food and raw materials. Any delay could cost the planet billions of credits. Okafor, like most the Logistics Corps, were from Nubia, Kush, Carthage, or the moons of Atlanta in Nubian system. They cared deeply for the wellbeing of the system and took great pride in its success.

Rodriguez sent a message to Okafor through the military network on a private channel using only her thoughts to create the message. Her bright pink eyes locked with the large brown eyes of Okafor as the channel opened.

"What the fuck can shut down all ER gates and bridges in a system? I have been in space my entire career and I have seen anything do that before," said Rodriguez via the channel.

"I have no idea. I don't even have a guess. The readings are like he says. Space is heavy. Space is thick. It is like space time went from the thickness of a piece of paper easily punctured by our ER gates and bridges to 3-meter-thick block of steel. The readings don't make sense at all but we will figure it out. Give us time," Okafor replied as she turned her eyes down to the console.

Rodriguez had faith in Okafor. She was one of those women that you are jealous of because they are so successful but once you meet them you can only wish them the best. To the male officers, she was one of the guys and to the female officers she was motherly even though like the men she went into the service once she applied. The woman had five children and only 2 years left on her 50-year commitment. Apparently, it all could be done Rodriguez would think from time to time. That was the high regard the Rodriguez held for her.

Rodriguez walked to stand next to Okafor and gave her an audible encouragement. At the end of the one-on-one talk she engaged the rest of the room the same way. Rodriguez was the type of officer that was tough but extremely fair. She was open enough that any officer from any branch could bring a problem to the forefront with the knowledge that they would get rewarded for the presentation of bad news if they had solution to fix it rather than being forced to conceal problems until they large and unforgiving.

One by one along the north wall of the command center the 12 Space Command officers in the dark gray uniforms completed the last of the weekly tasks assigned to them. Each terminal on the command deck was support by at least ten stations and officers elsewhere in the building. The officers sorted and pushed only relevant information up to the higher stations to prevent information overload. The Sentinel 7 operations station then exploded with information. The light from the Poveen incursion reached the first Sentinel 7 unit. He quickly sorted the information and sent the information to the console of Rodriguez and Okafor.

System Quasar Rodriguez looked up from her console at Logistics General Okafor. Suddenly Rodriguez didn't feel well. The two officers traded private messages to each other discussing the implications of the actions while they waited for verification of the Poveen incursion from a second unit. Time stopped on the bridge and it was so quiet that you could hear every person breathe. The station blinked to life with verification of 14 Poveen cruisers in the system.

Okafor quickly cross referenced the Poveen incursion to occur .122 seconds before all the ER gates and bridges stopped working. The women nodded to each other and then they triggered a yellow alert. At first the duo thought the thickening of space was a natural disaster but now it was clear that it was an interdictor system. Rodriguez, the veteran of over thirty space battles, understood the implications immediately. Human spacecraft could use the ER bridge drives to reposition around the Nubian system. Any battle would be fought without the aid of that tactical ability.

Space Command officers stood from the chairs they worked from as the work stations rose when the yellow alert activated. The chairs retracted into the floor as the officers welcomed the rising consoles to the standing position. The rest of the room turned to look at the Space Command officers as the team worked frantically trading information both verbally and via network. An officer of the Comet Corps along the west wall that didn't receive the information of the incursion by the Poveen yet said what the rest of room was thinking, "This can't be good."

Quasar Rodriquez requested Vice Commander Kahn return to the CIC via network connection. In the time that it took Kahn to reach the CIC deck Rodriquez and Okafor had compiled information and shared the initial report. Vice Commander Kahn walked onto the deck with focus and determination. Rodriquez loved the confidence and power that she showed. Kahn always commanded to attention of the room and that was an aspect of Kahn that Rodriquez tried to mimic.

"Space Command I need you forecast possible vectors of approach and get me up to date on the movements of that constellation, interrupt me if necessary, I need to know who is in danger and what they are doing. Also, I need to know what assets we can deploy quickly. Thirdly, provide a threat assessment of the enemy constellation and the force needed for overwhelming victory.

Logistics Command, find out why our damn gates and bridges are not working. If you can't figure it out I know scientists from the university that can help. Acquire them if you need to. Start the process of identifying if any commercial starcraft are along the Poveen vectors, update Space Command and me when it is completed," said Vice Commander Kahn as she walked on the deck. The confident officer walked over and stood next to Rodriquez at the console after speaking to the officers on the deck.

"Sir. Sentry 7 is reading a tremendous electromagnetic radiation coming from the ships, but that can't explain the loss of Einstein-Rosen capabilities. This is localized jamming of EM transmissions. I fear they may be operating in an area of science, math, and physics that we have yet to obtain but I am starting the process to acquire the scientist needed to assist the problem," said Quasar Rodriguez as she passed the information via network to the commander while it simultaneously updated the main projector on the deck of the CIC.

"Quasar Rodriquez, pass the ER problem to General Okafor. Continue to monitor the enemy constellation and ready your stars to engage in combat. We don't have to solve this problem right now but I will solve the 14 Poveen cruisers in my system. General Okafor, I don't need you to solve the problem of heavy space, but I will settle for a method to block the effect of the interdictor tech. Can we do that?"

"Sir, I can't even detect the technology. It's currently too advanced or it operates outside of normal detection systems. I recommend that we bring online Orunmila to give us solutions for detecting the interdictor technology and a possible method to defeat it," said General Okafor as she stood stoic next to the main console while she processed the information flooding into her mind from the network from the various stations on the command deck and in the building.

"Understood, keep trying to figure out what is interfering with the ER Gates. In the meantime, tell the corporations that we are aware of the problem and we are working on solutions now. Secondly..." said Kahn before she was interrupted by the Quasar Rodriguez.

"Sorry for the interruption sir but we have activity. The constellation has split up. Three of the vessels have increased speed and are moving toward Carthage. Another three vessels have vectored toward the Atlanta planetary system. Three more have vectored and accelerated toward Kush. 4 continue on the original vector toward Nubia and one cruiser has come to complete stop in the black," reported the Quasar Rodriguez.

Vice Commander Kahn sucked her teeth as the holographic map of the system updated the path of the Poveen cruisers. They are now vectored to engage the 4 largest population and economic centers in the system. Rodriquez could not understand why the force separated and vectored the way they did because those planetary systems were heavily defended and the approaching force would not survive an engagement.

"That can't be it. Something is at play here," Rodriquez said out loud on the deck to no one in particular as her thoughts escaped into the world.

'What? What do you mean that is not it?" asked Kahn.

"Something more is at play here. Do you really think the Poveen would show tech like this and only send 14 cruisers? Something is at play here and I don't know what it is. Vice Commander, you taught early space battles. You know better than anyone that the race with the better tech always uses it to defeat the race with the lower tech in space. Well, they are not just showing better tech, they are flaunting it in our face," said Rodriquez as she looked almost eye to eye with Kahn. Kahn processed that bit of information quickly and reacted.

"Command deck prepare to execute Protocol 1. Ping your station when you are ready to execute," said the commander as she stared defiantly at the 3D display of the system in contemplation on the repercussions of her decision. The data was clear in her mind. The Poveen entered the system with hostile intentions and she was going to give people of the system as much time as possible to defend themselves.

This was Rodriquez's third Protocol 1 since she was stationed in the Nubian system. All three times it was due to a Poveen incursion. The pings from the various station and operations confirmed that preparations were nearing completion around the CIC. The command deck was eerily silent as the last station pinged for readiness. Vice Commander Priyanka Kahn gave the command to execute Protocol 1.

The protocol system was created during the Great Push Era after first contact. It is a system designed to provide a threat assessment and then apply the appropriate response. Protocol 1 is triggered when hostilities with an alien race are imminent. The actions of the previous 15 minutes indicated that those conditions existed.

Protocol 1 recalls all active duty officers and soldiers within 12 hours to report. It allows the military to take over the system wide internet, holonet, and commination channels. Any corporate asset that is vital to the defense of the system can be conscripted. It also places the military leadership of the system in control over all military assets in the system over the civilian government.

“Ops, what is our current readiness?”

“We estimate all forces will reach 100% readiest in 14 hours. Sir, we have been contacted by the Civilian government and the representatives from the major corporations. They want to know why we are in Protocol 1 and they are reporting malfunctions in ER gates. How do you want me to respond?”

“Set the briefing time for the corporations and government for 04:00. Logistics command send craft to the homes or current locations of the command staff. Work the problem people. Your lives and the lives of your family may depend on it. Quasar Rodriquez you have the deck until I return,” said Kahn as Rodriguez was updated on the timing of the cruisers.

“Sir, the cruisers have stopped accelerating. They are all set to arrive in 95 hours and 45 minutes give or take a minute or so,” explained Rodriguez. Kahn nodded and then the Vice Commander walked back into the private unit down the hallway from the command deck to communicate with Lord Commander Malcom Masters and change into the battle dress.

PLUS 20 MINUTES
COMMAND CORPS LORD COMMANDER
MALCOM MASTERS
TITUN LEGOS, NUBIA
MARCH OF THE KLAXON

The klaxon jarred him from a deep sleep. The sudden rush to consciousness disoriented the usually calm and focused commander. A couple of seconds passed before his brain could let go of the vivid dream of Masters battling an alien with his bare hands. The klaxon marched his brain to clarity. It marched with the steady and unrelenting purpose to activate the Lord Commander to action. It marched defiantly into this subconscious and conscious mind without permission to do so. It marched because the Nubian system needed it to march. It marched to signify the importance of the moment and the need for Masters to get his ass out of bed.

Masters leaned forward in the bed and wiped his eyes. He silenced the klaxon with a thought and toggled the alarm to the visual setting only. This action placed a flashing red bar in the bottom right of his line of sight as to not obstruct his movement. The floor was cool to the touch. He stood facing floor to ceiling glass. The amazing view from the penthouse showed the bustling coastal city of Titun Legos. Masters arrived at the glass section of the room and moved a portion to side with a simple command from his mind to provide access to the balcony.

Once on the balcony the glass wall retracted. Masters turned to look back at his sleeping wife to ensure he did not wake her. A torrent of information flooded his mind the second a connection was made with the military network. "Okay, this is not a drill," he thought. With the precision of a computer his brain processed the information and categorizing the items that he thought were the most important. Masters walked down the timeline of events that occurred over the proceeding 20 minutes. A pending request for communication flickered into his field of vision and he quickly accepted the communication.

Masters' avatar appeared inside of Vice Commander Kahn's unit to her and in the field of view for Masters. His avatar appeared in the black uniform of the Command Corps while his real mocha skinned body stood naked on the balcony.

"Lord Commander Masters," greeted Kahn.

"Vice Commander Kahn. It looks like you are having one hell of an evening. I have reviewed your initial report. What is your assessment of the current situation? What do you think the Poveen are doing?" asked Masters. The report was just facts. Masters wanted some insight on the discussions on the CIC. He needed to know what assumptions were being made to ensure his officers operated under the same assumptions that he held.

Khan knew her commander well. She was going to provide the evidence that she had and some of the top line conclusions. Masters does not like assumptions not based on fact. This was beaten into his commanding officers daily and she was going to present the facts as she knew them with confidence.

"Commander, I have noticed 3 areas of note.

The first area of note is the Poveen formation. The Poveen entered the system in a standard formation. Alien constellations usually maneuver in formations of seven stars and currently 14 ships have entered the system so that is not unusual. What is unusual is the fact that they split into 5 separate constellations on separate vectors. In the 27 engagements humans have had with Poveen they have never displayed an action like this.

The Interdictor Field. We have lost the ability to use every ER bridge and gate in the system. Our forces are limited to push propulsion only. The interdictor technology limits our ability to react quickly and to consolidate forces at speed. It also limits some of our weapon systems and the functionality of our devices. If we are not able to counter the interdictor field, we will be at a disadvantage to the Poveen. Currently the Sentry 7 System has not been compromised by the interdictor field.

Poveen tactics and strategy. The incursion into our system displays tactics we have not encountered before and new the usage of new offensive technology presents a fundamental challenge. We face a dilemma. Is the interdictor field the only use of new technology or will they continue to use more advantaged technology during this engagement? We need to show patience of movement and action if we are going to determine the extent of the technology they hold. If we rush we could make a tremendous mistake," said Vice Commander Kahn.

Kahn made sure not to include any emotion in the response, only assumptions based on fact. Masters hated assumptions not based on fact. Over the course of his studies of military combat with alien races, most losses could be attributed to false assumptions and the lack emotional control. Kahn knew this was how he thought because she was the one who taught him. Masters was once her student at the military college and started active duty 13 years before she did. They used to battle in class daily. Masters would sit in the front middle seat and come into class seemingly ready to fight every day. That is why she trusted him now to make the right decision. She didn't trust him because she taught him. Kahn trusted him because she knew the man he was and his relentless work ethic.

"Thank you for your assessment Vice Commander Kahn. But, what do you think? I know I pounded it into your head and the rest of the team to not make assumptions not born by fact, but if theories are floating around in the CIC, I would like to hear them. Do any historical battles parallel this one? What could be the reason for them to break doctrine? We need to get inside the heads of these Poveen. We need to know why," said Masters. The statement settled Kahn. The rigid Commander rarely broke his protocol. This small change informed Kahn of the greater truth that he was feeling the same anxiety that the rest of the CIC was.

"Masters, to tell you the truth I am terrified of the unknown. I assume that the use of new tactics and equipment means this is fully functioned and supported engagement by the Poveen government or large Poveen faction. I assume that as we engage the enemy they will continue to bring forth new abilities and tactics. I assume that we will be tested to an extent that we have never been tested before. I assume that we will shortly have to order people to die. I assume all of this because the only other logical explanation is that 14 Poveen cruisers are engaged on a suicide mission with one of the most advantaged interdictor technologies we have encountered and that doesn't square with me. What say you? Are you troubled?" probed Kahn.

"Priyanka I have come to the same conclusion. We must keep our wits about us and stay focused on the task at hand. We can't let our emotions cloud our judgement or let assumption creep distort reality. We will not fail those that depend on us. Did you sleep?" asked her commanding officer.

"No, but I just took stims. I can give you another ten hours before my body gives out. That should be enough time for the entire command staff to be on deck. We have dispatched transport to your location and to the location of other high ranking officers. The bird is ten minutes out. Do you need anything else from me, if not, I will get back to the CIC?" asked Kahn. Masters informed her that he would speak to her again once he reviewed the information further or when he arrived at Ogun Station.

Malcom Masters was a mountain of a man. He stood a little over 2 meters in height. The product of both the muscle and bone density augmentation and the enhanced strength and power augmentation. He weighed for hundred and fifty pounds with 2 percent body fat. His muscles rippled under the skin and they flexed with the slightest movement. Masters had a top running speed seventy kilometers per hour and could jump 15 meters in the air unaided by technology. This was the brand of soldier the Meteor Corps produced.

Masters didn't have to receive the life extension augmentation. His mother was born with the augmentation and his father received it without needing to commit to the military at 18 from the United Planets of Humanity Science Authority because he tested extremely high in mathematics. It was now common in the Human Sphere that anyone that placed in the top five percent in their age group in one of the nine intelligences receive the life extension augmentation.

Augmentation is not limitless. Human DNA can only change slightly before it breaks down and causes massive deformity and death. An augmentation scale was created to rate the degree of change. When an induvial reaches a score of 100 they are banned from more augmentation. This stops over-augmentation and provides safeguards against abuse. Masters, unlike other recruits, was born with the life extension augmentation and didn't take the 40 Aug points hit that most recruits take when they join the service.

The strength and power augmentation and the density augmentation required by the Meteor Corps only used 50 Aug points combined. The usually soldier with a life extension augmentation would have reached 90 and stopped. Masters had the unique ability to add more minor augmentations to make him a better soldier. He added hyper-mental processing, enhanced sensory and perception, and advanced recovery. Almost immediately upon entering the Corps he was fast tracked into special operations command and spent his entire career in that division before he was offered an officer commission in the Command Corps.

Masters took a deep breath of the humid Nubian air and felt the warmth on his skin. Everything looked so peaceful from the height and the city in general bustled with excitement and energy. He loved the city of Titun Legos and couldn't wait until he could enjoy it free of his military commitment. Wonderful beaches, elite restaurants, and cultural activities provided the ultimate backdrop to Nubian living. It could be weeks before he returned home so he stood watching the night life and absorbing the energy radiating from the city.

Soft caramel hands wrapped around his waist. His wife woke up and walked behind her husband while he engaged in the conversation with Kahn. The intoxicating smell of her fruit-based perfume relaxed the warrior. Her long black curly hair gently brushed against his back as she gently placed her head against his back between the shoulder blades. She squeezed him as hard as she could. She didn't know if he was having another nightmare, taking a quick stroll, or if he was called to duty.

"Another test? Could they schedule one of these things when you are on duty. This is the fourth one in last fifteen days. I wonder if they suspect something. Why do they always have to take you from me when you are home? This is not fair. I don't like losing days with you. I hate it," said Layla Light-Masters as she held him tighter probing for the answer of why he was awake.

"Layla, you know I love you, right? I love the boys and I love our daughters. I love this place. I love all that we have become. I love our life," he said while he continued to look out over the city.

The first crackle of energy shook his wife. The second and third crackles shook the people below in the city but it was something he was waiting for it. The man-made thunder boomed and echoed in the caverns created by the skyscrapers. Energy powered into the massive shield generator as the top of the energy projector breached the surface of the water 5 kilometers out in the ocean. Layla walked around his massive muscle-bound body and looked to the Southern Ocean.

"Shit. Is this real? How bad is it? Tell me," she said as the implications of shield activation set in.

"We are in Protocol 1. The public will be notified shortly. Poveen are in the system. Currently we are trying to retrieve our forces and deploy police before panic sets in. I am leaving and I do not know when I will be back. I need you to go to the base. I need you under the same shield that I am under. Can you do this for me? I need to know that you are safe," he said in the calmest voice that he could.

"What? What is happening? Tell me now! Oh, my universe. What is going on? This can't be happening," Layla said to her husband as she turned to him on the balcony. Her outburst was interrupted when he pulled her close to his body. She fought his embrace for a second but then settled on his chest as tears fell from her eyes onto his mocha skin. The last time Masters was engaged in a Protocol engagement he almost died. Memories of that engagement now haunt his memories and hers.

"We are under attack. I am sure your family will be contacted shortly if they don't know already. We will need their support in controlling the corporate delegation. Can you reach out to your father and uncle to make sure that happens? If this escalates to a P2 or P3 I will need to know the machinations of the political and corporate class don't undermine my commands. I love you. I love them. I don't want us to be on different sides like I was with the corporate interest at the Battle of Butcher Bay," he said to her.

He leaned in a placed a soft kiss on her forehead. Two pleading green eyes looked up at him and he struggled not to give into the plea. He opened the silk white and gold night gown to run his hands along the soft skin of her hips and stomach. Long powerful arms cup her butt forcing her to her tippy toes and a kiss. This pressed her skin against his. Masters was tempted to savor the moment as the countdown until the transports arrival ticked down. If they hadn't made love three times in the last ten hours he would have made the request but even heavily augmented humans still had limitations.

"I promise not to do anything stupid if you promise not to do anything stupid," said his wife. Masters nodded in agreement. It wasn't like he was going strap himself to a Caladbolg rocket while it burned at 25gs only to jump off a thousand feet from the ground watching it impact an enemy formation and then land in the ashes of the impact firing on the enemy, like he did at the Battle of Butch Bay. He was 85 now and that was something he did in his late 60s.

Layla assured governmental assistance however she could. Due to the political implications of enacting a Protocol 1 his wife understood the seriousness. Her family, the wealthiest on the planet, could have valuable assets seized by the Lord Commander at any time to help with the war effort. The importance of the marriage between Malcom Masters and Layla Light 48 years prior could not have been anticipated. Many planets have tremendous conflict between the military and the corporate elites of the planets. In the Nubian system, this is different, due to the personal relationship Masters has forged with Layla's father, uncles, and grandparents. They have steered the system away from the usual political strife and setbacks because the sides respected and cared for each other on a personal basis. On the flip side, the two opposing parties have grown because of the relationship of the Masters and Light families. Master needed to keep a close eye on those factions without having to worry about being attacked from behind by his own family.

Unwantingly he moved from the warm embrace of his wife into the massive penthouse master suite. The massive closet doors opened from an apparent solid white wall to present his black uniform. Masters grabbed a large go bag. After one last kiss, he moved swiftly to the landing pad on the roof of the building.

PLUS 30 MINUTES
COMMAND CORPS SUB COMMANDER
MIKE RODGERS
JOHNSON BAY, NUBIA
LAST CALL

300 kilometers east of Ogun Station, Sub Commander Mike Rodgers drank away the evening with his lovely fiancé. Rodgers just turned 175-standard Earth years old standard earth days prior but Mike insisted that he party the entire 44 hours of the Nubian day. One of the most decorated soldiers in the history of the United Planets of Humanity Armed Forces could party however he felt, thought the crafty officer. He served in one compacity or another in the seven major engagements with an alien species.

He was born on the moon Houston, orbiting the planet Texas, in the American system at the turn of the 25th century. Pectoral muscles poked out of the open white linen shirt as his biceps tested the very limits of the sleeves. Massive thighs protruded from blue flower printed board shorts. A pair of brown sandals that had seen better days balanced the 7-foot-tall man on the stool. Though he had been in the sun all day his olive skin didn't burn, something he told his fiancé on more than one occasion.

Laura Oban, soon to be Laura Oban-Rodgers, sat the across the elevated bamboo wooden table. Though not as large Rodgers, Oban was slightly over two meters tall, with the clear markings of military augmentations. Her orange skinned glowed in the Caribbean themed bar light. Short blue hair and piercing blue eyes highlighted her angular face and full lips. Though muscular she maintained a womanly shape.

Oban is a protocol 5 human. The alien race known as the Lovick invaded human space 36 years ago. The conflict was the product of a Lovick Lord's insistences that Humanity owed it a solar system as payment for not asking for permission to settle close to Lovick space. Humanity lost 6.8 billion people in the conflict and Lovick lost 1 starhip. Humanity, understood after the conflict, it was not equipped to fight any alien species it had already encountered. We could be eradicated if the Lovick wanted it so. Losing a prospecting ship or a lone spacecraft to aliens was one thing but when three alien craft ER bridge into a system and destroy all human life in the system in a matter of three hours, the calculus for survival shifted. We also can't forget the 3rd and the 6th Galaxies ER bridged into the system only be rendered to atoms.

When a Protocol 5 is engaged the United Planets of Humanity Armed Forces trigger a force replacement plan. Every soldier that enters the armed services provides sperm or egg samples to ensure that they can have children if they are exposed to radiation in space or if they lose the ability due to injury. During protocol 5 a subset of the preserved material is used to create replacement soldiers. Three types of soldiers are created.

The first batch of soldiers are rapidly aged so that they can begin reinforcing human ranks after 3 years but they only have a 30-year life span. Another group is aged a little slower and they are ready to fight in 7 years and have a life span of 80 to 90-year life expectancy. The third group grow normally and have a normal human life span of a life extent human. Oban is a 3rd wave Protocol 5 human. Three hundred million soldiers like her were created at the end of Lovick incursion. They are required to serve until the age of 40 years of age but must stay in the reserves until they are 100.

Oban was born with double the augmentation that Rodgers had implanted currently. The only non-military augmentation was the "beauty" augmentation. It was extremely difficult to tell the difference between female and male P5's when they were first created. Public outcry and an extremely high suicide rate from the female soldiers forced the military to develop an augmentation. The augmentation gave the P5 women a more feminine appearance. Rodgers, would argue the augmentation worked beyond expectations and now even though Laura Oban was muscle bound she had an extremely attractive body and face.

Rodgers had 3 years and Oban 5 years left on the commitment to the military. After the service, they planned on buying a space craft and travelling the human sphere visiting all the planets. Mike's long service, frugal life style, and investments provided a mighty nest egg.

Until Rodgers retires from the service they both lived a comfortable lie. Laura Oban told her fiancé that she wasn't a high-ranking soldier and he accepted that explanation on the surface. The Sub Commander once searched for her profile and couldn't find it. That meant she was spec-ops, special forces, Dragon corps, or Mantis Corps. If that was true she would be court-martialed for telling anyone her identity. Rodgers feared that one day she would be called to an assignment and never return. That is what happened to special operations forces all the time and P5s received the most dangerous missions. Rodgers understood she was violating the rules because she was involved with a commanding officer but he was not breaking the rules because she wasn't technically under his command.

Rodgers made Oban feel like a human for the first time. She was born as a tool of war completely expendable. The love and affection from Rodgers was the first real human thing she had known. She had no family and her only friends are the other P5s. Oban was the first person that Rodgers loved in over 50 years since he lost his wife and two children. She pulled him out of downward spiral of drinking and carrying on. They both needed each other and the United Planets of Humanity Armed Forces was not going to take that from either of them.

Laura Oban signaled her fiancé that she need something else from him without making a sound. She seductively licked around her straw then sliding it up and down while peering into his eyes. Under the table her foot found freedom from the sandal commanded on a mission. It slowly crept up his leg until it found the target of the mission. Rodgers was not opposed to a little game footsie and the actions that usually followed it.

"Don't start something you are not willing to finish," said Rodgers.

"I finish what I start. I am ready to start now if you are," replied Oban as she seductively looked at Rodgers. He nodded his head in agreement to the start time. Eager to receive his birthday present Rodgers looked down at his drink to size it up. The man smiled and quickly connected into the bar account and paid the bill via the network. The popular peach beer was quickly chugged from the large glass mug. Rodgers stood from table visible excited from the foreplay though he tried to hide it with his shirt.

The protocol 1 klaxon jolted both from continuing. Over the military network top military officials were updated on the incursion of Poveen forces into the Nubian System. It was common for soldiers to cut off the active military feeds during personal time but the Protocol 1 klaxon didn't care. Sub Commander Rodgers triggered his implant to run a pre-selected program that prioritized the events since he cut off the feed. It also triggered the nanobots in his blood to start removing the alcohol from his system. The klaxon was silenced and placed in the bottom right of his vision. A message from Vice Commander Kahn popped in his main view. It was a brief thirty second general message telling anyone that heard the message that birds are in the air to them for extraction.

The information from the events of the past thirty minutes stripped the joy from his celebration. Rodgers knew the Poveen and he hated them. To date the Poveen killed 2,135,321 soldiers he commanded into battle. Not as powerful as the Lovick, the Poveen were still superior to the humans. Rodgers checked the timer that populated the lower right of his visual HUD created by the implant. It provided the landing locations of the transport and the time it was expected to arrive.

"Do you think this is a drill or this is real?" asked Oban.

"Hard to say. A lot of information on this one. Most drills don't have this much depth to them. I guess we will find out shortly," responded Rodgers.

The bird was eleven minutes out and he had to travel a short distance to get to it. Rodgers grabbed Oban's hand and walked to the taxi that he called. The network prioritized the taxi by passing the queues that would normal plague this area of Johnson City. The estimated trip time was five minutes. Oban looked at Rodgers and asked him if that was enough time. Though Rodgers had shifted focus from romance to duty quickly his fiancé hadn't. Rodgers wanted to dismiss the advance to prepare but when she started to undress he couldn't resist. Oban wasn't going to let the last moments of that wonderful day be spent gazing into nothingness sorting data files.

With one minute to spare the couple finished a passion-filled moment and put back on the clothing that was discarded recklessly. The large moon seemed to hang over the beach with its full reflection on the water. Rodgers couldn't help but think how beautiful Nubia was. It still wasn't better than Houston though and nothing ever would be, but it was nice. Men and women of the armed services approached from all angles toward the extraction point. An early extraction like this one was mostly high level officers only. Commanders, generals, admirals, quasars, colonels, and other high level officers would be retrieved before lower level officers.

Oban turned to Sub Commander Rodgers and said, "I have been activated. I hope this turns out to be nothing but it's realistic that we won't see each other for a while. Mike, I love you, remember that. If this does escalate to a Protocol 2, and Orunmila is activated, there is chance that our relationship will be exposed," she said with a calm but somber face. Rodgers turned and gave her a big smile.

"Laura, I don't give a fuck who finds out or what they do to us. When this is over we are getting married and that it that. Sparkle it is time for me to go. Take care," he said in a stern voice and unapologetic voice. Every minute more officers arrived to the beach. The same scene that played out in the taxi was playing out on foot, in taxis, or personal vehicles. It was time to say goodbye. Husbands kissed wives, wives kissed husbands, and they both kissed children.

Rodgers looked at the timer. The ship was two minutes out. Rodgers stepped out of the car as Oban cried from both eyes. He couldn't understand why as he tried to comfort her. This wasn't his first time leaving a woman he loved to go fight and he knew that once he left she would get it together and meet whatever transport would come for her in the coming hours. He was surprised when Oban followed him out of the taxi. He looked slightly angry. "What are you doing?" asked the Sub Commander. Rodgers wiped the tears from her eyes with his thumbs face and repeated himself.

"I have been activated. I am required to be on that transport too," explained Oban. The words hung in the air even though the weight of the comment was heavy. She wasn't just a member of a secret team. She was either the commanding or extremely high ranking officer. Rodgers looked stunned and then his face turned stoic and nodded to her. He could no longer hide the fact that he didn't know that she was under his command. The lie of omission was a lie of fact.

"Get out the taxi soldier, we don't have much time, he said to her as another officer walked by the taxi. Oban understood and stepped from the taxi. Together they walked to the extraction point. The officers saluted the Sub Commander as he walked to the extraction point. The other officers looked at Oban confused. Everyone knew each other but they didn't know who she was. One officer walked over and introduced himself to her. Oban stood and grinned slightly. She shook her head back and forth. The officer quickly understood. Oban's identity would remain secret to the rest of the officers at the extraction point. No one else asked after that point. Seven high ranking officers got onto the transport when it arrived in route to Ogun Station.

PLUS 40 MINUTES
COMMAND CORPS SUB COMMANDER
YOSEF AMIR
OGUN STATION, NUBIA
THE GANG IS ALL HERE

Amir entered the command and control building with a mass of soldiers and officers. He dipped and dodged running soldiers and maneuvered toward the officer's elevators in the lobby of the complex. Once inside only 2 or 3 other officers occupied the elevator. It stopped at the various departments and branch floors to allow the officers to exit. He was the only one left on the elevator when it reached to top of the building. Amir exited the CIC deck. A long hallway led to the CIC. Along the hallway were multiple doors on either side. These doors led to the private quarters of the command staff. Amir turned into his private quarters instead of onto the deck.

His height was slightly above average with a lean physic. He had an angular face, olive skin, and perfectly styled hair combined with confidence and bravado of a holovid star. Emerald green eyes and stunningly long black eyelashes made his gaze hypnotic. Recently he broke off a 5-year relationship with the number one model in the Nubian System because he wasn't spending enough time with her. It created a buzz around the CIC for the last two weeks, even stone cold Masters read an article or two to know what was going on.

He entered his command quarters and quickly got to work. The bag he carried was tossed onto the couch along with his white shirt. Bare chested he walked to the white wall. With a quick thought, he commanded a hidden door to open. Once invisible seams were exposed and then formed a door. It opened to reveal a combat closet. The dress uniform of the Command Corps hung to the right of the closet but those uniforms were no longer the standard.

Battle dress was now required and Sub Commander Amir grabbed his Command Corps exo-suit known as an CC-ESU. The suit was constructed of light carbon fibers and exotic nano fibers. Once equipped the wearer doesn't have to remove it to eat, sleep, or go to the bathroom for at least two weeks. Though after 5 days or so most soldiers will take it off to allow for the suit to clean itself. The suit feeds off the body heat, water, and waste to power its systems.

Amir grabbed his sidearm and placed it on his hip into the holster strap to the CC-ESU. Ready for duty he walked into the hallway and smelled Rodgers before he saw him. He turned to the drunk man that stumbled down the hallway in an open button down shirt and shorts. Amir thought the klaxon interrupted him during a bad time. It clearly caught Rodgers at a worse time. The old man smiled from ear to ear. Amir shook his head back and forth with a smirk.

"Wow you can't teach these kids nothing," joked Amir as he teased his 100 year elder.

"We need to kill these squids so I can go back to celebrating my birthday. They messed up my party," Rodgers joked back.

"Hey, word of advice, get a quick scrub down. You smell like shit. If Masters smells you like that on the CIC deck he will kill you. If Kahn smells you like that you will be court marshalled. She is on deck now. Watch yourself grandpa," Amir said as Rodgers laughed a little too hard at the joke.

"Sorry I don't shit roses and daffodils like you pretty boy," responded the grizzled vet in the only way he could.

"Rodgers you may also need to wait another ten minutes to ensure that the nanobots removed the rest of the liquor in your system before stepping on the command deck," said Amir as he moved toward the deck from the hallway. The other Sub Commander agreed and went into his room to sober up, shower, and get dressed.

Amir strolled on the deck and walked to his station. Within seconds he connected and booted it up. The process took about thirty seconds from the beginning to the end. He toggled to combat preset on the station and got to work. His task list was empty and he wasn't given any new orders from the commanding officers.

Amir pinged Okafor with a direct voice massager. Without raising her head, she answered his ping.

"Yes, sir?"

"What is going on here? My queue is empty. What are you all working on so intently?"

"Ask Vice Commander Kahn sir. I am not permitted to distribute yet."

The Sub Commander pinged Vice Commander Kahn and she denied his request. He tried it again and she refused again with a message, "one second". Amir wasn't going to be ignored.

"So, I see ladies night didn't go well," Amir said audibly. The Sub Commander received the response he thought he would receive. Amir signaled that he would not make it easy to ignore. Kahn looked at him like she was going to rip his head off, Rodriguez struggled not to smirk in an extremely awkward way, and Okafor shook her head the way she would towards one of her children.

It was meant to get the attention of the three high level officers at the rectangular command table. The response told him that this was not a drill. Until that point, he didn't know for sure, but it was now obvious to him that the officers were consumed with the work. A drill would not consume them to this level.

"Hey, in all seriousness, it is way too quiet in here. It is time to start pepping these officers up," said Amir as Kahn burned a hole in his face with her stare. Okafor and Rodriguez didn't outrank Amir so they remained quiet during the outburst. Amir knew Kahn wouldn't allow a second outburst.

"Sub Commander Amir why don't you go do it then," said Kahn. Amir agreed to his command. The charismatic man started to make his rounds around the command deck. He encouraged the officers while he looked at the station screens. Most of the officers on the bridge worked diligently on the problem and didn't think twice about hiding the work from a commanding officer. A minute into his rounds Kahn realized she got played. Amir wanted to make the rounds as soon as he saw that his queue was empty.

Kahn was much older than Amir, though they both entered the Command Corps Academy at the same. Kahn finished first in the class and Amir finished in the middle of pack. He didn't have of the experience as the other officers in terms of years but in terms of battle experience against the Poveen he was at the top. Amir served with Masters at the Battle of Butcher Bay. Masters gets most of the credit, and he should for the completely insane battle strategy, but his soldiers died executing it.

At the Battle of Butcher Bay he was a Colonel in the Comet Corps. He led an assault onto a Poveen dropstar, fought through waves of enemy soldiers, made it to engineering, planted 4 nuclear weapons, and then made it off the ship. He killed over ten million Poveen soldiers on that one mission. Those soldiers would have overwhelmed the defending soldiers on the ground led by Masters. Masters always felt he owed his life to Amir and he helped his career every chance he could.

He figured Okafor and Rodriguez were hard at work on the ER gate and bridge problem. Kahn was working on the readiness agenda in preparation of the arrival of Masters and he stood waiting for an assignment. Amir pinged Kahn again.

Rodgers walked onto the command deck with is CC-ECU. The extremely large human being walked over to the rectangular station hub and stood across in from Amir. He thought Rodgers looked much better than he had a couple of minutes ago, and the smell was gone. Kahn's eyes moved back and forth between the two of them.

"Do you need something from me sir?" asked Amir. Kahn stared at him wanting to say something but unable to find the words. The tension was thick in the room after his tour of the floor and the ladies night comment.

"What are you doing?" asked Kahn.

"Currently I am reviewing the hulls of the Poveen cruisers. I am attempting to identify the variant type of the spacecraft. I am wondering if we have a record of this type engaging us before. This is a new type sir. If they have engaged in combat with humans before it could provide some insight on what they are planning. Do you want to perform another task sir?" respond Amir.

"I need you on AI prep. Bring Orunmila online," said Kahn.

"Will do sir," replied Amir. He wasn't a fool and he was not a clown. Amir knew how to read a room. If people needed a joker, he would become one. If they needed someone serious because everyone else was joking, then he would fill the role. Kahn was the hard-noised disciplinarian, Masters was the warrior monk filled with revolutionary strategies and wisdom beyond his age, Rodgers was the soldier that would bash his head into the wall if ordered to do so, but Amir was the glue to held the command crew together. He could talk to an officer if they broke up with their wife or husband. If a child was sick or they needed help with a personal issue they all came to him. That was his value to the team.

"What the fuck is going on here?" asked Rodgers to Amir via a secure channel.

"Kahn is holding back some info. Probably waiting for Masters to get here before she shares. You know she doesn't want to say anything that may be wrong later. Okafor and Rodriguez know but are staying tight about it. Kahn has them wound up. I tried to ease tension but professor stick in the ass is not allowing it," responded Amir to Rodgers as he referred to Kahn's time as a professor.

"So, you are saying the chances she tells me what is really happening is slim?"

"Very slim."

Amir turned to Kahn. She starred at him with fury. She demanded Amir join her in the meeting room off the command deck. The duo walked to a door opposite of the hallway that led to the private officer's rooms. They entered the first room to the right of the hallway and Vice Commander Kahn exploded.

"What the hell is your problem Amir?"

"Excuse me sir? I don't know what you are talking about," asked Amir.

"Cut the shit. Professor stick in the ass?"

"I was wondering if you were listening. What is going on and what is your problem with me sir?"

"You will know shortly. Lord Commander Masters will be on site shortly. Can you wait that long or are you going to continue to be a problem? So far you have caused nothing but disruption," scolded Kahn.

"The way I see it sir you are the disruption. I walked on deck to a cold shoulder. I have no orders and I am in the dark on the true nature of the ER disruption. Is this a drill or is it not a drill?" responded Amir.

"Not a drill. This is real. This is very real."

"So why not task Rodgers and I to something meaningful until the Lord Commander arrives?"

"You will load the protocols to Orunmila. Don't you question my commands again. Do not disrespect me again to other officers. You need to fix yourself right now or go to your quarters," said Kahn.

Amir squinted his eyes. He wanted to challenge her but he decided that nothing good would come out of it. The situation was tense. It wouldn't be good for anyone to have the number 2 and 4 in command of the system fighting. "Sir, I will get the protocols for Orunmila ready."

"Thank you, Sub Commander."

"Sir, I apologize for the comment. I knew that you had access to that communication and I shouldn't talk about a commanding officer in that way. You deserve more respect than that. I also apologize for my previous comment about ladies night. That was uncalled for. I felt disrespected and I didn't act with the professionalism the Command Corps demands of us," said Amir.

This statement disarmed Kahn. Amir gazed at her with green eyes to further disarm her. Amir was an extremely handsome man that was blessed with the ability to have others forgive him for transgressions that others would not be able to be forgiven for. His only rivals are puppies, kittens, and small children. Kahn looked at him in slight confusion.

"Sir, do you accept my apology? I want to ensure that when we go back into the CIC you trust me," he said as his hypnotic gaze turned up the heat.

"Yes, I accept your apology. Just don't do it again," said Kahn as she walked out the room. Amir smirked to her turned back. He knew what he just did. Kahn liked to fight and argue. He took both away from her. The other thing he did was to give her a win. Kahn needed a win. Amir figured that would improve the morale on the bridge so he exposed himself to disciplinary action. One day his tricks would not work but today was not that day.

He walked back to the CIC and began to run the protocols to bring Orunmila, the massive AI, to life. Both Rodriguez and Okafor looked at Amir as he performed his task with a smile on his face. They looked to Kahn and she had a smile on her face. Confused by the sudden change in hostilities between the two confused the Quasars. They pinged him for an explanation but he gave them the same cold shoulder they gave him when he came to the CIC. Instantly the drama took the edge off the room for them as well. Amir's plan to relieve the tension on the CIC worked.

He asked Rodgers if he wanted to help with the prep work and he agreed. The two worked with speed to ensure that most of the preparation would be completed before Masters arrived. The inclusion of Rodgers insured that he would not feel left out of the process. Once again Amir provided what his soldiers needed. Rodgers would have went crazy without the assistance

PLUS 50 MINUTES
COMMAND CORPS LORD COMMANDER MALCOM MASTERS
TRANSIT TO OGUN STATION, NUBIA INVASION

Lord Commander Masters continued to study and categized the information for easy access if the situation changed. The steady stream of data into the implant filled the time to Ogun Station. He paid special interest in the extraction of military officers around the planet and the activation of police units, shielding generators, and other critical systems. So far everything ran smoothly. It was a testament to his officers that are coming on line by the second to process the data needed.

Masters was pinged by the Nubian System AI named Orunmila. It sought permission for its activation. Sub Commander Amir prepped the mighty program but Masters had to give the final say on its activation. He granted it permission to communicate with him and activated the protocols it would operate under. AI's with this level of power are illegal outside the government.

"Greetings Lord Commander Masters. I am here to serve. How may I help you?" said the manly robotic voice. Master replied mentally asking it to study the ER gate and bridge problem and provide an assessment of the possible causes. It agreed to the request and then faded into the background. He was pleased the command team already booted the powerful program. With any luck the AI will figure out a solution to the interdictor technology.

He was pinged once again. The constant communication delayed his thoughts from formation. This angered him at first until saw the origination. It was coming from the United Planets of Humanity Armed Forces main headquarters in the Victory System. He agreed to the request and his consciousness was thrust from his current location on the transport across the galaxy to the command center in the Victory System.

His avatar stood in row aligned with 4 other system Lord Commanders facing two senior officers. The Grand Commander of the United Planets of Humanity Armed Forces and the regional space commander stood facing them. The scope of the event was starting to take form. Masters examined out the side of eye the other commanders as they did the same. He was so focused on the invading forces in his system he didn't stop to think this may be a part of a broader event. Most of the officers he knew very well especially the Lord Commander of the Grant System.

Five months prior he was his Vice Commander alongside of Vice Commander Kahn before his promotion. Unfortunately, when he was promoted he took three other Nubian Commanders with him leaving Masters short staffed. Masters nodded slightly to the tall olive skinned man and he nodded back. The positions were set to be filled next month but it was clear now the Masters would have to engage the enemy with a short command staff.

Regional Commander of the Echo region of space Celeste Moon was of average height with light blue skin, short blond hair, and purple eyes. She moved forward to the collection of avatars and spoke, "All of you are experiencing the same phenomenon in your systems. All ER bridges and gates are not functioning. The Nubian and Indo are both equipped with the Sentry 7 systems and detected Poveen cruisers within 15 minutes of the disruption of ER activity. Sichuan and Siberian System, equipped with the Sentry 5 systems, have verified they also have Poveen Cruisers. We will assume until disproven that the Grant system also has Poveen ships or technology in the system. You won't have verification for at least 7 hours as light flies if they followed the same attack plan as the other systems.

The facts that are currently shared are these. Each system has an invasion force of 14 cruisers that are now heading on various vectors in the system. They are breaking standing operating procedures of the Poveen in not keeping in constellations of 7. All ER activity stopped .122 seconds after the enemy bridged into the system. At the current speed, they will reach all targets at 95 hours and 12 minutes. The Poveen are only heading toward planets, moons, and space stations with Galaxy class ER gates.

Your orders are to engage the enemy as far away from major population centers and areas of strategic importance as possible. Those of you with Sentinel 7 systems prep to launch all offensive weapons from the units and stop the enemy before they can inflict losses. Since this is now a multisystem conflict we will raising the Protocol level to 2. Do you have any questions?" asked the regional commander Celeste Moon.

"Sir, can you clarify your recommendation? I need to ensure we are all in alignment," asked Masters.

"What clarification do you need? Once the targets are acquired you are to burn constellations toward the enemy and destroy the squids. Fire missiles from the S7s and destroy your enemy," barked Celeste Moon.

"Sir, we are not to consider ourselves Dark Sentinels? You would not consider our systems behind enemy lines without means of support? Don't we have to protect all our military forces now at the cost of civilian forces? That is the disconnect," said Masters. The Supreme commander of Galactic command stepped forward. He was an extremely tall man with light skin and a grey beard.

"We have not lost 5 systems and I appalled that you would say something like that. Why do you feel like you are a Dark Sentinel? Be mindful of your answer. I do not tolerate officers that cannot follow orders. Your answer will determine whether you will be relieved of command or not," said the Supreme Commander. Masters never flinched or waivered mentally at the threat.

"Sir, we attempted to establish an ER bridge half a light year from the center of the system and it did not work. The reach of the interdictor technology is extensive. Best case scenario you find a way to bridge to that location and enter the system and reach our location in six to nine months. Worst case the interdictor field is a light year or more in distance. That would translate to two or three years before any support can reach the system.

We have also assumed that because we can't form ER bridges or gates that the enemy can't form ER bridges or gates. Ten minutes from now a thousand cruisers can jump into our system and we wouldn't be able to do anything about it. This is currently a form of blockade and since the beginning of time blockades have been considered an act of war. It is considered that because of its ability to deny access to resources. My system is self-sufficient but what about Grant and Sichuan. We provide them with half the food they consume. If we burn away from our fortified locations now toward the targeted attack vectors and more enemy starships bridge into the system or the current cruisers bridge in the system they could cause tremendous damage. If we use our S7 missiles we also run the risk of giving away the locations of our defenses.

If you cannot support us when we need assistance than we must be considered Dark Sentinels and proceed with preparation for a long siege. I don't like it any more than you do. I understand the political ramifications for you and for us. We need to prepare for a long unsupported defense of the system without resupply. I am also aware 14 cruisers is not a force that any of us should fear. They would need a multiple of that number to do any real damage. We know that and they know that.

I recommend the consolidation of forces around population or strategic centers and wait for the Poveen to attack. This provides us with the needed time to prepare for defense, to organize the population, to research the tech that is negating our systems. We need time more than any other resource at this moment," said the Nubian System Lord Commander in confidence.

"Interesting. How do the rest of you feel about that opinion? What action do you feel that we should conduct? Speak now," said the Supreme Commander. The rest of the room was silent. "We all have to be careful in a moment like this that our Egos, past performance, and personal deference do not interfere with our judgement. We all need to respect the chain of command, is that clear? Do I need to tell you all what is at stake here? Work the problem. Masters speaks some truth. I do not feel that you have lost the systems and I will not declare you Dark Sentinels. However, I agree that we should not move our military assets out of fortified positions until we know more. We will reconvene in two hours when we have a clearer picture of the Poveen aggression."

The Region Commander Celeste Moon then spoke. "Do not jeopardize the safety of the systems that you command. We are placing the defense of the system in your hands. Everyone is dismissed, I know you have a lot to contend with now. Lord Commander Masters I need you to stay behind," requested Regional Commander Moon as the other four system commanders and the overall Galactic Commander faded from the virtual meeting room.

Once everyone was gone she spoke, "Why didn't you take this job again?"

"Because the most terrifying force in this galaxy is my wife. I believe if I am stuck at the command center and I don't come home for a week she will get in a spacecraft and destroy the Poveen herself to get me home," said Masters as the two old friends spoke.

Masters was offered her job as Regional Commander 5 months prior and turned it down because he wasn't renewing his contract with the United Planets of Humanity Armed Forces when it expired in 2 years. 50 years of service was enough for him. They offered the job to Moon after he denied it and she accepted. This created the vacancy in the Lord Commander position in the Grant System. At first the UPHAF offered Vice Commander Kahn the position but she turned it down respectfully because she wanted the Nubian job when Masters retired. So, they offered the position to the other Vice Commander under his watch, Anthony Manzoni, and he accepted. Then he took three Sub Commanders with him.

"Masters, I understand the dynamic at play here. I need to know you will follow my orders. I am the commanding officer," demanded Moon.

"I will follow orders. I have fought the Poveen three times sir and every time they surprised me. They are not to be taken lightly. This attack is not what it appears. I know it," explained Masters.

"I need you to do better than that. The others will follow whatever you do no matter how hard I try. I am asking you to please not do that to me again," demanded Moon.

"This is not about us. This is about the people of the system. Sir, my wife is here, my son and daughter are here, my father is here, and I will not risk them. If you can't handle input from you Lord Commanders than you should not have taken that position. We are going to make you angry, but in that anger, will come truth. Only the man without bias can see the truth. The only outcome I care about is the protection of the people in this system. 95 hours from now we be in combat with the enemy.

I am looking at the best case or worse case scenarios. Best case I have 14 cruisers in my system. We engage them in 40 hours and win the conflict but sustain a minor loss of military men and equipment. In the worst case those 10 ships turn into 70 ships or 490 ships and they can jump around the system engaging how they see fit. Orunmila, our military computer, estimates that it will take at least 305 Poveen capital stars to break our defenses on Nubia and 105 to defeat the systems on Kush without the aid of Space Command. Both require them to land soldiers on the surface to disable the planetary shielding and the planetary gun's systems.

They are in control and that is not something that we are comfortable with. I had a sister that was addicted to a drug. She couldn't get the help until she understood that the drug was stronger than she was. Once she realized that she became something great. They have the element of surprise, better technology, and integrated coordination. They know how this is supposed to play out and we don't so we are striving to gain some control over the situation but we do not have control. I want them to feel in control. That is the only way we gain the upper hand.

If we are too aggressive we will feel in control but we will not be. We must make decision that force the enemy commanders to make decisions and commit forces. We must ensure that they are the one that are guessing our tactics. I want them to have to press to win. When they do that I will crush them. Though we feel like we are under a lot of pressure, the commanders of these invasion forces are also under pressure from their command structure. They follow and the population that they serve. They have declared war on another race. A race that is one of the most apex predators that they have faced so far," he said with tremendous confidence.

We are in trouble. We are in danger. We are not in control."

"I understand your perspective. We will speak again in 2 hours. Good Luck Malcom. You are going to need it."

The transmission ended and Masters consciousness returned to the transport. He stood from his seated position and walked down the ramp onto the roof of the command building. For a moment, he looked at the stunning view of the military base and the city nearby. It would still be hours before the sun rose but since almost every light in the city and on the base the horizon had a glow. It had a beauty to it. This could be the last time that he sees it like this again.

PLUS 55 MINUTES
COMET CORPS QUASAR
RYU TANAKA
OGUN STATION, NUBIA
FORM UP

Quasar Tanaka exited the officer's elevator and walked toward the command deck units. The tall lean man reviewed the latest data. Orunmila was now online and the AI filled his queue with requests and access permissions. The smooth gliding movements subtlety demonstrated his extreme athleticism. Tanaka was preparing himself mentally for the coming battle. The Comet Corps was one of the three rapid response branches alongside the Astro and Meteor Corps respectfully. Within a few steps he entered the room and prepared for combat.

Unlike the command corps officers Masters, Kahn, Amir, and Rodgers, the Generals and Quasars of the branches bunked up. These units had the same footprint as the other suites but a bedroom replaced the open dinning space and the master bath became a Jack and Jill. His roommate, System Meteor General Morris Solis, equipped his MC-ECU in preparation for the coming conflict. Like Rodgers and Masters, who also served in the Meteor Corps, he was a mountain of a man. His neck was thicker than Tanaka's and his biceps thicker than his quads.

Tanaka was raised in the Japan System on planet Tokyo. He could trace the purity of his ethnic heritage to the year twelve hundred. Solis, on the other hand, seemed to possess a mixture of every ethnicity from Earth. The man had blue skin, and his bone structure was the densest type of any human, due to the 1.6gs on his home planet of Atlas. The people of Atlas embraced the new era with the extensive augmentations. Tanaka didn't feel that his people was doing so. They were not racist by any measure but it didn't feel like they were truly committed to the future the way other systems were. The old ways still dominated.

Tanaka married his childhood sweetheart at 18 when he joined the service. Initially, he served in his systems Planetary Force, he excelled as an officer. Eventually he was selected to become a member of the elite Samurai squads. This elite unit participated in a rescue mission on the planet Holiday. The planet was overrun with a genetically created creature in an act of xeno-terrorism. His army group was noticed for its bravery. Shortly after Tanaka was offered a commission in the UPHAF Comet Corps. Until that point, he didn't even consider leaving the Japan system. He saw this as a great honor so he left the Japan system and accepted the commission.

He has lived on Nubia for the last eight years and he feels that the family is better for it. He never would have imagined when he was child that he would come home to his wife dancing to reggae music. The first 3 of 7 children left the home before he left Tokyo and are married living in the Japan system. His forth joined Space Command and is on a spacecraft somewhere. His fifth and sixth are both married to Nubians, breaking the cycle of ethnic exclusion, and that pleased him. Some of his children passed on the tradition while others joined the broader universe. It was the balance that he sought. His youngest son now dates General Okafor's youngest daughter. Kahn joked that they could marry off the last of the children with one marriage.

"General Solis. I hope this didn't ruin your day as much as it did mine," joked Tanaka.

"Actually, it did. Remember that girl I have been dating, Jamie Juelz. It is getting a little more serious. Thinking about marrying her. We were having a nice night. I was going to propose but this cut that short. I hope we kill these squids fast and get back to living," said Solis.

"Great, congratulations big fella."

"She hasn't said yes yet."

"I have seen the two of you together. She will say yes."

"Hope so. Anything exciting with you Tanaka?" asked Solis.

"Nothing. I was sitting at home watching a movie. It wasn't a good one. My wife was forcing me to watch it. This got me out of it," respond Tanaka as the two men laughed.

"I thought you said it ruined your day?"

"The last couple of months I haven't spent much time with my wife. Even watching a trash romantic comedy sometimes is good."

Tanaka quickly dressed in his CC-ECU. The orange highlights were indicative of the color of the Comet Corps and contrasted the blue highlights of the Meteor Corps and blue skin of General Solis. The two men traded ideas on the coming conflict and shortly moved into the hallway. The System Planetary Forces General Jamal Nasir and System Orbital Guard Quasar Kevin Johnson just left the unit across the hallway. The four men greeted each other in the hallway trading pleasantries as they turned toward the command deck.

"Where is all that beef going? It is like a supermarket in this hallway. Yo, what am I going to eat today? You have dark chocolate, milk chocolate, blueberry, or sashimi on the menu. What is a girl to do?" said System Astro Quasar Natasha Might. Most of the time you heard Might before you saw her and this time wasn't any different. If you needed a joke told or not a joke was going to be told if you were around Might. Her brand of humor rubs everyone wrong eventually.

"Sashimi? Might, you can do better than that? What happened to lo mein," asked Tanaka as he fired back while the other three officers snickered. Quasar Might walked toward them with long deliberate strides. Her six-foot seven-inch lean frame was the byproduct of growing up on the low gravity world of Brooklyn in the America System. She had porcelain skin, fiery red short hair, and eyes like the clearest ocean water.

"Sorry, I didn't expect you guys to be in the hallway and I had to work on the fly. Besides lo mein is Chinese and I want to be accurate. What do you think about all of this? Crazy yo? Squids raiding again," encouraged Might as she flawlessly maneuvered from the brass to. Even though Might is annoying at time Tanaka was always impressed by the way she fought and conducted herself on duty.

"Seems different. I have been hearing a lot of chatter about something being wrong with the gates. I think something more is going on here. Hope we find out soon. Hey, has anyone else been contact by Orunmila?" asked Tanaka.

"Orunmila contacted me as well. He needed permissions of ER gate control and other subsystems," responded Orbital Guard Quasar Johnson.

"Me too," said Planetary General Nasir.

"Yep, seems like it is more. I think we can rule out drill. Too many people have been called up. This is real. Squids are in the system. Just don't know how real. I only track 14 cruisers. Does anyone else have something different?" asked Tanaka. The rest of the soldiers agreed that they saw the same information that they received.

"Anybody fought Squids yet?" asked Tanaka.

"Once. We lost. The only time I ran from a battle. We were engaged in a scouting mission father down the spiral arm. We found a system that was just smaller than Victory. We wanted to scout more. Poveen jumped into the system with a couple of cruisers. We only had 30 starvettes, 5 dreadstars, and a bunch of science spacecraft. The energy weapon they have ripped into our formation. Worst defeat I have ever experienced. Barely made it out. Squids don't play around when it comes to killing humans. 14 cruisers aren't enough to take out the system but whoever is sent to stop them will suffer losses," said Quasar Might.

"I fought them in xeno-terrorist attacks in the Holiday system. Five-meter-high tall devilish creatures. My men stopped the advance of those creatures but we took losses. Saved two hundred thousand people though before we had to fall back," said Tanaka as they reached the end of the hallway.

The five officers walked onto the command deck and moved to the rectangular table with the work stations in the middle of the room. The entire officer team was now in the room except for Masters. He was on the roof speaking to UPHAF command. They all waited for the better part of ten minutes before he pinged the team that he was on the way down. Tanaka waited patiently when watching the various spacecraft under his command flicker to active duty from non-active.

Masters walked into the CIC. The entire deck saluted the Lord Commander and he saluted back. Masters walked to the front of the room and took his position at the head of the rectangular workstation hub. He activated the terminal and looked up at the men and women in the room and spoke.

"Everyone here is the deal. I am sorry that I have not shared the information I know with the broader network. I needed to know for sure before we decimated the information. I returned from a meeting with the Regional Commander of Echo. We are not the only system that is going through this. Four other systems in Echo Region have been compromised by Poveen cruisers. Each one has 14 cruisers in the system on vectors to intercept major population centers that have Galaxy level ER Gates.

Some of you may know this already but for those who do not know. We have been denied the use of our ER Gates and bridges. At first, we thought the problem was a natural disaster of some kind but we have confirmed that the Poveen have some sort of interdictor technology that is disrupting space and time.

Indo, Grant, Sichuan, and Siberian have been denied the use of ER gates and bridges as well. The cruisers will make contact in approximately 95 hours. We will start receiving real time information from those systems shortly via headquarters.

Shortly HQ will raise this conflict to a Protocol 2. I believe that if this only escalates into a Protocol 3 we are lucky. Be prepared to be declared a Dark Sentinel system. I want all of you to think in this manner. We are behind enemy lines without the means for support. Military assets are to be placed above civilian. We could be stuck behind enemy lines for a day or for 10 years. We need to prepare for both," said Masters as an audible gasp fell over the room.

Amir turned to Tanaka and sent a private message, "You ready for this T?"

"I think so," responded Tanaka. A new batch of information was downloaded from Lord Commander Masters. In the new packet of information was the initial information on the ER gate and bridge closure. It also contained the information from the other systems affect by the growing conflict.

"Is this all the information?" Tanaka asked Amir.

"I think so."

"This doesn't feel right. Poveen usually jump in and attack. Why the slow play?"

"Don't know. Vice Commander and the others are spooked too. This is something new. Funny how that works. If they jumped into the system and started attacking we would be calm. The fact they didn't makes us nervous. Something else is happening. I wonder what it is."

"We are going to find out sooner or later. I vote later," said Tanaka.

PLUS 65 MINUTES
ORBITAL GUARD QUASAR
KEVIN JOHNSON
OGUN STATION, NUBIA
THE HIDDEN DANGER

"Johnson, Nasir, Kahn, and Okafor with me. Everyone else continue working," said Masters as he began to walk to the door from the CIC toward the meeting rooms. Quasar Johnson locked the terminal he was working on and walked behind Masters. Confusion was painted on the faces of the four officers called by Masters. Johnson felt like he was being called to the office of the principal.

Masters walked into the hallway and then into one of the communication rooms. He ordered them to connect to the network and get ready for a meeting with the Regional Commander. Johnson quickly toggled his communications array to accept the transmission from the room. Masters had the ability to connect to HQ by himself but the others did not. Within a couple of seconds Johnson found himself connected to the system while he looked at a new 10 second countdown. The rest of the team connected as well.

Masters used the link once again and he was virtually transported to the Victory System but this time he brought his team with him. Instantly they stood in the virtual world created by the room. Master appeared in front of the slightly to his left and the rest of them stood in a line facing the regional commander. She greeted the team and then the short light blue woman spoke.

"We have three new developments we need to discuss that cannot wait until the previously scheduled update. First, the Grant System has detected Poveen in the system. Apparently, the Grant Corporation, didn't register a quantum communication device on one of luxury space stations. They detected the spacecraft and then called in for help. It detected 14 Poveen cruisers in the system and contacted the government. It may be prudent for you to sweep for rogue quantum devices as well. You are to find and commandeer these devices.

Secondly, in the Sichuan System, the Luzhou Sub Space Research Center is the leading developer of sub space detection systems. The Sentry 5 system in that system has experimental subspace tracking technology. When they used this technology on the invading fleet they detected 805 cruisers in subspace trailing the cruisers in normal space that we couldn't detect on the EM band. We contacted the Grant System, who has 6 battlenova capital ships equipped with the experimental arrays. We asked them to use the systems and they did. The Grant system detected 1425 cruisers hiding in subspace vectoring toward major population centers and the two battle clusters in the system.

Lastly, you and Indo system can adjust the Sentry 7 to detect any subspace cruisers in your system with a slight upgrade. That upgrade is being sent to your system AI as we speak. Those S7s will probably go off line and for some time. That is the reason we tested with the Grant system spacecraft first. I don't mind the loss of a couple sensor arrays on starships but I didn't want you to lose your Sentry system. We have not found a way to detect the ships with normal detection yet and unfortunately the Siberian System will not have any means of detecting the approaching force. Keep this information to yourself until we figure out what to say to them.

We will declare all your systems Dark Sentinels within the hour. This should give you the time and resources to prepare for the engagement. We plan to upgrade this to a Protocol 3 at that time as well. When you make contact with the enemy the Protocol with escalate to 4.

Prepare for battle and send your battle plans once they are ready. Everyone remembers the Lovick invasion of 36 years ago. Expect the same level of panic in your system. I will not take up anymore of your time. We will reconvene in 3 hours as a group. May the universe provide," said Regional Commander Moon.

The signal ended and Johnson's consciousness was thrust back into the room on Nubia. The room was quiet for over a minute before Masters raised his head and told them to keep the information between the five of them until detection. He ordered Johnson to work with Okafor to upgrade the S7s. General Nasir was tasked with activating the police force and National Guard in the cities. Kahn would oversee this task.

The five of them walked out of the communications room back into the main room. It is hard to hide bad news and it is even harder to hide terrifying news. Johnson did his best to mask the information that he heard but the looks from the rest of the command staff at them signified that they were not doing a good job. Johnson stepped to the terminal happy to look down and away from the eyes of the other officers.

"Hey, what did you Nubians talk about? You look scared shitless," asked Quasar Might via direct message and not audibly. It was true. Only the 5 Nubian born members of the command team went into the communication center. Johnson tried to ignore her as the download for the S7 units ended.

"Come on Johnson. You guys are freaking me out," pleaded Might. Johnson, figured that if he was going to get any work done he needed to silence Might before she moved into the realm of annoying.

"You will know in 15 minutes. That is all I can say. Now let me work," he barked back. She responded with an agreement and now he was free from that distraction. He opened a channel to Okafor and the two discussed how they would separate the duties. Masters jumped into the group chat in a passive mode to monitor the situation but not to micromanage. It took a little over 2 minutes for the two elite officers to finish the preparation. Johnson looked up at Masters when he mentally asked to shut down the Sentry 7 system to apply the upgrade. He agreed and the system went down.

10 seconds after the system went down Quasar Rodríguez looked up at Johnson with questioning eyes that said, "Hey was that you or did the Poveen take down the S7"? Johnson gave her a strong nod and then proceeded to monitor the update. Rodriguez pinged him. Johnson thought it would just be her double checking the fact that the S7 was now down but when he answered Amir and Might were also on the group chat.

"Hey, did you just shut down the S7? I need to know you did that," asked Rodriguez.

"Yes, it was me, it will be back up in 8 minutes. No, I can't tell you why and yes I was ordered to do it," he said before they asked anymore questions. Johnson closed the line and went back to work.

"How many cruisers do you think will be here?" Okafor asked Johnson in another channel.

"I don't know. The Poveen are not stupid. Enough to win probably," Johnson replied cryptically.

Over the next five seconds they all formed a group to ping him all at once. Johnson was getting a little angry. Why couldn't they let him do his work. He went into the channel.

"What the fuck do you want? You see that I am busy," yelled Johnson into the channel. The group fell silent.

"Hey Johnson, sorry buddy. We just…well to be honest we are having a hard time here. We are trying to figure out what in the hell could get Okafor that spoked. I never thought that could happen," pleaded Might. Johnson looked up at her and then asked himself, "Why in the hell does

Might always do the talking?"

"Stop bothering Quasar Johnson," yelled Kahn out loud. That is when the table took a turn for the worst. Sub Commander Rodgers responded.

"No, we will keep annoying him until you tell us what is going on here," demanded Rodgers. Masters picked his head up suddenly and told everyone not on the command team to leave the room. Every officer not at the rectangular command station in the middle room walked out of the room and into the hallway.

"Sub Commander Rodgers do you have a problem following orders?"

"No sir."

"Then why in the hell did you just disobey my order?" asked Masters. Johnson watched the two men square up. He didn't know who would win but he didn't want to see them fight. That wouldn't be good for anyone. One minutes left before the update and then another five minutes of data collection. They had to last that long at least.

"Listen up, all of you. You will listen to my orders and obey them without question. If you cannot handle that you are free to relieve yourself of command. You don't know what is going on because I don't want you to know what is going on. If I did, you would know. If anyone challenges me again I will kick your ass up and down this damn room. That means you Sub Commander Rodgers. General Solis don't think I can't square up against you either. Is that clear?" yelled Masters as he stared at Rodgers.

Rodgers apologized to Masters and then was ordered to stand at the door and apologize to every officer as they returned. Johnson had never seen anyone get in Rodgers face before and not get put down. Masters must be the man of legend. A message arrived from Might to Johnson in text form. "Sorry Johnson." Finally, he could work in peace again.

Johnson admired the way Masters handled the situation. He could have let Rodgers outburst slide but he didn't. He wasn't going to tolerate that behavior in this situation. He set the terms for emotion for the conflict. Adversarial outbursts would not be tolerated. Johnson took a mental note as the data from the upgraded Sentry system populated the system. Johnson asked Masters if he should keep the information to the select team or let it populate naturally. Masters told him to let it populate naturally.

"Everyone listen up. General Okafor and Quasar Johnson have worked on an update to the Sentry 7 system. This update will allow our sensor system to access subspace. We will not be able to determine much but we have reason to believe that the Poveen are hiding cruisers in subspace," explained Masters to the rest of the deck. Johnson was relieved that he didn't have to hold that information from the group.

Nightmares come in all shapes and sizes. Occasionally you might stare down a nightmare and make it bend to your will. You look it in the eyes with unwavering will and not flinch. You fight the beast with its teeth snarling and clacking. You summon inner strength that forces you not respect the danger. Everyone standing on the CIC deck now had to stare a nightmare in the face. Instead of 14 Poveen cruisers they faced 861 cruisers of various sizes. Johnson looked at Masters and he just snarled. Johnson then turned to the work station in attempt to mentally change the number of cruisers to a smaller one. His early prediction that they would summon a force that would win was correct.

"Sir, we are now tracking 861 inbound cruisers. Updating threat assessment and information," said Johnson to the group out of habit. His voice cracked like a teenage boy meeting puberty for the first time. Emotions swirled in his body. "How could they defeat 861 Poveen cruisers he thought to himself."

"Thank you, Quasar Johnson. Everyone, as you can see, the enemy was attempting to surprise us but we now have the element of surprise. They do not know that we know. Let's keep it that way. Control your need to tell people outside the military. Leaks can get the very people you are leaking to killed. The people in this room are the only people standing in the way of victory and death for this entire system. In the next hour, we will begin to formulate a response. Command team we will meet back in

90 minutes to formulate a plan. Prepare a list of your assets and your battle readiness," said Masters.

Slowly over the next ten minutes the team got back to work on the problem one by one until the entire team was hard at work. Over that time, Johnson worked with Okafor, to refine the upgrade. They studied the readings and tinkered with the resolutions to produce a better picture of the alien craft. They concluded that the ships travelling in subspace were not originally built as subspace vessels. To use the analogy, it was like the Poveen sealed all the windows and doors on ship to allow it to submerge. Since they were not originally designed for subspace they cannot go deep into which allows for the detection. These cruisers are only roughly 2 centimeters deep into subspace. That is the reason why we believe they are not moving as fast as they can. Subspace is fickle and they may want to ensure they don't lose any ships in subspace.

Johnson updated the system and then pinged the Orunmila, the planetary AI, to receive the updated projection of victory. Orunmila gave them a 3% chance of stalemate. Johnson than asked the program why it didn't provide an assessment of victory and it merely responded that it didn't see a logical strategy that would lead to victory in the system if they could not establish an ER bridge or gate to bring forces from outside the system.

Masters pinged Johnson and asked him to meet him in the meeting room. Johnson closed out his work station and walked into the meeting room. The Lord Commander followed him into the room a couple of seconds later.

"Sir," said Johnson eager to understand the nature of the request. Lord Commander Master hesitated slightly before he spoke.

"I need you to go to Oya Battle Station for the duration of this conflict. The enemy has displayed a higher level of technology than we expected. I don't think we will be able to conduct operations from this location. I want to be prepared for anything. I called a transport. Load up. It should be here in 10 minutes," said the Lord Commander.

Johnson didn't expect the Lord Commander to order him Oya Battle Station. Oya Battle Station was the largest battle station in the system. It was in Nubian orbit over the vast ocean. It was the backbone of the planetary defense grid. As the Orbital Guard Quasar, Oya Battle Station was the largest asset under his direct control. It was also the exposed asset in orbit around Nubia. Any attacking force would seek to destroy it first when they approached the planet. Johnson was just ordered to become the tip of the spear.

"Yes sir," responded Johnson. Emotions flooded his body as he processed the command further.

"Take a minute Quasar Johnson if you need it but I need you on that station before the Dark Sentinel order. I don't need panic on the station. I don't need panic in Orbital Guard. You are not the only one that will be asked to travel to forward operating bases. No one will escape danger," said Masters.

Johnson gathered his strength and followed Masters out of the meeting room. Instead of returning to his station he walked passed to the other command level officers to the hallway. Johnson went into the room and gathered his personal affects and armor. The travel package hovered next to him as he made his way to the roof and onto the shuttle to Oya Battle Station in orbit.

PLUS 85 MINUTES
COMMAND CORPS LORD COMMANDER
MALCOM MASTERS
OGUN STATION, NUBIA
POLITICS OF WAR

Protocol 3 and the declaration of 5 Dark Sentinel systems were enacted later than expected. The President of the United Planets of Humanity wanted more time to prepare the people of the human sphere before he declared the invasion. The general population until that moment was in the dark about the invasion and the real reasons the gates and bridges did not work. Minutes after the universe wide announcement the request for a meeting by the local government and the elite of the system was received by Lord Commander Masters.

Masters responded with a call for a complete meeting of the leadership consul. It was a collection of the top political, financial, and corporate interest in the system. Masters wanted to present transparency and fairness. Any resistance from one or more of the individuals in the meeting could lead to delays. The last thing Masters wanted was to fight a war against the Poveen and a war against his own people.

The designation of "Dark Sentinel" to the system meant that Lord Commander Masters was now in full control of the system. All rights and privileges of the governmental body were now revoked. The entire system was now under military rule. Masters could seize property, take assets, and dictate without a check and balance as he saw fit. This was terrifying to the politicians and corporate interest alike that suddenly lost control of what they worked so hard to gain. Masters saw the effects the stress of this situation had on his leadership team with Rodger's outburst and Okafor's slight breakdown.

Masters stood on the command deck finishing the last piece of work before he connected. Khan, Rodgers, and Amir entered the virtual meeting space before him. He would be the last one in the meeting. His political training from his wife's uncle was paying off and no doubt his command level officers were under fire from the leadership that had arrived. Vice Commander Kahn sent a message signally that everyone that was invited was now in the meeting area.

The cacophony of yelling and unrest surprised him. The leadership of the system were not handling this very well. Masters understood that this would be contentious but he did not expect this. Those in control will always fight extremely hard to stay in control or to feel like they are in control. This group wasn't any different. Lord Commander Masters held his right hand high as he looked around the virtual auditorium. Stadium seating placed them facing him while his team stood on a raised stage facing them.

The environment was artfully designed to present the leadership team as the authority of the room.

In return, each seat was artfully negotiated by the participants. For instance, the President of the Nubian system was in the chair directly in front of Masters at the same elevation to him so he could look him directly in the eye. The game of politics was in play but Masters was ready to take his ball and go home. He didn't move or say a word. They would calm themselves or he would leave and toss them all in jail until the end of the conflict, if they survived. After a minute of yelling the crowd finally silenced when they understood that he wasn't going to engage in the bickering.

"Thank you for coming on such a short notice. I understand that you need answers to the current situation. We will do our best to paint the picture and answer your questions. 85 minutes ago 14 Poveen cruisers bridged into the system. .122 seconds later they activated an interdictor field that disrupted our ability to use ER gates and bridges. This maneuver occurred in four other systems at the same time with the same result. The enemy forces split into five constellations. 4 cruisers are headed toward Nubia, 3 cruisers are headed toward Carthage, 3 cruisers are heading toward Kush, 3 cruisers are headed toward Atlanta, and one cruiser stayed stationary at and the incursion point. We followed procedures for a hostile incursion and we entered protocol 1.

The reason why we entered protocol 2 is because we are not the only system to come under attack. The Indo, Grant, Sichuan, and Siberian systems have also been invaded. Once we had confirmation that in 4 of the 5 systems that had ER disruption, Poveen cruisers had entered the system, we identified the threat increase with an increase in the Protocol. Make no mistake this is a coordinated attack.

Lastly, an innovation in technology allowed us to conduct another type of scan. This subspace scan revealed something even more sinister. Instead of the 14 cruisers visible with EM scans, the subspace scanners revealed a true force of 861 Poveen cruisers," explained Masters as the room suddenly exploded with shouts and yells. Panic spread in the room as the people yelled solutions, questions, and wild statements that than devolved into rabble. Master held his right hand up once more and stood quietly. He prayed no one left the meeting. If they did he would have to send his soldiers to collect them in the real world. The raised right hand was used to inject calm into the room.

"We have to keep our calm now more than ever. The events of the last hour and a half are extremely terrifying. I know this sounds cliché but we can only win together. We can't win without you and you cannot win without us. I am Nubian. I know you, I know your children, your wives, your husbands, your businesses, your hard work, and our amazing culture. I will defend it with my life and so will my officers whether they are Nubian born or not because they are honorable men and women of the United Planets of Humanity Armed Forces.

First, we are trying to determine how they created the interdictor field because solving that problem would allow the UPHAF to send more forces into the system and crush our enemies. Orunmila, our military AI has come on line and is increasing in capability. Once fully active we are hoping that it will be able to shed some light on the subject and provide a way to stop the interdictor field or find a work around.

With that said, many of you have begun to feel the loss of computing power, restrictions on electrical power, communication channels, and other services lost. You will continue to experience the loss of systems until all the necessary systems are in the hands of the military on Nubia and across the system. Make no mistake we are under attack by an alien race. We are cut off from support and reinforcements. We are on our own.

We will distribute talking points shortly that you will use when you talk to the public. The way you react to the situation will determine our short-term effectiveness. If you decide to go to the media and seed mistrust that we cannot defend the planet or we are being somehow unfair to one faction or another I will end your ability to seed mistrust. Do any of you have any questions?" asked Masters. The ten seconds of silence was eerie until the President of the Nubian System stood and spoke.

Masters knew the man very well because he was the uncle of his wife and the man that consistently tried to get him to run for public office in the Peoples Political Party. He was unsuccessful until his wife told Masters that she was not going to renew another 50-year marriage commitment unless he left the UPHAF and run for office. She wasn't going to spend another 50 years with him travelling the universe fighting aliens. Reluctantly in the end he agreed to run for Nubian System President when his uncle's term was over in 3 years. This truth leaked out six months ago. Masters thinks they leaked it on purpose to get an early buzz.

"Malcom, so are…."

"That is Lord Commander Masters President," yelled Sub Commander Rodgers. The outburst startled President Light but he instantly knew why it happened. If Masters would have allowed himself to be addressed as Malcom, and not Lord Commander Masters, the familiar would dominate the discussion. President Light took a quick glance at the pitbull next to Masters and wondered if that man was waiting for someone to call him Malcom so he could pounce. President Light held his hands out and bowed his head in a sign the he acknowledged his wrongdoing.

"My apologies Lord Commander Masters, we are a little on edge here, I want to let you know that you have the support of the Nubian government. Whatever you need to defeat these intruders you will have from us," said the President.

"Of course he has your support. You are trying to prop him up to replace you. We all know it. The Peoples Party will do anything to promote this man but this is terrible. Are we really scared of 14 Poveen cruisers? We have ten times that fire power in the system. You were a hero once Masters but this is beneath you. Burn out battle clusters now to the intruders and destroy them and be done with it," said the President of Planet Kush and probably his likely challenger in the election from the Rise Political Party.

"President Lawrence they have 861 cruisers," corrected Vice Commander Kahn.

"School teacher don't correct me. We can only see 14 cruisers. You tell me they have 861 cruisers. You are propping up the number so that when they are defeated you are a hero," said the man as he dismissed Vice Commander Kahn. Her face, even as an avatar, displayed extreme anger. That was the second time today something challenged her past as a professor.

"It is clear you have not learned anything from the Lovick Invasion of 36 years ago. The introduction of the system politics will not improve this situation. In fact, it will be the main reason any defense of system fails. I can control the military, but without the control of the people that you can provide, we will divert resources from the fight to fight you. Now you will apologize to the decorated soldier Vice Commander Kahn," demand

Masters.

"I will do no such thing. Her people have been the blight of this system since they arrived and it is the reason why you and your family have more power than mine and the others on Kush. I see this for what it is, a power grab, I will not use your talking points. I will not be silenced. I will be the voice of reason in the darkness. You will not control me boy," yelled the President of Kush. Masters paused before he replied. The room appeared ready to explode before the elder spoke.

The man was the son of one of the founders of the Nubian Corporation on Earth. He is known to most as the Patriarch, the oldest person on the planet, and the leader of the wealthiest family in the system. The Robinsons did not participate in politics but they tip the scales of power whenever they back one side or another. The man was old and frail. His face was wrinkled and spotted but his synthetic eyes pierced the soul of any that would look. Wisdom seemed to permeate from his skin and without saying a word the room instantly demanded silence and respect.

"So, we disrespect our own now? You will apologize to the Vice Commander. This woman has trained the best and the brightest on Nubia and Kush. Your grandfather would spit in your face if he heard you speak like this. You were not raised this way. I remember Nubia when it was a rock. I remember Kush when it was volcanic ash. I will be damned if we let these things come into my system and harm us and all of you. All of you will get in line and do as the Masters' child says. We know the ambitions of the man after he serves. If that is the obstacle for cooperation I ask the Lord Commander to commit to never running for political office. This action will demonstrate to all of us that he is willing to sacrifice the same as we are," said the old man. His gaze turned back Masters after his statements direct at President Lawrence.

Masters froze. His wife demanded that he run for office as a condition for them to stay together. If he agreed to the demands of Elder Robinson he would in effect end his marriage with his wife if she continued to demand that of Masters. Could he lose his wife, the love of his life, and the mother of his four children before first contact with the enemy. He knew what the right thing to do was but doing it was difficult. Alternatives to the only political problem he faced swirled franticly. He could not demand sacrifice and remain selfish himself. The political class demanded a pound of flesh, his flesh, for them to commit. Hopefully his wife would understand and they can find another solution to stay together.

"I hereby pledge that I will never seek the nomination, accept the nomination, or actively run for political office in the Nubian system. Now, President Lawrence, I would like for you to apologize to the Vice-Commander," said Masters now angered by the terms set forth by Elder Robinson. The smug Lawrence smiled happily that he boxed Masters into a corner and removed him from running for office in the future.

"Vice-Commander Kahn I offer my apology," said the President of Kush as he smugly sat down with a grin on his face. Masters stared at him for a minute without speaking until the entire room became uncomfortable. The glare was real and powerful. Masters wouldn't run for office but he would do everything in his power to punish that man when this was over and it was clear that everyone in the room knew it too. President Lawrence didn't care but he should have.

"Listen up. I do not have the time or the patience for this. 861 cruisers are moving toward our 4 largest population centers and this is how we are greeted. You insult the Nubian born Vice-Commander. You seek political concessions from me. You try to hurt us while we protect you. What is next from you? Huh? What else do you have in store for us," yelled Masters.

"Lord Commander Masters you should not overreact to this situation," said the Patriarch before he was interrupted by Masters.

"I have heard enough Elder Robinson. We toil in the room as alien cruiser move toward our home world. Your political games have been played and now it is over. You have all cleared the deck for the Presidential run 3 years from now but I am not sure if we will have a Nubia 3 weeks from now. Listen up and listen carefully. If I suspect, for one second, you are plotting against the war effort I will kill you. If without vital resources I will kill you. If you think for one second that you can play general or quasar I will kill you. That is my promise," said Masters as the entire room exploded at the disrespect that for the first time came from the officers toward them. The Patriarch gazed at Masters and Masters back at him. The old man nodded his head at him and then vanished from the meeting. Others did the same. The meeting was over and the support he wished he could have collected was not going to happen in this meeting.

Lord Commander Masters ended the meeting and everyone in the room that had not left was thrust back into reality. Masters turned to Nasir and spoke.

"I know you are preparing for Marshall law but I need you to create plans to remove any one of the officials from the office they hold. I believe we will need to remove some or all of them before this conflict is over," requested Masters. The rest of the officers that did not attend the meeting on deck took that as a sign that the meeting did not go as planned.

PLUS 3 HOURS
COMMAND CORPS VICE COMMANDER
PRIYANKA KAHN
OGUN STATION, NUBIA
THE RESPONCE

Vice Commander Kahn had a rough couple of hours. She was insulted two times that day. The first insult came from Sub Commander Amir when he told Sub Commander Rodgers that she had a stick in ass. Than he used his charm offensive that crippled her ability to reprimand him correctly. She was so mad at herself when she left the room. She was hypnotized by those damn eyes and she hated it. Kahn saw many male officers fall victim to the same effect from young female officers.

Kahn did it once or twice in the past. She promised this would never happen to her. Only Sub Commander Amir had that kind of power over her and she hated him for it because he knew it. When she was a professor at Light University the little boys would also try but they failed not only concur her but they usually failed the class. When she entered the room moments prior when she removed her clothing she could only think of him doing it. "He is a demon," Kahn thought to herself.

She was than insulted by the President Lawrence of Kush. The burly man also insulted her people. 125 years ago, a terraforming event forced the bulk of the population from a neighboring system to flee to the Nubian system. They were largely decedents from the ancient countries of India, Indonesia, and Australia. The people of Nubia graciously accepted the refugees but it came at a cost to the farmers of Kush. They were restricted from the export of the high margin foods to feed the massive refuge population. This held back the development of Kush for 25 years. During that time, the elite of Nubia grew richer as the elite of Kush remained stagnant.

The command staff officers argued how best to respond to the invasion for the previous forty-five minutes. They had 92 hours to figure out how to defend the system from 861 cruisers. Masters dismissed the team when the meeting descended into fight between two camps. Kahn went to her room equipping her exo-suit.

The black suit hugged her body's shape and features. It highlighted her powerful legs, wide hips, small waist, and disproportionately large breast. The modest dress uniforms could soften the disproportionately of her body and she liked that. Kahn was not conservative in her personal life at all but at work or in the military she was. Kahn wanted to be a powerful and competent officer, period. Whether it was real or imagined she always felt that when she wore the CC-ESU people were staring at her chest and rear and not her face.

The doorbell to her suite indicated a visitor at the door. She opened the door remotely and finished placing her side arm in the holster. Lord Commander Masters walked into the room and approached her at the closet door as she completed her preparation. Kahn could tell by his facial expression that he was coming to her to seek guidance but not approval. Masters didn't seek approval. He was a leader not a boss.

"What's troubling you?" she asked before he spoke a word. He smiled slightly and responded.

"That obvious huh? I don't know. I don't think we have approached this right. We keep trying to find a solution in which all we win but maybe our definition of winning is incorrect. The battleplans we keep trying to create are based on fairness. That all the forces should have an equal chance of survival. That is not going to work. We must pick winners and losers. We must not fall into the trap they want us to fall into. We don't know how good the enemy commanders are.

Their current battle plan is a successful one if we follow our standard response. I don't want to break convention just to do it. I want our strategy to be based on a solid plan and strategy. I think I have it. Before I presented it, I wanted to speak to you first because a lot of the plan will hinge on you and your ability to win a space engagement. Would you rather fight with Space Command forces or the Comet and Astro Corps," asked Masters?

Kahn paused. Why would she be in space? She would obviously be sent to Kush to defend the second largest planet in the system? Was he thinking of not doing that? Is it because of that President? She had to know before she answered.

"I am not going to Kush?" she asked.

"No. Is that going to be a problem?" asked Masters in that way you do when you are seeking to argue if the answer is not satisfactory.

"Why do you insult me? I have been insulted enough today I can't handle much more," she questioned. Kahn was probing to figure out the reason without presenting herself as disrespectful.

"This is what I was talking about Vice Commander. We have to think outside our preconceived notions. You think Kush is the second most important place in this conflict. You believe you should be on Kush. What if I told you that it isn't? What if I told you Nubia wasn't the most important," questioned Masters. Kahn thought carefully about the direction he was going.

"Okay I am game. What is the most important thing and what should I protect? That will determine which branches I want with me," responded Kahn.

"Hannibal Battle Station is the most important asset in the entire system. I want you to go to it and defend it," said Masters. Kahn's eyes moved to the left and down as she thought about the location and the ability to defend it.

"Why is it important Masters? Work with me please here," Kahn asked. The warrior wanted to know what Masters thought because Masters has a problem sharing information at times. It is not that he is doing it on purpose. When he speaks, or gives an order it seems odd, but in truth he has thought about it extensively and the reason for the odd request is perfectly reasonable.

"I have tried to get into the minds of the commanders of this mission. For a time, the attack didn't make sense. Why not just bridge into the system around Nubia with full guns blazing? Why hide your fleet? It all escaped me but I think I have figured out the true targets of the first attack. I think they aim to destroy the ER gates first. The only difference between the planets Carthage and Kemet is the two ER gates. In fact, Kemet has twice the population. Kush, Atlanta, and Nubia all have galaxy class ER gates. That is the only commonality.

I worked backwards to understand why that would be important. They have an interdictor technology that we don't understand. If we do figure it out I imagine that we would need our most powerful ER gates to breach it. That would explain why they are on the current vectors. They have cruisers hiding in subspace so we don't send resources to stop them from destroying all the galaxy class gates.

If the attack plays out the way they want it to. The battle of Nubia would be a slug fest to contain our forces here. That battle would stop us from moving our space forces. The planetary shield would hold on Kush. Atlanta and Carthage would be decimated and so would 3 galaxy level gates. Another one would be out of commission behind the planetary shield of Kush. They could than launch an attack at the last one around Nubia with full force.

Think about it. Why are no cruisers headed to Kemet? No galaxy level gate. I want to leave Nubia relatively unguarded. I want to Kush to hide behind the shield. I want them to get bogged down at Atlanta. I want you at Carthage to deny them the destruction of the two gates. I also want you to engage the enemy with equal force and win the conflict. Unless you want to turtle under the Kush shield. If that is the case I will send Sub Commander Amir," he said.

Now it all made sense to Kahn. He didn't think less of her. In fact, Masters placed her at the most critical part of the mission. Deny the enemy the original objective and the local commanders must improvise. Masters was betting on all of them. She smiled. Kahn loved the trust that he placed in her and the rest of the team.

"If I am going to Carthage I want Space Command with me. The Astro and Comet Corps will do better at Atlanta, with all the debris, the smaller craft will have an easier time in that environment. The larger stars of Space Command wouldn't do as well. I am requesting Quasar Rodriguez and Might to go along with me," responded Kahn.

"You have Rodriguez but Might is going to Atlanta. I will have the finalized battle plan shortly. The meeting with the rest of the command team will be held in 15 minutes. Get ready and say goodbye to Nubia for a while," said Masters as he turned. Kahn stopped Masters before he left the room.

"How are you doing? I know what you did in the meeting today. I know what that means for you," asked Kahn to Masters. Out of all the senior level officers she was the only one that could ask Masters these questions. They had a friendship that predated military service. Masters looked at her and shrugged his shoulders.

"I haven't spoken to her yet. I don't know where she will stand on this one. I hope she wants to continue but I am not sure. She really wants something different with life and hers. She doesn't want to be straddled to this life any longer and I don't blame her. Government service would have been an easy transition for me because most of this damn job is so political.

I don't know what I will do now. I guess that is something I will think about after we drive these damn squids out of the system," replied Masters.

"I understand. Around the time, you are at now I knew my husband wasn't going to renew our commitment. I knew that he would become my once husband. If you need a sounding board or a shoulder to lean on I am here for you," she said. Masters nodded and smiled in affirmation.

"How did you do it? How did you stop loving him? How did you move on?" asked Masters.

"I didn't stop loving him. I will always love him. I moved on to a new life filled with new experiences and challenges. With or without her you will be fine," Kahn consoled. Masters shook his head in agreement to her words.

"Thank you, Priyanka."

He left the room and Kahn started packing her personal effects into her duffle bag. She slid out of the wall the massive container that held her battle armor. The CC-ESU was just the base level of a set. Every soldier had a version of battle armor to wear over the exoskeleton. The modern battle field was too deadly for the human body to survive more than a couple of seconds without some sort of shielding or armor.

The BA 101 Dragon Battle Armor is the best body armor of elite soldiers in the United Planets of Humanity Armed Forces. Only the top special forces units in the Command Corps are assigned the armor due to the cost. The armor was nicely tucked into a large rectangular hovering box that would open to fit the woman when if the time came. She placed the armor into diagnostic mode. Kahn wanted to ensure that it was working properly before she left the room. When the light on the side flashed green that indicated that the armor was ready. Kahn pushed it back into the closet and gathered her clothing and placed it into the to go bag and closed it and walked out of the room. She returned the to the deck of the CIC ready for her deployment.

PLUS 3 HOURS AND 30 MINUTES
DRAGON CORPS GENERAL
DESIGNATION: A1D7 NAME: LAURA OBAN
OGUN STATION, NUBIA
DRAGONS

The transport landed on the roof of the command building at Ogun station. 6 Dragon Corps soldiers walked down the ramp onto the roof of the building in full armor. The heavy matte black armor covered the chest, shoulders, and thighs of the soldiers. Underneath the joints, scale like armor overlapped to create an armored lizard appearance. The overlapping scales was one of the reasons the armor was called dragon armor. The other reason was the helmet.

A long chin and a protruding head made the helmet resemble an outline of an ancient fantasy dragon head. The front of the helmet was featureless and smooth. The third part of the armor was stored on the back of the soldiers. If activated the soldiers would struggle to fit in doorways and in rooms so this part of the armor was collapsed and stored on the back making the soldiers look like they had a turtle shell.

The soldier's identities, true force strength, and missions were constantly hidden from the command team. The armor prevented an observer from identifying the user. Voice emulators changed the voice and removed any emotional inflections. The solders names were never used. They are replaced by assignment designations. A1D7 was the system General of all Dragon Corp activities. A1D7, whose real name was Laura Oban, lead her soldiers into the building.

They were called into building and the meeting by Masters to participate in the briefing. When the UPHAF declared the Nubian system a Dark Sentinel her rules changed. It is the first-time Masters had access to all the Dragon Corps information. It was weird for A1D7 because she was used to having complete control over the forces under her command. Now she would have to answer to Masters. She didn't know how she felt about that yet but she knew she did not like the loss of control.

They walked onto the command deck to stares from the lower ranked officers. It was a surreal experience for A1D7. She knew most of the command staff by name and they knew her. Oban had dinner and drinks with most of them. She has laughed and joked with them. Yet, not one person knew it was her under the armor, even her fiancé. Rodgers stood tall in the room with his arms behind his back watching the soldiers with pride.

She just wanted to reach out to him. Say hello. Hug him. Being this close to him without being able to speak to him was torture but this was the life of a P5. A couple more years she thought to herself and she would be able leave the service and live a normal life. If they survived this she thought only to regret the image she placed in her head of Rodgers death. A1D7 walked up to the large rectangular workstation hub that dominated the room and stood in an open spot.

All the branches of the military had the top officer on the planet at the table except for Quasar Johnson of Orbital Guard. He was on Oya Battle Station and join via holo. One by one they shut down the terminal in front of them as the briefing time approached. The officers at the workstations that lined the room also stood and placed hands behind the back. A1D7 followed the action and waited for Lord Commander Masters to present the battle plan. He walked into the room and stood at his position at the head of the room.

"Today the Poveen have declared war on us. They have not declared war by communication but by action. They have invaded our system and disrupted our sovereignty with hostile technology. We are called upon to drive these invaders from our space, from our planets, and our homes.

All of you will receive an update of the current situation when this meeting is concluded. This room is filled with a lot of brilliant officers and soldiers. Over the next 90 hours all of you will be able to contribute to the plan of action. The details of the plan will not change but I would like to hear solutions or suggestion to your area of operation.

The Poveen have entered the system with 861 spacecraft of various sizes. Our current estimate of the force strength suggests that they have enough fire power to destroy all of forces and take control of the system. Orunmila only gives us a little over a 3 percent chance of reaching a stalemate if we cannot find a way to open an ER gate or bridge. I tell you this because the last time I faced odds this bad I gained the nickname the Butcher.

At the Battle of Butcher Bay the military AI provided me with a 6.8 percent chance of victory. This freed my officers and soldiers to think differently. In the end, we won the conflict. I lost a lot of friends and colleagues during that battle. We also lost more civilians than we would have liked. The hard truth is that we will not all make it to the end of this battle. Make no mistake. This is the last time we all stand together in this room. We all need to face the reality. We are all dead in my mind. Everyone. All of us and our families. Once you understand this truth, you will be able to find ways to save them.

Perspective is everything here. If you believe yourself to be alive, you will cower to protect yourself and those you love. If you believe those you love are behind enemy lines you will strike out. I need all of you to strike out. I need you to believe that the only way to save those you love is to punch a hole in the face of any squid you come across. I ask you again to fight for your life. They have stolen it from you.

All the forces in the system will now form 4 commands. Nubian Command will operate out of this location. This will also serve as the fallback location if any other command succumbs to hostile forces. I will remain here along with the System Planetary General Nasir and the System Orbit Guard Quasar Johnson.

The second command will operate on the planet Kush. Kush Command, will be headed by Sub-Commander Rodgers. System Meteor General Morris you will be assigned to the planet with the rest of the Meteor Corps. Together with the Kush garrison you should have enough firepower to hold off the Poveen. Your mission will be to deny entry of the enemy to the surface of the planet. If they land on the planet you are to repel the invaders.

The third command will operate in orbit above Carthage. That command will be led by Vice Commander Kahn. System Quasar of Space Command Rodriguez and Logistics Corps General Okafor you will join her. Your priority is the protection of the two ER gates, Hannibal Battle station, and Barca Staryards. General Okafor it is extremely important that your combat engineers assist in making the current carriers under construction able to contribute to this fight.

The Atlanta command will operate in the Atlantean planetary system on the moons Buckhead and Peachtree. This command will be led by Sub Commander Amir. Comet Corps System Quasar Tanaka and Astro Corps System Quasar Might will support Sub Commander Amir. It will be your duty to protect the refineries and mining operations in that planetary system. In terms of departure and readiness you currently have priority over the rest. You need to get going if you are going to make the party.

Details will follow this briefing. Good hunting," said Masters as he looked out across the officers in the room.

A1D7 pinged him to meet in private when the meeting was over. Masters agreed and they exited the main room into one of the side meeting rooms. The meeting room should be able to fit fifteen people but with the 6 soldiers in heavy body armor the room felt much smaller. Times like this A1D7 wished she could just walk around as Laura Oban like everyone else.

"Commander, we noticed that we were not involved in the initial battle plan. We feel that we can make a difference," said A1D7. Masters nodded in agreement at A1D7 but he didn't move. Masters and Kahn were torn between sending them into the first strike or holding the forces in reserve.

"I want to use you as well but I am trying to decide what would benefit our forces the most.

"I would like permission to create a Dragon Task Force with the various Dragon Corps unit in the system. We have a constellation of 6 heavy stealthstars roughly 4 AU from Kush. Each one of the heavy stealthstars hold two dragon brigades. The force is well equipped. Those soldiers were tracking mercenaries smuggling Poveen and human tech in and out of the systems in Echo region. The trail went cold here in the Nubian system but we still have reason to believe that those mercs are still in the system. We are attempting to find those individuals now because they may have a role in all of this. Those soldiers should be on the ground. Soldiers of that caliber sitting in space will do no one any good.

Here on Nubia, the personal guard that protects you and the command level officers, number over 1000. We can create another brigade with those ground forces to bring the total to nine. The 8 stealthstars would join the other heavy stealthstars to form a formidable stealth constellation space forces that can hit and run enemy formations or reinforce another unit.

Masters mulled it over for five minutes in complete silence. Then a light went off inside of his head. Masters looked up at the elite soldier. I know how I can use your assets. Send all ground forces to Kush, after this meeting report to Sub Commander Rodgers for your assignment. I think you can make more of a difference on Kush than Nubia. You can take 6 command stealthstars. I still want the other two for the transport of our senior officers to Atlanta and Carthage. Rodgers will ride on the stealthstar assigned to him to Kush and once he is safely on Kush then it will join the rest of the stealth constellation.

That constellation will have one mission. I need them to destroy one of the CIC cruisers. We have designated the 14 visible cruisers as the CIC cruisers. We have concluded that the interdictor field must be produced by one or all the 14 CIC cruisers. We need you to destroy one of them to find out before we deploy our forces in mass against those cruisers. The destruction of one of the CIC cruisers will determine our long-term battle plan in the system. Make sure your officers understand the importance of that mission," described Masters.

A1D7 nodded the massive helmet in agreement. Masters left the room as A1D7 sent an update on deployment to her soldiers. The strategy was sound. Kush didn't have the infrastructure nor the level of heavily armored soldiers because they had the planetary shield system powered by the ring. It would take the Poveen months to burn threw the shield. If they found a way passed the powerful shields than A1D7 would join forces with the rest of her soldiers to help repel the enemy. The best part of it was the fact that she would travel to Kush with her Rodgers.

PLUS 4 HOURS AND 15 MINUTES
SYSTEM ASTRO QUASAR
NATASHA MIGHT
OGUN STATION, NUBIA
DEPLOYMENT

Fiery red head absorbed the white light of the CIC. Freckles bounced on her otherwise pale skin as she traded orders with members of the Astro Corps. Might pushed the officers under her command. They had to get off the planet and out to the Atlanta planetary system soon and the pressure was starting to mount. Light blue eyes assaulted excuses without mercy. Such things would not be tolerated today. She moved back to the rectangular table in the middle of the room to coordinate with the other two officers that would also head to Atlanta, Quasar Tanaka and Sub Commander Amir.

Might received calculations and readouts from the AI Orunmila and she quickly passed them to the consoles of the officers of the Astro Corps. Extreme confidence radiated from the Quasar. The Astro Corps had two prominent roles in the United Planets of Humanity Armed Forces. The first role is to establish systemheads with advanced ER gates and bridges into hostile systems or regions of space. The second mission is to destroy hostile ER gates, ER bridges, and respond rapidly to any incursions into human space or region. It is a spaceborn force that never operates inside of gravity well.

The vessels under her command are heavier than the same class of star in other branches. The stars are made to take a beating because of the roles they serve. This limits how fast the ships can travel which is the reason that Lord Commander Masters prioritized it. Quasar Might commanded a supercluster of 20 warstars, 20 gunstars, 20 dreadstars, 20 heavy starcruisers, and 200 starfrigates. The bulk of her force was in a trailing orbit around Nubia. 100 of starfrigates that were stationed near Ogun Station at Ogun Starport lifted off 15 minutes prior and reached greater orbit in anticipation of joining forces with the rest of the super cluster.

Quasar Might watched her screen with pride as her well-trained soldiers and officers mobilized the force into an efficient formation in trailing Nubia orbit. The vessels of war also carried relief supplies and enough provisions for the two moons to last another 6 months. The commander of the Super Cluster sent a message to Quasar Might that indicated all the stars were aligned and they were ready to execute burn to Atlanta. Might lifted her head from the console and looked at Lord Commander Masters right after she gave the command for burn.

“Sir, the super cluster is on the way to Atlanta at maximum burn,” yelled Quasar Might. Lord Commander Masters held his right fist in the arm and cheered. The rest of the CIC cheered loudly. The first response to Poveen aggression is underway. The mighty engines burned hot as the vessels moved out of orbit. Over the next hour, the spacecraft would slowly increase speed until it reached an acceleration of 20 g forces only to stop the burn once the spacecraft travelled at 20 percent the speed of light.

Sub-Commander Amir Yosef, her current direct commanding officer, turned to her and smiled and spoke words of encouragement. Might smiled back, how could she not, the sub commander was definition of handsome man stood flanked by the other two generals. His angular face and sculptured features focused intently were extremely pleasant to look at. Might sent a message to General Tanaka asking if she could help him with the assignment.

With her super cluster under burn the next group of stars to leave the Nubian orbit are the spacecraft of the Comet Corps led by General Tanaka. Two hours wasn't a lot of time in the world of planetary deployment but the three elite officers worked diligently with Orunmila to optimize deployment, loading, and launch order of the forces. Both Might and Amir are otherwise humorous and boisterous but during this process they were nothing but humble and sober. The responsibility now placed upon them reflected in the level of professionalism on display. People's lives were on the line and it wasn't time to play. In hours, over 50 million souls would depend on them to prevent the Poveen from killing them.

Might didn't like remaining behind as her forces left but she would catch up to them in moment when she departed with the other two high ranking officers. The later flight would also place a substantial personal cost on the noble woman. Most Astros are from low gravity worlds like she is. The weakness of the body due to the low gravity means that they have a much harder time, even after the heavy gravity augment, of matching the high gravity counterparts during high gravity burns. Most of the low gravity people can only top out at maximum 25g burns. The Astro corps will accelerate at 20gs toward Atlanta but the Comet Corps will accelerate at 25gs for over an hour and decelerate at the end at the same g-force. Though she is technically rated for 27gs Might is not looking forward to the experience. This will test her physical condition and could break her bones, collapse her lungs, create a stroke, or something worse if her gravity rating was off.

The other reason she stayed behind was that the mission to Atlanta would be conducted at relativistic speeds. They would experience less time during the trip and the command staff needed to finish preparations for the arrival plans before they left for the Atlanta system to ensure the solutions arrived before they did. Now that her forces had launched she supplemented the actions of the Comet Command the same way the System Quasar Ryu Tanaka help her.

General Tanaka kicked into motion with the focus on soldiers and officers under his command. The olive skinned, brown-eyed black haired main focused on the mission and the process. The Comet Corps was tasked in the United Planet of Humanity Armed Forces as the tactical low gravity assault and defense force. If you need a space station controlled, you send in the comets. If you need a ship boarded you send in the Comets. If you need a mining installation on a moon shut down, you send in the Comets. On the flip side, if you need any of those defended you also send in the Comets. Unlike the Astro Corps the Comet Corps had provided on the ground support.

In countless military actions the Astros and the Comets worked side by side in assaults and defenses. Might helped Tanaka and his forces ready for deployment. Quasar Might's soldiers left with the spacecraft and General Tanaka's forces were doing the same. Around the room as time passed the various station officers would close the stations they worked on and leave without a replacement. Across the planet on almost every sky elevator was carrying fully equipped comets to space stations to board 2 troopstars to the Atlanta system. 200 thousand human Comets and 800 thousand artificial human soldiers loaded the massive transport stars.

The ground force the Comet Corps was supplemented by a complement of 20000 interceptstars 200 starbombers, 2000 starpuppets, 700 breechstars, 100 speedstars, 200 starfrigades, 12 dreadstars, and 40 warstars. The assault force is based on speed and quick strike ability. The bulk of the forces are designed to be small enough to evade the larger caliber weapons while still large enough to take hits from smaller ordinance and keep going. This would allow them to land on the surface of the assaulting target, breach the hull, and destroy it from the inside.

The process took a little over an hour and the time for departure was coming quickly for the team. Once the last soldier boarded the last sky elevator they knew it was time. They would depart from Nubia bound for Atlanta. They would come back victorious or they would not come back at all.

Sub-Commander Amir nodded to Commander Masters acknowledging it was time to depart. Masters saluted the officers. He then walked around to the Sub Commander Amir and gave him a hug. The two of them had gone to hell and back once before and it was clear that they were going to have to go to war again. Might smiled, she rarely saw emotion out of Masters and it was good to see that the man cared for his people outwardly. Might thought about making it a three-way hug but decided she shouldn't.

Tanaka, Might, and Amir then walked off the Command Deck. It took a little less than five minutes for the trio to reach the roof of the installation. Inside the deep black transport their personal effects and outer layer of the armor kits waited for them. Dragon Team escorts in full armor assigned to the stealth ship transporting them to Atlanta flanked them on all sides. The cabin was silent for the first minute of the trip until Amir spoke.

"How are we doing? Tanaka? Might? How are you two holding up? You ready for this? Say something before I go crazy in this silence," said Amir as he tried to lighten the mood on the transport. They were currently done with the planning segment of the mission for the moment, and Amir wanted to ease his officers.

"You asking me to dinner or something? If you are, you better take me to a holo-movie first. A good one too, not one of those romantic comedies. That dinner better be curry too. None of this Victory System food I want only hard core Nubian food. I know your soft stomach can't handle it but that's what a growing girl like me needs. Can you handle that? Probably not," said Might as she picked up on the tone of the question from Amir. She was finally free of the oppression of the CIC command deck and set free by Amir's question.

Amir smirked and said "Only if you are putting out. I am a busy man. I don't want that weak stuff either. If I must eat curry I want butt stuff. If my butt is going to burn later so is yours," responded the only person in the command staff that could trade jabs with her and not get offended.

The cabin of the craft burst into laughter. That was the goal. Amir had to relax the troops and he knew Might could help him do that. The battle with the Poveen was still 90 hours away and he couldn't have his senior staff tense for the entire trip. He knew they wouldn't be able to joke like this for much longer so he wanted to get this out of the system now.

"Watch out Amir. That's my girl. Keep hitting on my woman and I will challenge you to a dual. Since you can't shoot for shit I feel confident in my victory. After, that I will claim my prize. The fiery maiden from Brooklyn" said Tanaka as he put his arm around Might. She then snuggled close to him while making the pouty lips toward Amir.

"Well I guess I can't compete with the legend of Tanaka. Defender of Tokyo and master of the realm of humanity," Amir said in a revertant voice as he raised his hand and waved it in the air.

"Gentlemen, you can share," said Might in a sultry voice that confused the two men. They didn't know if she was serious or joking. In a way, she was joking, but if they said yes, she may do it. The two fake suiters laughed again and it remained a joke. Unless they changed their minds later of course. In that situation, she would tear them up. Might laughed to herself internally at the thought.

"Sub Commander Amir, how did you destroy a Poveen droopstar at the Battle of Butcher Bay? You are the only Comet to ever to pull off that maneuver. We may need to do it again," asked Tanaka as he shifted back into serious for a moment. Soldiers didn't like to ask other soldiers about something so personal. Tanaka knew that asking Amir would trigger memories of those he lost that day and all of those he lost during the battle but it was relevant information for the coming battle.

"It's simple. Aim for the sphere on the back of the cruiser. Attack the rear of it at the connection point where it meets the rest of the superstructure. You can't see the seam but it is underneath the hull. Once you puncture it, you will be sucked inside. The Poveen starships run off a controlled singularity. Drop your ordinance close to the containment sphere and get out. The explosion will disrupt the containment and the gravity will collapse the vessel. I have done it multiple times. Each time I almost died. Every time at least one member of the team died. But, I took those bastards down," said Amir as the two locked eyes. This wasn't bravado or braggadocios. This was the truth. Amir was the most decorated officer in the Comet Corps before he was promoted into the Command Corps.

Tanaka nodded his head. He quickly realized that he shifted the mood slightly. Might quickly cracked a joke about Tanaka and the mood was once again lightened until the ship landed at the space port. Clearance allowed the elite officers to land right next to the stealthstar. This variant of the star was for command and control. It is equipped with quantum communication to connect to the officer QEN and all manner of EM jamming.

The stealthstar measured 400 meters long and looks like a handleless smooth black dagger. The hull was absolute black. The material that lined the hull absorbed light completely. Underneath sat three layers of carbon composite armor before a layer of titanium armor. The spacecraft was extremely hard to detect and made it the ideal transport of senior officers.

The trio and accompanying soldiers took an elevator up to the side of hull and walked into the star. The dark and close quarters were common on starships like this. The powerful vessel packed a lot of equipment, projectiles, and shielding into every corner and crack. It took 35 minutes for the star to lift off and join the rest of the Comet Corps in space. For the second time in 2 hours a major force departed from Nubia headed toward the massive gas giant Atlanta. Thousands of ships ignited engines and burned toward the futures.

The planetary system centered around the gas giant Atlanta. Its light orange and green gases make it look like a large and powerful marble. It is roughly ten times largest moons from a population standpoint. Defense of the area will start with those two moons.

Buckhead is the 8th moon from the planet and it is larger than Mars but lacks an atmosphere. The moon boasts a population of roughly 35 million on the moon in various cities. The moon has a planetary ring system that projects a magnetic field to protect the people on the surface from the radiation from the gas giant. The moon is a major mining facility. It has one of the richest deposits of rare earth minerals ever found. This moon not only supplies the Nubian system with rare metals but six other systems as well. The moon moves around the planet in the opposite direction of the other moons and must have been captured by Atlanta after it formed.

Peachtree is slightly larger than Buckhead and is the 17th moon in the system. This moon is also devoid of atmosphere but unlike Buckhead this moon primary purpose it to refine metals and not mine them. It also contains the command and control center for the planetary system. It has a slightly smaller population of 17 million people but the planet has twice human footprint as Buckhead.

The Atlanta system boast one of the largest Orbital Guards in the Human Sphere due to the wealth of the Buckhead moon. Pirates, smugglers, and criminal organizations target the moon daily. That harassment may have provided the means in which they can defend themselves. This is going to favor the defenders of the area. The station has 6 starcruisers, 50 starvettes, 12 starfrigates, 200 star puppets, and 200 interceptstars. When combined with the Astro and Comet forces they will present a challenge to the Poveen cruisers burning toward the system.

Quasar Might understood this information already but she reviewed it again as the engines of the craft pushed it forward. She was trying to find some way to take her mind off the g forces that now pressed against her body but she couldn't. The force of the acceleration pushed down on her body with tremendous force. The burn lasted for almost an hour before the formation caught up to the previous formation. When they arrived at the Atlanta system they would decelerate at a lower g force. The worst was over for the moment.

PLUS 10 HOURS
COMMAND CORPS LORD COMMANDER
MALCOM MASTERS
OGUN STATION, NUBIA
SCOPE OF WAR

Two hundred light years away the command was initiated to place the Nubian System and the rest of the Human Sphere into Protocol 5. The message traveled via quantum entanglement to Ogun Station and then into all the systems of the planet. The Protocol 5 notification appeared on the individual HUDs of the soldiers and officers in the Nubian system and it finally portrayed the scope of this conflict.

In the Victory and Sol System the massive military computers were beginning to match the most suitable candidates to begin the creation of more Protocol 5 humans. Corporations would start winding down production of the civilian equipment and begin building the designated military equipment that they would be assigned to them. Any staryard in the human sphere that was constructing a craft of leisure would have to rapidly finish the construction of the craft or push the unfinish hull out of the construction facility and start building the designated military starship.

For the first time in 36 years the human sphere was in a state of war with an alien race.

Masters was pinged by the Nubian government and from Orunmila almost at the same time. Masters quickly set up a meeting in 15 minutes to give all the representatives from the Nubian leadership group time to attend. Everyone on the list agreed to the meeting within seconds. It seemed that the age of tricks and posturing may be at an end. It was no longer Masters the one that told the elite of the system what to do. They all felt that they could handle that. Now the human central government would tell them what to do.

Orunmila needed permission for expanded access. The Dark Sentinel designation allows for the massive computer intelligence to begin the process of resource management. Protocol 5 allows the AI to use 80 percent of the planetary computing power. In this case, the request was made to reach the 80 percent threshold and remain at that level until the end of hostilities or the removal of the Dark Sentinel designation.

Besides the computer power threshold increase the Protocol 5 had less of a meaning to the people of the Nubian Systems since Dark Sentinel was already activated. Protocol 5 was a major wakeup call to the rest of the Human Sphere. On the news, some pundits were calling it a false flag, a means for the government to spend more on war, but now they would all see this for what it really was. This was a threat to humanity itself.

Fifteen minutes later Masters walked off the deck of the CIC and into the communications room to join the call. This time he would arrive first to reassure the leadership of the planet that he was prepared to fight the enemy. He was nervous that the meeting might go sideways again. They all needed to be on the same page after this meeting or the chances of them winning this conflict would be small. The leaders arrived early and the entire arena was ready two minutes before the meeting was supposed to start. This was extremely rare. Usually one party or another would arrive late to force the others to wait to prove some point but today no points needed to be made.

"Okay let's get right to it. The Poveen have invaded this system with enough firepower to take the system from us. All of us are in extreme danger and we can't win the day if we work together. I cannot release all the information yet because we are still securing our communications networks. Poveen have been known to create artificial humans and deploy them in our systems. Any attack of this size would include a scouting force of this type. Orunmila is currently working on finding any such machines in the system. Once we have the go-ahead from Orunmila the military feeds will begin to be distributed information to you.

All your satellites have been instructed to move to one of the Orbital Battle stations. They will dock and will be protected during the engagement. When those assets are safe and secure we will launch the battlite network and all communications will go through our systems. In 2 to 3 hours the AI Orunmila will have complete control of our system and actively monitor any attempts to invade our communication network. Until that time, you will need to remain patient.

We started the process of removing civilians in the system out of immediate danger. We are tight beaming all your deep system corporate, mining, refining, communications, and luxury operations instructions on how to prepare for the coming conflict. Those that can make it to one of the protection zones are being directed to do so. Those who are not able to make it to one of the 4 zones are being instructed to hide and await further orders. We have begun the process of sending resupplies to those deep in the system to ensure they can survive for at least year. The unmanned drones we have launched will arrive to most installations in a day or two and since they are relatively small and unpowered after the initial burn we suspect that the enemy will not declare them a major threat.

These are trying times but you have an excellent team of Officers and professionals working for you that have faced odds like this before including myself. Just know this. If we ask you to do something for us we it done. We may not be as forth coming with as many answers or explanations that you would like because the order will be based on extremely calculated understanding and knowledge thus making the time to explain wasteful. I want you to want to help yourself and the rest of the people of the system.

I am going to be as honest as I can. If you do not work with us we die. If you think that you can hold back critical resources so that after the conflict you can have a strategic advance over your competitor we die. If you think you are more important than others we die. A safe zone does not exist in the system and panic at any level means we die. Our ancestors that came to this system knew of the Poveen risk when they travelled to the system and they braved that danger and we must now do the same. We have to be strong," said Masters as he awaited a barrage of questions.

President Light, his uncle-in-law, stood and spoke. "We spoke before this meeting and you will have all of our support in this matter. We are here for you and we are ready to help in the fight." Masters nodded in agreement until another question came from the corporate section. The woman that asked the question was very familiar to the Lord Commander. They shared 4 children together, they shared 48 years of marriage together. It was his elegant wife and former Nubian Senator Layla Light-Masters.

"How is the Lord Commander? How are all the commanders doing? What is the morale of the troops? Tell them they have people that care for them out here regardless of what decisions they make," said his wife. For hours, she debated the future of the marriage in her head until she felt guilty that her husband was trying to save all of them and she was merely thinking of the best way to help the Light family gain more power or influence. The Light family had dominated the politics of the Nubian system and were looking to push into the galactic political scene and that was the reason she needed her husband to win office in the system while her uncle became a galactic senator. All of that was still important to her but not as important as the man. Her husband needed to understand that she was behind him now and forever.

"The Lord Commander is nervous but confident. Every decision I make will cost the lives of my soldiers and officers. The burden of command has been accepted by the commanders and me. Morale is high because they believe in the command staff. Our record against the Poveen is better than any other system in the Human Sphere. Sub Commander Amir and I have fought the Poveen before and won. The rank and file soldier is confident that we can do it again. To be honest, most soldiers and officers are more worried for our family's safety than ours," said Masters. It was good to see his wife and he would give anything to walk over and give her a kiss and a hug. But it was not so. Such actions would have to wait until the conflict is over.

The meeting ended without incident. For some reason this troubled him. No one overreached or took a misstep. Not one of the leaders pushed back in the slightest. Either everyone was on board or they were making plans in secret to "solve" the problem. Masters was suddenly uncomfortable. Orunmila pinged him again once the meeting was over. Masters agreed to speak with the AI as he still contemplated the meeting.

"Hello sir, I hope you don't mind but I monitored the meeting. The actions of the representatives do not match the communications traffic. The Kush President is not in agreement with any of the action taken by your administration. Furthermore, 4 of the major corporations are moving to hide pivotal assets and changed reporting systems to hide them. How do you want me to proceed?"

"Continue to monitor but do nothing unless it poses a threat to the system or the soldiers. If it does pose a threat contact me immediately. We need to understand who is against us and what their end game is before we move on them," said Masters as he paced around the communications room. Orunmila communicated directly into the machine connected to his mind so it was disorienting at times when he didn't have anything to look at or talk to directly. Many chose to create a projection or an artificial face created in the line of sight to solve the problem. Masters did neither.

"Do you have time to review what else I have found or do you want me to send it to you in a report," asked the AI. Masters agreed to the request and sat down in one of the chairs that lined the room. He didn't know how long the meeting would last so he sat ready to hear the information at hand.

"Sir, I have found hidden signals within all of our networks. They are extremely sophisticated and will take some time to crack but A1D7 was correct. The Poveen have alien agents on this planet. I have yet to find any indication that the infiltration is on any other planet or moon in the system but I will continue to follow the trail. If I Identify a problem on those planets I will update you. Once the battlite system is up and running to 100 percent I will be able to identify the enemy agents at that time.

Kush has an extremely high amount of activity from a communication and logistical perspective that cannot be explained by any orders given by military command. The actions on the planet need to be watched carefully. It appears something is happening on the planet that might pose a threat to the outcome of the battle to take place on Kush. I am analyzing the data and once I have calculated a reason the movement and communication I will present it," said the AI as it was cut off by Masters.

"Leverage. President Lawrence is trying to get leverage. Right now, he is out of the decision-making process. To regain power and return to the planning process, he needs more leverage. He needs something that he knows I will need in the future. Once he has that then he set his terms and I would have to comply. Orunmila I need you to secure the orbital ring, planetary shielding, and planetary weapon systems first," demanded Masters and he rubbed his chin contemplating the extent that President Lawrence may go.

"I will prioritize sir. Also, Lord Commander, there is another issue that I would like to discuss. It was not an important factor in your planning until you ordered A1D7 to Kush. I believe the command structure is now compromised," said the AI. Masters sat up in his chair wondering why that could be so he interrupted the program.

"What is the problem. Can it be fixed?"

"I do not understand human relationships enough to know if it can be fixed. A1D7 has broken procedure and is now in breach of command. She is in an unlawful relationship with a commanding officer. His records indicate that he is unaware but he suspects. I do not recommend disciplinary actions against him. A1D7 should be relieved of command. I have withheld names to save you from making an emotional decision," said the AI. Masters was angered that the AI would say that about him and his decision-making process but clearly, he knew both people in question.

"Orunmila I need more information than that. I am ordering you to unmask the names. I understand the ramifications of unmasking a Dragon Corps member and the senior officer," replied Masters.

"I understand. A1D7 is Laura Oban and the senior officer in question is Sub Commander Mike Rodgers. The names are now unmasked. How do you want to proceed?"

"Shit. Give me a second," said Masters as he contemplated what he heard. Laura was A1D7. The thought never crossed his mind. Instantly he understood Orunmila reasoning for not telling him. For five minutes, he weighted pros and cons. Than a simple question was poised to the machine.

"Would our combat effectiveness drop if A1D7 is removed from command?"

"Yes, B1D7 is not the same caliber of commander," responded Orunmila. Masters thought about it some more and then responded to the machine.

"Do nothing. I will handle this. I am disagreeing with you to maintain the best commanders in the field. We will have a conflict but I can live with that until the invasion is over. We will prosecute the crime at that point in time. Having A1D7 in another role during this conflict would hurt our chances of victory but I will give Rodgers and Morris the chance to decide when the time comes. Send a report highlighting all the major avenues of concern and I will follow up on them," said Masters as he stood from the chair.

"Okay Sir. Do you need anything else from me?"

"No, we will reconvene in 2 hours for the update," said Masters as he walked out of the room toward the CIC deck. The machine agreed and the conversation was over. A lot had changed in the last twenty minutes and now it was time to create a plan to prepare for the fallout.

Before he could stand he received another message. This time it was from the SciTech ambassador on Nubia. The Nubian Government and the SciTech government have worked side by side for over 150 years. The Nubian system is only one of four systems that have a SciTech embassy.

"Ambassador Suman how can I help you?"

"Lord Commander Masters I have come to lend my aid to you. I was just briefed on the situation in situation of the military commander. I just wanted you to know that our scientist is working on the bridge and gate problem. When we have a solution, we will provide it. Also, we have five hundred elite soldiers here. They can be of use," said the ambassador.

"How did you get briefed?"

"Once protocol 3 is enacted the agreement between the SciTech and the United Planets of Humanity triggers. They have briefed us and the mutual line of communication is now open. Our QEN with our home system is providing us with updates from the Victory System. We know what you know. I think we will be able to help in the conflict. If I have any solution I will share it with you. I just wanted to ensure that you knew we were holding up our commitment of joint defense with the UPHAF," said Ambassador Suman. Masters agreed to the help and closed the channel. Access to the most advanced corporation-state in the galaxy was a bonus that Masters did not expect. Relieved it wasn't another political stunt, trick, or deception Masters stood and exited the room. It was time to get back to the war effort.

PLUS 20 HOURS
SYSTEM LOGISTICS CORPS GENERAL NAKIA OKAFOR
OGUN STATION, NUBIA
MOVEMENT

General Nakia Okafor of the Logistics Corps monitored the movement of her combat engineering brigades as they boarded the massive space elevators to the space stations for deployment to Carthage. Twenty thousand of the best logistics soldiers in the system prepared to launch into the black of space. The mission on the Logistics Corps was simple in scope but difficult to accomplish. They will have a little over 40 hours to prepare the starships still under construction at the Barca Staryards for combat against the Poveen.

The general was in the shared personal quarters meters from the CIC command deck preparing the last of her personal effects for the trip. The starship she was assigned to will take off and bring her to Carthage shortly. Exhausted from the events of the day she battled the fatigue with constant movement and focus. The stimulants that once flowed freely when the Poveen entered the system were wearing off and the systems that monitored the body refused to dispense more. She needed to sleep, nap, or sit down to break the 24-hour grind that she was on.

General Okafor was happy that she found a couple of minutes to speak to her husband and children fifteen minutes prior as she packed for departure. Seeing his face and long dreadlocks filled her heart with joy. His powerful words of encouragement were the very thing needed in a time like this. Okafor wasn't called on to fight much anymore and this entire experience was new for her. Early in her career when she was crazy and dumb the combat engineer would take all the most dangerous missions. These actions helped her career progression and forced her behind a desk before she was ready. She found it ironic that when she was forced behind a desk she didn't want to go but now that she has spent the better part of two decades behind one the notion of combat was terrifying.

In between monitoring the movements of her soldiers the officer prepped her combat protocols and refreshed combat inside a vessel. This was second nature to the officer once but now it was if the tactics were brand new. 24 hours ago, Okafor was enjoying a lovely evening with her husband drinking tea and people watching on Johnson Bay. Now she packed to travel over 5 AU away from Nubia to the Barca Staryards to get starships still under construction into the fight against an alien species. "What a difference 24 hours makes," she thought.

Preparing the deployment of the forces to Carthage was not her only assigned duty. Over the last two hours civilian starcraft offloaded goods once meant to leave the system by ER gates were now redirected into the war effort. She cataloged and transported the materials to the areas that needed them the most. Okafor had to make all the hard decisions on resources like water, food, and equipment. Orunmila assisted all using most of the vast computing power in the efforts. Soldiers moved across the planet placing materials and equipment where they were needed.

The tall lean officer left the quarters and made her way to the command deck with her personal effects in the yellow personal effects bag assigned by the Logistics corp. Okafor arrived at her station and activated it after placing the bag under the console. The sign in was quick and within moments the status of the deployment was front and center. The fight against sleep was getting more intense by the minute.

Next to General Okafor stood System Quasar Valerie Rodriguez. The woman from the Azteca system via the planet Farragut was on duty when the Poveen invaded. Just like Okafor, she battled sleep, dark purple circles formed under her pink eyes.

"I am so tired," said Okafor to Rodriguez in a low voice.

"Me too, I could sleep on the console right now. I don't think I have ever been more excited to get off duty. I think I have just stared at the console for the last thirty minutes without doing any more work. I don't feel I can. I believe that if I did anything now it would be wrong," responded Rodriguez.

"Me too. I am trying to make it to the transport and that is it. I will also finish the prep work when I wake up. I wish this damn machine would allow me to pop some more stims but I guess we have had our fill," Okafor joked. Rodriguez tried to smile but couldn't. She was too tired and so was Okafor. The two zombied onward reviewing the updates while not making any changes that could affect the broader mission if they were not time sensitive.

Quasar Rodriguez spent the last six hours ensuring that all space assets were positioned around the system. The bulk of the starships were already surrounding Carthage in port at Hannibal Station or on the way. The 2 massive nova class ships were on opposite sides of the system. One of the enormous starships would travel to Kush while the other would arrive at Hannibal station.

The rest of the Space Command assets bound to Carthage will depart in forty-five minutes. Reservist and active duty spacers on vacation were all called to active duty on the planet to crew the vessels still under construction. The transportation for them had to be found and used. Okafor conscripted any starship that they could find to fly to the Carthage system. Each minute that passed it seemed like they found more veteran spacers that could assist in the war effort. Nubia had an excess of assault craft that required pilots.

It was dangerous to leave Nubia with thousands of pilots in unarmed starcraft but they simply didn't have the time to burn to Carthage, return to Nubia, and then burn to Carthage again. The strategic reward of having those pilots reach Carthage and pilot the assault level craft was so high that they had no choice but to risk the deployment of those assets in civilian starships. The trip would take about 25 hours and once they arrived it would take another 20 hours to prep all the starships for battle. They would have another 20 hours to prepare for combat. Plenty of time if the enemy kept the schedule it currently presented.

Vice Commander Priyanka Kahn walked onto the command deck with her personal effects and her dragon armor hovering behind her. She was fresh from eight hours of sleep. Kahn would be the one required to stay awake during the trip to the Carthage system while Okafor and Rodriguez slept. The team was beginning to manage sleep cycles. The rotation would become more important as the Poveen approached and they needed to have fresh command officers. The dynamic leader was cycling through the progress during her sleep. She always valued the professionalism of the General Okafor and Quasar Rodriguez and they have not disappointed her.

Okafor nodded to the commander as she made eye contact with her. Kahn looked so fresh and rested and the face Kahn returned toward Okafor indicated that she understood how tired the two of them were. Kahn walked over two officers and thanked them for the work that they have conducted when she was rested. Each highlighted improvement to the plan and the progress that was made. Kahn nodded in agreement and then looked at the time.

Masters walked onto the CIC deck as the time for departure neared. He walked over toward the three women that were on duty when the Poveen bridged into the system. Okafor was pleased with his leadership to date and the confidence he instilled in the command staff. This was not the time to shrink in the moment and he was not. Okafor always wondered if the stories of his bravery and composure were true and if the last 20 hours was any indication they were.

"Vice Commander Kahn, General Okafor, and Quasar Rodriguez. I received confirmation that your preflight tasks are completed on time. You all have performed extremely well during this crisis so far. I need you to keep it up and keep the rest of your team focused," he said as he stood from the couch and walked to his armor that stood by itself on the deck. It hissed and closed quickly.

"Sir. We will be leaving shortly. Do you need anything else from me before I leave?" asked Kahn as Okafor cheered inside. Leaving meant sitting and sleeping. Currently, that was all she could think of. Masters agreed that it was time for them to leave. Okafor and Rodriguez picked up the travel bags they packed on the floor. The floor erupted with cheer once again as the officers walked for the door. The cheering provided a sudden rush of energy to the tired officer. A quick smile and nod to the crowd ended once they arrived in the hallway.

They travelled to the roof and then to the Spaceport to depart from the planet. General Okafor didn't make her way to the bridge of the vessel instead she travelled to her quarters where she strapped herself into the crash couch and promptly feel asleep. The Stealthstar they travelled on took to the sky and then meet with the remaining force bound for Carthage. The mighty vessels accelerated at 2gs. This was much slower than the vessel was capable of but it was the fasted speed of the slowest starship in the convoy.

PLUS 35 HOURS
PLANETARY FORCE GENERAL
JAMAAL NASIR
FORWARD STATION, NUBIA
HIDDEN PLOT

"General Nasir, how long until you land?" asked Lord Commander Masters.

"I land in 5 minutes sir," replied Nasir.

"Good. I need you to go DEFCON 1. Call up 100% of the reserves. We just refined the subspace search again. We can see those cruisers in subspace now. One more refinement and we should be able to see the variant types. We are comfortable with full deployment. When you land get your forces ready," said Lord Commander Masters.

"Okay sir. We will have everyone ready to go. When the Poveen arrive. Sir, anything else?"

"Yes, I am sending you a packet of information. Orunmila started to process the information from the Dragon Corps. It is starting to get interesting. I need you to put a team on it. I think it is something. Need one of your people in the loop on this one," said Lord Commander Masters.

"I got it. I can put Colonel Nduwke on it sir," said Nasir.

'Yes, good. His team will do nicely. Have them look at it and then respond," said Masters.

"Yes sir," said General Nasir before Masters closed the line. Nasir sat on the transport and received the information. It was packets of well-organized information. It outlined a group of men and women that are in the Nubian system. The actions of the cell were legal and illegal. At first glance Nasir couldn't make sense of the data he saw. The answer to this puzzle was not obvious and he didn't have time to figure it out. Quickly he used the system to setup a meeting with Colonel Nduwke when he landed.

The transport landed on a massive airfield at Forward Station. The early signs of an enormous military effort were evident. In the sky above Forward Station massive numbers of drones hovered and circled the base. Currently the priority went to the massive transport aircraft that landed. Each transport was filled with thousands of soldiers. Battle trains lined the airfields. Soldiers would disembark the planes and head into equipment hangars to get outfitted into the land mechs that regular infantry of Nubia wore. Then they boarded the massive trains to the area of deployment.

Nasir stepped off the transport and walked toward the command center. The Planetary Nubia General Bello stood in anticipation with 4 military police soldiers in full armor. She was born on the low gravity moon of Buckhead and it was the reason the woman almost stood 2 meters in height. Military augmentations hardened her otherwise brittle bones and muscles. Bello stood with power and elegance. Coffee skin, light brown short hair, face full of freckles, and smiled greeting her commanding officer.

The two traded salutes and then stood side by side as they walked inside the massive bunker structure. The giants of the command for the Nubian system have been friends for a long time.

"Sir, what are we facing here? Information has been limited," said Bello.

"We are still trying to find out. We are out teched. Squids ER bridged into the system like a raiding mission. This time the Poveen used an interdictor technology that nullifies starships ability to use bridge drives and ER gates from punching a hole in space-time. It is like they can't generate enough power to punch through. That is not the whole thing either. In subspace, they have over 800 cruisers in hiding and trailing the visible craft. We don't want to transmit that information. I just received word that we are going DEFCON 1. This is real.

Our techs are confident that they can handle the situation but I don't know if they will handle it in time. We need to be ready down here. How is the team coming along?"

"The team is all here. Everyone is waiting in the bunker."

"Excellent."

The two elite officers walked onto the elevator and travelled to the bunk deep underground. They exited on the command level and quickly moved to the rear of the structure to the complex. Command officers greeted the duo when they entered the command center. The room was a massive complex with hundreds of officers monitoring troop deployment, enemy movements, and combat status. The room felt different than the command deck at Ogun Station.

The room was staffed with over ninety percent Nubians. They moved with a purpose that wasn't seen in the other room. The United Planets of Humanity Armed Forces required that each system provide at least ninety percent of the System Planetary Force. This is to ensure systems don't leach off other systems. The Nubian System was one of the richest systems per capita in the Echo region of space and the entire human sphere. They did not run from the commitment either. The armed forces were fully staffed and well trained.

Nasir reached the command deck and quickly moved with General Bello to the officer war room. He entered the room and the officers inside stood to salute. Nasir saluted back and the men and women of the room sat down. He knew all the officers in the room well. They have spent the better part of the last thirty years together. Nasir trusted every officer in the room with his life and they trusted him.

"Okay everyone. I know information has not been very forth coming. The reason for that is we are having a hard time finding out what we are dealing with. The technology they are using is much better than the technology that we have available. From what we can tell 301 enemy cruisers are on a vector for Nubia. It is hard to tell the type of cruiser but for now we are confident that they have 301 moving toward Nubia. The estimated time of arrival is in sixty hours.

I am going to need us ready in forty hours. Full deployment. The chances the Poveen will be able to launch a successful mission is likely. Our only space support will be the orbital stations. We will not have Space

Command, Comet Corps, Astro Corps, or Meteor Corps. Our mission is to hold the line. Our mission is to make sure those squids don't take one inch of Nubian soil. I will remain here for the entire conflict. I am also in contact with General Jones on Kush. We will coordinate accordingly. Any questions?"

"Sir, why did the space force leave?" asked the Carthage born Airforce General.

"I am going to be honest because I need you all to understand your part in the broader mission. We can't win a starship to starship battle with the Poveen at the numbers they entered the system with. The plan is to have Kush turtle under its shield. This action will hold the Poveen forces in orbit for weeks. We need the force that is currently burning to Atlanta to delay and harass the Poveen force around the gas giant and moons. The Nubian force needs to bloody the enemy so they call for help from one of the other locations. The force that is burning to Carthage needs to win a starship to starship battle. They will have the numbers to win the straight up fight," responded Nasir.

"So, we are putting the entire war effort to protect Nubia in the hands of non-Nubians?" asked the Admiral of the Navy in his raspy voice.

"Vice Commander Kahn and Quasar Okafor are on the leadership team headed toward Hannibal Battle Station. The entire station is Nubian. The Barca Staryards are Nubian. In the end that doesn't matter. Those officers will do the job they are commanded to do. They are all good soldiers. I need all of you to know that. Those officers will put their lives on the line and die for the people of this system. We have to be ready here. We have to be ready to defend this planet."

For the next twenty minutes the room shifted from deployment questions to strategy and the defense of the planet questions. With the limited information, they needed a flexible plan. The command officers of the services devised a three-tier plan. The first part of the plan would consist of the rapid response smaller forces. The force will move to the front and counter attack any invasion and the attempts of the Poveen to create a planethead.

If the Poveen can establish a planethead the second tier of the force will engage en masse on the enemy. This response is responsible for stopping the enemy advance and collapsing the lines of movement for the enemy army units. The third tier of the attack are the cavalry forces to reinforce breakouts and support units under attack by enemy advances. The officers left the room to prepare the forces for the coming conflict when the meeting concluded.

Nasir told Colonel Nduwke to take a walk with him. Nduwke agreed and the two men walked out of the room and into the elevator. The duo remained silent until they got on a transport tran a couple of minutes later.

"I have a mission for you. It is of the highest importance," said General Nasir to the most trusted intelligence officer. Nduwke wasn't from one the political families on Nubia. No one in his family is connect to any of the major corporations. He was one of the only subjective men in the intelligence service. A straight shooter that will get to the bottom of any inquiry. He will follow any thread that he discovers and won't be afraid of those he has investigated.

"What is it?"

"I am giving you access to Orunmila. When you receive access, let me know," said Nasir as the man next to him searched the network for the access that he required. Orunmila allowed him to enter a contained informational environment. Nduwke could research anything within the area of the investigation but was cordoned off from other information. Nduwke accepted the terms of the mission. Packets of information downloaded straight into his brain.

The mission became perfectly clear at that moment. The Poveen had agents on the planet and it would his job to find and suppress them. Nasir told the man to take a minute to absorb the information before the two men parted ways. Nduwke agreed. When the train stopped the duo left the train and walked along a railing.

They were in the puppet hangars. Nasir started his career piloting puppets. He loved them. The thirty-meter-tall machines captured his imagination so many times in the past. The machine resembled a man. In the past, they called such machines gundams, mechs, mecha, and a host of other names. Now they are call them puppets. Nasir started his career with the normal army tactical puppet. After three years as a pilot the service understood they had an adept pilot.

Nasir joined the elite ranger battalions. Again, his talent was evident. Once again, he was promoted and elevated into the elite ranks. Orga puppets are the most advanced puppets in the human sphere. These wonderful pieces of machinery are grown and not built. They are grown from a mixture of pilot DNA and tactical constructs. Those who pilot these wonderful machines command one of the most powerful land units in the human sphere. For 25 years, he led orga puppets into combat.

He liked to come down to the puppet storage area. He liked to look at his former orga puppet. It stood 25 meters tall. The machine had his face and features mixed with that of his former co-pilot. The skin of the machine was a dark grey with gold highlights. Its armor still looked viable and the machine lifted its head to look at the former pilot. It generated its own energy and was somewhat consciousness even without the pilots on board.

"You know that is creepy as shit sir?"

"Yep. But it's my creepy so it isn't so bad," responded Nasir. Nasir smiled at the machine and the machine squinted its eyes back at him. Nduwke laughed slightly at the response. The walkway put the two men just below the eye level of the massive machine twenty meters away. Drones hovered around the machine and those around him. They ensured the machines were in working condition. Some of these machines could be called back to duty during this conflict. All hands on deck Nasir thought to himself.

"Sir. I have reviewed the information and I think I am ready to execute the mission. How close to the vest should I keep this?"

"Just you if possible. If not only those you trust. Only you will have access to Orunmila though. We need you to find out what is going on."

"Got it. I will speak to you once I learn more."

PLUS 37 HOURS
SYSTEM METEOR CORPS GENERAL
MORRIS SOLIS
OGUN STATION, NUBIA
COMPLICATIONS

Masters was in his ready room reviewing data. The planetary AI Orunmila told him a truth that could not be avoided. Two of his senior officers were in a forbidden relationship. To pretend the relationship wouldn't affect the overall mission would be foolish. He kept the secret long enough. The planning phase for the mission Kush needed to move. For that the happen everyone needed to have all the cards on the table before they travelled to Kush.

The Meteor System General Morris Solis walked into the room. The massive muscle-bound military veteran entered the room unaware of the reasoning of the meeting. He wore the full black matted battle armor kit with the angular helmet under his right arm. Dark blue skin defined Atlas as his system of origin. A bald head reflected the light in the meeting room giving Solis a subtle glow. A nob of respect for his commander indicated he was ready to proceed with the conversation.

Masters stood from his seating position and walked over to the man. Masters was only one or two inches taller but Solis was clearly more massive. Masters needed to consult with the General because he will be directly affected by the decision that needed to be made. Solis loved the fact that his Lord Commander started in the Meteor Corps before being offered a commission in the Command Corps. They were cut in the same fire and shared many of the same traits. Solis saw the meteor in Masters, in the way he walked, in the way he talked, and the way he handled the soldiers under his command. This made his command style familiar and comfortable.

Meteors are a hard outfit to be accepted into. The author Bob Olsen coined the phrase Space Marines in the short story "Captain Brink of the Space Marines" a long time ago. He was the first man to describe a solider that operates in space, land, and sky. But, if you called a Meteorite soldier a Space Marine, he would cut out your heart and feed it to you. There is no water in space. They don't travel in a space navy. They are of space, they come from space, and they land on planets causing damage just like a meteorite.

Meteorites are the crazy sons of bitches that jump from a perfectly good space craft to enter an atmosphere at over Mach 40. They fall thousands of meters to the ground to start a fight. Next, they are expected to establish a planethead and hold that planethead until follow-on forces arrive. Sometimes they land in the desert, sometimes in the mountains, and sometimes on water. They are the most highly trained soldier in the UPHAF. Only people that do not value their own life call them Space Marines. Marines primary mission is to travel from a boat to the shore to secure it while meteorites are expected to do the same thing after falling from space with minimum space and air support.

"General Solis, I have to speak to you about a subject that might seem trivial at first but it could mean the difference between life and death to you and your men. How well do you know Sub-Commander Rodgers? Do you know his home situation? Have you met his fiancée?" asked Masters of his officer of 3 years. Solis paused after the question. It made him extremely uncomfortable and he really didn't know what direction the line of questioning was headed.

"Yes, we all had drinks that one time. You were there too. Though I don't remember the entire night. Getting old Commander. I have met Laura on many other occasions after that as well. Laura had lovely friends if you know what I mean. I would like to say the Rodgers and I are friends," he replied in a deep baritone voice. He was still a little unsettled but Masters didn't appear to be judging him or the relationship that he shared with them. Masters doesn't ask questions like this in the command deck which solved the question of why they were in a meeting room and not on the deck.

"General Solis let me tell you what this is all about. When we received the Protocol 5 I was given access to files that I wouldn't otherwise see. Orunmila alerted me to the identity of A1D7 because of a conflict. A1D7 is Laura Oban and the fiancée of Mike Rodgers. Both of which will be commanding the defense of Kush alongside of you. I am not sure if Rodgers knows the identity of A1D7 but clearly Oban knows she is in violation of the rules. What will happen if he needs to command the Dragon Units to death to defend Kush?

At this point in time it is too late to change his, hers, or your command for that matter. The only solution that removes them from serving in the chain of command together will be to send General Nasir instead of Oban but I need him here and getting him to leave this planet will not be something I don't think I can even do. I need your perspective. Your force will make up fifty percent of the force you have the right to know what is happening in the command structure," said Masters as he gauged the reaction.

The General stood motionless as he processed the information. He looked at Masters to gauge what decision he made but couldn't read his stone face. It was clear that Masters wanted his real opinion and not the opinion that Solis thought he wanted to hear. General Solis didn't care who Rodgers was having sex with and quite frankly didn't know how big of a role A1D7 would play on the planet. The Dragon Corps only had 10 thousand or so troops. They could defend a city or an installation but that was it. He had millions of soldiers and so did the Kush Defense Force command by General Jones. Though he did understand that in the heat of battle when emotions were heighted it could play a role but Rodgers was a man of honor.

"Sir, it doesn't bother me at all. I don't think it will make a difference. We all have our missions and they will be expected to complete them. She doesn't out rank me so if something happens to Rodgers I would take over and I don't see a situation in which Rodgers would override any of my orders. They both have a service record that dictates that they can handle this," said Solis confident in his decision to agree to the service of the soldiers.

Masters called for Sub-Command Rodgers and A1D7 into the meeting room. Moments later the two soldiers walked into the room. Masters and Solis stood tall with chins raised and stern faces. Sub-Commander Rodgers looked at the two men as he entered and could tell that something was up. Solis did all he could do to blank his face but unlike Masters he hadn't conquered that skill. Something serious had just been decided without him. Rodgers was tried to contain his anger. He wondered what plan of action his commanding officer and his future number 2 just decided without him. Did Solis just go behind his back to make something happen thought Rodgers?

Rodgers' brow lowered as he scanned the faces of the two men looking for any sign of what was just decided. He couldn't find any. Rodgers moved forward and stood in front of the two of them with his eyes darting back and forth. A1D7 walked into the room next in complete dragon armor from head to toe. The soldier walked into the room and stood next to Rodgers facing the Masters and Solis. The tension in room was thick and Solis wondered how long Masters would make them all stand before starting this meeting.

"A1D7, take off your helmet," said Masters in a calm and collected voice. Even under the armor Solis could see the change in the demeanor of the soldier. A1D7 knew that the game might be up. A1D7 didn't move, speak, or respond to the order. Masters just calmly stood watching her and letting her work her decision in her head. A1D7 choose to stall instead of obeying the order.

"I am not allowed to take off my helmet unless it is damaged sir. You know this," she stated but Solis knew it to be a plea to Lord Commander Masters, her friend Malcom, to please not do this to her. Masters' face was stoic. He was focused and unflinching. This was not going to end without that helmet coming off. Solis hoped she didn't do anything stupid like try to flee or lash out. That would be unwise and it would cause her to be removed when she wasn't going to be dismissed.

"I am not going to ask again. Either you take that helmet off or I will shoot you in the head to damage it and then take it off," said Masters. General Solis wondered if he would shoot but this confrontation was becoming more entertaining than expected. He watched shamefully slightly amused at this point. Rodgers was getting angry at A1D7 not responding to the order. A1D7 was terrified of the future now. Solis just wanted it to be over so he could get back to work.

A hand canon was suddenly unsheathed and pointed at A1D7 by General Rodgers. The old enlisted man had habits that would never die. Solis stepped back slightly but when Rodgers didn't fire the weapon he stopped moving. Rodgers' commanding officer gave an order twice and he would not be made to give an order a third time. A1D7 turned the faceless helmet to look at the hand cannon and slowly raised hands in a sign of surrender. Rodgers took a subtle step back in case A1D7 lounged at him but that was not something she was planning on doing. Rodgers looked for affirmation from Solis and Masters but he didn't get any. This confused the man.

The monstrous hand cannon didn't move one inch from the helmet on A1D7. It hissed for a second as the outside air pressure matched that in the helmet. A1D7, Laura Oban, removed her helmet slowly. Tears were already flowing from her eyes to her chin. Waterfilled eyes moved over to look at Rodgers as if to ask for an apology. Her secret was out. The thing that she never wanted to be revealed was. In that moment, Solis felt sorry for her. The raw emotion of the event tugged on his heart strings in a way that he never knew.

It took Rodgers a couple of seconds to realize what happened because his heart rate was so elevated after he pulled his weapon. He stood staring at down the barrel of his terrible weapon at the one person he loved. The gun slowly lowered as the shock processed through his body. Rodgers turned back toward the two of them and Solis signaled for him to lower the weapon with his right hand. Rodgers nodded slightly and the gun moved down to his hip.

Disappointment and fear dominated Rodgers' face. It was clear he didn't expect it to be her. Solis turned to Lord Commander Masters as he moved from his side toward the two of them. Masters placed his left arm on Rodgers shoulder and right hand on Oban's left shoulder and dropped his head slightly in a calming gesture.

"Orunmila told me of your relationship after the protocol 5 went into to affect. Ironic, considering the last time a P5 went into effect you were born Laura. I don't know what you are feeling or what you are thinking but there is no way in hell I am will be getting rid of any of my top officers before the biggest invasion in decades. You both will continue in your current compacity. You have my support and the full support of General Solis in the coming campaign. Don't make me look stupid," said Masters.

Oban looked up at her commanding officer and friend with relief. She wiped the tears from her eyes and straightened up her back and thanked him. Masters laughed and said, "Well there was no way in hell you would stay here. If something happened to Rodgers on Kush I wouldn't want you standing behind me with a hand cannon," the rest of the room laughed though the mixture of sadness, shock, joy and nervousness that bounced around the room.

Solis walked out of the room with Masters leaving the two of them to work out what happened. Solis was suddenly saddened by the conversation. He wondered if Jamie Juelz, one of Laura's friends, was also one of the Dragon Corps as well. A couple of hours ago he was going to propose to her. The man didn't have much in way of relationships to speak of. Though he was 115 years of age he had never married nor had any children. The early part of his life was committed to the Meteor Corps.

Solis remembers being stationed deep in unoccupied space on lifeless rocks waiting for enemies that never came. He spent way too much time in the virtual simulators, the only thing that kept him and his men sane. Solis fell addicted to the virtual world for decades. Spending time in that world was so much better than the real one. A shattered home life and an estranged family crippled the normal adult progression. The service was his family and the virtual world was his home. Solis' life was as empty as it sounded and he knew it.

The horrible dependence to the virtual world was severed fifteen years ago. Relentless focus on building personal relationships with people has been his primary objective. At first, he struggled, but over time, he made tremendous strides. The virtual world he knew was gone but the one that was under development meant something more. The love between Rodgers and Oban was something he sought with Jamie Juelz. When the moment presented itself, he would ask Oban if she was also in the Dragon Corps.

"Are you having second thoughts General Solis," asked Masters?

"No Sir, sorry sir, that moment triggered a past memory. Sorry for the delay I will pick up the pace," said Solis as he sped up to catch the Lord Commander. The duo reached the CIC deck and once again the man was worked on the mission to Kush. The loading of forces was almost complete. After Kahn and Space Command left seventeen hours prior his soldiers began preparations to leave the planet. The bulk of Meteor Corp space assets were in a trailing orbit behind Nubia. Those starships arrived on station as soon as the Space Command vessels left.

Those craft took turns resupplying at one the designated space stations. Once topped off they moved into formation to wait for the rest of the task force to fall into formation. The task force prioritized spare parts, weapons, ammunition, and raw metals. These materials would be scarce on Kush and needed in any siege of the planet. Civilian spacecraft will also accompany the fleet. They are sent to Kush to deliver heavy machinery and then bring back food supply for the coming sieges of the two planets.

The plan was for the entire task force to burn to the planet Kush. Once they reached Kush the planetary forces would either disembark onto the massive planetary logistical ring to take space elevators to the planet or land on the planet with dropstars. The space-based force would than remain until the commercial spacecraft were loaded with food stores. Once they completed uploading all the material the combined force of Meteor space forces, commercial spacecraft carrying food, and the battlenova would burn back to Nubia while the people of Kush hid under the planetary shield.

General Solis was not one for hiding but he was one for staying alive. So far this was the best plan to keep him alive so he would go along with it. A1D7 clad in full dragon armor and helmet closed followed by Sub Commander Rodgers walked onto the CIC deck twenty minutes later. He nodded to the two of them and they continued to work for the next half an hour.

The three officers left the command deck CIC just like the two task forces before them. They left building via the route to the starport that was now eerily empty. Almost 80 percent of the starcraft stationed at the port left the planet already with more prepped to launch. In less than 40 hours almost the entire space traveling members of the service would have moved or be on the move. It was truly amazing. Tens of thousands of craft big and small alike moved in preparation to fight. He wouldn't be any different than the other soldiers.

PLUS 45 HOURS
SPACE COMMAND QUASAR
VALERIE RODRIGUEZ
BATTLENOVA PLANET ENDER, CARTHAGE
TACTICS

Twenty hours after the starships left Nubia they reached Carthage and its two moons Hannibal and Hamilcar. The stealthstar carrying the three senior officers docked with the massive space station. Once on board the ship Vice Commander Kahn made her way to the bridge. General Okafor moved at speed toward the docking bay to get a transport to the largest carrier. Rodriguez moved to the dock as well but she would enter the battlenova named the "Planet Ender". It was currently docked with the station getting loaded reserve armaments and fuel before it would set the tip of the defensive formation.

Quasar Rodriguez left the stealthstar and ran as fast as she could down the hallways of the station to toward the dock with the Planet Ender. The now well-rested officer bounded and dove between other officers at speed in the hallways. The station was a buzz with activity and anticipation. They had timed the docking of the Battlenova Planet Ender with that of her arrival. On the way to the battlenova she received the last confirmation. It was fully supplied and now they just waited on her. Once she was onboard and they could pull away another three ships could dock.

It took her a little over five minutes to reach the ship. A quick trip through the airlock placed the Quasar inside a long white hallway. As she entered the hallway she instantly felt the loss of gravity from 1 g to .5 g. Space command ships didn't waste energy on anti-gravity, air, lights, or any other amenities found on all other craft. Travel on a Space Command starship meant travelling in pods. This type of construction allowed for denser, faster, and more capable starships.

The battlenova moved slightly as it drifted away from Hannibal Station. It was ordered to do so to allow another starship to the dock for loading. The Quasar bounded to the end of the hallway and entered the officer pod section. The metal door closed behind her and a pod slid down from the ceiling. It stood roughly 3 meters in height. Transparent steel morphed and opened to present an entrance into the pod. The body of the pod was a pure white just like the floor and the walls of the compartment. Rodriguez stepped into the pod and placed her personal effects in a compartment to the rear compartment and watched it slide shut.

With a quick turn, she faced outward as the pod shut. The floor of the pod flashed from white to a bright green color and then back to white as the machine scanned her body and took all the information it needed from suit currently equipped. A light green liquid with the consistency of honey entered the pod from the top running down four channels along the side. Warm liquid contacted the SC-ESU suit dissolving it. The SC-ESU was made of reactive nanobots just like the liquid. While in the pod she would not need the suit and thus it is dissolved. It will reconstitute the SC-ESU before she departed the pod after the mission.

The nanites in the liquid began building new equipment that will supply her body with everything it will need during the duration of the deployment. Hoses, masks, and other materials suddenly formed around her naked body as the docking process was completed in less than five minutes. The Quasar floated in the middle of the pod as the it retracted into the ceiling on the track system. The system took her pod deep into the battlenova into the protective cavity.

For the duration of the battle Rodriguez would command from the pod. Her body would be sustained and protected by the pod. It was the ultimate system. Eventually the pod stopped moving and slid into place next to the other officer pods behind shielding. She was now deep in the battlenova and she awaited connection to the broader matrix.

The port in the back of her neck was connected shortly after to matrix of the starship. A booting screen gathered all her information like rank, height, weight, skin color, birthplace, and any other personal setting she had stored for the computer to generate her avatar in the virtual environment. Thirty seconds into the connection Quasar Rodriguez's avatar was standing in a loading area of the program. The white room resembled the pod room without the pods. Dark grey dress uniform covered her purple skin. One by one the systems from the battlenova began to input into her personal HUD as access was granted by the ship's computer. One minute later a door opened and she walked onto the bridge of the ship.

The crew was lined up saluting the officer.Once dismissed they all returned to duty. The bridge was stunning. If the bridge was constructed in this manner in real life it would be impractical and too costly but in the virtual world the cost was nothing. The bulk of the team sat in smoothly curved white chairs to the right of her location complete with elegant consoles in front of them. To the left a long walkway protruded outward and almost 360-degree view of space. Each object in space was marked and each officer had the ability to pull up more information if needed. That is when she saw the three dark red dots and the and 154 more dots on approach with a timer and distance readout.

Captain Reiner walked over to her and extended his hand. She shook the tall man's hand and smiled slightly. He was an elegantly pale man with soft features. Captain Reiner was trained since birth to become a Captain of a starship like this. Rodriguez studied his background to discover he grew up on a starship collective and didn't step foot on solid ground until he was 14 years old. That experience prepared him for a life in space.

"Quasar Rodriguez, it is my pleasure to introduce you to the best starship Space Command has to offer. The Planet Ender was the second vessel constructed in the Space Hunter class Battlenova. We are pleased that we will have the opportunity to kill more squid. The crew is ready and in good spirts," said the man as he stood with a smile on his face. Rodriguez smiled and then walked with him down the long bridge considering the black of space asking about the crew and recommendations of attack plans, vectors, and counter-attacks.

"I am glad you were in the system. What was your original mission out here? I couldn't find it anywhere and I didn't have a chance to ask Masters," questioned Rodriguez.

"We were on a deep space reconnaissance mission. I believe the United Planets of Humanity Colonization Authority is looking to perform another push outward. The battlenovas, Planet Ender and Star Killer, were accompanied by ten dreadstars and a science vessel. We mapped twelve potential systems until we engaged the Poveen. A constellation of 7 cruisers engaged our constellation of 12 and they were taught them a lesson.

We destroyed three and heavily damaged the rest. We lost three dreadstars as well and we took some minor damage. The constellation ER bridged to the Nubian system for repairs a week ago. You are truly lucky we were still in the system when this happened. All the dreadstars are repaired and we are topped off with fuel and ordinance," Reiner answered.

Rodriguez shook her head in agreement and requested the battle information. She understood the specs of the battlenova and all it was capable of but she wanted to see the raw data. She wanted to know how it really functioned. The elegant man passed the information to her and asked if she needed anything else.

Ten minutes later Rodriguez left the bridge with a thought and arrived in a ready room. The office was sleek and smooth. Beautiful white-lined office was large and complete with a leather couch, fur rug, stunning paintings, and a wonderful view. Rodriguez walked to the window and looked out over the magnificent planet-sized ocean of her home world Farragut. Rodriguez opened the door to stand on the balcony. They got it all right. The light breeze, the animal life, colors, the people walking far below, and the smell. The designers of this simulation were good. Maybe too good.

Quasar Rodriguez turned from the view and walked to the desk and sat down. The chair leaned back kicking her feet into the air as multiple readout displays initiated. The Barca Staryards were furiously trying to bring systems online on the many starships under construction. Rodriguez watched as new combat ready vessels came online. Over the next five hours this activity would increase dramatically. The convoy they travelled with to Carthage contained thousands of pilots, navigators, and spacers of all kind. The station military AI Imilce has been furiously matching crews and assigning vessels.

Once they were matched and ready Rodriguez assigned local commanders new assets to include into battle planning and operations. It is likely that this process will continue to occur until the first missiles are launched and combat begins. Force projections flooded into her station and the opportunity presented for the coming battle was clear. Carthage would be the battle in the system in which they could win. Suddenly the genius behind Masters' plan was clear. The reason why they didn't leave any space forces around Nubia was to stack the deck at her location.

The plan was bold and aggressive. It would take such leadership by all of them to pull this off and Rodriguez was happy she would have a chance. On the flip side, Atlanta looked to be seriously outgunned and outmanned. Rodriguez couldn't help to think that she might not see Amir, Might, or Tanaka again. She quickly pushed that out of her mind and focused on the task at hand. They would win at Carthage and then reinforce Atlanta just like the plan dictated she thought.

Her brilliant mind finalized the coordination of the forces. They would assemble 2 battle groups made up of four super clusters each. The first super cluster is constructed of fast attack vessels constructed into 4 battle clusters consisting of starfighters, starbombers, starvettes, and starpuppets. Two super clusters of 2 starcarriers, 30 starcruisers, 100 starfrigates, and 60 dreadstars. The super cluster will consist of the heavy hitter ships that can all standoff with a Poveen cruisers. It will be led by the Battlenova "Planet Ender" and it will be supported by 10 warstars, 10 gunstars, and 20 dreadstars.

The other battle group is tasked with the protection of the Hannibal Battle Station and the ER Gates. 2 super clusters will protect the station. That force is supported by the 4 starcarriers that are still under construction at Barca Staryards. Each of the vessels have fully functioning power plants and though they lack propulsion the entire vessel is almost complete. 2 of the carriers lack the installation of weapon systems and propulsion while the other 2 lack sensors and many of the redundant systems needed to survive a long engagement. The other 2 have no weapons systems or engines but the fighter bays are complete. General Okafor's teams are on all four carriers now trying to complete as many systems as possible.

Gunstars and warstars will protect Barca Staryards and the unmovable spacecraft still under construction. Those two classes of ships lack the high maneuverability of the other spacecraft and are designed as standoff weapons meant to slug it out with enemy forces. The last super cluster in the battle group would consist of a Calvary force of interceptstars, star puppets and starvettes. The mission of this super cluster is to prevent any Poveen landing craft and troop transports from infiltrating the staryards, starships, or Hannibal station.

Hannibal Battle Station, one of the largest and capable battle stations in the human sphere, will support both battle groups. The station was riddled with offensive and defensive weapon systems. It had the capability to not only defend Carthage and the two moons Hannibal and Hamilcar, it could also defend Nubia, with long range missiles and kinetic weapons. Rodriguez factored that into her combat strategy as she worked with the military AI to predict tactics from the enemy.

PLUS 60 HOURS
COMMAND CORPS SUB COMMANDR
YOSEF AMIR
BUCKHEAD STATION, BUCKHEAD, ATLANTA
NERVES

The trip to the Atlanta gas giant planetary system was uneventful. The area was bustled with activity. Spacecraft of all shapes and sizes evacuated people from the moons of Atlanta that would be left unprotected to, Buckhead and Peachtree, the two moons that would be protected. Any valuable equipment, materials, or assets were also broken down and moved to the moons. A spacetilla of luxury, corporate, and older spacecraft burned for another gas giant in the system to hide. These vessels were too large to land on the moons to be stored and too fragile to mount weapon systems onto to fight.

Amir wanted to load the craft with explosives and send them on the suicide mission into the Poveen fleet but he was overruled by Masters. Those spacecraft would house the political and corporate elite of the Atlanta gas giant planetary system away from the planet into a safer location. Masters told Amir that it was a blessing in disguise that the political class left the moons. He could now engage the enemy without worrying about the politics of the engagement. Amir agreed and two hours ago the rich and elite fled the two moons.

When the stealthstar docked with the Buckhead Space Station above the moon of Buckhead only Sub Commander Amir disembarked from starship.

The other two high level officers stayed on the vessel. Tanaka would head to Peachtree, the other moon that would be defended, and Might would stay on the stealthstar to command the Astro Corps forces. Amir moved down the hallways of the battlestation until he reached the space elevator and took it to the surface. In about two hours the battlestation would untether from the moon in preparation for combat. It took Amir another thirty minutes to reach the CIC deep inside the massive moon.

Atlanta, the massive gas giant, was three times the size of Jupiter with 72 moons. Buckhead was the first moon developed in the planetary system. It was almost as large as Venus at .6 Earth mass and .72 Earth gravity. The moon was largely dense rock and metals. The moon boasted a powerful magnetic field provided by an orbital ring that blocked the radiation from the large gas giant and sun. 35 million people lived on the moon with plans to increase the population to five hundred million people.

Amir was connected his CU into all the subsystems of the station and the moons. It would take another hour or so for everything to connect with the equipment that his forces brought to Atlanta. Time was ticking away and unlike the other commanders he didn't have the same amount of time to prepare. The convoy that burned to Atlanta was traveled at relativistic speeds to reach the installation before the Poveen. They experienced time much slower than the rest of the Nubian system had and it effected his ability to properly prepare. Travelling at that speed also created communications challenges. It was impossible to communicate real time at those speeds even with quantum communications and instead he had to communicate by data packet.

The Poveen cruisers closed in on the planetary system. Amir set the deadline for his staff to be combat ready in 5 hours. The man barked commands and coordinated the best he could with the ragtag staff of commanders. He motivated relentlessly but provided criticism where needed. The level of micromanagement could not be helped because time was the enemy. Normally, he would encourage those under him to find solutions to problems on their own with guidance but this battle would allow such luxuries.

The battle force around the Atlanta gas giant was constructed of Astro Corps, Comet Corps, Orbital Guard, System Police Forces, and corporate security forces. Coordination between the services were critical to the success of the mission. Amir knew how the Astro Corps, Comet Corps, and Orbital guard forces would perform in battle but the other two forces are wild cards in his planning. No matter what he did it just didn't feel like the numbers added up. Every strategy he inserted into the military AI produced an outcome of total defeat.

The only variable was time in the results. While travelling to Atlanta the three senior officers decided that they would attempt to make the battle as long and bloody as they could. Masters confided in Amir during the trip in one of his messages. He told Amir that they needed to hold Atlanta if they could. Only once Carthage was safe would they send support. This wasn't the first time Masters gave Amir bad news. The first time was at the Battle of Butcher Bay. The news was worse that time. That time he told Amir that he was going to die. At least this time Masters told Amir to merely dig in.

Amir monitored General Tanaka's landing and the preparation on Peachtree. It was the only other moon that would receive a massive defense force during the siege. Tanaka prepared and deployed the Comet Corps forces around both planets. They embedded local police and security forces into the Comet regiments to ensure the forces would have the local knowledge of tunnels, subsystems, and defensive positions for the coming defense. Hundreds of thousands of humans and artificial soldiers poured off the massive troopstars.

Peachtree was a completely different moon than Buckhead. It was slightly larger that Buckhead at .62 Earth diameter but with less gravity at .58 Earth gravity. Peachtree didn't have the density of Buckhead and it had a much weaker magnetic field forcing the bulk of the population into underground cities. The natural cavities and spongy crust of the planet made the construction of these facilities much easier and contributed to the logistical nature of the moons economy. It was also destined to become the main food production moon for the broader Atlanta Planetary system. Peachtree would provide all the protein needs of the planetary system in the future.

Quasar Might stayed in the stealthstars and would remain on that spacecraft if it was operational. Might managed the space forces in orbit around Atlanta. The team benefited for the current relative proximity of Buckhead and Peachtree. The moons were currently on the same side of the planet. The plan of defense was for the larger ships to orbit the two moons in a figure eight pattern between the gravity wells. This would give the starships momentum and allow them to strike the Poveen on approach vectors and then move away from the attack to be replaced by the starships next in line like a conveyer belt. This maneuver would reduce the amount of damage any ship would take. When the enemy appeared they would be constantly engaged in combat with various ships.

The smaller starships can't stand off with the larger Poveen craft and hope to survive for a long period of time. A stand-up battle with the forces would get the forces decimated. That is why they conscripted eight huge mineral haulers. They have been reconfigured to launch pay loads of diamond, steel, iron, gold, and other heavy materials in small building sized cubes at the Poveen spacecraft. This is meant to break up Poveen formations and force them split up. Once split up the smaller craft would be able to pick off the larger spacecraft.

Starfighters, interceptstars, starpuppets, starvettes and other small craft are split in two groups attached to each moon. These forces will intercept any large craft that break the figure eight lines and make a run on the moons or the space stations. This smaller force will stay in the shadow of the larger craft to hide themselves from the line of sight attacks from the Poveen.

Amir took another look at the AI estimate of the tactical ability to win the engagement and it ticked up to 6 percent from 4.2 percent in the last hour. They strategic changes provided the perfect opening if the Poveen commander performed one of three stupid maneuvers. The goal was to work on the number until it was at least ten percent before the battle. A ping changed the train of thought from management of the percentages to one of leadership. Quasar Might pinged him. Amir placed his right hand over his heart and accepted the communication. The gesture was to allow everyone on the deck to know he was speaking to someone.

"I am glad our communications are finally working. How is everything going down there," asked Might as the two of them joined the virtual environment.

"Quasar Might, things are going smoothly for now. I must be honest I am feeling a bit uneasy. It has been a couple years since my last combat operation. The feeling is familiar yet unwanted. Just to think I used to get excited for combat," said Amir in a calm manner.

"So you are scared too? Good. I have been nervous shitting for the last two hours. Do you do that too?" asked Might as she once again made the simplest conversation awkward.

"Not scared and thank god I don't have what you have. I do identify that fear is near but son of bitch can't hold me back. I know it will do its best when the attack begins but we must remain strong Quasar. We can't buckle or be seen buckling one inch. If we do, our soldiers will fold. Have you seen the new estimates?" asked Amir. Might nodded making the avatar's red hair bounce slightly.

"This is the first time that I have ever felt that I could die. I don't like this feeling. Mortality is not fun. I am supposed to live forever Amir," she said in a jocular manor. Amir laughed a little too hard but they both needed this conversation. In effect the two of them were saying goodbye without saying goodbye.

"We are all supposed to live forever. Natasha, find something to live for. That is what I have done in the past. I do not have children yet so I am fighting for them because I want a couple of them. I will continue to fight for that dream family and life that I will have after this is over. I want that one day. I am fighting for that," he reflected.

"Kids are great. I have two. I don't think I will have more but I do want to see them again. I get it though. I need to find mine I guess. Wait a second. Are you saying that you want to have a family with me? I see you flirting Amir. So, unprofessional," she joked. Amir laughed harder then he should have again at the joke.

"Maybe. I just want you to survive to find out. Maybe I will try my luck," said Amir. For the next ten minutes the two officers spent comforting each other with jokes. They needed the tension relief. Unlike the other soldiers and officers who have piers that they could easily speak with to deal with the emotions of the situation the commanding officers didn't have many people to confide too.

PLUS 70 HOURS
COMMAND CORPS LORD COMMANDER
MALCOM MASTERS
OGUN STATION, NUBIA
BEHIND THE LINES

The Lord Commander walked into the combat control center on the command deck. Most of the officers at the station had left to engage the Poveen at forward operating bases so Masters decided to engage in the war effort from this location. He had returned from resting, eating, and washing. The room wasn't that large but it had everything that he needed. It connected him to all the readouts and feeds that he would need to command his soldiers. He would not need to leave the room until the conflict was over if necessary.

The chair that he sat in was large and white to match the rest of the room. The massive commander sat in the chair and connected to the military network. A preset virtual environment populated. The virtual construct provided the Lord Commander with all the information he would need from each of the forward battle locations and on Nubia. The Poveen cruisers were getting closer to engaging the military and civilians of the system. The Lord Commander was ready to take on anything that stood in his path. He was ready for the war.

Masters was pinged from the Victory System QEN relay. The ping request was from the Siberian System, one of the other systems under attack by the Poveen. He accepted the ping request. The woman on the other end of the ping seemed extremely frazzled. Vice Commander Lee once served on Nubia under his command. She took the Vice Commander role 4 years ago.

"Vice Commander Lee. How are you doing?"

"Lord Commander I need help. They are gone. My Lord Commander and ranking Vice Commander are gone."

"Where did they go?" asked Masters. Vice Commander Lee sent him pictures of two officers laying on the ground with gunshot wounds to head. Masters paused not understanding the images that he saw. "Did Lee mentally crack and kill her commanding officers?" he thought to himself. He searched for an answer to his question when Lee returned in frame.

"They killed themselves. These cowards killed themselves. I am in charge now. What should I do sir?" asked the frantic officer.

"First, calm down. You do not serve anyone well if you are not calm. Next, you need to follow the plan that was laid out by you Lord Commander and approved by Regional Commander Moon. You need to keep it together. Take control and lead the people of the system," said Masters.

"People are scared here Lord Commander. We don't know how many of them are out there. All we can see is the 14. I don't know how we are going to do this. What if they stay in subspace? What if they can attack us from subspace without coming into normal space?"

"Lee, get it together. Those cowards took the easy way. You will not. The enemy is vectoring in your system to the ER Gates just like they are here. They are coming to you. Get your forces ready. Prioritize targets and break out the siege. You can do this," inspired Masters. Over the next thirty minutes he talked the Vice Commander into a better state of mind. Masters felt for the Vice Commander. In many ways, she was correct. They were at a tremendous disadvantage. They didn't have any way of seeing the Poveen in subspace because they only had a Sentry 5 system.

Masters prepared to make a personal call to his wife. He wanted to speak to her before the conflict ramped up in couple of hours. Unfortunately, he was interrupted again. The ping this time was from General Nasir. He had an update on the information the Dragon Corps came to him. Colonel Nduwke, with the aid of Orunmila, tracked down the base of operations of the smuggler operation.

"Sir, we have tracked down the criminal network of smugglers. We think we know what they are up to. They are planning a xeno attack. Nduwke will be on station momentarily to assess the situation but this is what we know. The organization has shipped various elements to the system over the past two years. During that time, they refined and moved those elements to a building in downtown Meroe. When we researched the elements and chemicals they have secured we discovered that it was consistent with the trace elements left behind on the planet Holiday during its xeno terrorist incident.

Quasar Tanaka lead the soldiers that saved the people of the installation. We contacted him and he could provide us with the after-action report on the incident. The Poveen spread the contagion through the air. Once a human host is infected it spreads rapidly. The infection can overwhelm our nanites. For the first hour people do not notice any symptoms. After two hours the infected become extremely hostile and aggressive. They will attack anyone close by. Over the next five hours the body starts to change into a beast. After 24 hours the body is almost fully transformed into a raging beast.

We have units moving to the location now. Colonel Nduwke's team is getting into position. We may need to execute an orbital attack on the building. We will need your permission to conduct such an exercise. Orunmila calculated that if they release that contagion in the city of Meroe now, we will have one million infected in the next hour, and seven million infection in the next two hours. In three hours, we will lose the city to the infected and the outer areas. The Poveen plan is clear. Release a contagion on Nubia and watch us tear each apart other," said General Nasir.

"Okay. Let's work the problem General. I will connect us to Quasar Johnson. We are going to need his assets," responded Masters as he connected he configured the communication for the mission. Johnson and Nasir would connect to Masters via the Nubian QEN in one channel while they had a broader channel for the rest of the team currently via the military network. Masters pinged Regional Commander Moon in the Victory system and informed her of the mission. She kept the channel open to see the progress of the mission.

Colonel Nduwke moved to the roof of an adjacent building with ten of his most trusted soldiers. They launched a package of seeker drones on the roof of the building. The drones were autonomous and the size of marbles. They moved with speed along the roof of the building and entertained the ventilation shafts and other areas of access. Within the next couple of minutes the drones moved throughout the building providing a picture of the area.

It was just as they thought. The top three floors had large containers of a liquid. Four of the floors under that floor had people strapped to chairs. The infection was detected on these floors. Some of the people were already showing the effects of the infection. Artificial humans, probably of Poveen creation, walked around the floors of the building shepherding people into the forced infection areas. The men were heavily armed and seemed to control the entire building. On the ground floor ten transports lined the parking area.

"General Nasir send in your team. We need to stop this," said Masters as the full implication of the situation settled in. Colonel Nduwke and his team jumped from the adjunct building's roof to the roof of the target building. They moved along the roof of the building under full camouflage. Four of the soldiers took up positions along each corner of the roof. Four other soldiers jumped off the side of the building to the street along the corners. They had standing orders to shoot anyone that walked out of the building. Those soldiers were in full camouflage on the bustling street in the middle of the most populous city in the system. Any gunfire would cause a massive panic. This entire situation could go south extremely quickly.

A large force moved into position a couple of blocks away from the target building and held that location. The armed forces had to ensure they did not to spook the terrorists inside. To do so would trigger the infection's release. Masters commanded Quasar Johnson to have a firing solution on standby. Battle Station 37 was positioned over the city and had the direct line of sight. Johnson took control of firing control of the laser artillery mounted on that station. They targeted the entire block the target building was located on. Ten thousand people would die if the laser fired.

Regional Commander Moon entered the QEN channel with Nasir and Johnson via the connection on Nubia. Once she was inside the channel Masters updated her with the current movements of the team and the overall state of the plan. Almost as Masters Informed Regional Commander Moon the line with her went dead and terrorists in the building seemed to move with urgency. Unlike the previous ten minutes of activity in which the artificial humans stood in guarded positions, they all seemed to move collectively at once.

"Colonel Nduwke, what is happening? Did they get spooked?" asked Nasir over the mission channel. He agreed that the enemy was spooked. Colonel Nduwke and his team then went hot. The four men on the corners outside started to fire into the lobby of the building. Panicked civilians fled from the gunfire. The bullets ripped into any human or artificial human in the lobby of the building. Large panes of glass exploded and fell to the ground. Bullets ripped into all the people that stood in the lobby until everything in the lobby of the building was dead. They moved to the transports next with RPGs.

The special operations soldiers moved with such speed and grace they secured the ground floor in less than two minutes. On the roof two of the soldiers moved into the building to support Colonel Nduwke's team that maneuvered to the tanks of the contingent on the top three levels. The enemy units that outnumbered them ten to one raced to the three levels.

Colonel Nduwke and his team fought with discipline.

The dormant tanks sparked to life. An audible hissing sound filled the room as the tanks opened to push out the contingent. On the roof of the building four large doors opened and it flooded out of the building. They watched in horror as the gas was released upon the citizens of Meroe. They didn't have much time if they were going to stop this.

"Quasar Johnson fire the weapon," yelled Masters on the line. Johnson hesitated. Firing on the enemy was one thing but firing on Nubians was another. His ancestor was one of the founders of the Nubian corporation on Earth. Johnson City and Johnson Starport were named after his family. He was from one of the six power families of the system. He was taught his entire life to protect the people of Nubia and not kill them. He couldn't give the order. Masters sensed his hesitation and understood it.

"Orunmila give me control of firing controls for Battle Station 37. Target the building and fire for effect when ready," commanded Masters. Three seconds later Battle Station 37 used the powerful laser artillery to obliterate the entire block. Smoke rose in the middle of city as the powerful laser stopped firing down on the city. Masters quickly checked the readings from the forces outside the blast radius. No sign of the contingent was detected.

He just killed about ten thousand Nubians. His own people were dead. Emotions flooded his body. Guilt, duty, honor, and logic wrestled for control of his mind and spirit. Sometimes you must do what you need to do as a commanding officer. He knew he made the right decision but it didn't make it an easy decision.

"Sir we will continue to track down the leads generated by the Dragon Corps. Excuse me I need to find a new officer to lead the operation," said Nasir. He needed to get off the line. He just lost one of his best friends. The man needed a second to mourn the loss. Masters allowed him to drop from the channel.

"Sorry sir. I froze. I just couldn't do it," apologized Quasar Johnson.

"Prepare for the Poveen Quasar. I understand," responded Masters. He would keep a close eye on Johnson. Any signs that he could not perform his duty and Masters would relieve him of command. Masters didn't have time for emotional officers that couldn't make the right decisions regardless of difficulty. The channel closed and Masters wanted to reach out Regional Commander Moon who was disconnected from the network right before attack. Before he could set up the communication he was already being pinged by Moon.

"Lord Commander Masters. You have a problem. Your QEN is compromised," said Regional Commander Moon.

"Sir, how can my QEN be compromised? Isn't that impossible?"

"It is supposed to be. When you linked me to the network with Johnson and Nasir the AI noticed a hostile attempt to corrupt my network. Our network is highly encrypted and our anti-intrusion technology is to prevent humans from spying on us and not alien. It triggered a defense and that is why the line went silent. Here is the thing. The AI tracked the location of the breech and it wasn't from the planet Nubia but from space in the system. Somehow, they can hack into the Nubian QEN network. I know most of the commanding officers are off world and are using this network to conduct your planning.

We are currently working on a workaround for you and the other systems. The chances that this effect is only in your system is minimal. Let's reconvene in 30 minutes. I must pass on this information and the I need to warm the other systems of possible xeno-terror attacks in population centers. By the way Lord Commander you did the right thing. You saved millions of people with your actions," said Regional Commander Moon as she disconnected the line.

Coordination with his forces just got harder. Keeping the political forces on the planet inline would get even harder since he just fired on a major city without even giving them a warning. The investigation of the terror group would slow down now that Colonel Nduwke was dead. A new team lead would have to be brought up to speed and that takes time

PLUS 82 HOURS
COMMAND CORPS SUB COMMANDER
MIKE RODGERS
OKO RING STATION, KUSH
KUSH BURNS PT1

Rodgers remembered the outing of his fiancée forty-five hours ago. Rodgers pointed his hand cannon at her head. He told the soldier to remove the helmet and when they did it was his Laura Oban. After the discovery, Masters told the two of them to take 20 minutes to talk it out in the room before they returned to duty. Rodgers nodded and thanked his commander and friend. Rodger couldn't help to think that humanity was still human.

Oban was dusky orange, Solis was navy blue, Masters was golden brown, and Rodgers was olive skinned but they were all humans and all on the same team. Friendships still mattered. Honor still mattered. Love still mattered. They would all have to answer for this when the conflict was over, if they survived, but they all knew that the coming fight would be harder than anything they would have faced in the past and something like this could wait.

Rodgers remembered that Solis walked out first followed by Masters. Rodgers locked the door so they could discuss what just happened in private. She agreed, they would take the 20 minutes that was granted to them. They both needed it. Rodgers took off his armor and just stood in his exo-suit with his arms out toward her. Oban placed her helmet on a work station and stepped out of her armor until she was also in the exo-suit. She walked over and hugged the man she loved. Tears once again started to flow from her eyes.

"I wanted to tell you. For so long all I wanted to do is tell you," she kept repeating.

"I can't be mad at you Laura. I am glad you didn't tell me. If you did, I don't know how I would have reacted. I don't know what I would have done. Until this happened you were never under my command so to me it didn't matter at all. But, how did you square this? How did this play for you Laura?" he remembers asking.

"You made me feel human. Before that I felt like a machine. I felt empty. A tool made to kill aliens or die trying. I only think about our life after this. After the war. After the fighting. After all the shit. I thought about suggesting we run away and hide off the grid on a newly terraformed planet. But I knew you wouldn't go because you are you. Frustrating at times but that is the reason why I know you won't leave me. You stick to your word," she said as she buried her face into his shoulder.

Oban was massive but her size never bothered him. Rodgers was bigger than almost every human alive and any woman he dated would feel small to him. His 7-foot frame was still six inches taller than she was. He just kept telling her that he loved her and reassured that they would make it as soldiers and as a couple. They would get through the politics of love in the military service. In the end, everything would work out.

Rodgers rubbed her back trying to console his fiancée. 5 minutes later she finally calmed down. Rodgers moved his right hand just below the neck on her back. Every suit had an emergency release for combat medics to help the injured. Rodgers pushed the button and Oban's exo-suit suddenly released and retracted. Concurrently Rodgers lifted Oban placing her on the desk behind them. She was shocked.

Frantic movements tried to gather the exo-suits components. Oban thought Rodgers hit the button by accident but it wasn't by accident. Rodgers pulled the front of her exo-suit down revealing her bare breast and skin down to her naval. He pushed her down onto the desk and leaned down kissing vigorously. He migrated south from her neck to her navel kissing along the way. When he reached the bottom half of the exo suit still on he pulled it off. His fiancée lay naked on the rectangular work station aroused, confused, and compliant. He popped the emergency release on his suit and it fell to the ground.

Rodgers told her she needed to be taught a lesson for lying. She licked her lips and confirmed that she needed to receive the lesson because she was a very disobedient girl. The teacher was pleased with the ten-minute lesson and the student thought the curriculum provided was excellent. The20 minute grace period was coming to the end and Rodgers chuckled to himself when he remembered the two of them racing to put on the exo-suit and armor and return to the command deck. They made it with thirty seconds to spare.

Rodgers remembers walking to the console and returning to his work. Masters walked over and stood next Rodgers. He leaned in and asked him a question.

"Is your suit okay?"

"Yes, why do you ask?"

"Well Orunmila told that both your suit and A1D7's suit had an emergency medical release shortly after you ordered an end of video and audio recording. I just wanted to make sure you didn't need to get a new suit before you left," Masters probed.

"No sir, we needed to perform an inspection of the exo-suits sir. To ensure that they were working properly. We concluded after the inspection insured they worked optimally. They are good to go now sir," responded Rodgers.

"Good, I am glad everything checked out. For a second I worried your inspection may last longer than the 20 minutes. Men of your age usually can't inspect for that long," implied Masters to Rodgers as he smiled and then walked back to the other console. The conversation took place between the two CUs of the men and thus it was not audible for others to hear.

That all occurred 45 hours ago but to him it felt like 5 minutes ago as it played over and over in his mind. They arrived at Kush five hours prior and fifteen hours behind schedule. Three of the major supply spacecraft suffered engine problems during the burn and the entire taskforce had to travel at a slower speed than expected. The entire plan could be in jeopardy if they could not unload and reload the transport craft in the next hour.

The massive Sub-Commander Rodgers stepped off the stealthstar onto highest of three massive orbit rings that encircled the entire planet of Kush. The six elite Dragon Team members followed behind him closely. Power and determination rippled in the air and mixed with panic and confusion of the cargo hold. Massive crates of materials streamed off transport spacecraft. Rodgers knew they were fighting against time, the enemy that never stopped. Five minutes later the commander reached the top deck of the ring command complex.

The planet Kush was slightly larger than Earth but only had .85 the gravity of Earth. When it was discovered it had a weak magnetic field and barely had an atmosphere. Nubian corporation set to terraform the planet after Nubia as the agriculture planet of the system. The planet had a rich volcanic surface that was almost completely flat. The terraformers first constructed massive machines at the poles of the planet to increase the magnetic field.

Secondly, they constructed the first planetary ring. The ring encircled the entire planet around the equator. It was then connected to massive logistical space elevators from the planet equally distant around the planet. The first layer of the ring also proved another layer of defense against radiation and helped create a thicker ozone layer for the planet when the Nubian Corporation started to bring water, oxygen, nitrogen, and other gases to the planet.

It took roughly fifty years before the first plant sprouted but the product was worth the investment. Population centers popped up around the space elevators and major distribution centers but the planet remained mostly farm land as it was intended. Next, A second ring was constructed 400 hundred meters above the first ring once the export demand for the food grew. It was mainly used for storage, larger docking stations, and some point defense for the planet.

An unguarded planet rich in food soon found itself in the crosshairs. Pirates would perform quick strikes and raids on storage facilities. Organized crime organization extorted the distributors and threatened to destroy spacecraft. Alien races launched xeno-terriost attacks to destroy massive swathes of land and crops to stop human expansion. This lead to a gun and self-defense culture. The people of the planet banded together to form Black Squads that would respond to the threats from the outside.

Finally, the third ring was constructed 400 meters above the second ring. This ring was littered with point defense cannons, missiles systems, advanced targeting system, and a planetary shielding system. Planetary cannons were installed on the ground allowing the planet to reach out and touch any spacecraft that entered within 200 hundred thousand meters of the planet.

Rodgers stood at the edge of the observatory of the command and control facility of the entire ring system. The massive vertical installation reached from the lower ring to the top ring. The sight inspired awe in the heart of any spacer that saw it. The installation connected all three of the rings under one massive port that also allowed the shielding system of all three rings to be active while allowing ships to pass in and out of the planet's atmosphere. Dropstars maneuvered down to the planet's surface holding hundreds of thousands of soldiers ready to protect the planet to the death.

All 112 of the heavy lift elevators transported either the thirty million soldiers, 100 thousand armored vehicles, 100 hundred thousand mechs, equipment, ten million armor kits, or ten million guns. Kush had a standing army of 2 million active duty forces and 4 million reserve forces. Since the Kush rings were designed to move as much material as possible as quickly as possible the forces were quickly being moved from the massive transports onto the ring system and then down the planet. Since the ring systems encircled the entire planets, military forces could disembark around the strategic areas they would protect.

The sun breached the horizon of the planet casting the light down on that part of the planet. Rodgers nodded his head at the sight and vowed to protect the planet to his last breath. Such a jewel of Human engineering needed to be protected. He walked to the elevator on the observation deck and traveled from the top ring to the bottom ring.

The trip was quick and he stood on the active bridge of the ring system. Soldiers and officers of the Orbital Guard saluted Rodgers and his Dragon Corps guard solders. He nodded and the officer proceeded with the duties they were assigned. The tall and lean Orbital Guard Quasar for the planet of Kush walked over to update the Sub-Commander on the movement of man and material. The process of getting all his forces to the planet should take no longer than 45 minutes and then the process of extracting the food stores should take no more than 30 minutes. Rodgers hoped they made good time and are able to get the transports back to Nubia before the Poveen arrive.

PLUS 82 HOURS AND 25 MINUTES SYSTEM METEOR GENERAL MORRIS SOLIS OKO RINGS, KUSH KUSH BURNS PT 2

System Meteor General Morris Solis walked off the troop transport into the holding area on the top ring above Kush. The Meteor Corps forces were clad in heavy black armor and moved with the coordination of soldier ants. Millions of soldiers had to be moved to the planet surface at speed. Rather than travelling on a dropstar the General travelled on a normal troop transport to ensure that the rank and file troops would be taken care of. The convoy was delayed by faulty drive systems on corporate spacecraft. This forced an expedited disembarkation process. His troops would be at a disadvantage when the Poveen arrived. The deployment plan he envisioned took a little over 17 hours but he only had 10 hours to get his forces in place before the Poveen attacked. Everyone was feeling the pressure to get to the surface of the planet and Solis wasn't any different.

The soldiers moved in a rhythmic order from the cargo hold into the massive train system. They moved entire divisions out of the cargo hold at a time on the massive machines. Solis watched from a distance as the soldiers moved out. A slight grin dominated his blue face. The precision of movement and the confidence of mission pleased him. Morale was high and it reflected in the body language of the soldiers. It was real now. They would defend Kush. The Poveen are coming and this was no longer a drill.

The General and other commanding officers moved with him into the last train. The cargo hold would fill with pallets of food and water for transportation back to Nubia in moments. He moved into the car he was assigned to on the train. This particular train car was designed to transport cattle but instead today it would carry the various officers of the Meteor Corps. Magnetic boots stuck to the metal floor and gravity stabilizers kept the officers from bouncing into each other on the train. Darkness filled the train car with only a couple spotlights on the roof of the train car. Some of the officers activated the lights on the black matte armor to provide more light.

The train was mildly quiet with a couple of loudmouths talking about how many Poveen they were going to kill. While most of the men and women on the train recorded goodbye messages or updates for family members. Communication after the start of hostilities could not be expected. The military network was also currently overloaded with communication and file transfers. It may take an hour or two for a message to get out and most of the soldiers would be moving nonstop until the Poveen arrived. Unlike the planetary forces the bulk of this force was from somewhere else in the human sphere. In fact, slightly over 90 percent of this force was from another system.

Only five percent of his force was even from the echo region of space. This made communication even harder since the gate system, including the communication gates, would prevent real time communication with other systems except for the leadership with the ability to the QEN. Solis was connected to the QEN, Quantum Entanglement Network, this updated his CU with continual updates on the movement of all his forces as they moved around the rings and those that landed on dropstars, troopstars, or basestars down to the planet. Solis knew his soldiers would do their jobs when the time came.

Basestars, the massive landing vessels used by the Meteors Corps, were almost all on the ground. These spacecraft were designed to land on enemy planets or friendly planets and create a base of operations. The spacecraft would transform into a barracks, airfields, resupply locations, logistical hubs, and production facilities. Twelve of these massive craft will land shortly on the planet around major population centers and strategic locations to support the forces on the planet.

The heavy dropstars, almost the size of the basestar, would land close to the basestars and unload the 2 regiments of soldiers or a battalion of mechanized and armored forces to support the basestars and then travel to logistical locations to pack food and provisions for the return trip back to Nubia. The lighter dropstars were a little different. These were smaller craft and usually were designed to breach planetary shielding systems to provide the first troops on the ground of a hostile planet. These vessels travelled to established starports around the planet to reinforce these locations with heavy equipment and more soldiers. They would remain on the planet to provide a military transport network and provide close air support to the ground troops they are assigned to.

Thirty minutes after the train ride started it stopped. Meteor soldiers got off the train and walked onto the massive space elevators. Kush boasted 147 space elevators making it the third largest network ever constructed by humans. The view of the planet was magnificent. Fifteen-meter-high transparent walls allowed the meteor forces presented an epic panoramic view once the elevator began the decent to the planet. The black of space faded to reveal the light blue upper atmosphere. The trip took a little over fifteen minutes to reach the base of the elevator on the planet surface.

Large warehouses surround the base of the elevator. Solis could see the larger corporate buildings that managed this logistical hub in the distance. Massive storage facilities, train stations, and gravity truck stops bustled with activity. This was a normal day of operations for this city and it would not be any different today. They were people and product movers and today they had to do both.

When the massive door opened, Solis watched his forces march out and follow the directions of the men, women, and machines that guided them to the exit and the proper transport. The soldiers moved with precision in movement and in focus. Solis was surprised with the emptiness of the cargo hold they exited into. Where were the pallets of food he thought to himself? He expected the walls and every inch lined with pallets, boxes, and shipping crafts but he saw nothing. Solis walked over to the highest-ranking doc officer.

"Boss, where are the food stores? This place looks extremely empty?" he asked. The officer at first dismissed him. When the dock worker looked closer at the large blue man's rank after he would leave the dock worker's personal space he discovered the rank.

"Sorry sir, they are behind the doors. We didn't know what would be coming down here so we had to ensure that you had enough room to maneuver. If tanks or puppets came down the elevator we would need the space. This elevator is going right back up without loading. It can get back to the station in just under 5 minutes unloaded without people. Our orders are to get all of you to the surface as soon as possible," said the man nervously and in an apologetic tone.

Solis nodded to the man but could not help to feel like he was being deceived. He took a couple of steps and then pinged Sub Commander Rodgers. It took a couple of seconds for Rodgers to respond which was expected in the middle of such a mass deployment.

"Sub Commander Rodgers something is off. I just reached the surface and the elevator room was empty. An officer tried to tell me a truth that didn't square. Something is off. Something is happening here that doesn't seem right. The people are not acting correctly," said Solis to his commanding officer.

"I thought it was just me but I am feeling the same thing up here as well. Something is a little off. Let me check with A1D7. She is about to land at the Johnson Space Port in River City. I will contact you if we find anything but for now continue your deployment. We are running out of time here. I need your forces to be ready when they arrive. Let me worry about this but if you see anything else let me know. Thank you for the information," said Rodgers.

PLUS 82 HOURS AND 55 MINUTES DRARGON CORP GENERAL DESIGNATION: A1D7 NAME: LAURA OBAN JOHNSON SPACEPORT, KUSH KUSH BURNS PT3

"A1D7 have you witnessed any suspicious behavior at the space port? General Solis has noticed that some things are out of place. I have noticed things that are out of place up here as well. What are you seeing?"

"Nothing, we still haven't landed yet. We are in a holding pattern waiting for an open port. I just tapped into the optical sensors on the dropstar. It looks like all the docking births are filled with spacecraft. Also, around the spaceport thousands of speeders, buses, and other ground vehicles are littering the area. If I would guess, it looks like an evacuation of some sort. I hope these people don't think they can make a run for it. They are safer under the shield," said A1D7 in the augmented electric voice.

The pilot once again asked for landing instructions from flight control. A1D7 cut into the line and told the officer to clear a port for them. The officer responded a minute later with instructions to hold and to be patient. It was clear that they were delayed it just wasn't clear why. Any controller would have ordered one of the craft to leave the port a let the high ranking official land. They didn't want them in the starport, but why? What were they hiding? Could this be another attack like the one on Nubia?

"Sub Commander Rodgers they have denied our request to land again. What are you orders," asked A1D7?

"Okay, we don't have time for this shit. Find the biggest spacecraft you can find and hover above it. Combat drop into the Starport and figure out what is going on. I have a bad feeling about what is happening here," said Rodgers to A1D7.

A1D7 sent a message to the pilot of the star and they maneuvered above the largest ship with all weapon ports opened. The long sleek stealth dropstar was coated in the darker than black paint. The paint absorbed almost all the energy produced in the electromagnetic spectrum. It looked like an eerie blackhole in the sky as it descended from a thousand meters at speed. In the rear of the craft A1D7 readied Alpha Company for the combat drop. Weapons heated up and the armor clacked snapping into place forcing sound to echo in the drop hold. The pilot yelled ten seconds as the craft activated all the stealth and evasion systems on the elite vessel.

The starships weapon ports burst opened and targeted anything that looked hostile on the ground as the rear and sides of the craft burst open. The 250 soldiers of Alpha Company jumped from the openings to the ground. The gravity repulsors in the heavy armor ensured they landed softly. The elite solders moved with speed outward from the base of the spacecraft, weapons drawn pointing at port security. Full kitted and with restriction the dragon armor was glorious. Each soldier stood nearly 3 meters from the ground to the top of the helmet. The police forces in the spaceport moved onto the spacepad when the disturbance was reported only to greeted by the barrels of elite weaponry. The police officers stopped and placed the weapons on the ground.

The spacepad was packed with people. Everyone had suitcases and other bags loading the spaceship that was docked. The full company of dragon corps soldiers froze everyone and forced silence on the crowd as they waited for orders from the terrifying soldiers. Seconds later two more stealth dropstars reached the starport. Beta and Charlie companies landed on the starpad as Alpha company moved into the broader space port. The elite soldiers moved with speed along the corridors and corners, prepared for anything.

What they found was disturbing. Thousands of people lay huddled along the walls and in the many various holding areas. It looked like a mass exodus was about to take place but they had not received any indication that a mass movement of the people of Kush to another location was authorized.

A1D7 reached the command and control center for the Starport. Kush Orbital Guard regulars quickly responded. They didn't have the dragon armor but they were in military grade combat armor and guns drawn. UPHAF soldiers were now pointing weapons at each other before a shot was fired against the aliens threating the sovereignty of the system. A1D7 walked right up to the commanding officer without even acknowledging the Orbital Guard soldiers. Unless they had the top of the line armor piercing rounds and five minutes of continual fire they could not penetrate the dragon armor. In that time, she could kill every person in the room ten times over. The Orbital Guard knew that as well and it was the reason why they didn't fire weapons. They just continued to point the guns at A1D7.

"What the fuck are you doing?" asked A1D7. A plain clothed woman that A1D7 identified as the leader took a step back and looked around the room for support. "Okay, I will not ask again. Tell me what you are doing or I am going to snap your neck," said A1D7 as the massive mountain of human and armor leaned over the woman. She looked around the room again looking for support to not find it. The officer quickly calculated that her life was more important than the orders she received not to tell anyone.

"We have our orders to get as many people on the spaceships as possible. Why do you ask?" she said giving a half truth. A1D7 lifted her hand and gripped the neck of the woman picking her off the ground.

"I don't have time to play with you. Tell me what you know now?" yelled A1D7.

"Okay, we received orders like fifteen hours ago that the plans had been changed. We were to focus on loading people and not food. The spacecraft would go to Nubia when the task force arrived," she explained.

"Who gave the order? Why would you disobey an order from your commanding officer during a Protocol 5? During a Dark Sentinel. Are you stupid?"

"We tried to get the message out but I didn't have access to the QEN. My commanding officer said that all messages to Lord Commander Masters, Sub Commander Rodgers, and General Solis were scrubbed. It would have been impossible to get the word to you. The order came from the Planetary Force General Jones and President Lawrence. I am sorry but many of the commanding officers were relieved of command when they protested. I figured that I would serve my soldiers better to remain on duty and do what they told me to do," said the woman as she pleaded for her life in the hand of A1D7.

"All spaceships leaving should be filled with supplies not people. Get these people out of the spacecraft and get them back to the cities and shelters," said A1D7 in anger as she let go of the woman. Even through the voice augmentation software scrubber the inflection of anger couldn't be expunged. A1D7 pinged Sub Commander Rodgers in orbit to give him an update.

"Sub Commander Rodgers the leadership at the port have informed me that the spacecraft are filled with people and not food and resources. They received orders from the Planetary General and President Lawrence to put as many people as possible in the spacecrafts to leave with military starships on the return trip to Nubia. Apparently, this is planet wide. What are your orders?"

"Stop all craft from leaving. Get the rest of your team on the ground.

Take it over the Starport and start ordering spacecraft you suspect have people on them to the ground. If all the spacecraft in orbit are filled with people and supplies we have a major problem on our hands. That port is now your port. Bring the orbital guard soldiers back into the fold and standby for further orders," said Rodgers as he ended the call.

A1D7 called attention to everyone on the bridge of the Starport and said, "Okay Everyone this is the plan," she said. For the next fifteen minutes, she gained control of the port and the soldiers in the surrounding areas. They ordered all the people off the spacecraft and started the process of recalling some of the spacecraft that were already airborne.

PLUS 83 HOURS AND 15 MINUTES
SUB COMMANDER
MIKE RODGERS
OKO RING STATION, KUSH
KUSH BURNS PT 4

Sub Commander Rodgers snapped his head to look at the commanding officer of the Oko Ring Station. The helmet slammed shut into full combat mode. The trusted hand cannon was pulled from the holster on his side. The barrel of the weapon was trained right on the face of the ring station commanding officer. Rodgers knew a mutiny or treason was at hand and he wasn't going to tolerate any deviance from the orders given by Lord Commander Masters.

"What are you doing here? Play with me boy and you will no longer have a head," barked Rodgers as the security force raised weapons to point at the other officers on the deck. The was terrified and continued to retreat backward until he hit a work station. With the retreat halted the armored Sub Commander walked closer and closer to the commanding officer with the gun drawn.

"Sub-Commander Rodgers, please do not fire that weapon in here, I need you to calm down so that I can understand what you are asking. My standing orders are to facilitate the unloading of your forces to the planet. Then I am supposed to load the people on the spacecraft bound for Nubia," said the station commander.

"That wasn't the order given by Lord Commander Masters. What are you doing? You know as well as I do that those spacecraft must accelerate at least 15 gs to make it back in time before the assault. Are you telling me that those people can handle that kind of acceleration? You are committing treason during a Protocol 5," yelled Rodgers as he moved even closer and the anger grew.

"I do not know anything about a change of orders all I know is that I was instructed by General Jones and President Lawrence. People began to arrive a little over 7 hours ago, and I was told that your spacecraft would unload soldiers and then we were to load the people. We started the loading process five minutes ago. The people were on the second ring and we are now bringing them up to the 3rd ring. Now can you please lower your gun," said the man. Rodgers lowered his weapon and his helmet opened again.

"How many people do you have on the second ring?"

"About 2 million people. Do you have enough room to take them back to Nubia?" asked the man. Rodgers just stared at him. The officer was completely oblivious to what was happening.

"General you are following illegal orders. You were supposed to load food and supplies bound for Nubia and not people. Get those people off the spacecraft and this ring. Get them back to the planet as fast as you can. They cannot be on those spacecraft," yelled Rodgers as he moved back from the officer thinking of the next steps. He had to get the convoy spacecraft back to Nubia while the window was open. They wouldn't have the time to find and bring food stores on Kush and get them back to the Nubia like the plan dictated but he needed to protect those starships and crews docked with the rings. Rodgers order the military spacecraft that came in the task force to prepare to depart for Nubia without cargo.

When the order to return to the Nubia travelled around the rings something happened to the citizens of Kush that had waited for hours. The people on the ring panicked and ran toward the open cargo holds of the military craft. The entire ring system was engulfed by hordes of scared people trying to ensure that they received a place on the starships on the return trip to the Nubia. Soldiers and officers on the starships were overwhelmed and pleaded to leadership for answers. Rodgers saw the increased chatter from the captains of the starships docked with the ring, he tried to process how bad the current situation was. Unaugmented humans on board those starships would not be able to burn back to Nubia at the acceleration needed to and land before the Poveen fleet arrived.

On the planet's surface tens of thousands of spaceships took to the sky and began to burn for orbit. It appeared from a quick glance that any space worthy craft took off from the planet. Rodgers HUD lit up when the sensor data was relayed to him from the commander of his space force. This is getting worse by the second he thought. We are exposed. Very exposed. Rodgers needed to gain control of the situation and he needed to gain control now.

Evolution demanded that humans needed a mechanism to quickly and reliably alert the group to recognize danger and move as a collective. That mechanism was fear. This hardwiring took full effect on the ring system and on the ground. When the news that the spaceport was taken over by the Dragon Corps people at other spaceports feared that they would not be able to leave. The resulting panic launch without air traffic control or computer guidance was chaotic at best and deadly at worse. Midair collisions were common at the many of the spaceports.

On the rings, the meteor regulars tried to stop the flow of people on to the cargostars and dropstars but the people would not accept this. Safety was in the cargo hold and the people would not be denied. The population of the planet felt that Nubia was much safer then Kush when the reality was the opposite. The people knew this would be the last military shipment back to Nubia until the war ended. The calculation was simple. Get back to Nubia and you and your family would be safe or stay on Kush and die.

Sub Commander Rodgers struggled to regain control of the planet which had descended into mild anarchy. He barked orders and started to open direct lines of contact with the commanders on the ground that received the treasonous orders from the Planetary General Jones and President Lawrence. Rodgers in his struggle to regain control of the situation finally noticed that he was being pinged by Lord Commander Masters.

"I apologize Lord Commander we have a situation here. President Lawrence and General Jones changed our orders. Instead of food they were trying to send people. We uncovered the plot and I am trying to lock down the planet now. Can you give me a minute sir?" asked Rodgers.

"Okay that would explain the reports that we are receiving here. We are getting a lot of orders verification requests. Orunmila is working with the AI on Kush to purge a rogue signal. Just get a handle on it and remember Sub Commander. The military assets are more important than the civilian," said Masters. A chill ran up the spine of the Sub Commander after that statement and he knew why he said that. If the panic continued, he would be forced to start making tough decisions. Some might include force.

The command center at the ring continued to tell the starships rising in the atmosphere to go back to the port they originated from but no one was answering hails or responding to the commands. Thousands of craft maneuvered for the exit to leave the planet but Rodgers order it closed. Military craft can easily pass through human shielding with the combination of transponder codes and dynamic shielding systems but civilian spaceships lacked the military transponder codes and would die if they tried to pass through the same as an enemy projectile or starship. Rodgers was systemically pinging the commanders on the ground and the infrastructure to stop the movement of people but the panic was overwhelming every institution on the planet. They caught this way too late.

Seconds later he was pinged by President Lawrence. Rodgers took the call quickly.

"Commander Rodgers, why are you denying the people of this planet a safe journey to Nubia? Did Masters tell you to reject us? Do the Nubians only want the food from Kush and not the people? These liberals have gone too far this time. We have changed the plans because the plans did not suit us. The people of Kush will be allowed to return Nubia with the convoy and you will not stop us. If the people of Nubia need food so much they can risk another journey. The people of Kush will not be left to die," said the President. Rodgers hated nothing more than politics during war.

"You changed a lawful order given during a while we are designated a Dark Sentinel while also under Protocol 5. This is treason. You are ordered to turn yourself in and face charges of treason for your actions."

"I didn't see anything lawful about an order that took our resources while you fail protect us. Yet you send entire fleets to protect the 40 million people of Atlanta and the 200 million people of Carthage. You Liberals have been trying to take power from us since we entered the body politic. This is Masters and his wife's family trying to use the Poveen invasion to push us out of power. You will open that shield and you take the people on the ring," yelled the man as he felt that his point must be heard and understood. He was in control of Kush, not this outsider.

"So be it, "said Rodgers in a cryptic voice.

"You are going to arrest me. Boy, you are funny. This is my planet boy," said the man as he laughed deeply. President Lawrence had a couple moves up his sleeve. Within a second of the end of the communication the planetary shielding system went down. Spacecraft from the planet now raced out of the atmosphere and started to take up positon close to military vessels in orbit. The situation was now completely out of control. Rodgers yelled at the planets AI to put the shield back up but it was not responded to his commands.

Rodgers yelled at the orbital commander but they were locked out of the system as well. The officers of the command deck yelled suggestions back and forth until they settled on the best solution. The only solution they could come up with was a hard restart. Rodgers yelled for them to implement the solution. Purple lights and a mighty klaxon sounded throughout the ring system. The purple alert was to inform everyone on the station that they would lose gravity shortly. Rodgers magnetically secured himself to the ground. Thirty seconds later the power, gravity, atmospheric systems, trains, and every other system went black.

They had to perform an emergency start of the ring system and it would take 10 minutes for the for the systems to start coming back online but a full 30 minutes for the entire system to be at 100 percent.

Around the control center cups and other lose debris that could not be stored in time floated around the command center. One by one the systems were rebooting slowly. First the emergency lighting came back to life with the environmental controls. Next the gravity reignited slowly to allow all the debris to fall back to the deck slowly. That is when chaos and panic hit a new level. Some people were injured during the loss of gravity and more were hurt when it was restored.

Broken bones, cuts, and bruises stoked the flames of panic like an accelerant. People rushed from entrances of the starships docked with the stations. Others raced for the trains trying to find a better location, while yet others ran for the elevators to try to return to the planet seeing the chaos and not wanting to become a part of it.

Sweat was poured down the face of the Sub Commander Rodgers. Okay, solve the problems, one at a time, and then move on. Quickly he ordered all the starships to close all doors and undock. They were ordered to push out all people in the cargo holds with exception. Next, he ordered his Meteor force to reach a higher orbit outside of the shield when it comes back on. They are ordered to go hard burn with high G maneuvers so that they can lose any civilian stars that decided the best place for the them was next to Meteor starship.

The word "BREACH" flashed across his HUD. It was impossible for Rodgers not to see the bright red letters that dominated his field of vision. Did something break the ring, was the air getting out, did explosive decompression kill people? He toggled off the warning and turned to the commanding officer to find out where the ring system had a breach. The commander responded by telling him that the ring system was in perfect working order.

The Poveen cruisers that were once approaching in subspace had breached into normal space. The telemetry information dominated his HUD thanks to Orunmila. He yelled louder than he ever yelled before in his life, "Get that fucking shield up now, incoming!"

The people on the command center clicked buttons and used the CU on the back of the neck in attempt to speed up the reboot process and they couldn't. Rodgers never saw the enemy cruisers blink into orbit but he heard the energy fire. When humanity took to space a long time ago the silence of space was a problem for human brain. The silence of space combat was so disorienting to humans that engineers assigned sounds to each enemy projectile, energy fire, acceleration, deceleration, turning, banking, and other actions. Not only did the assignment of sound help the ease the disorientation of space it also provided valuable information to pilots, soldiers, and officers alike.

The extremely loud sound of the energy indicated to Rodgers the power and distance of the assault. Explosive decompression from the blast pulled him outside the command center and outside of the ring system all together. He fell down the gravity well toward the Kush with his back to the planet. Arching white energy struck the ring system at the hub and continued to burn large swatches in the hull. Explosive decompression occurred around the entire ring as Rodgers panned his face from left to right.

His systems tried to identify all the objects falling around him and the cruisers in orbit but it struggled with the volume of debris. Once in the vacuum of space his suit reacted and closed completely. It took less than a second from the time breach flashed on his HUD until he was falling toward the planet. The magnitude of the calamity that was taking place could not be measured. The planet was under attack because of political infighting. Rodgers turned to the planet and pulled in his arms and legs and prepared for reentry. The sight he saw chilled him to core.

A woman holding a small child was less than 2 meters in front of him between him and the planet. Her body and the body of her child were already frozen from the cold of space. They died in space of decompression. Extreme pain was etched on the face of both parent and child. They should both be safe on the surface of the planet behind a planetary shield and space guns but instead the misguided leader marched them and the rest of the planet to death. Moments later the bodies thawed from the frozen husks into burnt figures as they hit the upper atmosphere. His shielding system ignited for protection during reentry. The elite battle armor that the man wore had the meteor space diver system for times like this and he was extremely thankful. Without that system, he would be seconds from death.

Rodgers turned to face the ring system now that he was in the atmosphere. Orunmila reestablished the connection that was lost when he as ripped out of the space station. The command center was destroyed and the enemy cruisers moved along the ring cutting piece after piece out of it. The enemy cruisers dominated his field of view. A list of possible countermeasures flooded his HUD.

"Why are we not firing? Fire on the enemy cruisers," yelled Rodgers to the now acting Orbital Command General at one of the reserve command centers.

"Starships and spacecraft are in the way…"

"If it is not a military vessel I do not care. We need to push them now before the they destroy the entire ring system. firing now," yelled Rodgers once again. Two seconds later the massive planetary gun system ripped through the atmosphere and started to hit the Poveen cruisers. The cruisers began to preform maneuvers to save themselves from the powerful energy weapon systems on the planet.

The Meteor Corps starships from the task force mobilized into action around the three pillars of the force. The first pillar is the Meteor Carrier. The small but fast meteor jeep starcarriers unloaded starships from the hull. Each carrier carried 1000 star puppets, 200 starfighters, 50 interceptstars, and 20 starbombers. The carrier is supported by 50 starvettes, 25 starfrigates, and 5 starcruisers each to create one Meteor Carrier Constellation. The task force contained 10 of these constellations that formed 2 clusters of 5 constellations.

The enemy was broken into 8 constellations of 7 cruisers. One constellation of cruisers moved east raking the ring system while another constellation moved west. 2 moved north and south respectfully as the spread from the former center location of the ring system. The remaining two constellations fired upon the vessels docked to the ring and any human space craft in local space orbit. The first of the carrier clusters met the Poveen cruisers travelling north.

The first line of engagement was the SAP – 2 Mesos Starpuppet. The standard starpuppet for the meteor corps in human sphere raced into combat. Each Mesos was piloted by two human pilots and array of AI systems. The craft mimicked the human autotomy and looked like a metal human with a jet pack on his back. The small and agile craft easily penetrated enemy defenses with speed and agility usually unable to be intercepted by the large caliber weapon systems.

The massive Poveen cruisers fired on the small but nimble anatomical human machines without the desired result. The Poveen cruisers were in the heavy weapon configuration. The rail cannons from the puppets raked and punched small holes in the hulls of the cruisers as they attempted to kill a fly with a hammer. Dipping and diving in and out of the formation forces the Poveen cruisers to take notice that the response to the attack on the ring system would be swift.

Next in the fray were the SAF – 7 Iron Starfighter. The fast attack vessels moved in masse. Thousands of Irons descended at speed. It utilized the same maneuverability and quickness as the Mesos Star puppets but had more armaments to cause offensive damage. The fighter force focused fired on one of the cruisers causing massive damage to the vessel. By this time Poveen cruisers returned to the standard allocations of variants. The point defense anti-space craft variant appeared quickly on the battle field and started to decimate the formations of the fighters and puppets.

The Poveen cruiser had three configurations. The first configuration was the assault configuration that was used by all the spacecraft when they attacked the ring system. In that configuration, the cruiser pushed all energy toward the primary weapon making it extremely powerful, but the cruiser is unable to fire point-defense energy weapon systems. The standard configuration allowed for the use of the point defense weapon systems and reduced power to the primary weapon system. The defense configuration focused on increased shielding and added point defense platforms. The typical Poveen constellation of seven cruisers consisted of two assault, four normal, and one defense configuration. The enemy was now trying to battlefield configure into the standard configuration. During this process, the enemy cruiser could not fire at all.

The larger human vessels moved in after the smaller attack craft engaged. They would not have been able to stand off with the Poveen Cruisers if they remained in the heavy attack configuration. The starvettes and frigates moved closer. Rail cannons blazed and missiles burned toward the enemy constellations. The swarm of ordinance and vessels overwhelmed the Poveen attackers. Missiles slammed into the hulls of the Poveen cruisers to create massive damage. The game: attrition. The same battle played out with the other carrier clusters and Poveen forces that moved along the west, east, and south.

The second pillar of the Meteor Corps was the force of heavier starships that were geo synced above the north pole of the planet. 20 dreadstars and 40 starcrusiers moved on the Poveen quickly. They burned south toward the ring system once the cruisers blinked into Kush orbit. The battle cluster of human spacecraft engaged directly with the enemy forces. The two-traded fire with the Poveen sending high bolts of energy fire at the powerful human starships with extreme disrespect. The humans retuned returned fire with energy, missiles, and railgun rounds.

The third pillar of the force Meteor Corps was the landing force. The task force arrived with 15 troopstars carrying 15 million soldiers. 13 of the troopstars were docked with the rings and two were not but still contained the full complement of soldiers waiting for their turn to dock on the rings. The last two troopstars reacted quickly when the enemy jumped into the system. They broke from the upper atmosphere and opened the massive doors that dominated the sides of the vessel. The soldiers jumped out the hold with the vehicles, mechs, and equipment. The troopstars dodged each other and equipment the best they could to avoid enemy fire with only cover from the two starcruisers that are assigned to every troopstar.

Millions of soldiers dove to the planet from space. The equipment and heavy machinery followed closely behind. All equipment, vehicle, armor platform, and resource was capability of orbital entry and that was being tested under fire. Arching beams of energy only subsided with the human starcrusiers engaged the enemy cruisers. That support only lasted for two minutes before those starships were ripped apart by the force fire of the enemy. Both troopstars took critical damage and fell into the atmosphere of Kush on fire.

The 13 troopstars that remained that were attached to the ring when the battle began took fire from the Poveen as soon as they blinked into orbit. Those troopstars had more difficult decisions. Some of the troopstars were loaded with civilians when they rushed the officers in cargo the holds. Any high g turn or maneuver would kill everyone on the troopstar that was not military or ex-military. Two troopstars broke from dock and tried to maneuver slowly and they were destroyed along with the cruiser escorts. 5 other troopstars made the only decision they knew they could make and survive. 3 went into 30 g turns and maneuvers to escape the fire from the Poveen but it crushed and killed all the people in the cargo hold. The craft then opened the cargo hold door causing explosive decompression and forcing all the mangled bodies out of the hold to burn up in the atmosphere.

4 other Troopstars were docked with the station when the battle broke out. The Poveen energy weapons cut through the rings causing decompression and sucking all the people and soldiers on the station out toward the planet or into deep space. The troopstars exploded and destroyed more of the ring and other systems. The rest of the craft scattered in all directions trying to find and angle of retreat. This all happened in the first minute of the engagement.

The massive battlenova Star Killer was under a hard burn to slow down to enter Kush orbit before the Poveen blinked into battle. Instead of the continued breaking the craft turned and accelerated toward the planet. It would have arrived in 30 minutes if it continued the deceleration profile. The craft turned and increased speed to reach the engagement in five minutes. The only drawback was the battlenova would not be able to enter the orbit of Kush because it would be travelling too fast. It would fly by and rake the enemy force and turn to hard burn back to the fight.

The Star Killer launched the nova class kinetic missiles toward the enemy. The speed of vessel provided the missiles with tremendous starting momentum. Star Killer launched over one thousand missiles of the total 4 thousand missile compliment. The constellations in the northern hemisphere was the target to receive the twenty-meter-long rods of depleted uranium and tungsten. The battlenova vectored the massive primary weapon system that ran along the entire length of the 3-kilometer-long starship toward the Poveen craft attacking the rings.

The Star Killer was only within weapons range for 1.7 seconds as the speed of the battlenova dictated such a short fly by but the damage it caused was extensive. The 1000 kinetic missiles ripped into the 7 Poveen cruisers in the northern constellations disabling or destroying all of them. Next the massive primary weapon struck out against 3 heavily damaged Poveen cruisers finishing them off. This was only the second engagement the Poveen had with a human battlenova and they learned quickly that it was not a starship to be reckoned with.

The massive weapon system fired intently on three cruisers in the rear of the attack. Two of the cruisers took damage while one of the cruisers shield failed and it collapsed under the gravity of the controlled singularity in the sphere at the rear of the cruiser. The massive human battlenova travelled past the enemy and kept going. It would now take two hours for the vessel to slow down and get back to the planet but its impact was felt.

Its attack signaled a turn in the battle. Most of the Poveen Cruisers had at least light damage and some had heavy damage. The planetary gun system was coming on line and firing at a greater pace. Some of the ring systems were coming back online. Missiles and point-defense rail cannons fired on the enemy cruisers. The Meteor Corps response was swift and overwhelming at times. The volume of fire from the humans increased on the Poveen cruisers.

One other force was snuck into battle unnoticed by the Poveen. The constellation of heavy and light stealthstars moved into combat. The stealthstar force identified one of the command in combat cruisers and they moved in to destroy it. The CIC cruiser remained largely away from the combat which made it vulnerable. The human stealth force launched equally stealthy missiles. They were kinetic rounds similar to the missiles launched by the battlenova except they cost thirty times more because of the stealth configuration. Unlike the other missiles that would be able to travel at the same velocity due to the relatively low speed of the stealthstars, the warhead was more powerful. The completely stealthy missiles slammed into the sides of the cruisers without them knowing.

For the second time in the battle the enemy lost and entire constellation. The stealthstars ravaged the cruisers that flanked the CIC cruiser and the CIC cruiser itself. The Poveen struck a major strategic victory in the battle but they suffered for it in the loss of cruisers. 40 percent of the planetary ring system was destroyed with more of in need of major repairs. The most dangerous military weapon platform in the system. Over half the attacking Poveen cruisers were destroyed. All the remaining Poveen cruisers were damaged but they would fight again.

Rodgers continued his freefall to the surface now joined by tens of thousands of meteors that were sucked into the vacuum during the battle, spit from the troopstars before they were destroyed, or those who just jumped to survive. The ionization of his suit prevented him from contacting his forces on EM bands until they cleared the atmosphere. On the other hand, he received a battle update via the QEN through his CU. The masse of soldiers angled for Oko Base outside of Oko City. He would land in a little over five minutes at his current decent rate.

He may have just lost the ability to defend the planet. The enemy was gone for now. They lost a lot of cruisers but the humans lost the planetary shield, thousands of starships, and millions of people. The Poveen clearly won the first engagement at the Battle of the Nubian System. Rodgers could see debris from the station and starcraft hit the surface of the planet exploding in massive megaton explosions. How many people were dying on the ground? How many people just died in space? Fire could be seen all over the horizon in every direction. Kush Burned.

A ping came over his CU from Lord Commander Masters. Rodgers answered the call.

"What happened?"

"Planetary General Jones and President Lawrence deactivated the planetary shield. I don't know how but they locked out the command crew. Poveen blinked into orbit thirty seconds later," answered Rodgers.

"How bad?"
"Bad."
"How many dead?"
"Millions."
"How many starships did we lose?"
"Thousands."
"Okay, it seems like you are being short with me Rodgers."
"Sir, Kush Burns."

PLUS 85 HOURS
COMMAND CORPS VICE COMMANDER PRIYANKA KAHN
HANNIBAL BATTLE STATION, CARTHAGE REVENGE

Vice Commander Kahn watched the video again of the Kush for the fifth time. She watched as the ring system broke and fell to the planet's surface. Kahn watched as human space forces responded with hate and spite against the Poveen attackers. The invasion was real. The large masses in subspace were starships and they were trying to destroy all human life in the system. Humanity engaged in the first battle with the Poveen in the Battle for the Nubian System and lost it badly. That was not going to happen around this planet and under her watch.

Carthage was the tenth planet in the system roughly 5.3 AU from the sun. Carthage was easily within the Goldilocks Zone since the Nubian sun was over three times that of Sol. The super earth was composed of relatively the same make up as Earth. Large continents and deep water oceans covered the large planet. Humans could never settle on the surface due to the crippling 4.5 Earth Gravity at the surface but that didn't stop their machines from journeying to the surface to mine the seemingly endless source of metals and minerals.

In its orbit were two moons named Hannibal and Hamilcar after the powerful warriors of the ancient nation of Carthage. Both moons were currently being terraformed into habitable worlds. Hannibal, had roughly the same size and gravity as Venus. It lacked an atmosphere but that the process of taking the needed materials from the parent planet of Carthage to Hannibal was underway. Once Hannibal was finished terraforming they would move to Hamilcar. Hamilcar was two thirds the size of Hannibal and did not have a magnetic field.

Hannibal Battle Station orbited the moon of the same name ready for combat. When the enemy breached into normal space and then used the blink drive to seemingly teleport 10 AU to Kush from the previous location the station has prepared itself for attack. Every starship in the Carthage planetary system opened weapons ports and activated defensive shields. The carrier decks exploded with activity as starfighters, interceptstars, starbombers, and starpuppets launched into the black. The smaller spacecraft launched and dove toward the planet Carthage to maintain speed by orbiting the larger planet. They would use the gravity of the planet to sling shot them into combat when the enemy arrived. The number of starships grew from zero to 10 thousand, 20 thousand, and 50 thousand.

Vice Commander Kahn sat in a crash couch on the command deck of the CIC. Her helmet was closed shut because the air was pumped out of the room. The entire space station except for the medical bays and some other select locations waere placed into vacuum to prevent fires and explosive decompression during the battle to come. Though the massive battlestation would need to take substantial damage for the compartment that she was to have a breach reach space the Poveen force approaching did contain enough fire power to do so.

The Poveen force in route to Carthage breached into normal space ready for combat. 154 Poveen Cruisers moved at speed toward the Carthage planetary system. Everyone on the bridge could see the starships break the subspace barrier and enter normal space but when the sensor operator yelled "Breach". A cold chill still ran down her back. It was time for combat. How dare they come into this system, her system, and attack them? "These cowards, yes cowards," she thought to the herself "have no honor." Kahn was prepared to kill every one of the Poveen.

Status reports filled Kahn's HUD. One by one the massive military force around the planet activated readiness alerts. 85%....90%...97%...100%. Kahn was impressed that in less than two minutes the entire fleet responded and was ready to fight with all missile ports open, laser charges, and rail guns sparking and twitching with stored electricity ready to send the neutron tip tungsten rounds into the bellies of the Poveen Cruisers.

"Contact," yelled the sensor operator as the display lit up with Poveen Cruisers blinking into the planetary system. Kahn sucked her teeth and went into action. Unlike the attack on Kush the Poveen commander kept its forces tightly bunched. Blinking into battle was a strategic disadvantage for the enemy units. In normal conditions once a Poveen Cruiser blinked into combat they couldn't blink again for 57 minutes and 23 seconds. That meant any attack from the station and the craft could not be simply dodged by the performing another blink.

The massive arsenal of the angry Hannibal Battle Station bristled waiting for the enemy force to come into optimal firing range. The mass of fighters, interceptors, puppets, and bombers rounded the planet and headed toward the moon Hamilcar for the final burn before combat. Hamilcar was on the opposite side of the planet than the Poveen attacking force. All these attack craft burned at 20g acceleration and rounded the moon at various angles changing the return vectors toward the enemy force. Three distinct columns of craft cut burn and zipped toward the Poveen Cruisers 20 minutes away from contact.

"Vice Commander Kahn, I have studied the trajectory of our projectiles as it pertains to the enemy fleet and it seems the angle of approach is not random. If we fire our guns and miss 10 hours from now those rounds will hit Nubia. How do you want us to proceed," asked the Chief Weapons officer?

Kahn studied the information and quickly managed the situation and made a quick decision. The larger weapon systems will speed up the rounds to ensure if they miss they will not intercept the orbit of Nubia hours from the battle. Tactically it will slow down the fire rate of the larger weapons systems as launching projectiles faster will take more energy and thus take more time to recharge the systems to fire again. The medium and smaller caliber rounds will continue to fire at normal rates of fire. Vice Commander Kahn send Lord Commander Masters a message that merely stated "In ten hours you might have some rain". Seconds later Masters replied with "I have an umbrella, good hunting".

Kahn snickered slightly and then ordered the adjustments and told her officers to fire when ready. The super cluster of starships burned into to position and changed the engagement angle. When they attacked, they hoped to push the Poveen force off the current angle of approach and down into the gravity well of the planet. This would force the Poveen forces to slug it out with the human forces at close range or blink away from battle.

Kahn was confident in the ability to outthink this Poveen Commander. It already showed a degree of hubris believing that it could stop the larger weapon systems of the battle station from firing because of an attack vector. This was a fatal flaw in the strategy and the sign that the Poveen commander is either a show-off, has a high level of self-esteem, or disrespected her abilities. She choice to believe that he was disrespecting her.

Kahn was not new to combat and in fact she studied warfare her entire life before engaging in it. the identification of the enemy commander's motives and then turning it against them was her strength. With the precision of the planetary AI she shorted examples of commanders that fit the profile that she now faced and engaged in countless scenarios in her mind as the battle as it played out. She was ready. She sucked her teeth once again and then smiled.

"3...2...1...Engaging," yelled fire control as the four mighty rail cannons unloaded ordinance at the enemy. The Battle of Carthage was now underway. A distant descendant of one of the mightiest warriors in human history, Kahn always felt that when in battle she channeled his energy. The station shook when the tungsten shelled depleted uranium neutron tipped projectiles raced at two percent the speed of light at the Poveen cruisers, heavy cruisers, and super cruisers. The overlapping shields of the Poveen cruisers absorbed the insane amount of energy that smacked into them.

Those shields didn't have unlimited energy though. At some point, they would have to silence those guns or suffer the consequences of not doing so. Ten minutes of fire didn't discourage the Poveen fleets approach. The lead Poveen starships absorbed damage and then rotated to the rear of the formation to recharge shields as other cruisers moved forward to take the beating the Hannibal Battle Station.

The smaller fast moving human attack force closed in on the battle. The first wave to engage the enemy formation outside of the Battle Station would consist of the SF-11 Tiger Starfighters, SB-3 King Lion Starbombers, and the SV-7 Saber Tooth Starvettes. The wave of attack craft fired the canisters of fire chaff. Fire chaff canisters were filled with a gas cocktail easily turned to plasma when heated by energy weapons and hollow steel balls designed to deflect or trigger explosions of projectile rounds fired on the small craft.

A massive wave of gas raced toward the enemy in front of the 1st wave. Once in range the Poveen cruisers opened fire hitting the gas. The heat from the energy fire quickly turned the gas into a wall of plasma and molten metal. Targeting computers of the fast attack force readied to fire weapons behind that wall of plasma. The first wave raced passed the Poveen force at such a high speed that they engaged for less the .5 of a second but the repercussions of that conflict was evident.

Impacts and secondary explosions from the missiles fired at close range at the Poveen cruisers were visible. The concentrated energy fire of the Poveen Cruisers ripped into the first wave attackers. Hundreds of explosions indicated that the enemy force found the small craft and obliterated them. Kahn instructed that every attacker ensure that they passed in the line of fire of two cruisers. One of the draw backs for the tight formation of the Poveen was that when weapon systems fired sometimes they hit one another.

Kahn understood that this had an effect as the Poveen cruisers began to drift farther apart. Just as she predicted. The remaining nine waves of human attackers approached the Poveen formation. Wave after wave of human attackers slammed into the Poveen formations for thirty minutes. After the ten waves of attacking craft each Poveen cruiser had some visible damage on its hull but it didn't stop the march toward the Hannibal battle station.

She knew that the fighters, bombers, and starvettes couldn't destroy those cruisers but when the super cluster engaged the Poveen cruisers they would have the advantage. Military craft benefit from the mass of redundancies built into starships. Entering combat with a lot of damaged systems and subsystems impacted overall survivability. The swarm of small starships only destroyed 3 of the 154 cruisers. The remaining 151 cruisers, on the other hand, were damaged. The cost of the victory was high with a causality rate among the small craft of 15% percent. The Sb-3 King Lion Starbombers turned and headed for the carriers for resupply after the strafing mission. SF-11 Tiger Starfighters and SV-7 Saber tooth Starvette too damaged to reengage also turned and head toward the carriers and shipyards for repair. Those that could fight turned to engage another attack run before resupply. It would take another 30 minutes before they could turn and reengage.

The second and third part of the battle was in effect. Just like the first part of the battle the second part was meant to weaken the enemy force. While the attack craft strafed the Poveen cruisers in the first part of the battle in the second part of the starcarriers, missile frigates, dreadstars, and warstars fired a barrage of missiles of all kinds at the Poveen force from standoff locations. The missiles burned at 90gs toward the enemy. They achieved extreme speeds before slamming into the enemy force. Ninety percent of the missile were destroying before they reached the target but some of them found the hulls of the enemy. 3 more Poveen cruisers burned in the void from the volley.

Kahn sat on bridge pleased with the results of the first attack while the count down for the enemy to blink once more reached zero. Five seconds after the countdown ended the Poveen cruisers blinked once again. The force split into two equal forces. One force encircled the super cluster and the other force encircled the Barca Staryards.

Kahn muttered under her breath a multitude of curses and insults. The move rendered the weapon systems of the Battle Station useless. Any fire from the station would have a high change of engaging and destroying her forces. On the other hand, they were now at pointblank range with the human starships erasing the edge their primary weapon system had to reach out and touch human craft at range. The first wave of fighters and starvettes shifted course to return the carriers while star puppets and interceptstars protecting the carriers engaged in combat.

PLUS 85 HOURS AND 30 MINUTES
SPACE COMMAND QUASAR
VALERIE RODRIGUEZ
BATTLENOVA PLANET ENDER, CARTHAGE
PRIME TARGET

On the virtual bridge of the Battle Nova Planet Ender System Quasar Valerie Rodriguez stood next to Captain Reiner. Poveen Cruisers blinked into surround space around the super cluster she commanded. Rodriguez sprung into motion and commanded the best of space command into combat. The starships she commanded had more weapon systems, more shielding, more missiles, more rail cannons, and more engine power than any other fighting service the system.

The enemy force encircled the human supercluster with the creation of a spherical attacking formation around the human space force. This formation created crossfire angles, denied the human starships the ability to angle shielding in one direction, exposed engines, and reduced the ability for the human forces to respond with overlapped fire. On the other hand, the Poveen cruisers could angle shielding to the front of the starships, keep drive systems from harm, and use overlapping fire angles. The blink allowed the Poveen to stack the deck for the conflict in their favor. The Poveen expected to pummel the human forces inside the encirclement at best and at worst it would constrain the human forces from assisting in the assault on the Barca Staryards and carriers.

Spacecraft to spacecraft the Poveen were much stronger than the human counterpart except in the case of the battlenovas. The battlenovas were designed and constructed after the previous incursion of an alien species.

The Lovick destroyed an entire human star system with 3 starships. The battlenovas were designed to repel the fire power of that type of craft long enough to strike the heart of the massive alien starships. The battlenovas were basically a moving energy weapon with engines and shielding. Today the Poveen would understand its power.

Captain Reiner ordered the Planet Ender forward toward the closest constellation of 7 Poveen cruisers. In support of the battlenova were 5 warstars, 10 gunstars, and 8 starcruisers. The human constellation burned toward the enemy cruiser formation and started to receive energy fire from the Poveen cruisers.

The chaos energy cannon on the Planet Ender fired for the first time in anger. The lead Poveen cruiser buckled from the energy fire. It was soon fired on by the remaining members of the constellation. It jarred and vented atmosphere for a couple of seconds before the singularity drive that powered the starship in the massive sphere to the rear of the vessel collapsed on itself destroying the craft. The Poveen quickly realized that the new massive starship of the humans was not like the others. Humanity welcomed the attackers to a new level of warfare.

On the simulated bridge of the Planet Ender they cheered after the craft was destroyed. Quickly the Planet Ender burned its maneuvering thrusters and fired on another Poveen Cruiser hitting it broadside after it turned to move away from the Planet Ender. Just like the previous engagement the rest of the constellation fired on the cruiser after it was struck by the chaos cannon as it tried to maneuver away from the battlenova. In less than five minutes the Poveen lost 2 cruisers. The Poveen cruisers tried to maneuver into a tighter formation to use overlapping shielding to repel the powerful chaos cannon of the Planet Ender but it did not work.

Rodriguez was shocked that the Poveen responded in weakness. This was the first time that she witnessed weakness on the part of the Poveen. That meant it was time to press the attack. Adrenaline filled the veins of the Quasar. "Run you fucks," she muttered. Quasar Rodriguez spoke words of encouragement to the bridge crew. The Planet Ender continued to turn to face one cruiser after another hitting them with the full power of the chaos cannon powered by 12 anti-matter reactors.

The human forces didn't go unscathed in the opening moments of the battle. While the Planet Ender carved a hole through the alien formations other human constellations in the battle were still at a major disadvantage. Brave human men and women were died from overlapping invader fire as the starships moved into new fighting formations to repel the encirclement. The fight was a slug fest, a war of attrition, a battle for the heart of the Nubian system.

The Planet Ender arched toward more and more prey. The chaos cannon ripped down two more Poveen cruisers while the support starships emboldened by the mighty battlenova attacked the other three Poveen in the constellation. They battled starships at close range obliterating the three remaining cruisers on the constellation that tried to hold the mighty Planet Ender. The encirclement was broken and the breakout was underway.

Rodriguez barked one command after another to the commanders of starships to give them a tactical advantage. Human forces moved in strategic grace to optimize the advantage the Planet Ender gave them. The battle would now swing on the capabilities of the individual commanders and leadership to identify and react to opportunities. She was suddenly pinged from an unlikely location. When the connection request came from Victory System both Quasar Rodriguez and Captain Reiner were surprised. Why would the leadership in the Victory system want to interrupt a captain and a quasar in the middle of an engagement? They both decided to dismiss the request and continue to command the fighting force.

After 30 seconds, they received a new message. This message stated that the CU attached to the brain stems of both the captain and the quasar would override the current connection to the virtual world in 30 seconds. A countdown started before they reacted. Quickly Reiner told his second in command to take control and that they would be back shortly. The second in command took command and continued with the current battle plan. Rodriguez prepared the rest of the formation for a brief absence as well.

At the end of the countdown they were relocated to another virtual environment with Lord Commander Masters and Regional Commander Moon. Why would Masters go through the central location when he could communicate directly? If he had to this then something was wrong, very wrong.

"I apologize for the intrusion and I will get you back to combat as fast as I can. We have been compromised. We have a firm belief that the Poveen can listen into our quantum communications. I do not know how they are doing it but they are. The question that you are asking yourself now is why is he communicating this from the Victory System? That is because the quantum communication between the Victory system and the Planet Ender is heavily encrypted to keep out prying human eyes. We have reason to believe they cannot hack the encryption.

You will be sent a new encryption protocol for your old system that will bring it to the standard of this encryption. Once that is in place you will be able to send messages directly to me in the system. Note, when you contact an unencrypted system the enemy will understand what you are saying. Use that to your advantage if you can. At the same time, when speaking to people on unencrypted systems do not relay any valuable information or any information discussed here.

Everything I am about to tell you now you will keep secret from Vice Commander Kahn until she has been made aware of the current situation. Hannibal Station does not have a QEN to the Victory system and we cannot speak to her directly. You will follow Kahn's orders unless I tell you different. Quasar Rodriguez you will do everything possible to be summoned back to the station to tell Kahn in person. Once on the station you will tell her to look at her personal military email. In those emails is the process to encrypt and purge the current quantum protocols.

Secondly, we have reason to believe that the 14 Poveen Cruisers that entered the system but never went into subspace are the only cruisers that possess the interdictor technology. At the battle of Kush your battlenova brother and the stealthstars destroyed one of those spacecraft. The strength of interdiction decreased by a factor of 1/14th. Currently you are engaged with two of these interdictor cruisers we are calling CIC cruisers. Your priority is to destroy those two cruisers. If we can take them down we will be able to open ER gates and bridges again. With support from one or two battle galaxies we would push the Poveen from this system. Also, you cannot tell Vice-Commander Kahn that you are now targeting the CIC cruisers until she is in the loop. Do you understand"?

The words from Masters did not surprise the officers. The Poveen had technology more advantaged than the humans. The fact they had the ability to hack into the QEN systems made sense. It also made sense that they could hack in and present false information as well. Rodriguez needed to know that she could test the message that she received. She needed some sort of verification but because a communication hack of this kind never happened and the protocols didn't yet exist.

"I understand sir but I need to know that I am talking to you and not to a Poveen. I have a question. Who won the Galactic Cup officers pool last year?"

"Well technically General Solis won the pool because they found out later that the champs cheated but Quasar Might was the one who collected the money. She also would not give the money back and told Solis that Brooklyn doesn't fucking care if my memory is correct," said Masters as both Reiner and Moon tried not to laugh at the comment. Rodriguez nodded her head in agreement satisfied with the answer.

They were suddenly back on the bridge of the Planet Ender. Rodriguez toggled the system to display the CIC cruisers. It took a second for the system to identify and display two CIC cruisers in the encirclement. Rodriguez liked to put her soldiers and officers in positions that would give them the best chance of succeeding. In warfare success was staying alive and failure most of the time meant death. She was now about to give orders that would put her officers in no-win situations. Commanders are always prepared to take losses. That is the burden of command. Ordering people to die, on the other hand, was a lot tougher.

Rodriguez hesitated twice before giving the order. She knew the captains of those space craft. She knew the wives and husbands. She knew the children that would grow up fatherless and motherless. Yet they signed up to defend humanity and sometimes the defense requires blood. Rodriguez gave new commands that plunged half the encircled starships into the fire. The Planet Ender and the cluster of starships angled toward the nearest CIC cruiser and another attack group moved toward the other CIC cruiser.

The vice quasar of the battle cluster pinged Rodriguez to ask for clarification on the orders. She didn't see the need to expose her starships and basically needed to understand why. Once the vice quasar received clarification and noticed the Planet Ender had also engaged in the same type of maneuver she complied.

The attack was more effective than Rodriguez anticipated. It startled the Poveen commanders into inaction. The attack was so brazen, chaotic, and against traditional human combat formations and tactics that they reacted with caution unsure if these crazy humans were going to reveal another new weapon. This inaction of the Poveen cost them the two highly specialist CIC cruisers while the human forces didn't pay the price they should have for the reckless attack. Shortly after the second interdictor cruiser was destroyed the enemy force blinked out of combat.

The Poveen forces around Carthage all blinked one AU away from the planet at the same speed and orbit as the planet to maintain the distance. Of the 3 CIC cruisers that entered combat at the Battle of Carthage only one remained.

Moments after the battle a light flashed on her HUD from a high-level contact. Quasar Rodriguez cringed is discomfort. It was time to explain to Kahn why she performed such a crazy maneuver ever without consulting her first and when they had the advantage in the fight. Rodriguez is a 35-year veteran of space command. Many officers and soldiers don't know how she became a system quasar so fast. It was not by luck, nepotism, or favoritism. It was due to the 7-year command of an intelligence group that tracked rogue human smugglers that traded with alien races.

Rodriguez knew how to lie, deceive, and outright send people in the wrong direction when she had to because of her training. Today she would have to use it on her own commanding officer. The audience was also larger than just Kahn. This would be monitored by the Poveen as well. They just lost 2 CIC starships around Carthage and one early around Kush. Rodriguez needed to ensure that they didn't suspect anything.

"What the hell was that Quasar Rodriguez? I have seen reckless behavior before but that was almost criminal. I am formally reprimanding you and if you perform another action like that again you will be relieved of command. Do you understand?"

"Yes"

"So, what the hell was that?"

"We noticed that two cruisers were not performing the same way as the others. They never took the place in the front of any rotation. Those were the only two cruisers that had not. We believed that they were special and had some sort of importance. I believe that we should identify these cruisers in the future as well. After the destruction of the second craft, they blinked out of orbit. In the next engagement, we need to ensure that we identify them before the blink window is over," said Rodriguez as she laid the trap for the Poveen.

The interdictor CIC cruisers never took a spot on the front line to absorb fire which was true. Rodriguez gave the enemy a reason why the tactics they used were flawed as a reason to attack. The human forces could identify the Poveen CIC cruisers without the tactical flaw but the Poveen didn't know that. Rodriguez presented the Poveen with a choice they didn't even have to make. The alien invaders could enter the CIC cruisers into the normal rotation exposing it for time, place it at the rear of a formation to ensure that it is protected, or continue with the current strategy and postpone the humans from identifying at the beginning of the engagements. Rodriguez hoped to bait the Poveen into entering the CIC cruiser into the normal rotation. This would expose the CIC cruiser to human fire and would be the easiest way to destroy the starship.

“Understood. This is powerful information Quasar Rodriguez. Next time I need you to bring information like this to me when it is discovered. Is that understood?”

“Yes sir,” answered Rodriguez confident that her quick and capitulation would end the conversation and make Kahn remorseful that she scolded Rodriguez before she understood the reasoning. Quasar Rodriguez could pass information along to Vice Commander Kahn by using the tactics of the Poveen to explain it. The Poveen listeners would blame the loss on poor internal planning and flawed tactics. Her deception worked the way Rodriguez wanted it to.

PLUS 86 HOURS AND 30 MINUTES
LOGISTICS CORPS GENERAL
NAKIA OKAFOR
BARCA STARYARDS, CARTHAGE
REPAIRS NEEDED

The battle ended over an hour ago but the carnage left in the wake continued. The System General of Logistics stood in the operations center that overlooked the main hangar deck of the largest carrier that orbited Carthage. A hoard of repair drones, artificial humans, and her team raced to repair the fighters, interceptors, puppets, and bombers as fast as possible. The ensemble of man and machine raced against time and the enemy to complete the assignments given.

The assault forces took the brunt casualties of the first attack. While the larger spacecraft only lost 5 percent of starships the assault craft lost slightly more than 40 percent. Readiness was low and morale was even lower. The teams of officers did the best they could to save as many vessels as they could but too many were damaged beyond repair onboard the carrier. On these dead and dying starships they stripped the craft of useful parts like engines, guns, ordinance stores, and operations systems. Discarded husks were pushed out the carrier to be retrieved later when the conflict was over.

Okafor sipped on a cup of freshly brewed Nubian coffee and continued to make adjustments as she saw fit to the orders given by the Hannibal Battle Station AI Imilce. The report was not good. It was going to take hours to repair and rearm the assault craft. The blink technology of the enemy presented an extreme advantage for the enemy. The Poveen could blink all cruisers into combat meters from the carriers at any moment. This forced the human carriers under constant readiness that sapped them of technicians and the needed space for optimum repair.

In response to the advantage Okafor's engineers prioritized the craft that needed the shortest time for completion. Once the starship was completed it was moved out of the bay to the planetary orbit or kept in the hanger in the launchers. The completed craft in the launchers created bottlenecks for the movement of damaged craft and repair machinery. In normal operating conditions, she would repair the entire wing first and then move on to the next wing maintaining the battle readiness of entire wings to preserve outcomes of the commanders.

Okafor moved around the deck reassuring the officers that they could complete the task. Her tall frame moved with grace and confidence but the truth was that for the force to return to full strength they would need to take a chance. The current progression of repair was taking way too long on all the carriers and in the repair yards. Okafor needed permission to shut down combat operations for 2 hours to repair and rearm without the burden of launch. Nervously, Okafor pinged Kahn to make the request.

"Vice Commander Kahn. To speed up repairs we need to close the bay doors and focus on repairs. Doing this will allow us to fix and rearm in 2 and half hours. If we continue to try the hybrid approach it will take over 6 hours. I need your permission to go off line for that time," asked Okafor.

"What does that mean for us?"

"It means that we will shut the doors on all the carriers. During that time, they will not be able to launch any attack craft. If attacked it would take roughly 15 minutes or so for the attack craft to move to launch. I think this gives us the best chance in the future. We will launch all craft currently on the deck and more craft already orbit Carthage. Most of these carriers can't move anyway and they are sitting ducks for attack if the Poveen want to attack us. These fighters are the only hope of defense," explained Okafor.

"I can't have them down for that long. Do better General Okafor," responded Kahn.

"You either get this half way approach we are doing now and in 6 and half hours you have full strength or you have full strength in two and half hours. Speed in the key here. We have to repair the damaged starcruisers too," said Okafor. Kahn stared back blankly.

"Crash repair for an hour and then go back to a stand back state. What would that do?" asked Kahn.

"That would speed up repair for an hour and then place healthy starships on the same deck as the damaged ones like we have now. I don't like it any more than you do but we need to do this," pleaded Okafor. Kahn punched the desk in front of her and agreed to the recommendation.

General Okafor gave the order to all repair faculties and carrier decks to suspend flight operations until repairs were completed. The mighty cargo bay doors closed and inert gases pressured the decks slightly. The burden was now on repair crews to fix the assault craft as soon as they could. Healthy starships were stowed in lower deck hangers while more space was given to the damaged craft for repairs. It took fifteen minutes to rearrange the deck but after the reconstruction the efficiency begun to show.

Okafor had been on the front lines before as a combat engineer. Unlike most in the Logistics Corps she fired her weapon in anger and was on a mission where people died. This was the first time that she witnessed carnage of this scale in decades. Mangled and crippled bodies with arms and legs jutting at impossible angles were removed from the damaged craft. This was war. That bitch was unforgiving. Cold, relentless, and focused on your destruction.

They needed to move and they needed to move and move fast. The sudden ping on her CU from Masters startled her. Why would Lord Commander Masters contact her now? Okafor didn't need a pep talk. She didn't need him telling her she was doing a good job. She needed to work and he was stopping that. Reluctantly she answered the ping.

"General Okafor I will make this short. I know you have a lot of work to do and this is an interruption. Being that you have children the same age as mine and like my children some are off system. Please take this time to send a quick message to them via the military network. I will have time here shortly to send these messages to the Victory system. Given the events of the last couple of hours I don't think we will have time later. I know this might not feel like the right time but we may not get another one," said Masters. Okafor was stunned by the message. The main Poveen attack force was within blink range of Nubia but he focused on her communication with her out system children? That was not what she was expecting. She knew Masters for too long and something else must be taking place.

"I didn't consider that sir, thank you for reminding me. I applaud your humanity. Do you need anything else from me"?

"No, you are doing a wonderful job. I have forwarded you messages from your children into your military email account. You should respond to those first. Keep up the good work," replied Masters. Okafor opened her military email account. The top message was an urgent message from Masters. This was extremely confusing because it was sent shortly before the ping.

Okafor opened the message and read the message. She couldn't help but say out loud, "holy fuck." Other bridge officers looked over at her but when they saw her arm across her chest they knew she was in the virtual world completing a task. Though it did spark some CU to CU communication on the deck between officers as they contemplated what she saw. Okafor read the message about the compromised communication. Every conversation was compromised. The most secure channel was the most vulnerable and what we consider the most vulnerable was the most secure. She stumbled in place for second thinking about what she just said the Kahn. She just provided the timeline for repairs and defense of the carriers.

Okafor sent a response to Masters with confirmation that she read the mail that he sent. Okafor was pleased to know that Rodriguez knew as well. Somehow one of them needed to pass the information to Kahn. Kahn's stubbornness made this task extremely difficult. She might not take the bait that Masters dangled in front of her. Nervously she paced the floor of the command and control center while she plotted away to affect repairs faster than the time she recommended to Kahn. The enemy knew they now had 2 and half hours to repair the cruisers, they had and attack.

The mother of 5 suddenly pictured her children. The thought was fresh in her mind since Masters brought them up. 2 were on Nubia but 3 were out system. What if she never could speak to them again? What if she never could say goodbye? What about her sweet husband? She needed to send at least one more message to him as well. Okay, she would take the Lord Commander at his offer even if he meant it as a ploy. She couldn't focus now and in order to get back to work she needed to respond to settle her soul. When she was finished recording the message it felt as if a light burden was removed from the soul.

PLUS 88 HOURS
COMMAND CORPS SUB COMMANDER YOSEF AMIR
BUCKHEAD STATION, BUCKHEAD, ATLANTA
FIRST BLOOD

Sub Commander Amir called the joint meeting with Comet Corps Quasar Tanaka and Astro Corps Quasar Might. The trio quickly reviewed the battle of Kush and Carthage. Each highlighted battle tactics used by the enemy and possible solutions to the battle. The Atlanta battlefield would be different than the other two battlefields. The orbit of Atlanta was filled with debris left over from the planet and moon formations. The enemy had to approach or exit down lanes created by the humans when they settled the moons. Even if the enemy used the blink drive to bypass most of the debris they needed to reappear into normal space in one of the lanes if they didn't want to risk being struck by debris.

Amir highlighted tactics to his two officers. The three discussed the proposals in a virtual environment that mimicked a small room. Readouts and displays populated every wall of the room and could be summoned on command mere thought. Sub Commander Rodgers lost the first engagement around Kush but Vice Commander Kahn clearly won the first engagement around Carthage. Sub Commander wanted to put another victory in team human's column during this battle. They solidified the plan of action and ended the session.

Amir returned to the CIC in Buckhead station from the virtual environment. He proceeded to run down the checklist of actions once again before combat operation begun. Anger, doubt, and fear battled with his constitution for control of his mind. The overly confident man had faced terrible odds before but he never faced them as the commander. He imaged that Masters must have felt this way years ago at the Battle of Butcher Bay. The internal conflict overwhelmed him slightly as the moment of battle approached.

Amir was pinged by Might shortly after the meeting. Amir wondered if she needed to add something before the conflict that was missed or a new strategy. The commanding officer quickly accepted the call.

"Did you forget something? What is happening Might?"

"Sir, I just wanted to tell you in private that it has been an honor serving with you. I think you are an amazing commander. I know this isn't a great time but if we live past this I would like to continue our relationship. I would like us to become more. I know you are getting over a break up but I want you to give me a chance. I sent you a little something via email for you to look at. I hope it provides you with the motivation you need," said Might seductively to her commanding officer. Amir didn't even know how to respond. The communication caught him totally off guard. The extremely handsome man was used to advances from women but not right before combat. Might was a wildcard but this crossed the line.

On the moon Buckhead, Sub-Commander Amir went into full panic mode. Quasar Might cracked. She lost her ability to function as enemy forces approached. He needed to relieve her of command now before she killed people. Amir pinged his commanding officer. Quickly, Masters answered the ping.

"Lord Commander Masters I need relieve Quasar Might of her command. I just received a communication from her that was disturbing. I don't think she is fit for command."

"What did she say?"

"She just professed her love me and told me to look at my email. I believe she may have sent me nude imagery or video. I can't have this on the eve of combat."

"Did you look at the pictures? Are they any good? Take a quick look at the images and ping me back. It could be something you need to see," said Masters. Amir almost fell ill. "What the hell was going on," he thought. His heart raced as panic started to settle in. Amir knew Masters and this was not like him. Something was happening and Might and Masters have to be in on it together. They are both acting too weird. He pushed the conversation from his field of vision to the right sight of his field of view. It was stacked on top of the channel directly with Might. Amir pulled up his menu for his military email.

The top message was from Quasar Might with the title "All you ever need". When he clicked on the image it was a revealing image of Might in a seductive pose of her face and what appeared to be a naked body from the shoulders up. One hand pointed downward with the caption "more in the next image" but that was the only image. He closed the message frustrated with the current situation and opened the message below her message because it was from Masters. Amir clicked on that message and that is when he learned the Poveen hacked communication. Suddenly it all made sense.

The Sub-Commander Amir toggled back to the communication with Masters. "Lord Commander, the image was impressive. Maybe I was rushing to judgement. I believe she can still be of service. I must sign out and prepare for the battle. Thank you, commander," said Amir as he closed that window. The CU opened the channel with Quasar Might.

"Impressive Natasha. I think your timing could have been better but I understand though why you told me now. I am flattered. I didn't know. When this is over we must go to dinner or something. Also, you owe me another picture. That one was not enough. Does Tanaka know you feel this way? I know he likes you," said Amir.

"No, he thinks I am crazy. I imagine he will speak to you shortly. Give him my best," she said. Amir snickered to himself. Over the next five minutes Amir convinced Tanaka to check his messages and he finally did. Once that was completed the entire Atlantean planetary system could move to a more secure form of communication. The entire process took a little over twenty minutes but it was completed. Amir returned his consciousness to the bridge from the virtual environments he was just engulfed into.

The operations officer on the bridge moved the launch countdown to the front of the CIC. The massive wall displayed seven sectors on the battlefield. Intercepstars and star puppets burned from the surface of the moons into orbit when the countdown reached zero. These smaller attack craft would stay in the orbit of the respective moons until they were call on.

The larger capital starships of the United Planets of Humanity Armed Forces already travelled in a figure eight pattern between the moon Peachtree and Buckhead. The crews on board these starships were now fully awake and in combat assignments and battle positions. Until this point the battle was theoretical to Amir. He watched it from a far on monitors and over displays. It wasn't real to him until now. The enemy approached and the base bustled with activity. He could feel the rumble of the starships taking off. He could hear the fear in the voices of the officers. Amir could see hands shaking and nervous ticks. The battle was now upon them.

Amir pushed confidence into his officers with encouragement. He cited the Cartage battle and displayed video of the Planet Ender chasing down Poveen cruisers. The enemy force that was hiding in the depths of sub-space breached into normal space. The once invisible force of 77 cruisers and 21 heavy cruisers approached the two moons. The enemy maneuvered into position and split into three groups. Two of the of the groups were of equal size and headed toward the two moons. Each of these groups consisted of 35 cruisers, seven heavy cruisers, and 1 CIC cruiser. The remaining group consisted of 7 cruisers, 7 heavy cruisers, and 1 CIC cruiser.

Suddenly the two equally sized formations of Poveen starships blinked. One formation blinked above Peachtree and the other above Buckhead. The smaller formation remained back at roughly one tenth AU from Atlanta outside the debris belt of the planet. The action stations sparked to life and so did the human response to the incursion.

The human starships that raced around both moons in the figure eight pattern fired first. Laser cannon barrels poured energy into the vacuum of space toward the Poveen cruisers as they raced by. The Poveen craft were stacked in tight formation and fired back down the gravity well onto the human defenders. The arching white energy slammed into the hulls and shields of the human starships. The first formation of human craft could absorb the energy with shielding and escaped before they collapsed. The plan was working. The human starships could handle the barrage of fire and escape before collapse. Amir was happy that the plan survived first contact without having to change. Now it was time for part 2 of the plan.

In orbit around Buckhead, the first converted ice and rock hauler launched a barrage of building sized cubes of iron and diamond at the enemy. That was followed by more haulers that launched other heavy metals at the enemy. The haulers were protected by the overlapping shielding from the capital starships that raced around both moons in the figure eight pattern. The Poveen cruisers responded by firing at the building sized cubes. This drew weapon fire from the human starships and missiles launched from the capital starships. The second part of the attack was going as planned as well.

The Poveen followed the standard configuration of seven cruiser constellations in a 3D wedge shape. One vessel was dedicated to repealing smaller craft, four vessels had the rear of the starship dedicated to anti-assault starcraft and missile while the front two sections were dedicated to the primary weapon, and two ships focused all energy on the primary weapon. They continued to move closer to the moons at a constant pace. Both sides were cautious. Neither had inflicted significant damage on the other. It was like a boxing match in which the boxers feel each other for the first round.

The anti-assault craft configuration of the Poveen cruisers moved to the front of the enemy formations. Tasked with the destruction of the building sized material moving into the Poveen formations at speed. Unable to destroy, deflect, or deter the buildings sized cubes the Poveen simply moved out of the way. It took too much time to burn through materials of that thickness. This was the behavior Amir looked for. He wanted to break up the enemy formation to engage. His smaller craft couldn't slug it out with the much larger Poveen cruisers. If his craft could swarm one Poveen cruiser with overwhelming force they had a chance of destroying it.

The Poveen continued to march down the gravity well. The dreadstars, warstars and gunstars could absorb the hits from the enemy formation at distance but as they moved closer every pass around the moon was getting harder on the starships. It started when a constellation of 10starfrigates rounded Buckhead and launched the full missile complement onboard. The Poveen fired back on the constellation destroying 5 of the starships and crippling the other 5.

Sub Commander Amir understood he had to act and act now before his fleet was gutted. He quickly ordered the frigates to enter lower moon orbit with the starpuppets and intercepstars. This maneuver created a massive hole in the figure eight design. The larger human starships moved to abandon the figure eight formation and form into fighting formations. The Poveen firepower was too great to continue the current battle plan. Quasar Might, under orders from Sub Commander Amir, reformed the units on the fly and created battle formations to combat the attackers.

On Buckhead Amir studied the readouts and knew that the battle was going in the wrong direction. They would have to step up the plans before his constellations were reduced to slag. Larger starship constellations plunged into lower orbit following the frigates. They picked up speed and then used the moons to push the large vessels toward a nearby Poveen formation.

The smaller attack craft that a moment ago orbited the planets matched velocity and followed the larger craft creating a larger attack formation. Rockets launched from the surface of the moons burned toward the enemy formation while the haulers launched more of the building sized pieces of metal and material at the enemy formation.

The combined formation burned at speed toward the enemy. Speed was the weapon they had and they were going to use it to fullest. The same soup of chaos formed around Peachtree. Amir watched with trepidation in the CIC on the moon.

The military wing of the Nubian Corporation produced the SI-10 Hyena interceptstar. The craft functioned as a high g interceptor that engaged small enemy fast movers and supported bombers on attack runs. 2 thousand Hyena burned toward the enemy formations. Massive moon based rockets burned past the first wave of Hyenas toward the Poveen cruisers. When the Poveen cruisers fired at the rockets because they posed the greatest danger, but this allowed the Hyenas to move in close and start to fire on the much larger vessels.

The fifty-meter-long ships fired the compliments of hard kinetic missiles and railguns at the hulls of the Poveen cruisers. Most of the Poveen cruisers shrugged off the small weapons but some didn't. Flashes of light marked the impact of the fast-moving missiles and railguns rounds of tungsten, uranium, and hard carbon. These rounds seemingly without end smashed into the sides of the Poveen cruisers. Twenty five percent of the fighting force was destroyed in the first sixty seconds of the conflict. The small craft took a beating before the Hyena's turned and burned back to Buckhead and Peachtree to resupply. The second mass of 2 thousand more Hyena launched to replace the wave on the way back to the moons. In all 20,000 Hyenas were on the moons and they would continue to fly in the formations of 2 thousand until the battle was over.

Before the Hyena force broke from the engagement the Nubian SP-7a, b, and c variant Scarab Starpuppet burned into combat. Puppets anatomically looked like humans wearing armor with jet packs strapped to the back. They were once called on ancient earth mechs, mechas, or gundams but now across the human sphere they are known as Puppets. Starpuppets, like the Lion, are designed as an infantry force for space. The long barreled Assegai Railgun was as powerful as one of the railguns from the Hyena but they had a much smaller footprint.

The debris from destroyed Hyenas and rockets created the soup of dangerous debris for the Scarabs to maneuver inside of. They hid behind debris on attack approach. The high energy shielding of the Poveen Cruisers were mainly focused and angled to stop the energy fire from the larger starships which allowed the smaller craft a path to approach. The Scarabs landed on the surface of the cruisers and fired the massive Assegai railguns into the hull. It took a couple of rounds but if given time the Scarabs could breach the outer hull and drop explosives inside the super structure of the large craft.

They acted like fire ants taking down a large predator with thousands of bites and extreme pain. It shouldn't happen but it did. Before the first wave Puppets burned back to Buckhead for re-supply, one of the Poveen cruisers vented atmosphere in the vacuum of space. The sphere at that the housed the singularity was penetrated. Slowly the superstructure crumbled until the singularity pulled the cruiser upon itself.

The Nubian built starfrigate SF-110 Hippo burned into combat in the next wave. Two hundred and fifty-meter-long craft was heavier than the galactic class cousin. These craft were only system class ships and thus didn't have an ER drive. This space was filled with missiles and another shield generator instead to make the Hippo as powerful as a Heavy Galactic frigate.

They formed up into constellations of twenty and then burned for the Poveen cruisers. The debris fields around both moons grew as every wave between the galactic foes created more damaged and destroyed craft. The Hippos fired the forward energy weapon that dominated the starships design while missile bays spit missiles en masse. The Poveen formations were overwhelmed by the previous formations smaller craft and strained to intercept the missiles. More and more were finding home on the hulls of the Poveen ships. The Poveen ships were not dying but they were all bleeding.

Hiding among the star frigates and missiles were the building sized projectiles from the haulers. Thousands of deadly cubes approached the Poveen formations in waves. It was the cubes that finally broke the tight Poveen cruiser formations. They didn't have time to burn down the materials with the assault craft and missiles attacking en masse so the only solution was to move out of the way before they hit the hull.

Poveen cruisers moved apart creating more gaps in the overlapping fire. When a forty-meter-long gold cube slammed into a Poveen ship the aliens knew that the game had changed. Not even the ten inch Neutron armor couldn't stop that much kinetic force. It ripped through the super structure of the ship and exposed the inside of the forward cone of the Poveen craft. The exposed insides were quickly hit by three nuclear tipped missiles launched by nearby Hippo frigates. One more Poveen cruiser was sent to Poveen hell.

PLUS 88 HOURS AND 30 MINUTES
COMET CORPS QUASAR
RYU TANAKA
PEACHTREE STATION, PEACHTREE, ATLANTA
COMET SWARM

Peachtree's defense held for the moment but that wasn't going to last. Quasar Tanaka stood in the makeshift armory of the installation. Tanaka finalized the placement of his armor. The orange matte metallic heavy armor of the Comet Corps soldiers visually dominated the room. The click clacking of weapons echoed in the large space as equipment locked into place and magazines of shapes and sizes entered receivers. A low mumble of the soldiers provided the bass for the song of war.

The mission details were still a little murky but all the soldiers in the makeshift armory knew what they would be asked to do. They are the Comet Corps. They are routinely asked to do the craziest shit in the galaxy. This mission was a step above the usual. Tanaka read the mission orders from Sub-Commander Amir and it was simple. They needed to take out one of the CIC cruisers of the Poveen.

Orunmila, the system AI, calculated that his forces would have a ninety percent casualty rate for the coming mission. That number troubled Tanaka as it would trouble any commander. This was a war of attrition and technology. The human forces in the system could not resupply but they could limit the technology of the alien enemy and they needed to. If not, this conflict would not last long.

Quasar Tanaka received the order and passed it on to his commanders and they started to process of arming the troops. Over the next ten minutes Tanaka paced the floor of the command deck before he decided to lead his soldiers into battle. In good conscience, he couldn't stay behind after he ordered nine out ten soldiers to die. Commanders that order such attacks are cowards to him. They are without honor and they do not deserve to command. If you are brave enough to order ninety percent of the men under your command to die than you should be brave enough to die with them.

After ten minutes of furious assembly the large area quieted as the soldiers of the Comet Corps formed lines ready to exit the holding area. Each commander pinged Quasar Tanaka readiness and once they were all complete he sent the final command order on the location of the target and the mission specs.

The mission was simple in execution but extremely dangerous in practice. The comet soldiers would mount the building sized cubes of raw material and ride them into combat. Their cubes would follow one round of unguided cubes and a second round of guided cubes equipped with small thrusters attached to them. These guided projectiles would confuse the Poveen cruisers and lead to the cruisers moving farther from each other. Once the Poveen cruisers moved enough they would launch the third wave.

Strapped to the back of the third wave of cubes were Comet dropstars. The DS-2 Anteater would ride the massive cubes until they were close enough to make a drop run. The dropstars would land on the service of the cruiser, gain entrance into the superstructure, and detonate the nuclear weapons inside of the cruisers. This mission would not be easy but it could be done. This mission was necessary because Quasar Might was taking her Astro Force into the heart of the enemy to destroy another CIC cruiser. The taskforce around Atlanta simply didn't have enough starcraft to punch a hole into both formations.

Fifty thousand fully kitted soldiers moved to large elevator system that took them to the surface of the moon. The armor made all of them at least a meter taller in height. Large engines hung from the back while massive 4-meter-long rifles rested on the shoulders of the soldiers. They marched in unison onto the platform to be taken to the surface. When the last group of soldiers reached the end of the platform Quasar Tanaka walked onto it with them. It was time.

They reached the surface in less than thirty seconds to a long row DS-2 Anteater dropstars. Each craft held two thousand fully kitted Comets ready to descend on an enemy cruiser. Tanaka looked at the black sky above as small flashes of light flickered in and out over the horizon. Humans and Poveen alike died every second in orbit. Tanaka knew it would soon be his time to test fate with them. The soldiers entered the Anteaters in rows of ten very quickly and then the massive doors that spanned seventy five percent of the 300-meter-long craft closed shut.

Tanaka felt the dropstar take off. The force of gravity faded and the soldiers in the hold secured themselves to the deck of the craft with magnets. Tanaka patched into the command and control of the dropstar and followed the progress of the mission. The dropstars burned into orbit taking positions behind the cubes. Each cube would conceal two dropstars. Via his CU embedded into the brain stem he gave the command for the operation to begin.

The massive haulers that remained silent for some time tossed the building sized cubes at the Poveen cruisers. The heavy cubes moved at speed toward the enemy formations above the moon currently engaged with human spacecraft. The dropstars that carried the soldiers maneuvered into position behind the cubes that they would take into combat and readied themselves.

The Poveen got better at avoiding the massive cubes. The formations moved apart while they continued to fire on the small assault craft that battered them. Tanaka ordered the second wave to start. The Poveen did not expect what would happen next. The first guided cube slammed into a long 3-sided long pyramid like protraction to made up the front 2/3rds of the cruisers. It completed ripped the vessel into two pieces. The Poveen cruisers didn't break the greater formation until the second cube hit a Poveen cruiser.

The gaps in the Poveen formations caused by the new threat of building sized cubes of raw material that moved opened more and more. Quasar Tanaka order the third wave to start. The cube his dropstar was attached to launched first. The sudden acceleration was jarring the man and the other soldiers as they all smashed against each other in the cargo hold. Twenty five percent of the attack force launched before the Poveen counter attacked.

Seven Poveen cruisers blinked into low orbit around Peachtree less than ten thousand meters from the fifteen haulers that launched the massive cubes. The energy arched from the spacecraft onto the hulls of the haulers. They buckled and tore into the commercial vessels. The spacecraft didn't have the protection to deflect energy of this magnitude and in less than one minute all the haulers were destroyed.

On the other hand, this left the enemy cruiser exposed. The 75 percent of the force that remained would not be able to join the attack but they could wreak havoc on the Poveen cruisers. The locust like swarm moved on the cruisers at speed and quickly opened the by doors to release the soldiers. Comet Corps soldiers burned at speed to the hulls of the Poveen cruisers as they did everything they could to stop them. Within a minute the hulls of the Poveen cruisers were covered with soldiers.

The cruisers attempted to fire weapons at the small soldiers but it failed. The Poveen then resulted to firing on each other to burn off the Comets on other cruisers. This tactic also failed. A couple of minutes later nuclear devices were placed deep inside all seven Poveen cruisers that blinked into low orbit. One by one as the Comets cleared the blast radius the nukes went off tearing apart the Poveen cruisers from the inside. This came at a tremendous cost to the soldiers that engaged and the dropstars that carried them into combat. The force was almost destroyed. The causality rate that was provided by Orunmila held. Only 1 out 10 of the soldiers survived the conflict.

Tanaka cringed as the casualty totals mounted on his HUD. He was glad that no one could see his face because he was struggling to hold back tears of grief. They won the conflict from a strategic perspective but could have just lost Peachtree. On the other hand, the seven Poveen cruisers that blinked into low orbit around Peachtree only to be destroyed were the main picket cruisers for the CIC cruiser that they targeted.

The building sized cube of iron Tanaka's dropstar was attached to was not fired upon during the trip to the enemy lines. He cringed as the cube started to hit debris. Engines, superstructures, and other elements of the smaller assault craft destroyed in earlier combat bounced off the iron cube. The twenty-minute journey into combat riding the cube allowed the Poveen to spread out their cruisers to make them harder to hit with the thrusted cubes that launched in the second wave.

Tanaka sent a message to the commanding officers that they entered the combat zone and that the drop was going to begin shortly. The large doors on the side of the craft opened to reveal space and the battlefield for the first time. Streaks of the arching light from enemy cruisers seemed to never end. Streaks of laser fire and missiles from human military starships raced passed the cube toward the enemy. The scene was madness thought Tanaka. What the hell were they all doing? Billions of star systems in the universe and they were fighting for a small moon around a gas giant in this one. It didn't make sense.

Magnetic restraints decoupled from the iron cube which allowed the dropstar to move away from the object. Quasar Tanaka checked his equipment one more time and then looked to the right of him at the soldiers lined up along the edge of the craft like he was. A moment later the dropstar burned from behind the protective cover of the iron cube towards the CIC cruiser. It raced at speed maneuvering in all directions to prevent the enemy fire from getting a direct hit. The first ten seconds only produced two minor blows to the shield but as they got close Tanaka knew that the enemy would soon find the range.

It was time to get out of this transport. When the dropstar reached drop speed Tanaka jumped out. The other soldiers followed behind. Within seconds the soldiers started to spread out from the dropstar mildly accelerating from the spacecraft to allow other soldiers to exit. Arching energy blasts started to find the range. Two dropstars on approach exploded under the fire. The current approach was taking too long. Tanaka ordered all the soldiers to speed up the approach and for the dropstars to peel away as soon as they dropped the soldiers.

The Poveen fire was too strong at this range for the dropstars to provide the proper cover. They would use speed to breach the defenses of the enemy. Tanaka increased speed with the use of the two engines strapped to his back. The standard attack speed allowed for a break stop on the hull of enemy craft at 10 gs. The current approach would be around 29gs because at 30gs he would die. This fact was not lost on Tanaka as the warning lights flashed in his HUD as his acceleration profile increased and the danger to him and the rest of the soldiers also increased.

More danger signs appeared on his HUD because it was time to slow down. The HUD insisted that he slow down. For first time, he could see the CIC cruiser. The distance to target indicator flashed one warning after another. Tanaka readied the breaking maneuver after he said a short prayer. Tanaka mumbled to himself, "This is going to hurt."

Tanaka flipped over so that his feet faced the cruiser and fired the thrusters from his feet, hands, chest, and back engines. His body compressed on itself with a force he never felt before. Tanaka screamed as his body compressed under the pressure of his deceleration. The armor absorbed most of the impact to the surface the cruiser. For a second everything went black and then his systems came back online. Pain ran around his body like children at the park. Under tremendous pain the suit reacted and provided pain killers and stimulates to keep him going.

He stood to his feet and detached the rifle from his back and began to move toward the large sphere that dominated all the Poveen spacecraft. All around him soldiers were hitting the hull at great speeds. Some got up and rallied to his position and others didn't. In all about two hundred soldiers rallied to the edge of the sphere and triangular part of the superstructure. Large breaching machines in the last wave of soldiers slammed into the hull. Once inside the hull the arms of the machines expanded to allow the fully kitted soldier into the breach.

Tanaka jumped into the hole first and started to run down the wide hallway with his rifle out. The Poveen were much larger than the human so even in the full kit they easily moved down the hallway. The hallway was white with dim blue lighting. He reached the first "T" junction of the incursion and stopped as the other soldiers split up and headed into the two directions. Behind him more soldiers raced toward the rear of the cruisers. At the breach, more soldiers borrowed downward onto new decks of the craft.

Tanaka placed his small nuclear device on the wall under the breach. He would wait for the men and women of the invasion force to place more bombs and get out before he left. For five minutes, he monitored his soldiers advance into the spherical section and the placement of more bombs. They moved up and down the floors past obstacles and danger to vital systems inside the cruiser. He listened as two teams of soldiers were torn apart by the Poveen security drones. Every second that passed felt like an eternity. Tanaka just checked his devices and kept calm. One, two, three, and more bombs had been placed and the soldiers were moving to return to the breach they created. Once all the bombs were placed he triggered all of them to detonate in ten minutes.

One by one squads of soldiers returned to the breach. They insisted that Tanaka leave the breach first and return to the surface for safety. He argued for a moment but when the hallway started to fill up he complied with his soldiers. On the hull of the cruiser he could look out on the battle. It was hard to tell what the state of the battle was. The distances involved in space combat were too vast for the human eye and he didn't have time to connect to one of the greater military feeds to receive updates. Of the 231 soldiers that went into the breach 42 remained. Six fought with security forces in the hallway below the breach as the rest of the team readied to push off from the hull of the cruisers.

This was fun part Tanaka thought to himself. The United Planets of Humanity Armed Forced called the maneuver a Strategic Combat Extraction but the unofficial name in the Comet Corps was "Nuke Riding." The soldiers had to wait until nuclear weapons would detonate because if they pushed off too soon they would be shot as they left the surface of the cruisers. Since space was a vacuum the soldiers didn't have to worry too much about a shockwave as they moved from the craft. The comet armor would also shrug off the EMP and radiation ejected from the multiple explosions. The real danger to the soldiers was the spherical section of the Poveen cruiser. Inside of that cruiser was a singularity and when the sphere is destroyed that contained singularity will destroy itself. The gravity created during that destruction could suck the team inside and crush them.

Comet soldiers moved around the hull of cruisers and gathered the dead teammates that hit the hull too hard. If the engines worked they would lift the soldiers and bring them to the breach. When the countdown hit a minute the six soldiers at the entrance to the breach dropped grenades and left the hallway to the surface of the hull. The soldiers connected themselves to each other and the dead soldiers. Tanaka synced all the suits and accelerated from the hull of the cruisers. They expended all the energy from the engines of the dead soldiers and then cut the soldiers from the pack as all the Comet soldiers separated from each other and burned for Peachtree to make for smaller targets of Poveen fire.

The cruiser only fired one shot before the chain reaction of explosions ripped and buckled the enemy cruiser. Shockwaves could be seen moving along the hull. Secondary explosions and explosive decompression engulfed the cruiser before the spherical section collapsed. The singularity that powered the vessel and provided the propulsion collapsed onto itself with most of the cruiser. The entire process took a little over 30 seconds and then it was over. They completed the mission. Another CIC cruiser was destroyed.

Tanaka floated toward the moon of Peachtree. His computer estimated that it would take him two hours to reach orbit. The mission was a success but the prediction was correct. He lost almost the entire attack force. So many good men and women died that day and so many more would die. Tanaka opened the QEN once more and sent a message to Sub Commander Amir about the mission. He fixated on the battle over Buckhead as Quasar Might tried to destroy another CIC cruiser.

PLUS 89 HOURS
ASTRO CORPS QUASAR
NATASHA MIGHT
STEALTHATAR, ATLANTA
TARGETS IN THE OPEN

Quasar Might studied the read outs and the other information that was feed into her systems. She spent the bulk of her early career in the 12th Stellar Group on task force Freedom Watch. This taskforce fought human trafficking from failed or failing terraformed planets left over from the Great Push. The only engagement with an alien race was a year prior in the Nubian System when they destroyed a Poveen probe that entered the system.

The opportunity to meet aliens in combat is one of the reasons she took the command in the system. That romanticism could cost her life. If given the choice she would rather chase slavers in poorly outfitted ships rather than facing the complete destruction of a human system with a less, then ten percent chance of winning.

Quasar Might's battle cluster had 16 gunstars, 32 dreadstars and 60 warstars broken into 4 constellations of equal size. Sub Commander Amir yelled over network, "Prey in the Open". This signaled the call for the massive starships of the human forces to break orbit and engage the enemy cruisers. The unique attack of the building sized cubes made of pure ore worked the destruction of the enemy formation.

Might moved the stealthstar from the holding location to join the battle cluster. They identified the first Poveen cruiser that broke formation. Like a pack of wolves, the human starships attacked the lone Poveen cruiser. It fought back with bravery but in the end the cruiser was out matched. The missile and rail gun fire was too much for the cruiser to repel and after a two minute exchange the cruiser was destroyed. The pack then went on the hunt again in search of another victim.

The same engagement played out three more times before the Poveen regrouped and started to mount a defense for the powerful cluster of UPHAF weapons. The cruisers did not expect the building sized cubes. The battle plan they used when they engaged the moons has fallen apart. The Poveen commander was trying to switch formations and tactics on the fly. The Poveen forces lost the coordination that they were known for.

"Might. I have a mission from Masters. Make a run for the CIC cruiser now. It must be destroyed. We think they may be the best shot. Quasar Tanaka is getting together a large force of comets to make a run at the one around Peachtree. Oh, Masters also said to try to make it look like you are targeting something else if you can," said Sub Commander Amir.

"What is more important?" asked Might.

"What do you mean?"

"Is it more important that I destroy the CIC cruiser or to make it look like I didn't want to?" asked Might. She wasn't going to get people killed over foolishness.

"Destroy that damn cruiser Might," said Amir.

"Okay consider that asshole dead sir," replied Might as she mumbled a curse under her breath. The current mission of picking off strangler cruisers was easy and productive. Might gave the order to the cluster and the 4 constellations gathered to make a run at the CIC cruiser.

The constellation burned toward the enemy formation of 14 cruisers around Buckhead. The formation currently battled the smaller attacker forces and a small amount of Hippo missile frigates that reentered the battle. Quasar Might signaled the intent to engage. Starfighters, starpuppets, inceptstars, and starbombers that were on approach to reengage with the enemy revectored to join the combat behind and after her constellations. The big guns were going to enter the fight.

Might still preferred her chances more than Tanaka. What the Comet Corps was about to do was insane. She watched on the monitor as a massive deployment of dropstars left low orbit around Peachtree. Those crazy bastards were going to land on the CIC cruiser, crack it open, and destroy it. She liked the safe confinements of the stealthstar a lot more than jumping onto a moving cruiser to plant a nuclear device inside the hull and then jump off.

The 14 Poveen cruisers were not all the standard cruisers. Half of the cruisers were the larger heavy cruiser. They boasted 2 massive spheres at the rear of the cruiser with two singularities to power them. They presented a problem for the attacking starships in her cluster. Its main weapon was powerful enough to take out all the craft in the cluster with only three direct strikes. If they coordinated fire they could burn through most of the humans before they even reached the CIC cruiser. Might understand a standoff assault with a starship versus starship battle would not end in her favor. Her brain processed the battlefield. Though to her it seemed like an eternity, only a couple seconds passed.

"Constellations break and head on the vectors of approach I send. We can't take the Poveen head on and hope to survive. You are going to split up and hit the cruisers on the fringes. With any luck the Poveen will spread out. This will allow the stealthstar to sneak in and destroy the CIC cruisers with our missiles. If this doesn't work chances are I will be dead," said Might and she sent the new vectors to the four constellations in the battle cluster. One second after the receipt of orders the four constellations begun to move on the new vectors.

All four would reach the enemy on opposite sides vertically and horizontally on the same plane. The Poveen heavy cruisers will then have to decide to focus fire on one constellation or even spread out the fire among the four constellations. Might hoped for the later because that meant more of her crews would survive that day. They would all find out in a little more than ten minutes.

Might ordered for the stealthstar to fire missiles. The long stealth coded missiles left the fire tubes almost undetectable with subspace and in the EM band detection systems. Each missile cost more than three dropstars but they were extremely effective at the neutralization of a singular target. One after another the kinetic missiles launched from the stealthstar slowly gained speed. The missiles eventually caught the 4 constellations that burned for the enemy at speed.

The enemy moved to engage the human force. The 14 Poveen cruisers, 7 heavy cruisers and 7 standard cruisers, formed a defensive formation to ensure the railgun projectiles and missiles had to penetrate at least three layers of shields before they struck the surface. The enemy didn't move enough. The chances that the missiles would be detected was high. Might ordered the stealthstar to move in closer. When the first wave of her missiles was intercepted she would go to full burn and fire the rest of the complement at full burn as well and pray that they make it out the scrum alive.

The stealthstar was outfitted with strong shielding and poor armor that belonged on a commercial transport rather than a starship of war. That was the cost of the stealth. Even a standard Poveen cruisers could destroy the stealthstar with 3 or 4 direct hits. The heavy cruiser could destroy them with one hit if it was in a critical system. Quasar Might planned to keep the stealthstar at distance but she readied the starship to plunge into the heart of the enemy if the first wave failed.

The four human constellations readied to engage the Poveen formation when one of the constellations changed course. The commander of the Charlie constellation quickly performed a twenty g turn into the heart of the Poveen formation. The maneuver forced the Poveen cruisers to move quickly to intercept the maneuver. Instantly Might understood why the commander performed the maneuver. The Poveen cruisers that protected the CIC cruiser had to move to engage them. The path for the missiles was now clear.

The human constellation fired all the ordinance onboard each starship. Explosions and destruction littered the Poveen formation. In the end, one after another, the human starships fell to the arched energy weapons of the Poveen cruisers. The concentrated fire of the enemy destroyed the Charlie constellation but spared the other three. The massive use of energy also prevented the cruisers from the detection of the stealth missiles. During the height of combat with the Charlie constellation the missiles slammed into the side of the CIC cruiser. Secondary explosions rocked the front of the starship but the death of the CIC cruiser was the impact of one of the kinetic missiles into the massive spherical part of the Poveen cruiser.

Once the sphere was breached the contained singularity in the heart of the sphere unleashed a gravity wave that pulled the cruiser upon itself. Since three more cruisers in the area were damaged and another cruiser was destroyed the enemy might consider it bad luck. The battle was over for her and the Astro Corps forced. They were ordered to return to Buckhead. In less than an hours' time Quasar Tanaka destroyed one CIC cruiser and Quasar Might destroyed another.

The cost of victory was high, maybe even too high for her taste. The Astro Corps didn't have a lot of capital starships left from the engagement. Husks of the starships burned in orbit as crews rapidly tried to save the spacecraft and then themselves. Pieces of the small assault craft fell to the surface of both moons. Almost every starship that entered combat suffered damage. Most starships were pot marked with massive burn marks on the hull that indicated the spot where the arched energy fire of the Poveen cruisers hit the side of the vessels.

Might read the damage report and the casualty list. She scanned the number of available starships and the number seemed too low. "More starships had to be left," she thought to herself. The battle currently stood at a stalemate but they clearly got the worst of it. She stood from the crash couch and gave the bridge back to the captain of the starship as she walked into the ready room. Might sat on the white couch defeated emotionally. The force she commanded was decimated. She couldn't contact Quasar Tanaka and wondered if he was alive or dead.

Her force would not survive another attack by the Poveen and clearly Sub Commander Amir and Lord Commander Masters had to know this. They should burn out of the Atlanta orbit and make a run for it. After ten minutes of decompression Quasar Might pinged Sub Commander Amir. Thirty seconds later Amir responded to the ping.

"Quasar Might. How can I help you?"

"What the hell is going on Amir? You must have seen the causality reports. We lost too many starships. We need to fall back to Carthage or Nubia. If not we are all going to die up here," said Might to Amir.

"We can't."

"Why not?"

"Because some asshole decided that they were going to drop the shields around Kush. Now Kush is on fucking fire and the starships that would have backed up the force on Carthage and forced the Poveen to divert the force that attacked us to Carthage never left Kush Orbit. We have to hold until Carthage wins the battle. Only then will the enemy be forced into deciding," pleaded Amir. He knew like she did what the chances were of survival if they kept trading blows with the Poveen.

"I need more than that."

"I don't care. You won't get it. Stop complaining like a child. We must hold Atlanta and its moons. Period. If you don't feel that you can do that than I will relieve you of command and find someone else that can do it," yelled Amir.

"Okay. I just…I got it, sir."

"Look Quasar Might I don't want to die here either. This is the mission. This is what we must do. The millions of people in these domes depend on our protection. Quasar Tanaka just went on a mission that had a causality rate of 90 percent. He completed his mission and didn't complain one time. The only thing he did that pissed me off was go on the mission even though I told him not to. I need you to have the same fortitude," said Amir.

"Hold on. Did you question my bravery? Who do you think you are?"

"Your commanding officer. That is who. Now stop whining and get your starships repaired and ready to fight. Do you have anything else," asked Amir?

"No, sir," said Might as Amir closed the channel. Might was so caught up in the micro picture of the battle field she didn't process the broader macro war of the Nubian system. Sub Commander Amir was under extreme pressure and Quasar Might playing doctor obvious with the diagnoses of the clear problem didn't help. The entire system was at war and they needed subordinates that made it easier and not harder. Might stood from the couch in the ready room and walked back onto the bridge and sat down in the crash couch. It was time to make her mark on this war.

PLUS 97 HOURS
OBITAL GUARD GENERAL
KEVIN JOHNSON
OYA BATTLE STATION
PROTECT NUBIA

The mighty Oya War Station prepared to receive incoming fire from the massive Poveen Fleet bearing down on the planet Nubia. Oya Battle Station was in geo synchronous orbit over the massive ocean of the planet Nubia. The planet was roughly eighty percent water and would remain so for at least another fifty years until the terraforming took hold on the planet. The three major land masses were on the other side of the planet. The vast ocean made it difficult to construct planetary weapon systems to support the planet.

Ogun Station was on the other side of the planet. The continent that based most of the military was easily defendable. The moon was in geo synchronous orbit with that land mass and it was one of the reasons that all the continents were pulled to that side of the planet. The gravity from Luna Nubia pulled the continents and slowed the tectonic expansion. The moon was also a massive weapons platform. If the Poveen tried to take on the moon and the military continent they would struggle to land forces en masse without taking major losses.

The Poveen understood the tactical disadvantage of engaging the moon first on the other side of the planet so they approached on a vector to engage with Oya War Station over the massive ocean instead. 12 other battle stations would be able to support the station in range when the Poveen engaged with the war station.

The station was massive. It was 44 kilometers long, 12 kilometers wide, 15 kilometers across the base. The war station didn't try to pretend to be anything else but a weapon of war. Most battle stations had some civilian uses but Oya War Station didn't have any. These types of war stations were designed as a response to the Lovick invasion. They are common in up spiral human systems where the Lovick threat is real and terrifying.

The Nubians improved on the thirty-year-old design with the addition of 10 Zulu cannons to replace the original 10 Thor cannons. These cannons increased power output by 7 percent per cannon. They also added twenty more antimatter reactors and another layer of neutron armor. Oya War Station was ready for war. It housed two hundred thousand Orbital Guard soldiers and officers. The best of the best from the Orbital Guard ranks flooded to the station to train and fight on the most powerful station in the region.

Quasar Kevin Johnson stood in his ready room. For the last ten minutes his stomach betrayed him and he had to vomit into the officer's bathroom toilet. He was confident that the last of the vomit cleared his system and he was free to return to the bridge. The tall lean man walked from the bathroom to the bridge. The officers prepared for combat. They locked into crash couches, work stations, and placed helmets on their heads.

The countdown for the loss of gravity and the loss of atmosphere was displayed on his HUD. The man sat down in the commanders crash couch and readied himself for combat. The large white metallic crash couch station wrapped itself around his body locking him into place. He connected to the system behind him and readied himself. To his left was the station commander and to the right was the second in command of the station. Thirty more stations littered the bridge with the heads of the all the departments. The air left the station and gravity relaxed. It was time for battle.

Outside the 10 Zulu cannons started to target Poveen cruisers. 301 cruisers now moved toward the planet. The events of the past ten hours have been extreme. Kush burned. Carthage fought to a victory and Atlanta held their own. It was time for Oya War Station to send Poveen to hell via Zulu cannon. 98 heavy cruisers continued to move in a tight formation toward the station as the rest of the Poveen formation stopped. It was time for the battle to begin.

Oya War Station rumbled to life when it fired the first salvo of kinetic weapons. The three hundred rail cannons fired at the Poveen. They slammed into the tightly bunched Poveen forces. Missiles from the 400 missiles tubes fired in unseen at the force. The Poveen cruisers absorbs the first salvo of fire. The lead cruisers started to move to the rear of the formation to allow cruisers from the rear of the formation to move to front with fresh shields.

The second salvo slammed into the fresh cruisers. One cruiser exploded from the powerful energy fire. It was the first kill for the station. Johnson coordinated the attacks of Oya War Station with the other 12 battle stations in the area that could help in the conflict. Another salvo launched and then another salvo launched. Six more Poveen cruisers were destroyed by the fire.

The remaining 91 heavy cruisers fired on the station together with the arched energy beams of the cruiser. The station shook violently as the shields of the station fought the onslaught. Johnson growled in his helmet angered that the aliens would fire on the pride of Nubia.

"Return fire. Fire Zulu cannons for effect. Target lead cruiser!" yelled Johnson.

The ten mighty Zulu cannons fired at the lead Poveen cruiser. It disintegrated upon contact. Zulu weapon command placed the countdown timer into the HUD of the officers on the deck until the next time the weapon could fire. The station commander to the left of Johnson searched for another target for another salvo of missiles and rail cannon until the Zulu cannon was ready. The salvo rocked the Poveen formation.

The countdown ended and the cannons fired again. Once again, a heavy Poveen cruiser was gone. "We have to keep this up," Johnson thought to himself. Rockets from the planet and Luna Nubia raced to the battle to join with large range missiles from the other 12 battle stations in the battle. Ten more Poveen cruisers were destroyed. Despite losses they continued the march toward Oya War Station. When the Zulu cannon was ready again they fired. This time they missed the target. All the cruisers blinked.

Suddenly the entire Poveen force blinked around the station in constellations of 14. They fired on Oya War Station from various angles. The aliens were in front, behind, on top, and below the station. Arched enemy weapon fire pounded the shield at close range. The Zulu cannons swiveled to engage with the spread-out force. They could no longer toggle all ten cannons to fire on a single target. The Poveen cruisers could absorb a single shot from the cannon once or twice before destruction.

98 more Poveen cruisers moved into combat. 49 heavy and 49 standard Poveen cruisers moved into combat. The rail cannon moved to focus on the invading force while the missile commanders targeted the heavy cruisers that blinked around the station. Once the 98 cruisers reached firing range the writing was on the wall. The shields on the war station could not hold off that level of fire power. They needed to break the siege.

"Zulu control fire on the incoming cruisers. Force target one heavy cruiser until it is destroyed and then find another one. We need to increase the cost of taking this station. Turn rail cannon fire to the cruisers in the local area of affect with the missile bays. Battle stations 1 through 12 we need you to fire on the cruisers in our local space. The Zulu cannon can take care of the cruisers that approach," ordered Johnson. He opened another channel to the Lord Commander. A brief second later the channel opened.

"Keep up the good work Quasar Johnson. You have bloodied them."

"Sir, we can't keep this up. Our shields are failing. We can last about another twenty minutes or so," responded Johnson.

"How many more cruisers would you destroy by then?"

"About 50, sir unless we can get some support. Can you launch attack craft from Luna Nubia or grant us use of the S7 missiles?"

"I can't do that. Fight with what you have. I have faith that you will come with a solution," said Masters. Johnson closed the line in anger. They didn't have anything else. The station shook as another salvo of missiles left the station. The gravimetric effects of destroying Poveen cruisers so close to the station had detrimental effects. The release of positive and negative gravitons when the sphere that held the controlled singularity collapsed and damaged the station. It broke relay stations, conduits, bullet feeders, missile feeders, and all manner of systems.

Johnson was angered when the first Zulu cannon failed from gravity damage. One by one missiles bays and rail cannons went dark from direct energy fire from the cruisers or from gravity damage. Oya War Station was being ripped apart. Shield warnings flashed on the bridge as more and more arched energy blast defeated the shields and hit the station. The station shook not from offensive weapons fire but from the enemy dispensing arch energy blast.

"Orunmila, take over firing for the station. All hands abandon the station," said Johnson. Officers from around the station made their way to escape pods and transports located around the station. Eight Zulu cannons remained and fired another salvo that destroyed another cruiser. They needed to keep up the fight until they could get the soldiers off the station. One by one the transports left the station into heavy enemy fire. They engaged in extreme maneuvers but most of them didn't make it past the Poveen cruisers that encircled the station.

Johnson cursed under his breath as another two Zulu cannons were damaged. The bridge officer hadn't moved since the evacuation orders. Command staff don't leave until all those that report to them get off the station. Another salvo and another cruiser was gone. A graviton wave rocked the station and disabled three more Zulu cannons. Another massive graviton wave hit the station again. Two of the heavy cruisers dropped one of two spheres located at the rear of the craft at the station. They threw two controlled singularities at the station. Not even neutron armor could stop an attack like that.

Only one Zulu cannon was functional. It fired but it lacked the punch to destroy any more enemy cruisers. Like sharks smelling the prey the Poveen moved in and attacked the long cracks in the armor that now dominated the superstructure of the might war station. The energy beams entered the hull of station destroying systems and equipment. Targeting went down first. It was quickly followed by sensors and shielding. At any given time fifty Poveen cruisers were firing on the station.

Finally, the station cracked and the antimatter reacted with normal matter. When the chain reaction started, the enemy cruisers blinked out of blast range. Oya War Station was the pride of Nubian defense no longer. The station exploded above the might Nubian ocean. Less than five percent of the crew made it off the station and safely to the ground.

The Oya War Station didn't go without a fight. It took out 72 Poveen cruisers in the battle. At Ogun Station Masters could only wonder what would have happened if they would have allowed him to order 3 of the mighty war stations like he wanted. .

/

PLUS 101 HOURS
PLANETARY FORCE GENERAL
JAMAAL NASIR
FORWARD STATION, NUBIA
FIGHT DAMNIT

The command center of Forward Station went quiet when Oya War Station exploded. The pride of the Nubian defense was destroyed by the Poveen in the assault. General Nasir, a combat veteran, wouldn't let the destruction of the station break the morale of the soldiers. He rallied the soldiers and officers on the command center. The impassioned speech and commands inspired the team and got them re-focused on the mission at hand.

General Nasir wasn't any stranger to loss and death but this was the first time in a long time he lost people close to him in rapid succession. First, he lost Colonel Nduwke in the laser attack on the xeno terrorist facility. Next, he lost his good friend Quasar Kevin Johnson on Oya War Station. They served together for decades. He looked around the command center and wondered how many of the officers in that room would still be alive when this entire conflict was over.

Three more battle stations fell shortly after Oya War Station so Lord Commander Masters ordered the space stations to move closer together over land. This action opened a large lane for the enemy to breach the atmosphere and land on the planet. Masters ceded this avenue of approach. It is the hardest location on the planet to affect a sustained invasion because of its distance to land on all sides. The Poveen seemed to accept the tacit agreement as well. They didn't press the attack once the space stations retreated. They lost a lot in the initial attack. Nasir imagined that a lot of Poveen lost friends that day as well.

"Okay people. Here we go. We now know where the enemy will enter the atmosphere. Admiral, start steaming your fleets toward to the invasion locations. When the enemy assaults the planet, I want submarines, aircraft carriers, destroyers, battleships, aircraft harassing the landing craft. Let's get the Marines on trains and moved them to the shoreline. They will hold the beaches and access lanes. I want airborne soldiers in the air in ten minutes. We need to drop them twenty kilometers from beach lines on avenues of support for the marines.

When that is finished, I want armor, mechs, gravity copters, and puppets to support artillery forces. We need to be ready to move in support of the troops on those beaches. We must keep them off dry land if possible. Let's move people. We know where the enemy will land so let's give them hell. Airforce, you will be up first. Get ready to launch everything we have. When those troopships hit the atmosphere, I want you ready. Okay everyone let's move with a purpose," said Nasir as the command center exploded with activity. Officers moved back and forth around the room as they made his commands into tangible orders.

"Can I have a word with you sir?" asked the Nubia General Bello. She was a powerful leader and commander. The two were extremely good friends that also fought in combat together. They walked off the command deck into a meeting room.

"What is it?"

"Sir, I need you to allow me to do my job. I know you want to be here in Forward Station to monitor the situation but we need to maintain our cohesion here. The next time I need you to provide me with your orders and then I will pass it on If you get distracted with another battle on another planet and are not available for contact I need my officers to know that I can make the decisions. If we don't hold to the chain of command than I may lose my officers if you are not around. It also allows for me to make adjustment to the plan of action before it is presented. I do not have objections to the current plan but if I did it would now be a problem," said the tall dark skinned woman.

"Agreed and allow me to apologize. I know this is your shop. If I don't back off drag me back into this room," agreed Nasir. Bello was one of those officers who will be Command Corps material one day. She was the perfect blend of grit and intelligence. She was in charge of the Nubia Planetary Forces and Nasir was in charge of all Planetary forces in the system.

"Thank you, sir. Now let's get back to defending this planet."

The two officers started to walk onto the command deck when Nasir was pinged by Masters. This is the very situation that Bello described to him moments ago. He told her to run the deployment while he communicated with the Lord Commander.

"Sir," answered Nasir as he travelled to the virtual environment to meet with the Lord Commander.

"General Nasir, how are we looking?"

"We look good sir. The shockwave didn't affect us much. We are ready to defend the planet. Forces are on the move now."

"Do you notice anyone acting funny or suspicious. We can't have another Kush."

"No sir. I don't see anything like that here. That virus may have only been on Kush but I will keep an eye out for it here. I know these people and I do not think they are capable of such an action. On the other hand, if you would have asked me yesterday I would have said the same about General Jones. Do you think that was political or do you think it was something else? Something about it seems weird to me. President Lawrence's name came up a couple of times in the terror case. I think somehow, they may be involved. Take out the population of Nubia with an infection and take out the planetary shield on Kush."

"You may be right Nasir. We will get to that when we can but for now do your best. I sent a messenger your way. Receive them. It is important."

"Got it," said Nasir as the conversation ended. He walked out of the communication room and on to the command deck. He told General Bello that he had a meeting topside that he had to go to. After ten minutes in the elevator he reached the top of the building. On the roof a transport waited. A man walked over to him and handed him a data pad. He turned around and got on the transport without saying a word and left the roof.

Nasir quickly downloaded all the information on the data pad. The data pad contained information that the Poveen can hack the Nubian QEN. Regional Commander Moon and the team in the Victory system were able to come up with code that would encrypt the communication going further. Nasir quickly downloaded the information on to the QEN on his side. The process took no more than five minutes. Orunmila pinged Nasir and informed him that his communications were now secure. Everyone thought the QEN was unbreachable but we thought a lot of things were impossible before. Humanity just received another education curtesy of the Poveen.

Nasir felt like he was going into a fight with a foot in a bucket, arm behind his back, and a blindfold on. They had every advantage and it seemed like they kept getting more and more of them. The past 24 hours have been extreme in so many ways. Death and destruction has consumed the system. A couple of days ago the planet was at peace. Nasir didn't know how but he would make sure to get his revenge on the Poveen for what they did, what they are doing, and what they plan on doing in the future.

He looked out over the horizon toward the location they would breach the atmosphere. They are going to face a lot of angry Nubians when they do. Nasir looked to his left at the sprawling Forward Station. The battle trains raced to the east full of Marines. Mechanized forces moved in columns over the horizon. Hovercopters full of soldiers and equipment transported them to the east. In the distance, you could see the massive combat aircraft getting ready for takeoff at the end of the runways.

Nasir thought the last time he went into combat would have been the last time. That battle cost him so much more than he ever could have imagined. His unit was a part of a regional taskforce sent to take back planet CA-112 overrun with an AI-terror attack. It is unknown whether the infestation was an alien or human engineered product but the effects were disturbing. What was known was the battle the ensued after they landed on the planet.

During the engagement, his co-pilot was killed when the orga puppet was hit while in a high gravity turn. The maneuver snapped her neck but only damaged his. The sudden removal of her mind from the Venus matrix did unrepairable damage to his mind. Since that day, he hasn't been able to love, show remorse, joke the way he wanted to, or use any other powerful emotion. He hasn't been able to keep a relationship since then or maintain that many friendships. It is like his emotion died that day. That battle took that from him and he couldn't help but to think about what would be taken from him this time. No soldier goes into war and comes out the same.

PLUS 112 HOURS
COMMAND CORPS LORD COMMANDER
MALCOM MASTERS
OGUN STATION, NUBIA
HOLD TOGETHER

"Ambassador, have your scientists reviewed the data yet?" asked Lord Commander Masters.

"Yes, the SciTech scientists have reviewed the new data. The destruction of the cruiser provided a lot of information. We have a hypothesis on the nature of the enemy interdictor field. The field is producing a time dilation effect. Our gates are not designed to calculate for time because it is assumed that time at all the locations is constant. For the lack of a better analogy, it seems that the Poveen are displacing time and then time is rushing back to normal.

This process is continuously repeating itself. We believe that if we can get a gate open we can match the disruption and keep the gate open. But, we would have to get a gate open first. We are working on a solution to detect the wave length they are using to push time out of balance but the math seems to be very advanced. We are doing our best. I haven't seen them this excited in a long time."

"Excited Ambassador? My people are dying."

"That statement was not meant to offend. It was meant to express the sentiment of my technical teams that were presented with a new challenge. A challenge that we have expected and that our people have worked tirelessly to solve once it was presented."

"We thank them for the service," said Lord Commander Masters as he held back a snarky response. He wanted to attack the man back but it was just his emotions getting out of control. The events of the day have forced him over an emotional edge. Masters has been trying to rein the emotions in for the last hour or so but it has been one of the more difficult things he has had to do. Unlike the battle of Butcher Bay when he was in the middle of the combat. In this engagement, he is a control room far from the conflict. He just wants to get out and do something, anything.

"Do you have a plan to get the gate open?"

"Finalizing it now. We have taken out a couple of the interdictor CIC cruisers already. They are the source of the disruption. Our chances of defeating all the CIC cruisers is better than defeating the entire Poveen force. Orunmila give us roughly a 37% change. Much better the current percentage against the entire Poveen force. Have you had contact with the Victory System?"

"Yes. We have offered the 1st and 2nd Battle Galaxies as support for this system. They can arrive through the gate as soon as you destroy the interdictors."

"Which gate?"

"Our gate. It seems that the Poveen know it is in the system."

"I don't know it is in the system. Did you construct it in secret?"

"No, the authority knows. They have been holding up our permit for two years now. We think they are playing politics with us. It is resting on the moon Camden Yards around the planet Baltimore. We can launch it and have it ready in less than hour. It is a Galaxy level ER gate and it will have enough energy to keep the gate open. Consider it your wild card.

"Thank you, Ambassador. I will be in contact as the time comes closer," said Masters as he closed out the channel. He couldn't believe it. They constructed a gate of that size and he didn't even know about it. Masters disconnected from the machine that he was connected to for the last fifteen hours. He needed a break from the interface.

The first engagement was over. Human and Poveen forces are keeping distance to repair the weapons of war before they relaunch attacks. He didn't know how long it would last but he knew that he had a couple of minutes before he needed to engage again. The man walked to his private quarters on the command floor. He removed the exosuit and placed it on the floor so it could self-clean. Masters moved into the shower and turned the shower on high heat.

The water was almost hot enough to scold. A dense steam filled the entire suite. Hot water rippled down his brown skin to the ground. The events since the invasion have troubled him. Master had to conduct a strike on his own people to save them. Ten thousand souls gone. He watches as the masterpiece of Nubian engineering was destroyed over Kush. Millions of people lost their lives. So many people. So many gone.

Oya War Station was gone. Masters questioned whether he should have held the Meteor Corps space force on Nubia. They could have defended the station after the enemy Poveen blinked. They could have helped in the defense. That force is now trapped in orbit around Kush and when the Poveen make another run on the planet they could all get wiped out. He ordered Quasar Tanaka and Might on suicide missions that they somehow lived through. The luck of Atlanta was at play for sure.

At the battle of Carthage, he had to withhold information from the officer closest to him. He had to lie to Kahn and he hated that. He needed to find a way for Rodriguez or Okafor to bring Kahn along. Normal tactics would not work on Kahn and he knew it. Masters struggled to formulate a plan so he moved on to the next item on his agenda. He couldn't bring himself to think about anything. His mind went blank until he was pinged by someone very familiar to him. It was his wife, Layla.

"Hello honey. How are you guys doing?" asked Master.

"Oh my universe Malcom what is going on? I just heard Oya War Station is gone. I heard Meroe was attacked. We heard Kush is destroyed. What can you tell us?" asked his wife. It took Masters a second to hear the word "us".

"Who are you with?"

"All of us. We are at the house in the mountains. I am here, my brothers, his children, your children, our parents, and some friends. We are all here. We are going to ride it out here instead of in the cities. We figured it would be safer," said Layla Light-Masters.

"Okay. I am glad all of you are together. Oya is gone. We lost Kevin Johnson. He was on the station. I just finished talking to his family. That one was tough," sad Masters. Masters' wife was a Light. One of the six founding families with the Johnsons. Layla spent her childhood with the Johnsons and Kevin. She went silent for a moment.

"Anyone else that I know? Anyone else in leadership?"

"No, no one you know. We lost a lot today though. It will get worse before it gets better. We will lose others. Prepare the people there love. A lot more people are going to die. A lot of people. Millions of people. This is going to get bad before it gets better. I will be sending all of them to die," said Masters as a tear ran down his face. He was happy that the discussion was in the virtual network. The tear wouldn't register.

"I am sorry Malcom. I am sorry you must carry this burden. But I don't think I would want anyone else to carry it. I have full faith in you. I have full faith in what you can do and so does everyone else here."

"I wish you were here with me. In this place, there isn't an escape. No way out. Just this war. I didn't ask for this war. We didn't ask for this war," said Masters.

"You don't need me there. You need me here. Remember when you told me during the battle of Butcher Bay you became something else. Something like a demon. Maybe you need to become that again. You can't do what you need to do if I am with you. I take that from you. You need to become that demon. Unleash that demon on those alien bastards. When it is over I will be here for you. I will heal you," said Layla. Masters thought about her words and she was right. So far in the conflict he was fighting his inner instincts. He would tap into that demon again and become the man Nubia needs to push the aliens out of the system.

He talked to her about the children and the grandchildren for a couple of minutes until he had to get back to his duties. For ten minutes, he could leave the building. To leave the war. His wife was right though. From this moment on he would become that hardnosed man that defeated the Poveen before. He stood from the bed and put the exosuit back on and walked back to the control room.

Thirty minutes later he received a ping from the Victory System. Masters joint the call and he was instantly taken to the virtual command room with the four other Lord Commanders that oversaw the systems. The commanders faced the purple skinned woman as she spoke.

"I am glad you are all here. You have survived the first wave of attacks. Some of you have performed better than the others. Some of you have a lot of work to do. It is time for everyone to share what they know," said Regional Commander Moon.

For 30 minutes the commanders traded ideas and solutions. Then the topic of the interdictor CIC cruisers arose. In the 5 systems, they destroyed 9 CIC cruisers and Masters had destroyed 6 of them. They asked him how he did it. He explained to them how he sacrificed ninety percent of his offensive Comet Corps force. Masters told the story about how he snuck a stealthstar into range only after an entire constellation sacrificed itself. He described the secret mission of the Dragon Corps heavy stealthstar and the Battle Nova Star Killer. Masters highlighted the deception he betrayed on one officer while the other maneuvered to destroy two more CIC cruisers.

The room was silent. It was apparent that the other officers were not ready to put forces in harm's way like he did. Because he didn't have that weakness, Masters, was much closer than any of them to reopening a gate or a bridge. The group dynamic changed after he spoke. The commanders reevaluated the force deployments. Masters showed them that they had to get more aggressive. They had to be willing to sacrifice. They must be willing to sacrifice themselves and others.

PLUS 135 HOURS
ASTRO CORPS QUASAR
NATASHA MIGHT
STEALTHSTAR, ATLANTA
YOU ONLY LIVE ONCE

"Lord Commander I can't give that order. I won't give that order. We are not going to sacrifice over forty million people around Atlanta. You need to provide a better plan than that," yelled Amir to his commander in virtual environment. Quasar Might stood to his left and Quasar Tanaka stood to his right. The three officers currently around Atlanta all faced Lord Commander Masters in the setting. Though the conversation was held via the QEN with computer generated avatars, the emotions of the event equaled an in-person event.

"By all means Sub Commander Amir provide me with a better solution. You know what the mission is. You know what the fucking target is. I am waiting Amir. Tell me how to defeat a force with three times our force ratio. Show me the low hanging fruit that I missed. Kush burns and Carthage flounders because of it. You are the only one that can turn the tide of this conflict and the enemy had realized this. They are moving back in to finish you off while the rest of their forces hold. Why is that Sub

Commander?

They know that your small but extremely fast force is trapped protecting Buckhead and Peachtree. The only hope for the billions of humans in this system is to open an ER gate. That is, it. No other path to victory. We open that gate or we all die. So please tell me another way to take out that asshole orbiting Atlanta and that little fucker that is 20 AU from you in the deep black. Please let me know," yelled Lord Commander Masters back.

Might was nervous. Masters didn't curse. Masters didn't lose his cool. He was exhausted. The man must have barely slept since the first round of attacks and the avatar presented his current condition. Were the orders he gave the right orders or were they the product of sleep deprivation. Might sent a message to the system AI Orunmila to get the answers. With brutal efficacy, the program responded to her request. Lord Commander Masters was right. There was no path to victory if the forces in orbit around Atlanta were destroyed.

"Do you believe me now," snarled Lord Commander Masters toward Quasar Might. Orunmila snitched on her. She was extremely embarrassed but she now knew the truth. That would be the last time she questioned her commanding officer. She was making a habit of it and it was not helping. Earlier she questioned Sub Commander Amir. She couldn't lose the trust of the officers that commanded her.

"Sir I apologize," said Might to soften the action. The fall of the Kush rings destroyed the entire plan and everyone knew it. The command staff all looked to him to correct the problem. Lord Commander Masters searched for path to victory but unfortunately those avenues left were horrendous. They needed to destroy those 14 CIC Interdictor Cruisers that entered the system one hundred and thirty-five hours ago.

"Yosef. You have been with me for years. I have never told you this. During the Battle of Butcher Bay I fully expected you to die. I expected you to die, I expected the meteor corps under my command to die, I expected to die. I also believed until the end that we would save the people of the system. We signed up for this. I know we didn't sign up to die. I know we didn't sign up to be fodder in a war machine. We didn't sign up to be pawns of glory of politicians.

We all signed up to become more. We received free augmentations that would allow us to live to be 300 years old. We received the best training and equipment. Ten percent of every tax credit goes to provide us with the best starships and weapons.

I am not asking you to abandon the people of around Atlanta. I am asking you to send your forces to destroy that asshole. Then I am asking your forces to solider up and bunker down to fight these bastards room to room and hallway to hallway until reinforcements arrive. They will arrive, I promise you that," said Masters.

"Okay. I understand. This is hard for me sir. I don't know how you do this sir. I really don't. Just thinking about giving this order makes me nervous. I thought I understood the burden of leadership but the last 100 hours have taught something different. I don't like this but I guess I am not supposed to. Can you provide us control of the local Sentry 7 systems?" said Amir.

"No I cannot. I am holding those in reserve. If this mission fails and we use our compliment of missiles we will have no other means of defending."

"Okay sir."

"I am going to tell you what a commanding officer once told me. Eat or be eaten. Hunt or starve. Kill or be killed. Welcome to the jungle. Welcome to the fucking universal jungle," said Masters as he left the channel. Sub Commander Amir took control of the channel with both Quasar Tanaka and Might to finalize the details of the mission.

"Quasars, we find ourselves having to make a bad choice between two bad options. We are losing this battle. Quasar Might I am going to ask that you take all the space assets on one wild ride. You must first destroy the Interdictor CIC Cruiser in orbit around Atlanta. Then we are going to need you to burn toward the other asshole in the deep black of the system and destroy that one as well. If you survive that I need you to burn to Carthage and place yourself under the command of Vice Commander Kahn.

Quasar Tanaka and I will be knee deep in Poveen by that time I don't expect we will be able to chat. Quasar Tanaka I need you to create a plan to defend these moons. We need to hold out as long as we can," said Amir. Tanaka and Might agreed that they would complete the missions and save the system after a moment of silence.

An hour later the human space force formed up in orbit above Buckhead. The bulk of the Poveen force burned toward Buckhead to meet the force that assembled. Quasar Might sat in her crash couch on the bridge of the stealthstar. She was unphased with the approach of the Poveen cruisers. Might barked orders and organized the constellations, battle clusters, and super clusters into a powerful fighting force. The big and heavy starships are all allocated into taskforce 1 and the smaller, faster, and more maneuverable starships are in the second in taskforce 2.

Might positioned the stealthstar at the rear of the taskforce 1. She would follow the heavy starships into combat and make the killing blow as they pass by the large Poveen formation. Taskforce 1 started to burn into combat. They were opposed by the 76 Poveen cruisers that remained in the system. They moved down the gravity well toward Buckhead in one large formation. The game was about to be played and both teams had taken the field.

The Poveen forces began to move. Unlike the first attack all the constellations are moving toward the moon Peachtree. 52 Poveen cruisers continued toward the moon on an intercept vector toward the human starships while 24 cruisers stopped their motion toward Buckhead. The interdictor CIC cruiser was among one of the 24 cruisers that remained behind. The humans burned into combat with 292 starfrigates, 30 warstars, 10 gunstars, and 1 steathstar. The warstars and frigates opened the massive missile bays and started to fire defensive weapon systems and offensive weapons at the enemy as they approached.

In thirty minutes the two forces will enter combat. The Human attackers launched missile after missile toward the Poveen hoard. The Poveen sent white arched energy at Taskforce 1. The Poveen weapon systems had a greater range than the human weapons but the human starships pushed forward as they were stuck countless times by the heavier weapon fire. Starships exploded until the massive cannons of the warstars and gunstars came into range. They fired the first salvo of weapons. The heavier missiles and railgun fire closed on the Poveen ready to return some of the damage that the human forces had endured but the enemy cruisers blinked away.

The Poveen starships reappeared in front of the 24 cruisers that had remained behind in the initial push forward. Taskforce 1 continued to push toward the Poveen on the original vector. Might had to decide. They fired missiles at the Poveen cruisers before they blinked. If Taskforce 1 accelerated those missiles could be a part of the next attack but the increased speed wouldn't allow Taskforce 1 the ability to turn around if the enemy blinked again. Taskforce 1's mission forced them to continue to burn into the deep black after the engagement without and having the chance to resupply. They couldn't waste missiles so the taskforce accelerated to catch the missiles.

Quasar Might punched her console so hard it cracked after she gave the order. They now had to accelerate at a rate that made the stealthstar detectable by the Poveen. It would only take five more minutes at the new acceleration profile to reach to Poveen. Missile bays and railguns were quickly topped off on the human starships only to be fired once more. More missiles were now in space heading toward the Poveen cruisers now in a formation of 76. Might ordered them to hold 25% of ordinance in reserve for the next mission but instructed 5 warstars and 2 gunstars to expend all ordinance.

Taskforce 1 engaged with the Poveen formation and thousands of missiles slammed into the hulls and shields of Poveen cruisers followed by rail gun projectiles. 24 Poveen cruisers blinked including the CIC cruiser. The 52 that remained could not blink again so soon. Those cruisers fanned out and waited for the human starships to pass by them at speed and they did. The two sides traded tremendous fire for about a minute and then the conflict was over. Taskforce 1 changed vector and headed out into the deep black of the system toward the CIC cruiser the farthest from the population centers of humanity.

Might ordered the stealthstar to flip around and fire the stealth missiles. After the first blink by the enemy she anticipated the maneuver. The missiles left the launchers until she was down to 25 percent of ordinance and then she stopped. The stealthstar reoriented to face the direction of the CIC in the deep black and Taskforce 1 was out of the fight for Atlanta. It was now up to Taskforce 2 and the guided stealth missiles from Might's starship.

She took command of the missiles at her console as the starships and the S7 system scanned for the 24 cruisers that blinked. The cruisers were located at the maximum distance jump from Atlanta. Might ordered Taskforce 2 to burn at high speed toward the location of the 24 blinked cruisers. The stealth missiles accelerated on a profile that would have them reach the Poveen cruiser in time to hit before it was capable of blinking again.

Taskforce 2 consisted of 16 dreadstars, 26 starcruisers, 100 speedstars, 900 starpuppters, and 4000 intercepstars. The starships accelerated at 30 gs toward the Poveen and would engage in 42 minutes. The missiles from the stealthstar burned adjusted the acceleration profile to match the impact time with that of Taskforce 2. Might opened a channel to Sub Commander Amir.

"We have to go loud. I must tell them all what is at stake. I am going to send everything that we have at that CIC cruiser. We only have 40 minutes until contact. They may only get one pass. If they fail than the entire mission is a failure and someone else will have to correct the problem we caused. Let me go loud, it is the only way sir," asked Quasar Might to Sub Commander Amir. He was silent for only 2 seconds but it felt like a lifetime to Might.

"Do it. Kill that interdictor," said Sub Commander Amir as he canceled the call. Over the next five minutes Quasar Might tight beamed information to the leaders and commanders of all the constellations that now moved into combat. At times, she communicated directly with induvial starship captains. They needed to understand the importance of destroying that star. Over the next ten minutes every Lion, Hyena Anteater, starbomber, speedster, and missile vectored toward the target vessel which had been renamed "Asshole" in honor of Lord Commander Masters' reference to the starship in the planning meeting. The rank and file pilots, captains, and officer enjoyed the moniker and quickly adapted it in the preparations.

That is when everything changed tactically. The Poveen cruisers that remained behind when the 24-cruiser blinked moved toward the CIC cruisers location at tremendous acceleration. The 44 cruisers that survived the melee with Taskforce 1 would reach the battle moments before Taskforce 2 engaged with the CIC cruisers formation. Once again, the human force would have to face the full force of the enemy. Unlike Taskforce 1, Taskforce 2, didn't have the massive shield complements and neutron armor. Taskforce 2 would take heavy casualties during the battle.

Thirty-eight minutes later the first human craft fired at Asshole. The battle had begun. The Poveen cruisers that traveled at high speed toward Taskforce 2 strafed it. Brilliant white arched energy ripped into Taskforce 2. In less than a second thousands of starships exploded. The Poveen cruisers were gone as fast as they came. Half the attacking force was gone but the missiles and ordinance they carried were gone too. Before destruction they hurled all they had at the Poveen formation that contained the CIC cruiser. Poveen cruisers moved in front of the CIC cruiser and took the full brunt of the onslaught.

The next wave consisted of the full complement of Hyena interceptors, Lion Star Puppets, ground based missiles, dreadstars, and starcruisers. They ripped into the damaged Poveen cruiser as hide behind the rest of the Poveen cruisers deep in the enemy formation. The picket line had tremendous overlapping fire and fired back when Taskforce 2 entered firing optimal firing range.

Losses on the Nubian side were staggering. Not one Star Puppet made it farther then the first line of Poveen defense. The entire force was destroyed. The same fate was met by the 4 thousand Hyena intercepstars. Unlike the puppets, they reached the target before they were destroyed. They took out a lot of the picket cruisers before they fell. That is when some pilots made the ultimate decisions. The Lion pilots started to yell over the coms statements like "No Lube" and "Fuck this asshole" before they plunged the starships they piloted at full speed into the hull of the enemy cruisers.

They pounded the picket cruisers and some of the pilots managed to hit Asshole too. The heavy cruisers were forced to stand off with the human dreadstars and starcruisers. The brave intercepstar pilots also set the new tone for the battle. Once out of ordinance the human starships plunged into the enemy. The Poveen cruisers were not accustomed to engaging with enemies with that level of determination but they would learn something about humans that day.

The missiles fired from the stealthstar slammed into Asshole. The picket crusiers faced Taskforce 2 but they exposed the CIC from attack from another vector. Might seized on that mistake and guided her missiles in. The CIC cruiser shock and rolled but it was still in the fight though critically damaged. The rest of Taskforce burned into combat.

It was the Dreadstar Epoch that fired the final blow to kill Asshole with its rail-canons. The Epoch punctured the sphere that dominated all Poveen starships. When it imploded from gravity of the singularity drive it went silent and the effects on the system were immediate. On Nubia Lord Commander Masters celebrated but around Atlanta Taskforce 2 tried to escape the battle once the objective was met. Two other dreadstars fired nuclear ordinance at the gravity crushed hulk to ensure the CIC cruiser would be out of the fight. It was dead.

All the starships from Taskforce 2 broke for the gas giant Atlanta. The plan was to burn toward the planet and receive a gravity assist to pick up speed and sling shot around the massive planet on a vector to join the force that burned toward the other asshole in the deep black. Not many of the starships made the trip around Atlanta into the deep black. The Poveen, now able to use the blink drive once again, blinked around the gas giant and fired upon the wounded and smaller starships as they passed by. The retaliation to the destruction of the CIC cruiser was clear but all three CIC cruisers that entered orbit around Atlanta were gone.

Quasar Might stood from the crash couch on the bridge. It had been over 30 hours since she rested and once the battle concluded she had nothing left. The officer walked down the hallway to her room barely able to process the trip due to exhaustion. When she reached the officer quarters she quickly entered and jumped into the crash bed for sleep and closed her eyes.

She could still hear the cries and yells of the men and women that gave their lives minutes and hours earlier. Her mind raced while at the same time it was shutting down all motor function to sleep. Every time she was close to sleep she remembered another horrible moment from the conflict. The seesaw of memory and sleep teetered for the better part of thirty minutes before sleep won. Quasar Might may have done the impossible but the people of Peachtree and Buckhead didn't have any space support. More people in the Atlanta system were going to die that day.

PLUS 139 HOURS
COMET CORPS QUASAR
RYU TANAKA
PEACHTREE STATION, PEACHTREE, ATLANTA
THE NAIL

Quasar Tanaka watched with the rest of the command staff as Asshole was destroyed. The command deck he stood in erupted in cheers and celebration. They completed the mission. This meant the Nubian System was one step closer to freedom. Tanaka looked at the casualty report to gauge the changes the taskforce would have against the Poveen in the deep black of the system. It didn't look good. They lost so many starships in the conflict.

Tanaka would never see the pilots he once commanded again. So many faces. So many soldiers he knew in passing and as people. All of them, gone. For what? What did the Poveen want? Did they really want this system that badly? Is this a part of something bigger? It didn't matter to him because the soldiers were gone either way.

He wanted to retreat to his quarters and meditate. He wanted to clear his mind of toxic thoughts and emotions but he couldn't. The Poveen cruisers continued to blink all over the planetary system. They chased down and destroyed the starships that had been damaged in the conflict. They blinked to destroy smaller installations around other moons in the system until every human installation was destroyed except for those on Peachtree and Buckhead.

Tanaka watched the enemy with a level of hate he didn't expect. He was truly angry at the Poveen's destruction of innocent people and equipment. Quasar Tanaka saw the pettiness in the Poveen that he thought was an exclusive human trait. Today he was proven to be wrong.

The Poveen formation moved toward Peachtree with 44 Poveen cruisers left from the 98 that initially travelled into Atlanta orbit. The fully armored Tanaka barked orders to the Comet commanders around the moon. Most of the fighting force was already in strategic locations around major population centers and vital equipment. The humans on the moon bunkered down and waited for the Poveen ground soldiers. Roughly 14 million people were protected by Comets, Policemen, and others who picked up weapons to fight the enemy that would soon be at the gates.

The Poveen cruisers entered orbit without much resistance and fired down with arched energy weapons. Planetary gun systems attempted to hold off the massive cruisers but couldn't. Tanaka watched the guns go silent one at a time. He looked around the command deck and he saw defeat in the eyes of the men and women. He felt it as well. The brutal helplessness of orbital bombardment. The command deck shimmied and shook from the shockwaves of secondary explosions and direct energy fire. Tanaka put on his helmet to avoid being knocked out by debris. Others on the command deck followed his lead.

All they could do was wait for the enemy to land. The Poveen reigned down fire upon the moon for two hours. High powered energy ripped through vacuum to hit buildings, mining facilities, smelters, construction equipment, and other machinery. In an act of spite the Poveen captured some of the building sized cubes that destroyed Poveen Cruisers. When Tanaka first noticed the building sized cubes he thought they captured the cubes to help in the repair of the cruisers but when he continued to watch the moments of the cubes and the cruisers he understood what they would be used for.

Tanaka would not get a chance to fight to the death against Poveen landing forces because it looked like he would be killed from orbit. The Comet Corps would not prove themselves to be the mighty guardians of Peachtree. The Poveen planned to destroy them from orbit with the same weapons they flung successfully into the Poveen cruisers. The alien invaders launched with a gravity accelerator down the gravity well toward the moon of Peachtree. The first cube slammed into the moon and released an untold amount of energy.

One after another the cubes impacted the surface of the moon. The Poveen launched reclaimed instruments of war and tossed them at the underground cities of Peachtree. The cubes were a brutally efficient method of destruction. One by one the massive underground shells that held up the rock from collapse buckled under the shockwaves. The Poveen method of underground city destruction worked on three of the five major underground cities. Ten million people were now dead or dying in the three cities. People either died from the explosion, shockwaves, vacuum, or fire that was produced by the massive objects.

Tanaka was disappointed that he failed his mission. The protection of Peachtree would not happen. No blaze of glory in a hopeless fight against the enemy in a hallway or on the surface of the planet. There would be no great honor in his death. He would get stoned to death by the very stones he sent toward the enemy. The mood on the command deck was somber. They did all they could do to protect Peachtree and now they all watched in horror as the 4th city fell to the bombardment of the cubes.

Then everything changed in the CIC. The officers in the room started to hug each other and shake each other's hands. They spoke kindly and told other people how much they meant to them. Officers traded quick stories of wonderful times that they spent together. The last goodbyes of fine officers. One after another the officers raised the right arm and placed it over the heart. The officers recorded goodbyes to loved ones and friend. Tanaka did the same.

He first sent a message to all his children. One by one he told them what they meant to him. A cold chill ran down his spine when he sent the message to the two children still in the Nubian system. Would they make it he thought? He wished that they all lived long and wonderful lives.

Once that was over he recorded a message for his wife. The message was long and heartfelt. Once it was completed his CU pinged. A link request from the QEN. He ended the message to his wife and joined the virtual environment. Lord Commander Masters, Planetary General Nasir, Orbital Guard General Johnson, Sub Commander Amir, and Astro Quasar Might faced him. Each one of them spoke for about 30 seconds giving him praise.

"Masters, Johnson, and Nasir I need you to promise that you will defend Nubia. I have two children and an amazing wife still on that planet and need you to give me your word that they will survive this," said Tanaka.

"They will survive. The Poveen will never take this planet," respond General Nasir. The response comforted him even though he understood they could not guarantee the safety of his family. For the first time in his life Tanaka felt helpless to change his situation. His unease was clear so Quasar Might's avatar walked over and hugged his avatar. The rest of the avatars walked over to the friend they had come to know and love over the years. Each one gave the man a massive hug. The warmth of the hug surprised them all. Even in this virtual environment the sincerity of the soldiers was transmitted. Then Tanaka's virtual avatar was gone in an instant.

Six cubes landed on Peachtree station. The station was destroyed. All 17 million plus people on the moon were now dead or dying. The Poveen continued to drop cubes on dead cities for another hour to ensure that they killed all the humans on the moon before they set off toward Buckhead. I guess they were making sure the attack worked or they are rubbing it in.

PLUS 140 HOURS
DRAGON CROPS GENERAL
DESIGNTION: A1D7 NAME: LAURA OBAN
OKO STATION, KUSH
CORRECTION

Outside of Oko City on Kush the fires raged in the distance. The horizon turned into a pale orange in every direction. Black and grey ash rained fell and coated the once green grass and will shortly cover the grass to the point in which you will not be able to see the green. The powerful Nubian sun struggled to break through the clouds. Streaks of lighting caused by the high level on ionization in the atmosphere sparked in the clouds and to the ground creating more fires. The response teams on the planet were stretched beyond the limits with the effects of nuclear winter unavoidable. The old terraforming equipment was close to reignition in hopes that it could stop the planet from descending backwards into a planet not habitable by humans.

Debris streaked through the dark black clouds as more pieces and sections from the rings, space stations, spacecraft, and Poveen cruisers alike hit the atmosphere and fell to the surface of the planet. Aircraft raced around the planet overhead to stop the invasion of Kush. Rescue craft also dominated the skies as they attempted to save people trapped by the fires and find survivors of damage spacecraft caught in the attack. 3-kilometer-long hover trains raced back and forth moving people and resources. The planet Kush was in chaos.

A1D7, given name Laura Oban, didn't have much knowledge of the spiritual elements of humanity. The government would never teach such things but she knew of the mythical place called hell. Kush now seemed to fit that description. She looked around and only saw death and destruction. Panic and anxiety swept through the people of the planet and the armed forces. A1D7 struggled to comprehend the reason for such panic but it escaped her.

35 percent of the ring system that was once the crown jewel of the planet remained undamaged. That section of the ring could shield itself and provide some planetary defense. Elsewhere repair teams tried to repair what they could or salvage parts for the intact sections of the ring system. Priority was given to shielding, communication, and weapon systems. The Poveen formation moved toward Kush after the destruction of the human forces on the moon Peachtree. A1D7 would miss Quasar Tanaka. She liked him. The man was polite and his sense of honor was extremely familiar to the one that she was trained under.

Many in the officer ranks believe that Peachtree was lost because Kush lost the rings. She followed the logic and it was sound. The planetary shielding system could not be repaired without a massive investment into the ring system. The damage inflicted during the first attack was too great. Without that shielding the cities would have to protect themselves with localized defense shields and systems. Over the past forty hours they rushed to move people and equipment into larger cities with larger shielding systems to protect them from Poveen attacks from space.

Kush was made up of small towns and suburbs. Only along the equator were there cities of any major size. Word was sent to all the people in regions to hunker down or move to one of the protect regions. They should also prepare to repel invaders. A1D7 and the officers knew that they would not stop the aliens from landing forces on the planet. The Poveen, on the other hand, must land ground forces if they wanted to take the planet.

A1D7 looked at Sub Commander Rodgers from the bleak horizon and smiled under her helmet. Rodgers survived the freefall from space during the start of the conflict. His armor had fresh pot marks from collision with debris and some temperature scarring from reentry but otherwise it was functional. It was now time to get to the mission at hand.

The president, congressional leadership, and military leadership all knelt in front of Sub-Commander Rodgers with the Dragon Corps soldiers behind him. Each of the Kushite leadership officers were bounded at the wrist and ankles as they knelt. Some of the men and women wept while others had the emotion of stone. A1D7's teams walked around the kneeling officers and stood behind them. One hand cannon pressed against one head.

Sub-Commanders Rodgers stood in front of the leadership cold. Over the last twenty hours A1D7's dragon corps rounded up the former leadership of the planet. Lord Commander Masters wanted all of them executed at one time while Rodgers struggled not to kill each one as they were caught. Masters' method proved to work better. Some members were captured and then told the Dragon Corps teams where the others were hiding. If they had been shot on sight A1D7 could still be in search of some of them.

"You have found you guilty of with treason during wartime. Your sentence is death. Do you have any last words for the record? History will not be kind to any of you. The best you can do explain your reason," said Rodgers.

"You have no right to do this to do this to us. You have no legal right. This military coup is treason. You have no right to treat me like this. You and Masters will burn for this," yelled the former President Lawrence.

"Your words are noted in the record. Make no mistake. This is all your fault. 23 million people were killed on Kush because of you. You decided that your political position was more important than the lives of the people of this planet. Your selfishness and insecurity did this and now they are dead. Dragon team aim…and fire," said Rodgers as the team readied the hand cannons.

One by one the heads of the former leadership exploded. The hand cannon projectiles were designed to penetrate armor and high energy shields. Bullets tore into the flesh and bone of the human heads. Violent decapitations occurred along the line of former military and political leaders of the planet. Limp bodies fell to the ash ridden field of grass one by one. The military officers turned from the treasonous Kushites and took to the sky with the use of the armor. It took five minutes to fly back to the military base. Rodgers sent a message to Lord Commander Masters and told him it was finished.

A1D7 was satisfied with the conclusion. She didn't truly understand the civilian criminal justice system. It took too much time to convict anyone of a crime and the death penalty was a relic of the past. The military justice system was quite different but she loved the efficacy of it especially during times of war. This justice was swift and meaningful. P5 humans weren't burdened by a life told not to kill, for them it was the opposite, they spent a life learning how to kill. They all pulled the trigger with emotional ease. Not one hesitated. Perfect soldiers she thought. The United Planets of Humanity Armed Forces should be proud.

Her cannon silenced the former president. Lawrence was the bane to the Nubian system before the conflict and could have set a chain of events to destroy it now. He gained power through division. It is a coward's method only used by politicians with low moral character. A1D7 hated killing humans in the past but this time felt completely different. It was justified.

A flash jumped on her HUD. One hour until contact with Poveen. The invasion force was inbound. Sixty minutes until Kush would fight for life or death. A1D7 sent a message to her forces to prepare to leave Oko Station. They are assigned to protect Napata City and the surrounding regions. The bulk of the Dragon Corps are already in the city supported by local troops from Kush. A1D7 and some members of the command staff were with her at Oko Station to oversee the execution of the Kushites. They needed to leave shortly to return to Napata City and ready the soldiers for ground combat.

The removal of the Kush planetary generals created a leadership vacuum that was filled by Sub Commander Rogers and his command staff. General Solis, A1D7, and Sub Commander Rodgers took on expanded roles in the defense of the planet. A1D7 liked the new role she played in the defense of the planet. Leadership on this level was never something she thought she would have a chance to engage in. Though she finished close to the top of her class she didn't finish in the top ten percent. Only those in the top ten percent were fit for command of this level but the battle field promotes who it pleased to. A1D7 had a chance to prove herself and prove those that doubted her ability to command and fight wrong.

A1D7 approached her commanding officer and spoke to Rodgers. "Sir, it is time for us move out to Napata City. Do you need anything from us? If not we will head out," said A1D7 in the robotic voice projected by the dragon armor.

"Yes, come to the ready room," said Rodgers as he turned to walk to the ready room next to main chamber. A1D7 walked to the door with two of her officers. Rodgers waved those soldiers off and A1D7 continued to walk into the room. Once they entered the room and the door closed Rodgers turned to her and she retracted her closed helmet to open. A1D7's helmet then slid back and she became the fiancée of Mike Rodgers again, Laura Oban. She walked over to him and stopped just short of contact. They both wore the fully kitted armor gear currently and they didn't have room for an embrace.

"Take care of yourself. If something goes wrong during the battle I will find you. Remember that. I will find you. Okay," promised Rodgers as he touched his forehead skin to her skin. She giggled slightly and nodded slowly.

"If anyone is going to need saving it is going to be you. We are Dragon Corps and you are old and slow. I don't know what caliber of solider you have around here," she said in a joking but serious manner. Rodgers smiled looking at Laura and chuckled. He wanted to savor the moment but he knew that she had to leave.

"About that. How are you soldiers holding up after what just happened. Are they okay?"

"They are fine. You must remember we grew up in the military. The military right or wrong is our code. The code that normal society has is jarring to us. Treason and munity are the enemy of every armed force. What they did was worse than those who pedal sex slaves to the P5 humans. Though that is disgusting as well. My soldiers are fine. They feel better knowing the cancer is gone and in the coming battles our forces won't have that kind of interference. They will be fine, anything else?" she asked.

Rodgers shook his head. The gesture ended the conversation. Laura Oban stood and waited for something from him. A departure gift of some sort. Rodgers leaned in and kissed his fiancé passionately for what seemed like hours but it only lasted ten seconds. They both fought tears when it ended. Laura took a step back and activated her helmet to close to cry without Rodgers seeing it. A1D7 was back and she would remain so until the conflict was over. She saluted Rodgers and he dismissed the soldier. Both hoped quietly that they would see each other. Rodgers stayed in the room for another minute or so until his eyes fully dried.

A1D7 moved to the roof of the installation. The stealthstar that transported her from Nubia to Kush hovered over the installation. The massive starship startled the commander at first because the sight of it was so unexpected. Why would the large starship be this close to the installation? Standard protocol recommended that a transport land on the roof. The docking bay door opened. A1D7 pinged the captain of the stealthstar and asked why her ship hovered over the installation. The pilot was under direct orders from Lord Commander Masters.

A1D7 used the dragon armor's propulsion kit and took to the sky toward the docking bay door. The ascension only took thirty seconds. A1D7 moved with urgency toward the bridge of the stealthstar but she was greeted half way to the bridge by the captain. The two moved into a small officer's room before the captain spoke.

"A1D7 I have an urgent message for Sub Commander Rodgers from Lord Commander Masters. He told me that you would be able to convince him," said the captain. A1D7 took a slight step back and reached for her fire arm. After the events that occurred on the planet over the past couple of days it was extremely difficult to trust anyone. The Captain raised her hands in air when she saw the movement and clicked on a button on the table.

A 3-dimension representation of the Captain of the Battlenova Star Killer in orbit and Lord Commander Masters appeared. A1D7 looked at the avatars and froze. Why would Lord Commander Master not just contact her through the QEN? She drew the weapon and pointed it at the captain of the stealthstar.

"A1D7 put that gun down," yelled the Lord Commander Masters' avatar.

"This is bullshit. You are not Masters. This is another attempt to infiltrate the command structure. Captain I need to get on the ground or I am going to fire this weapon," said A1D7.

"Laura put that gun down. Your name is Laura Oban. You are engaged to Sub Commander Mike Rodgers. You once ate the spiciest pepper on Nubia because you didn't know what it was and spent the next hour crying in pain. My wife helped you pick out your wedding dress," said Masters as A1D7 moved back slightly from table.

"Okay, let's play the game. Why are you communicating with me through tight beam instead of private communications threw the QEN?"

"I am using the Command Corps QEN to communicate with the Victory System. They are transmitting that message through Space Command QEN to the bridge of the Star Killer. The Star Killer is tight beaming the message to the stealthstar because the Nubian QEN has been compromised. If I contacted you threw that network we would have Poveen minders," said Lord Commander Masters. A1D7 lowered her gun and put it back into the holder on her right hip.

"Okay. Let's say I believe you. What do you need me to do?"

"I need you to have this very same conversation with Sub Commander Rodgers. I need you to install an encryption program to protect the Nubian QEN so we can directly communicate. I also need you to do this now. You have 50 minutes before the enemy arrives," said Masters.

"What did you say to me the first time we met?"

"I believe I told you I would toss you off my balcony if you hurt Sub Commander Rodgers. He was not a play toy to be chewed up and spit out. The man has been through too much," said Masters. A1D7 turned to the Captain and told her to leave behind a smaller transport for her and leave with the regimental commanders for Napata City. A1D7 received the code for the tight beam and told the captain of the battlenova and Lord Commander Masters that she would call them when she reached the ready room of Rodgers. A1D7 left the stealthstar and reentered the command deck of Oko Station to brief Sub Commander Rodgers.

PLUS 142 HOURS AND 30 MINUTES
COMMAND CORPS SUB COMMANDER
MIKE RODGERS
OKO STATION, KUSH
BREAK OUT

The mood in Oko Station was somber. Word of the destruction of Peachtree reached the rank and file of the military. Sub Commander Mike Rodgers paced the deck as the Poveen formation closed in on the planet Kush. The battle for the orbit above Kush would be decided shortly and the betrayal of earlier and loss of Peachtree were in the minds of the officers. Rodgers finished a riveting speech about honor and duty that fired up the officers on the command deck. The Sub Commander tried to will the men and women of the command deck into a better mind state. Morale was low. The humans in the system needed a victory. He wanted to give them that victory.

The front of the command deck projected two maps on the massive wall. The map on the left detailed the planet and the positions of all the military assets. On the right was a diagram of the planet Kush and the military units in orbit around the planet. The Battlenova Star Killer was the focal point of the space force and Oko Station was the focal point of the planetary forces. Hundreds of red triangles depicted the Poveen cruisers that moved toward the planet Kush on the right side of the map.

In total 180 Poveen cruisers approached in one massive formation. If you take out the 30 troop carriers, they still had 49 heavy cruisers and 101 standard cruisers left. The allied forces only had 36 heavies, 60 small capital starships, and a lot of smaller craft. This battle will be won by the cunning of the captains and local forces. Thoth, the planet AI, gave them a thirty-one percent chance of victory with optimal conditions. The Poveen commander would have to make mistakes for this to happen and the human forces would need to be ready to exploit those mistakes when they took place.

They would follow the standard plan of firing missiles, followed by smaller craft, and then splitting Poveen formations with the heavier spacecraft. Once split they would try to isolate and destroy the small formations until the overall combat of strength of Poveen prevented a threat to the planet. Splitting a Poveen force that size was the problem.

The plan was to bloody the nose of the fleet as they approached and delay the operation long enough that the scientists and experts on Nubia could crack the code of the interdictor technology. If they couldn't hold the force was directed to take out the last CIC interdictor cruiser and burn for Nubia. The scientist on Nubia learned a tremendous amount from the destruction of the other CIC cruiser. Sub Commander Rodgers understood that Lord Commander Masters didn't want to leave another population center unguarded after the events on Peachtree. The discussion with Masters that Rodgers had with him showed a man at the end of hope.

He ordered the Super Cluster around the gas giant Atlanta to destroy the CIC cruiser and because of that command over thirty million died. The calculus has changed. Lord Commander Masters and Sub Commander Rodgers both believed that the Poveen wanted to invade and take the land. They did not think they just wanted to destroy the human colonies. They proved this assumption wrong on Peachtree. Rodgers wanted, no Rodgers needed to give the military forces on the planet and in the system a win. They needed a win.

The command deck bustled with activity. Readiness of even the smallest six-man squad was checked and double checked. Officers tightened when the first visual evidence of the oncoming alien invaders was visible. The enemy was close enough to rely on the sensors from the planet and not a Sentry 7 system. Rodgers gave the orders for all units to engage.

The planetary guns located near major cities and strategic installations around the planet that had a fire solution discharged. They were at maximum effective distance but the enemy would learn that Kush would not give an inch to the enemy. Each gun unleashed ungodly amounts of energy into deep space at the formation of 180 Poveen spacecraft. The energy clipped the overlapping shielded formations of the Poveen. The alien spacecraft didn't slow down and kept the movement toward the planet.

When the Poveen reached 350,000 km from Kush the attack force split into four formations. The Poveen Cruisers kept charging to the planet until 35 of Heavy Cruisers and 60 of regular sized cruisers broke for the human Super Cluster above the north pole of Kush. The remaining 35 cruisers that remained moved for the undamaged section of the ring system. The third group consisting of 30 troop carrying cruisers broke for high orbit above what remained of the most damaged section of the ring system. The 20 cruisers that remained were mostly the damaged cruisers from the first battle and they took positions behind the first formation that moved toward the north pole of the planet. Rodgers audibly cursed. The commander of the Poveen taskforce was the most aggressive Poveen on record. Wargames predicted this kind of outlier but this was the first time humans engaged a commander that acted this aggressive.

The movements would allow for the rapid deployment of the Poveen. The only good outcome of the deployment, if an alien race landing a hostile force on your planet could be considered good, was that the Poveen weren't going to destroy the life on the planet from space. The troop variant cruisers of the Poveen force raced for an unopposed landing while the human space force was engaged over the north pole. The move also stressed his planetary gun defense system. The ability to focus fire was lost with the separation of the fire control system.

In orbit above the north pole of the planet the Poveen forces engaged the human super cluster. The human spacecraft huddled into a tight formation with the engines toward the planet. Shields overlapped with the most might starship, the battlenova Star Killer fired the first shot at the Poveen. The enemy approached from above the Human forces to pin it against the planet. Heavy cruisers led the assault and didn't fear the chaos cannon of the Star Killer as they should. The spread of the enemy forces indicated that they expected to trap the human forces and not allow them to escape the battle even if that meant they would lose a couple more cruisers.

Spacecraft that once tried to escape during the coup attempt were fitted with slave drives and controlled by the Star Killer. 1621 spacecraft loaded with fertilizer and other explosives burned toward the enemy force from the planet. They gained speed quickly when they reached space and vectored toward the heart of the enemy formation. Chaff and other defenses flew from the spacecraft to increase the survivability of the craft. The spacecraft belched extensive amounts of spare metal parts and chaff. The goal was the put so much junk in space the enemy would have a hard time sorting the starcraft out at distance.

As expected the Poveen fired on the civilian space craft as they approached. The thin hulled craft didn't stand a chance against that caliber of weapon. The chaff and debris began to clog the space in front of the human forces. The Poveen stopped unleashing the fire on the converted spacecraft and reacquired the human military starships that closed the distance on the Poveen as they fired on the converted craft. The Star Killer's chaos cannon caused more damage as it approached the enemy formation. Rodgers watched the screen and smiled. That would be the first break that his forces received that day.

Commandeered starships exploded at ten thousand meters from the Poveen formation. The explosion was the largest claymore mine ever constructed in human history. Debris designed to damage and maim the Poveen cruisers accelerated into the mass of Poveen cruisers. Millions of projectiles struck shields and hulls alike. Though the explosion didn't destroy any of the Poveen cruisers, sixty percent of the attacking force took damage in one way or another.

Through the debris, the starfighters, intercepstars, starbombers, and starpuppets rushed into combat. They needed to break the enemy formation but what they faced was a fully augmented Poveen Force geared to destroy the smaller craft. The incoming forces were decimated by the overlapping fire of the Poveen. The Poveen commander was different than the others. He adapted quickly and continued to anticipate the coming maneuvers. The reason why the Poveen stopped firing on the augment spacecraft was to change the variant of the cruisers. When the assault craft engaged the Poveen cruisers they faced and entire fleet that was equipped to defend against small craft. The guns of the Poveen once again went silent. The next time Rodgers expected the assault configuration of the Poveen cruisers.

Rodgers watched from the commander center as the UPHAF assault craft were obliterated by the unexpected change of cruiser variant. Rodgers and other commanders gave the order to retreat but most of the force was unable to retreat before they were destroyed. The plan was not working. Thoth, the Kush planetary AI, updated Rodgers with new predictions of victory in space and they were not optimal to say the least. Rodgers knew a terrible truth. The space battle in orbit was over. Without the planetary shield system Kush could not be defended.

Sub Commander Rodgers made the call to the commander of the force.

"Captain. This battle is over. You need to get your forces out of here with the minimal amount of damage. Burn to Nubia and help defend the homeworld," said Rodgers. The purple skinned woman didn't seem phased by his comments. She was expecting his communication and quickly answered with her solution.

"Sir, we have identified the CIC interdictor cruiser. It is at the rear of the formation. We need to destroy that cruiser on our way out. I will need your help to do that. We have run projections. If the ring system fired fifty percent of the missile complement at the Poveen formation as the super cluster burned out of orbit we would have the ability to make a surgical strike on the CIC cruiser on the way out. That would limit the ability of the remaining ring system to stand off against the Poveen cruisers that moved to take it out.

"Okay, I will make the call and slave those missiles to your system. Good luck Captain," said Rodgers as he closed the communication. Rodgers turned to the highest ranking Orbital Guard and told him to give the order to his officers on the ring system. Five minutes later tens of thousands of missiles launched from the operational ring system. They burned at high g toward the Poveen force that attempted to trap the human space force above the north pole of Kush.

The super cluster burned out of orbit and timed the interaction with the Poveen formation with that of the arrival of the missiles. The captain and Rodgers both hoped the Poveen would not use the blink drive to escape the attack before they could strike the CIC cruiser. In a stroke of luck the aggressive Poveen commander spread his forces out to ensure maximum damage to the retreating human forces.

Five minutes later half the Poveen formation was engaged with the tens of thousands of missiles that slammed into the flank that bordered the equator. The supercluster lead by the Battlenova Star Killer then moved into the second part of the engagement. The capital starships of the humans walked into a fire storm. The Poveen cruisers pounded the Star Killer and the other large starships of the human force.

The conflict lasted about two minutes before the distance between the retreating human force and the Poveen grew too large to engage but the battle for the orbit of Kush had been decided. The Poveen lost roughly 25 percent of the force and the CIC cruiser. On the other hand, the human force lost 75 percent of the force retreating. All the starships under the command of the Star Killer were damaged heavily. Some would struggle to make it Nubia without shutting completely down for repairs once they reached top speed.

Rodgers watched the screens as the enemy space force panned out across the planet to cement orbital dominance. The next phase of the battle was about to begin but Rodgers was still confused to why the enemy did not blink out of orbit. Thoth, the Kush planetary AI, informed him of the truth. The Poveen had also shifted priority. With the destruction of Peachtree and that force moving toward the deep black the humans would not be able to engage Poveen attack groups. Their plan was to destroy as many human starships as possible. Eventually the humans wouldn't have enough starships to fight back and they would not be able destroy the 4 CIC cruisers around Nubia.

The battle of Carthage just became more important than ever. The space force around Carthage needed to break out to help one of the other taskforces. If not, this entire conflict would end shortly. Lord Commander Masters also held the wild card of the Sentry 7 system. The ten thousand satellites each held at least ten powerful missiles almost ten times the size of the missiles that were launched from the ring system. Rodgers knew they would play a critical role in the conflict. Masters displayed great patience in the withholding of the vital weapons platforms but he would have to use them soon if they were going to turn the tide of the conflict. For now, the soldiers on Kush needed to prepare for combat because the Poveen troop cruisers entered the atmosphere.

PLUS 143 HOURS AND 30 MINUTES
METEOR CORPS GENERAL
MORRIS SOLIS
PIYE STATION, KUSH
HOLD THE LINE

General Solis and his team watched the display track four large Poveen troop cruisers breach the upper atmosphere 500 kilometers from the Piye Military station. Planetary gun systems fired on the large craft hitting the powerful shields of the craft. The craft kept coming unphased by the ground fire. The battle for the planet of Kush was about to begin and he would lead the resistance on this side of the planet. The Meteor force that he commanded and the Kush regular army were under his control.

The first order of business was to launch the mighty Airforce. Ten bases in the region exploded with action. Mighty AC-2D and AC-2M Condor air carriers raced down runways and took to the sky. The Condors were massive wedge-shaped black aircraft. The AC-2D variant held two thousand smaller diamond shaped Locust 2 fighter drones. The AC-2M condor was packed with missiles and standoff air to air and air to ground rail weaponry. 500 of each craft took off from multiple bases and vectored toward the Poveen landing craft.

The second wave of aircraft consisted of five thousand KF-3 Strike

Falcon Atmospheric Strike fighters. The versatile fighter was kitted for air to air combat missions though it could be fitted for bombing missions too. Five thousand Avian Skypuppets would also engage enemy aircraft. Like the space variant it had the appearance of human covered in armor with a large rocket pack strapped to its back. The Avian Sky Puppet went into combat with the long-range energy cannon especially suited to destroying incoming aircraft.

The human planetary forces needed to gain air superiority in this battle or this battle would not last long. The largest remaining piece of the ring system was holding its ground in space against the Poveen attackers which provided cover from space. If they could hold the ground, they might be able to hold out long enough for Nubia to find out how to open the gates again. General Solis finished the battle plan with Sub Commander Rodgers minutes prior and the two men were confident in the battle plan. They also discussed contingency plans for the loss of communication.

Solis watched for thirty minutes as the Airforce gathered for the attack. The Poveen did not waste any time. They created a planethead quickly with the troop-carrying cruiser. They launched a counter to the air attack. The aliens launched one hundred thousand aircraft. The craft were spherical in shape and didn't try to use any sense of aerodynamics. The craft ran off the same singularity drive that the spacecraft ran off. The rear of the aircraft had a cone that stabilized the craft and it was the only identifiable protrusion from the sphere. It measured 12 meters from the front of the craft to the rear making it much smaller than the human fighters but each of the craft were extremely formidable.

General Solis watched nervously as the two forces closed on each other. AC-2D Condors released the Locust 2 fighter drones from the massive holds of the ship. They darted and weaved as they reached the Poveen craft. Missiles, bullets, and energy weapons tore into the sky. Pops and booms rattled the ground below as the first casualties of the Battle of Piye began. AC-2M Condors opened doors along its massive wing shape to release a maelstrom of missiles. They ripped through the sky accelerating to extreme speed rippling the countryside with a cacophony of sonic booms.

Underneath the battle the ground shook violently from the falling destroyed craft, errant missiles, energy fire, and sonic booms. The soup of grinding metal was stirred finally when the KF-3 Strike Falcons and Avian Skypuppets entered combat. The high g-force units bolted and darted into the enemy formations as the slower Poveen craft tried to keep up. The Poveen continued to fight in large groups and the electric like energy bolts flung and flipped off the shiny circular hulls like lighting in all directions.

On the ground 2000 of the 200-ton Rhino tanks, 500 of the 500-ton Hippo tanks, and 20 of the 1-kiloton Elephant tanks raced to the front lines. Behind the tanks rumbled 25,000 Kangroo armored personnel carriers holding twelve soldiers a piece for a combined armored force of 3 hundred thousand angry soldiers. Above the armored carriers flew twenty-five thousand AG-3 Hornet Hover Copter. Another 20 kilometers behind the armored force approached 6 million Meteor soldiers and five hundred thousand Kush regular infantry. Reinforcing the line of infantry twenty thousand Meteor Land puppets and four thousand Heavy Mecha Puppets of the Kush forces bounded toward the enemy formations.

In all the battle front was about 110 kilometers long and reached 25 thousand meters high. Death and destruction was now upon Kush at the battle of Piye. The lethality of the modern battle field artfully etched itself on the world of the Kush canvas. Energy weapons scorched the ground and killed massive amounts of units with one broad stroke. With the beauty of scattered paint infantry soldiers lay on the ground dead and dying from injuries.

The battle in the sky turned when the KF-3 Strike Falcons had to rearm. Human projectile and missile weapon systems were the only system of combat that rivaled the energy weapons of the Poveen but they also became a major liability when the fighters and bombers had to retool. They were only out of the fight for 45 minutes but in that 45 minutes the Condors were ravaged by the Poveen craft. They darted and killed bombers en masse as the large lumbering craft could not repel the mass of enemy aircraft.

General Solis tried to command the units to victory but once the air battle turned it didn't seem likely that this battle would end in victory. He hoped that when the Strike Falcons returned the battle would turn back to a stalemate. Solis could take a stalemate but he couldn't take defeat. Not now. Not after the carnage that raged in space. Not after his friend, Quasar Ryu Tanaka, was killed by these squids. How could they let this happen? How could he let the aliens take the planet? He would not let them. He would channel the power to defeat them. He would because he was Morris Solis.

The Strike Falcons swooped back into combat but without the condors drawing most fire they had no way to defend themselves against the more powerful weapon systems of the Poveen interceptors. In the command station Solis ordered the base to begin preparations for combat. The battle wasn't close to over but Solis knew that the force could not hold it for much longer. Solis prepared to make a call for all forces to retreat to the base of origin.

The effects of the turned air battle started to manifest. With less human aircraft the Poveen air force strafed human infantry and armor. The lines broke and folded like paper. Solis ordered an orderly withdrawal but the human forces were folding and the enemy breached the lines and attacked the forces from the rear and the front. An hour later the lines crumbled and collapsed completely. Human forces retreated in all directions as they tried to flee the carnage that was now becoming the battle of Piye.

Piye base shook from the enemy air attacks. The personal guard of General Solis entered the command deck. Officers on the deck readied personal weapons and armor as the vid screen showed a relentlessly advancing army. Anti-aircraft energy and projectiles spit out of human weapons in defiance into the sky. Poveen craft strafed the base to probe the location of anti-aircraft weapon systems. Buildings continued to shake and rattle from secondary explosions and direct energy fire. Officers darted back and forth on the base to dodge the fire. General Solis gave the general retreat to all forces.

General Solis and the security forces ran to the roof of the command building. When they reached the roof his saw the true battle for the first time. The haze from the fires that burned on the horizon and now on the base hurt visibility. The temperature of the planet had also dropped by 2 degrees globally from the blockage of sunlight since the beginning of the conflict. Energy lighting rippled along the base from the swooping and dodging craft. The remnants of the human aircraft did the best they could to defend the Piye military base but they were systematically destroyed.

General Solis' top lieutenant told him that the hovercopter was on the way to pick him up and get him out of the base. Solis panned to the left and the right of the building and thought to himself that no one was getting out of this battle. Nightmares looked better than what he saw from the roof of that building. The blow to his ribs came unexpectant but it saved his life. The second in command tackled him as an energy arc hit the roof of the building. Three of the six security force members were instantly killed with another being thrown off the side of the building.

General Solis got to his feet. He turned to his second in command and told him they needed to get off the roof. The men ran and jumped from the building into a free fall. Anti-gravity repulsers broke the fall when they reached the ground. At times like this it paid off to have the top of the line Meteor kits. When your branch of the military expected you to jump from space, a jump from a building was easy.

They moved with a crowd of soldiers to another evacuation zone. Solis' fate would be the same as his soldiers and he was comfortable with that. Once again enemy forces swooped down the roadway killing hundreds of soldiers and officers. Solis stood from the attack and quickly recovered from the blast. When he stood, he realized he only held the leg of the security solider. He dropped it to the ground and looked for the rest of the body but it was nowhere to found. The leader of the security team was also missing.

At first, he didn't hear the humming sound but as more and more of the ground based spherical boxes entered the base it became deafening. The outer defenses had been breached. Damnit, the speed of the Poveen advance was unexpected. He reached to unsheathe the massive gun that rested on his back. It was time to awaken the Dragon Fire assault rifle. The intoxicating power of the rifle satisfied Solis's blood lust as soon as he pulled the trigger. Unlike the weapons deployed by the regular soldiers his railgun was loaded with rounds tipped with dense neutrons, tungsten shells, and depleted uranium cores. The drawback of this ammo was that it didn't have the range needed for front line soldiers but for commanders it was perfect. If a commander needed to use a weapon than more than likely the enemy was close.

The General fired round after round at the ball that hovered overhead. Slugs ripped through the alien armor plates. Secondary explosions rocked the craft as smoke and fire raged from its wounds. Smoke and debris lifted two blocks away as the craft struck the ground. Solis smiled in anger under his helmet. Escape now depended on getting to the underground rail system. The General rallied all the men and women around him to follow him to the entrance of the underground tunnel system. Bodies and debris lay along the ground but the soldiers bounded above the debris with determination.

On the way to the entrance he shot and destroyed two more of the armored ground units. Solis took up position against the wall at the entrance. The General would stay at the entrance and get out as many of his soldiers as possible. His Mantis Armor and advantage projectiles made him more survivable than the average soldier and he was going to get as many soldiers out as he could.

Tracer rounds filled the sky and the streets as the human counterattack raged. Mechs and drones fought relentlessly as the human soldiers geared up to fight. Poveen spheres darted and raced but were struck by small arms fire and shoulder mounted systems. The close quarters fighting turned to favor the humans. The base held. Street to street and block by block Meteor soldier fought to the death and didn't give an inch. Solis personally torched ten of the armored units and gleefully took pleasure in the combat. General Solis saved almost two hundred soldiers in the last ten minutes with many more soldiers on the way.

Those soldiers formed up and formed fighting groups that then retook a section of the city. Solis tried to listen to the reports from the field but it seemed that some of the armored columns mounted a successful counter attack with the remnants of the air force and some of the space forces that reentered the atmosphere after the capital starships left. Humanity was fighting back and they were fighting back hard. It has been said that one man defending his home is worth ten hired soldiers. Today Solis witnessed this in action.

Solis stood in the doorway of the tunnel complex. Most of the techs, non-combat officers, and civilians entered the tunnel system and were on the way out of Piye Military Base to rally points outside. The military units in the military complex formed new units and moved out of the base or continued to provide support until vital equipment was removed. The automated system fought bravely. The battle would continue out of the base.

The base had taken too much damage to be salvaged but the damage it inflicted on the force that attacked it was substantial. Solis believed that 40 percent of the of the first wave of Poveen ground and air units had been destroyed. It wouldn't be the overwhelming victory that he wanted but it was a stalemate at best and he would take that. The Meteor Corps fought well. A ping over his CU from Sub Commander Rodgers jolted him. Solis answered the request.

"Sir."

"General Solis, I will make this quick. The Poveen are targeting our satellites and I don't know how long we will have communications. Keep up the fight. We will not let them take this planet. Kush fights. Do you hear me? Kush Fights. Meteor Go," yelled Rodgers. Solis smiled. Rodgers was a Meteor before he accepted the command corps commission. He understood.

"Sir we will give them hell over here," responded Solis.

"Okay, you now have command of the Eastern Forces. Transfer all communications through the ring if you can. Orbital Guard is fighting its ass off in orbit and they are holding firm," said Rodgers.

"Yes sir. Is that all, I have to get back to work?" asked Solis. Rodgers chuckled and agreed the conversation was over and ended the communication. He quickly ordered his communications grid to the planetary ring system. Three minutes after the transfer the last satellite was destroyed. He lost all communication with Rodgers and he was alone.

The base was almost completely devoid of living soldiers. On General Solis' HUD he witnessed a group of seven soldiers moving toward him. Two of the soldiers were high ranking officers in the service. Solis checked his ammo on the HUD. He ran low on the powerful ammo and once he replaced it with the standard ammo his effectiveness would drop considerably. One of the officers carried the codes to various systems that would be needed in the defense of the region. Solis cursed to himself. Earlier he placed those officers in a safe location. When the Poveen attacked that location was the first to become overrun. Next time he wouldn't let those codes out of his sight.

Solis turned to the soldiers that guarded the tunnel. Most were junior soldiers without the heavier armor configuration. This mission would be suicide for them. One more time Solis would enter the soup of war. After a subtle curse under his breath the man raced from the concealed location. The armor worked brilliantly as the soldier ran, darted, jumped, and bounded down the street at considerable speed.

Poveen armored units moved in on his position. Four aircraft swooped and fired the rippled energy weapons as they passed. Solis took a knee and activated his hard shield to better survive the strafe attack. The Poveen struggled with accuracy as they darted in and out of the streets due to the reemergence of human fighters and anti-aircraft guns. The activation drained his energy reserves to 10 percent but it allowed him to survive that attack. Another perk of the mantis armor.

Solis moved to place he back on the wall on a corner. Down all three approaches Poveen armored units hovered down street. Solis jumped forward and fired the engines of the mantis armor. He accelerated at tremendous speed across the street while he fired at the armor units. The matte black armor looked like a black streak as he moved with tremendous speed away from the enemy. Advanced targeting system allowed the General to hit the targets. The explosion of one armored unit indicated the precision of the shots. Quickly he reloaded the clip. It was the last one. Eighteen rounds left. He turned to face the street once again and destroyed the second unit on the street.

Heat rushed through his armor and the man fell to the ground. Hisses and pops indicated the suit lost functionality as his hub flashed red. He was hit and it was bad. He laid on his back trying to get his suit to respond but it wouldn't. He yelled with fury and then opened the suit. He left the safety of the armor and tried to move across the street to the entrance of the underground station but the enemy forces laid down a constant fire along the road.

He needed to wait for them to stop firing before he could try. Sweat ran down his blue skin as his eyes darted back and forth. The soldiers that he came to save arrived at the corner but were pinned down by the last armored unit. The unit fired one arched energy barrage at them. The soldiers escaped the fire but they wouldn't for long. Solis jumped from his concealed location onto the street and fired on the armored unit from a prone firing position. Rounds from his gun punched holes in the armored unit. It shifted targets and focused on Solis. The soldiers sprinted down the street as the Poveen armor was distracted.

Once they reached safety Solis stood and left the rifle. He was lifted from his feet and tossed into the building by the shockwave of the energy blast. Solis found himself on his back once again. Rubble fell at the entrance of the building.

The barrel of the hand cannon pointed at the entrance. He told himself that he could still make it out. In his amazement, the energy moved like a hand across the floor. It arched under the debris and fallen supports to hit him. His death was instant as his body was suddenly cooked and burned into ash in less than a second. The General of the Meteor force was dead.

Elsewhere on the planet Sub-Commander Rodgers continued to try to reach his commander without response when his transponder went dark.

Rodgers tried and failed for a half an hour. They just lost twenty percent of the ground force in the first 4 hours of the assault but the enemy suffered tremendous losses as well. Solis provided the forces of the planet with hope. Rodgers sent a quick message to Lord Commander Masters that read, "We lost General Solis".

PLUS 148 HOURS
LOGISTICS CORPS GENERAL
NAKIA OKAFOR
BARCA STARYARDS, CARTHAGE
THE SACRIFICE

Fifteen hours passed since Okafor ate. The white beans and lamb smelled of heaven. The officer's mess was quiet. The slow burning high protein diet would keep her powered during the coming battle. Her chocolate skin hid the appearance of bags under her eyes but the woman was exhausted. The last couple days of combat and around the clock repairs was taking its toll on her and her teams. Updates from Kush, Nubia, and Atlanta were shared as rumors spread like wildfire around the room. She knew the truth and it was bleaker than the rumors.

Okafor ate and studied updates from the fleet. Over the past five hours her teams left the carriers to help repair the starships faster. Starships were damaged in the first conflict and her forces helped to repair at record speeds. Okafor just spent 10 hours with one of the high-level teams installing salvaged weapon systems from two dreadstars and attaching them to the Barca staryards station.

She almost went straight to sleep once she was off duty but she knew that if something happened while she was asleep it might be another 20 hours before she could eat again. Nanites would keep her powered with sugars, fats, and proteins but the human body had limits. Large brown eyes scanned around the room. Officers with folded arm pillows slept on the metal tables. In normal times, they would be disciplined but today no on woke them up.

Okafor switched to her personal device. She looked at the pictures of her friends that she lost during the conflict. She smiled at the picture of Quasar Kevin Johnson and her when they graduated military school. Okafor almost cried at a picture of the Okafors and Tanakas together in a picture. Quasar Tanaka had become so much to her since their children started dating. General Solis and Nakia's husband loved to watch boxing and MMA matches together. These people were dead now. Never again would she have a conversation with them. How many more of her friends would die during this conflict?

The klaxon blared in the mess hall and it didn't seem register at first. 5 seconds into the attack she awoke to the danger. The Barca staryards shimmied three times. The activity knocked the personal device out of her hand and the klaxon's loud alarm dominated her field of vision. Adrenaline flooded her body and she shot to her feet. Okafor activated the combat mode of the suit and an energy shield razed around her head and face for protection against the elements. The klaxon warned that the atmosphere would start pumping out of the station shortly to prevent explosive decompression.

She ran to her battle position on the command deck of the station. With precision, the men and women of the station moved to the battle stations. It was clear to Okafor that the enemy blinked into combat. If the Poveen would have approached the officers would have more warning of an attack. Another massive hit to the station's shields knocked her to ground with other officers and soldiers. She was hit by two other officers before a comet soldier picked her off the ground to her feet. Minutes later atmospheric units sucked the air from the hallways and walkways. Barca Staryards shock slightly but these movements were different. The massive weapon systems of the staryards started to fire on the enemy. Okafor smiled slightly with the knowledge that the humans were now fighting back against the squids.

She entered the command deck into the organized panic of officers as they barked orders, updates, and commands. Okafor took her station and activated her station. She turned to the large holographic display in the middle of the room showing the staryards and the 6 large birthing bays. Also displayed were the ten carriers that surrounded the staryards to protect it.

Against this formation was all 114 of the original 154 Poveen cruisers.

They blinked close to the staryards and the carriers and opened fire with the curved energy weapons. This placed the human forces at a major disadvantage. The direct line of sight from Hannibal Battle Station to the Poveen cruisers was blocked by the staryards. For the battle station to fire on the Poveen with direct energy weapons they would have to fire through the staryards and carriers. The super cluster of human spacecraft were 45 minutes away if they burned at full speed from the current location. When they arrived the entire Poveen force would be able to blink again to another part of the system.

Okafor looked down at her station and watched the commands flood in from Vice Commander Kahn and Quasar Rodriguez. The women went to work with speed. Missiles from the supercluster spacecraft had been fired and they approached en masse with an arrival in 20 minutes. Starfighters, intercepstars, star puppets, and starvettes once in orbit around the moon of Hannibal now burned to engage the Poveen fleet and will arrive in 30 minutes. The assault craft from the carriers launched and entered the soup of war.

The ten starcarriers and the Barca staryards were not helpless. Rows of energy weapon and kinetic weapon turrets fired at will into the Poveen cruisers that were all at point blank distance. The sustained and consistent fire from the staryards pounded the lines of the Poveen cruisers forcing them to rotate new cruisers to the front to absorb the blows of the stations. The Star carriers, the largest space craft in space command, activated the powerful shielding systems and all short-range defense systems to counter the Poveen's attack.

The aliens moved quickly toward the Barca Staryard Station. The usually timid and reserved Poveen forces closed distance while they focus fired on one carrier. The group of carriers identified the change in tactic and pulled closer to the staryard to get support from overlapping the shielding. The Poveen were so close that they were inside much of the overlap negating much of the tactic. This battle was more like a street fight than any of the previous battles.

The first human carrier fell in less than one minute. The cascade effect of losing the ability to use overlapping shielding with the following carriers meant that each carrier after that one would be destroyed much faster. The benefit from a close formation quickly dissipated. The carriers burned wildly in different directions to defend themselves. Assault craft launched from the carriers did the best they could to push back the enemy but they didn't have the numbers. Thousands of attack craft were eradicated by alien fire.

The missiles launched by the supercluster and the assault craft merged into the soup battle. The missiles smacked into the Poveen formations but nothing was stopping the advance of the fleet on Barca Station. Enemy energy weapons fire on the station grew as the last resistance of the carriers ended. Okafor stood in disbelief at the screen. It felt surreal but Okafor knew at that moment she was going to die. She watched helplessly hours ago when Quasar Johnson died on Oya Station. She wondered if he felt like this as well.

General Okafor was no stranger to combat. She performed as a combat engineer for years. On the other hand, this was the first time she was in combat as a mother and wife. She needed to help them fight the enemy because her children needed her. Okafor poured over the shielding data. If she could generate an extra kilowatt from the power systems she was going to. Widows were being born by the second at the second battle of Carthage. Okafor was determined not to make her husband one of them.

She worked tirelessly with the chief engineer. It would be impossible to defend the station against the Poveen attack fleet. The battle was over. In roughly 16 minutes the shields would fail and the enemy would then take another five minutes burning through the hull until the station died. The destruction of the carriers left the station as the target of too much assault fire. The Supercluster was over 25 minutes from maximum fire range.

Okafor received a direct communication request over her newly updated and encrypted Nubian QEN. Okafor responded to the message.

“General Okafor. We have mission for you,” said Lord Commander Masters. Quasar Rodriguez was also in the picture.

“I don’t know what I can do for you sir. It doesn’t seem that Barca Station if going to make it,” replied Okafor.

“I know. We need you to speed up the process.”

“Excuses me sir? What does that mean?”

“General Okafor would you step in front of bullet to save one of your children?” asked Masters.

“Yes, I would sir. I wound not even hesitate.”

"Okay, well I am asking you to take that bullet right now. The Poveen will regain the ability to blink in 15 minutes. We predict that the Barca Staryards will be destroyed in twenty minutes. This would allow for the Poveen to destroy the station and blink away before the shockwave of the destruction. I need you to destroy the station now. The shockwave will force the Poveen to blink early or be destroyed by the shockwave.

The squids that blink out of range of the shockwave with have antimatter on the hull. One missile could destroy an entire cruiser. We could take out the entire squid fleet around Carthage. That would free up Quasar Rodriguez's taskforce to break the siege of Nubia. We can retake the entire the system. I need you to sacrifice yourself and the station. To drop antimatter containment of the reactors for the station in needs two command staff level authentications. Once I authenticate I will need you to finalize," asked Masters.

"Why not ask the Station Commander," asked Okafor?

"He is not on the command staff. If we told him, he could stop you. I don't want to take that chance. You must do it. Are you with me," asked Lord Commander Masters. Okafor thought about the new mission. Okafor was comfortable with dying at the hands of the Poveen but killing herself and everyone else on the station was something completely different. She looked at the readout again and it was clear. Every person on the station was going to die. The only difference would be if the Poveen died with her or not.

"Okay. I will do it. What do you need from me?" asked Okafor.

"Enter the antimatter containment protocols. Once you are inside let me know. I will trigger the deactivation of the containment. An alert will sound. You will then be able to authenticate the deactivation. Once the alarm sounds everyone will know that I approved the deactivation of the containment. It will be up to you to finalize it," said Masters.

"Understood. Hold on for my signal," said Okafor She placed Lord Commander Masters and Quasar Rodriquez on hold. Her right arm feel to her side from her chest to let everyone know that she was no longer communicating. The chief engineer next to her asked who she talked to but Okafor continued to work at her station. The commander of the station frantically requested ideas on how to hold off the Poveen but Okafor just continued to work.

The smaller chief engineer placed her hand on Okafor's arm and yelled "What are you doing? Who did you talk to?"

The command deck crew turned to the commotion. Okafor turned and punched the smaller woman in the face and then told Masters that she was in the system. Lord Commander Masters initiated the removal of the antimatter containment on the station. Okafor quickly approved the command with secondary confirmation.

Okafor hit the ground before she understood what happened. An intense burning sensation ran down her right arm. Puncture warnings took over her field of vision on her private HUD as the suit reacted to the impact of the bullet. The general took a gunshot to her right shoulder from the Sargent at Arms on the bridge. With speed the chief engineer grabbed her collar as the commander of the station ran over to her. Anger permeated the bridge as multiple barrels pointed in her direction.

"Turn it off you idiot you will kill us all," yelled the commander.

"We are already dead. This is the only way we take them with us. If not we die and they escape. We will take out this entire section of the taskforce with this last act. Look for yourself," as she pointed at the large display. It indicated the blast radius and all the Poveen Cruisers were inside of the radius. The commander looked at the screen and was dumbfounded. Okafor was correct.

"But the enemy can just blink away you idiot," said the commander.

"Yes, they can. But, they all have antienergy on the hull of the cruisers. That is why they must wait before they blink again. The antienergy needs to dissipate because if they blink again it hardens into antimatter. If they blink the cruisers hulls will be covered with antimatter. If the cruiser moves it will ignite the antimatter. One missile from a starfighter could spark the chain reaction. The enemy taskforce will not last another thirty minutes. We will win. It just cost our sacrifice," said Okafor as she moved to lean against the wall.

The room was silent. Okafor was correct. The officers turned to each other and hugged and shook hands. The countdown reached ten seconds the commander picked Okafor to her feet. He saluted her and she saluted back. Moments later the antimatter containment on the 100 antimatter reactions shut down. The tons of antimatter collided with normal matter and created a massive explosion and shockwave. Barca Staryards was destroyed and General Okafor along with it.

PLUS 149 HOURS AND 30 MINUTES COMMAND CORPS VICE COMMANDER PRIYANKA KAHN HANNIBAL BATTLE STATION, CARTHAGE FOR OKAFOR

Kahn watched the icon for the Barca Staryards disappear. The computer system quickly turned the visual sensors to the location of the Barca Staryards. A brilliant explosion as bright as the sun dominated the view screen on the command deck. Death and destruction followed as the shockwave ripped into any and every starship in local space. The command deck was completely silent and Kahn just stood with her eyes trained on the screen.

What a loss. What a defeat she thought. Would this be her legacy? 100 thousand soldiers and officers were gone. The 6 carriers under construction and 2 more carriers with all hands lost. Ninety-two thousand fighters, 125 thousand inceptstars, 30 thousand bombers, one hundred and ten thousand starpuppets, and five thousand starvettes all gone. General Okafor, her friend Nakia, was also dead. The decades long friendship was over. The defense of the Barca Staryards was over.

After the moment of reflection, she jolted back to reality. Kahn had Poveen to kill. Accurate sensor readings of the local battle area were difficult for thirty seconds after the explosion. The antimatter shockwave had to dissipate before the accuracy could be believed. The Poveen cruisers were scattered around the planetary system. Most blinked before the shockwave but not all. Only half the Poveen cruisers remained. They were forced to break protocol to blink and they didn't have the time to coordinate the blink.

Kahn then received a ping from Lord Commander Masters. Kahn was still slightly in a fog from the explosion and answered the ping. Lord Commander Masters spoke on the unsecure QEN line. At this point he didn't care if the Poveen could listen.

"Vice Commander you have squid in the open. Kill them all. Don't let General Okafor's sacrifice be in vain. The Poveen cruisers are lined with antimatter. Hit them and hit them now," yelled Masters as the line then went dead. Kahn didn't know what to say when she heard the word sacrifice. Slowly Kahn started to piece it together. The destruction of the staryards already killed half of the Poveen fleet and the other half was severely damaged and exposed.

Kahn sucked her teeth and got to work. The taskforce commanded by Quasar Rodriguez split into various constellations and moved toward the Poveen. The ships dove into gravity wells to accelerate to attack speeds. Targeting computers on the battle station soon provided firing solutions on 15 of the cruisers. Kahn ordered them to fire. The deck of the mighty battle station shook as the railgun weapons, missile systems, and energy weapon systems unleashed hell on the 15 cruisers that the battle station targeted.

Kahn, once the preeminent military historian in the system, studied battles that turned from one extreme to another her entire life. The ancient battle of midway flashed in her mind. When the American aircraft attacked the Japanese carrier force at the very moment the decks of those carriers were filled with ordinance and fuel it created one of the greatest victories in naval history. One ten-minute attack turned the tide of the battle and the overall battle for the pacific. This was such a battle. They just lost the largest staryard in this region of space but its destruction destroyed half of the Poveen force and severely damaged the other half.

Quickly she pinged Masters back. She needed his help to end the threat. Within a second he responded.

"Lord Commander I need control of the Sentry 7 units in this sector of space. I can destroy them all if I have your help. If not some will get away. I think you know as well as I do the flexibility that we would gain from all the cruisers around Carthage to be gone," she said before a response. Master stood silent. Was it time to expose the secret of the Sentry 7 system.

"Guidance is coming to you shortly Vice Commander. Avenge those soldiers Vice Commander Kahn. Avenge them. Avenge Tanaka, Johnson, Solis, and Okafor," said Masters as the link closed. Kahn froze again. She received word of the battle that raged on Kush but she didn't know that Solis was dead. Ten seconds later the Sentry 7 satellites pinged with acceptance to the battle station. Every Poveen cruiser was targeted. From as far as five AU away from the Carthage planetary system the stealthy and mighty S7 satellites opened and fired the deadly missiles that they held. One by one the missiles lit up space as they burned at 90gs of acceleration toward the Poveen cruisers that they now had their sights on.

As each volley approached, more and more missiles launched to match the timing of the arrival of the missiles that launched from a greater distance. Boasting both kinetic and nuclear warheads they raced to the planetary system bent on avenging all the people that lost lives at the hand of the invading aliens. Kahn could see the response of the enemy cruisers as they realized the extent of the attack that was launched on them. They attempted at the last minute to reassemble into larger groups to benefit from the overlapping shields but it was too late.

12 volleys of fast moving missiles slammed into the hulls of the Poveen. They fired the arching energy weapons in desperation at the missiles as they approached but every Poveen cruiser was struck by at least one missile. The station fired in anger upon the wounded aliens. Vengeance was upon humanity and they would seize it. One by one the Poveen cruisers burned and imploded under the gravity of the singularity engine. Kahn yelled in anger on the bridge "DIE" in a fit of rage. It was contagious. The command deck was rife with the anger of the humans in the system.

The constellations of the massive super cluster burned into combat. The capital starships raked the damaged Poveen cruisers extensively. Cruisers tried to maneuver and accelerate from death but the hulls coated with antienergy and antimatter both sparked and exploded to cause massive damage. She turned to the commander of the battle station and asked why the 6 cruisers weren't damaged. After five seconds of research they found that the missiles that were tasked to destroy those vessels were diverted to another target.

30 minutes later every Poveen cruisers in orbit around Carthage was destroyed. Hands were raised in victory and celebration. Woots and hollers

could be heard all around the station. The humans in the system won a victory. They stopped the advance of the Poveen at Carthage. The mighty Hannibal station and the taskforce stopped the alien invaders. It was truly bittersweet thought Kahn. She wanted to celebrate but her friend was dead, hundreds of thousands of the troops she commanded were dead, and her commanding officer wasn't being straight with her. She knew these to be true.

Kahn ordered her officers to implement an aggressive sleep and recovery campaign on the station. The officers and soldiers of the station needed get rest and recovery and they would have at least thirty hours before the Poveen in system could launch another attack. They would use that time wisely. Kahn steeped off the command deck into the ready for a discussion with Masters.

"Lord Commander Masters. I need you to be straight with me. I know that I am out of the loop and I have been forced out of my own chain of command. Before the Barca Staryards exploded we detected a change of course by the taskforce. They knew the staryards were going to explode. That means you ordered it. You ordered both the destruction of the staryards and the redeployment of the force without me. Why?" asked Vice Commander Kahn.

"You still haven't done what I have instructed you to do since the last engagement. If you would have followed all of my orders and suggestions, you would know more. But you haven't so you don't. You are one of the most stubborn people I have ever met. It serves you good 95% percent of the time but that other 5% is going to get you killed.

Over 250 million people have died since the Poveen have entered the system. I don't give two fucks about who gets credit for killing the Poveen cruisers. I don't give two fucks whose feelings get hurt during the process of driving these damn squids out of the Nubian system. We need to kill them all and kill them now. Cut out this self-loathing now," said Kahn.

"With all due respect sir. Fuck you. You don't get to order my friend to die and my super cluster to disengage without telling me why," she yelled. Master knew that this line was still monitored by the Poveen and he had to be discreet. He had to tell her in a way that she would understand.

"Are you finished? I expect this from a junior officer and not someone of your caliber. We are losing Kahn and I need you to keep your head on straight. Eat, shower, sleep, and talk to your family while you have this break," said Masters. He hoped that calling her a junior officer would trigger her need to prove him and everyone else wrong.

"I hearby submit my resignation. You clearly do not trust me. I also do not trust you anymore," said Vice Commander Kahn.

"So, you are pouting now? I do not accept your resignation and if you try to give it to the commander of the station I will consider that a treasonous act. You will stay in command and you will continue to serve with class. Is that clear Vice Commander? I don't need this right now. I need you to be focused and ready to deploy the ER gates when the time comes. We will need them soon. We are going to win this and I need your leadership to do it. Also, since you no longer need Rodriguez's taskforce I will be taking them. You won the battle Vice Commander. You won," said Masters.

Kahn didn't know how to react. Masters didn't want Kahn to leave so that was a bonus. Kahn remained confused on what command she missed but she filed that away for another conversation. This conversation was over and in a way Masters was right. The battle was over though the war raged on. Kahn formed a plan of action. First, she would agree with her commanding officers. Secondly, she would find the best place to eat on the station and get something to eat, and third she would go back over the log of communications with Masters to find out what she missed.

"Yes sir. I will comply. Sorry sir," responded Kahn. Masters ended the communication. Kahn left the ready room and moved to her quarters. Before she did anything the woman was going to take a well-deserved rest.

PLUS 152 HOURS
SPACE COMMAND QUASAR
VALERIA RODRIGUEZ
BATLENOVA PLANET ENDER
THE HUNT BEGINS

The last of the enemy cruisers imploded under the force of gravity. Quasar Rodriguez and Captain Reiner stood on the immaculate virtual bridge with resolve. Invaders were silenced by the guns and missiles of the humans. They won. They defeated the formidable force that attempted to destroy Hannibal Station. The sacrifice of Okafor and the others would be remembered forever by the people of the system and of the entire human sphere. The battle had turned. Rodriguez and the others felt it. She was sure that the enemy felt it as well.

The discussion with Lord Commander Masters after they fired the last round in anger didn't last very long. A new mission more dangerous than the previous mission was given. The taskforce would burn from the Carthage planetary system to the Nubian planetary system. The mighty engines of the taskforce burned at full 25g acceleration. The battle would take place in a little over twenty hours and the crew of the Battlenova Planet Ender were ready for the engagement. Morale was high and the officers were equally as confident.

Quasar Rodriguez went off duty once the high gravity burn ended. The one perk of service onboard a Space Command starship was the amenities.

Officers were connected to a virtual environment the entire deployment which meant they lived, worked, and fought in a virtual environment. When they were not on duty they could use that virtual environment how way they wished. Rodriguez did just that when she sat at her favorite café in the city of Chapala, on the planet Farragut, in the Azteca System. Rodriguez drank one of the signature rum and passion fruit drinks while the warmth of the binary suns bathed her lavender bronze skin. Tropical pastel clothing made of light materials rippled in the light wind off the ocean.

Opochtli, a massive planet wide ocean, spanned in every direction. It contained slightly over ten times the amount of water as Earth. The planet was twice the diameter of Earth but only produced 1.2gs due to its lack of heavy metals. Farragut's economy was based on food production for export. It was the largest producer of ocean based food in the region. it was only surpassed by the combined weight of the dozens of planets that produced similar food in the Victory system in the human sphere.

Whales and dolphins breached the surface of the water as a warm breeze flew through her pink hair. It was hard for her to believe that she lived like this for 50 years while she was married to her once husband. She lived an entire life before her commitment to the United Planets of Humanity manifested. The tradeoff was fair she thought. We will extend your life by 250 years if you give us 50 of those years. The last couple of days highlight the joy she felt in her previous life and she wished for it or something like it again.

After her commitment was over she was going back Azteca to live out her life. The peace and calm of that life was something she was going to get back to after she was done fighting. Or Rodriguez would find herself a nice young stallion to travel the stars with. They would drink, party, travel, and have sex on all the luxurious beaches in the Untied Planets of Humanity. Or maybe she would stay in the Nubian system if General Nasir would pick up on one of her hints. He would sweep her off her feet with a pronouncement of love. She loved each scenario equally though she reserved the right to also travel the universe tumbling and fumbling around on each of the beaches with General Nasir. She giggled to herself she drank the cocktail.

Five hours ago she didn't believe a life after this conflict was possible. The mode on the starship and in the overall military was different. For the first time in the conflict the human forces are now moving on the Poveen forces. The task force she commanded would join forces with the other battlenova and the rest of the starships from Kush to form Task Force 1 to complete Operation Avenger. They were tasked with the destruction of the 4 interdictor CIC cruisers in the orbit around Nubia. The only problem was that that they were surrounded by 301 Poveen Cruisers.

All 4 CIC cruisers were positioned deep inside the massive diamond formation. Multiple layers of overlapped shields and weapons fire protected them. It would take the combined power of the entire task force to punch through the enemy lines and reach the four cruisers at which time they could just blink away. She gulped more of the drink and relaxed at the café. In a couple of hours after she relaxed and slept they would begin the planning for the assault.

Salmon mixed with an assortment of vegetables was brought to her table by a handsome shirtless waiter. Rodriguez smiled and continued to the cocktails. This was lovely. Space Command was much better than the conditions of the Meteors, Comets, and Astro corps. Those soldiers and officers would all gather in mess halls, hot bunking in cramped crash couches, and still feel the stress of the conflict. Rodriguez agreed with herself that this was much better.

In reality her body was suspended in nanite liquid. She was fed intravenously and with a feeding tube. Alcohol was not going into her system. The sensations she felt were induced by the computing unit attached to her brain stem. The water she felt as she swam wasn't real. The breeze wasn't real. The sun's warmth wasn't real. To her mind, on the other hand, it was all real and it felt good. Rodriguez spent the next two hours in the simulation before she rested for ten hours. Over the next two hours Quasar Rodriguez and Lord Commander Masters finalized the plan for Operation Avenger.

Operation Avenger would determine the outcome of the overall war for

Nubia and the conflict. Rodriguez will command the third wave and Taskforce 1. The first wave will consist of incoming fire from Carthage. The Hannibal Battle Station will fire the projectile rounds from Carthage to intercept the enemy forces over the Nubia over 5 AU away. The purpose of this volley is to make the Poveen Cruisers move. It is meant to break up the formation of the enemy or sap the shields of the enemy force.

The next wave will consist of missiles from the Sentry 7 system. Missiles from deep in the system have already been fired and they burn with anger toward Nubia. The once silent weapon systems of the Nubian System were now awoken. In all over 10 thousand missiles will strike the enemy force in the second wave. The S7 satellites within blink drive range of the Poveen cruisers however will wait to fire. If the enemy decides they want to blink out danger, the S7 systems in the region will rain missiles onto any cruiser that blinks. The trap was being set and the enemy would not dictate any longer the battlefield.

The mission of the 3rd and 4th wave will depend on the effectiveness of the second wave. If the Poveen blink away Nubia Taskforce 1 will redirect from a space battle to a space to ground battle. They would adjust the attack vector slightly and reign down space command caliber weapons onto the Poveen forces on the ground.

The forth wave will consist of the entire complement of starfighters, starbombers, interceptstars, and starpuppets from the fire base on the Nubian moon. Like the third wave, if the enemy blinked they would strafe the Poveen forces on the ground. Rodriguez liked the plan. When the soldiers and officers of the United Planets of Humanity went into combat they would understand the mission and the secondary mission. The Poveen were painted into a corner and the human forces would ensure they now stayed in the corner.

During the conflict Rodriguez didn't always agree with the actions of the Lord Commander but his leadership had placed them all in a position to win. They have turned the tides of the battle. He placed her Space Command force in a position in which they were never boxed in by the superior space forces of the Poveen. Even after Kush fell because of politicians committing treason he never faltered. Consistently he made the right call no matter how hard it was. He remained patient in the face of disaster and when they had the opportunity to turn the tides of war he did.

Rodriguez admired him and feared him. Masters ordered a senior member of the command team to kill herself and her soldiers. What if she was next? What if she was ordered to do the same over Nubia? Could she do it too? She would find out. Operation Avenger would decide the outcome. Her leadership would matter. She would matter. The Battlenova Planet Ender would matter. This terrified and delighted the officer. Legends were being made and Rodriguez did not want to be left off the list.

PLUS 154 HOURS
PLANETARY FORCE GENERAL
JAMAAL NASIR
FORWARD STATION, NUBIA
GROUND WAR

General Jamaal Nasir stood inside the control room of the largest military installation on the main continent. Forward Station has been home for so many in preparation of this moment. The massive Poveen force moved toward the shoreline of the main continent of Nubia. It stretched nearly 5 thousand kilometers from north to south. The continent was shaped roughly like the ancient country of Brazil. The long shoreline had millions of marines and airborne soldiers ready to repel the invasions.

The massive airforce raced to greet the enemy at the shoreline. Sonic booms rippled along the countryside. The sound broke windows and damaged buildings because of the scope and size of the airforce. The massive black wedged Condors blacked out the sun by sheer volume. Armor waited hundreds of kilometers behind the shoreline to close any gaps that were created. Legions of tactical puppets waited to exploit gaps in the enemy formations.

5 minutes until first contact. The control room was silent. You could hear a heartbeat if you listened hard enough. General Nasir felt helpless like all commanders do when they launch an attack. After the planning

phase the commander is helpless until the battle plays out. With 4 minutes left Nasir went to stand closer to General Bello. She was just as tall as the man and she seemed to enjoy the comfort of standing next to him would provide. This was it. This was combat.

On the shoreline the first missiles were launched by the human fighters that raced ahead of the rest of the force. Hundreds of thousands of aircraft crashed into each other. Poveen spheres swooped and darted in the sky battling the human airforces. Air combat took place from 1 kilometer to 10 kilometers high. It also extended 3800 meters down the shoreline as the two opposing forces clashed. The Condors released the dangerous missile and drone's consortium.

To look at the air combat was to look as a maelstrom of metal, energy, and fire. Nasir couldn't help to think to himself "Why are we doing this? Why is this happening?" Avian Puppets joined the fight when the fighter left to re-arm. They would not have a repeat of Kush when the Poveen exploited the lull in fighting. The puppets would stay in combat until the fighters returned. They protected the mighty Condors. The Condors in return unleashed hate and anger upon the enemy forces.

A constant rain of fire and metal fell on the ground troops as the battle for the shoreline started. Artillery from 50 kilometers away fired onto the beach. Gravity copters hovered and fired anti-armor missiles. Marine soldiers fired on any craft that attempted to make it to shoreline. For an hour, the enemy was contained by the hard fighting Marines and the airborne soldiers that filled any gaps when they were created.

The legendary beaches of Nubia were now a battlefield. Destroyed Poveen spheres, dead soldiers, metal, debris, sea animals, and destroyed buildings covered the land from the ocean to ten kilometers inland. The next wave of Poveen ground forces turned the tide of the conflict. The bioweapons hit the beach next. These beasts were constructed very like the orga puppets. They had strong skeletons constructed of metal. The rest of the beast was grown around he exoskeleton.

The four-legged monster hit the beaches en masse. The beast stood 3 meters tall on four legs. Its head was like a mix between a rhino and lion. The carapace of the beast was thick but the true value was the hard shielding that the unit had. It was designed to break through fortified positions like the shoreline and that is what they did. They swam up to the edge of the water and then they jumped out the water and bounded over the defenses.

The first wave of the monsters was almost all devastated but some got behind the front line and they started to wreak havoc in the rear of the line. More and more of these terrors jumped from the water and broke the human lines. Marine puppets race to front line the destroy the terrors and they did. The marines held the line once again. The line was holding but the line was getting thinner. They could not hold for much longer without support. The heavy tanks couldn't operate that close to the shore line. It could be time to pull back before the marine units collapsed.

"Let's pull them back to the second line of defense. They can fight with the army groups and the heavy armor," said Nasir via CU to Bello. She agreed and then barked the orders. The coordinated retreat lasted roughly three hours as the airborne and marines forces retreated to the forward positions of the army. The massive army tanks and armored vehicles pounded the chasing Poveen.

It was weird that the front-line soldiers heard the enemy before they saw it. With all the noise on the battlefield the hum of the larger Poveen units could be heard. The monstrous bioweapons landed on land in numbers. Hundreds of thousands of enemy units moved on the human line. Nasir watched on the live feed and it was hard for the human mind to wrap itself around that much carnage.

At times, it was almost too much to look at. So many soldiers died. Since the start of the battle ten thousand soldiers died per minute. The carnage was getting to the entire team of officers on the bridge. On the large screen, entire army groups just disappeared to never come back. Until it all stopped. The enemy stopped the advance to consolidate the gains they got. For six hours, they battled and fought to keep the enemy back but they conceded 200 kilometers of ground along the coast line.

General Nasir tapped General Bello on the shoulder and he told her to follow him. They walked into a control room. This wasn't a planning meeting. This was a decompression meeting. Nasir knew that if he walked into the room by himself they would think he wasn't built for command and the same would apply for Bello. They needed the meeting to look like a planning meeting so they both could decompress.

Once they walked into the room the two of them almost in unison took a deep breath and sat down in one of the chairs in the room. They both just stared off into space to ponder what just happened.

"I can't believe that happened. I can't believe it. So many of them are gone," said Bello. Nasir shook his head in agreement. He had seen war but he had not seen anything like this. This was something totally different.

"I know. I don't know what this is. This is something new to me as well. We have so many dead, dying, and wounded. Do you think Nubia will ever be the same after this? This place was built on love and hope. What will it stand for now?"

"Reliance. We will push them back. All of them bastards. Push them back into the sea. Where squids belong. Not here on land with us," remarked Bello.

"Yeah. I just hope after this we can go back to being us. Being Nubian. I think this may do something to us that can't be undone," questioned Nasir.

"I hope not. I love this planet," said Bello as her eyes began to water. Nasir looked over at her and he was slightly confused.

"What is it Bello?"

"You know the 117th Airborne regiment? My younger brother was in that regiment. We lost contact with them two hours ago. I don't think he made it. I don't think he is coming back. I am from Buckhead. These motherfuckers just destroyed Peachtree. Do you know how many people I know that live on Peachtree? My sister was on Peachtree with her four kids and husband. My mother and father are on Buckhead with my other sister. I might lose my entire family in this conflict. No one is out of the system. Everyone is here. We are all here. I am breaking apart here," said Bello.

Nasir stood from the ground and walked over to the tall woman and pulled her toward him. He wrapped his hands around her body and gave her the biggest hug. He just whispered into her ear "cry it out." Bello did just that. She cried as hard as she could on his shoulder for five minutes until the emotion passed.

Nasir couldn't be crippled by emotion either way. What he did understand was the emotion of others. He could correct his behavior to help them like he did with Bello. She was a fine officer and brilliant mind. But even the most gifted soldiers grieve when half of their family is killed violently. They had to. They are human.

She pulled back after the stretch of crying and pulled it back together.

That five-minute break from being the cool and composed officer ended and she was better for it. She wiped her eyes and hardened herself once again. She looked at her commanding officer with thankful eyes. She didn't have to say it he just nodded.

Just like that they walked back on the command deck. Nasir felt much better as well. It was if he absorbed her emotions and charged his own emotional batteries. He felt light and confident until he saw the battle trains return to the base. Hundreds of thousands of wounded and dead soldiers arrived back on the base. On every surface doctors, humans, AI, and drone worked on soldiers that they could save.

Reserve units marched onto the bloody trains off to the front. Nasir thought that was a good thing. The soldiers would know that they are walking into combat and not another exercise. He felt that they would be ready to fight when they arrived. The battle had slowed for the moment but it would go hot again soon and they all had to be ready. Nasir told the General that he was going to go off duty for 6 hours and when he returned he would relieve her. She agreed.

Nasir walked off the command deck and into the private officer quarters not too far from the level. He walked into the room and removed the exosuit. He discarded it to the ground. He laid on the white bed looking at the ceiling. He reached over and grabbed an energy bar that he had placed by the edge of the bed. He wasn't hungry but he knew his body needed food. The berry flavored bar was more flavorful than he expected and that pleased him. Nasir was then pinged by Lord Commander Masters. He answered.

"General Nasir. How is everyone holding up?"

"Sir, we are holding as well as we can. Everyone is shaken but they are acting like the events of the day are not affecting them. But we all know they are. I need you to be straight with me. How are we doing?"

"Good. I don't know how much you have had a chance to pay attention to the rest of the battles but we won the battle of Carthage. Quasar Rodriguez burns for Nubia as we speak. We took out a couple more interdictors. We lost General Solis. We lost General Okafor. We lost Quasar Tanaka."

"Okay. Thank you for being honest."

"We need you to hold the line for just a little while longer. We will get one of these gates open and we will take these squids down. Just believe. I need you to believe. Can you do that for me?"

"Yes sir. You have my support. Now I need you to let me go. It is my turn to bunk."

"Okay. Get to sleep soldier. You earned it.".

PLUS 165 HOURS
COMMAND CORP LORD COMMANDER
MALCOM MASTERS
OGUN STATION
DON'T LEAVE

Lord Commander Masters studied the readouts and updates from the first land battle on planet Nubia. The outcome was a stalemate but the number of soldiers that died in the conflict was unacceptable. Every minute the casualty count rise long after the fighting had stopped. The enemy is reinforcing the front lines for another push. Masters didn't know if they could stop another push from the Poveen.

Masters was pinged on his CU. When he looked at the person that sent it he didn't know what to do. It was his wife. He ignored it twice but she continued to ping him so he answered the call. He saw nothing but complete panic on her face. She was holding her communication device and her face bounced up and down in the feed. It struggled to reach him since so many satellites had been destroyed and military communication was prioritized.

"We need your help Malcom. We are on the diplomatic star. My uncle talked the kids into getting on the getting on the star so I got on it too to talk them out of doing something stupid and now we are lifting off."

"What are you doing? Land that star. Are you crazy?"

"Malcom says you are crazy. This is stupid put this star back on the ground. Do it now. Put it down!" yelled Layla.

"Get back on the ground," said Masters. Layla was running to the back of the vessel and handed the communication device to her Uncle, the President of Nubia.

"Good you have him on the line. Malcom, we need you to cover our escape. We know you haven't used the S7's around the planet yet so we need cover our escape."

"No."

"Excuse me?"

"I said no."

"You will let your wife, children, and grandchildren die? You would let you President die? What is wrong with you. You are going to use the S7 missiles when the time comes."

"No I will not. The S7 missiles will provide support to the planet of Nubia not to you. Do you know how Kush fell?"

"No I do not know how it fell. I heard that the outlander Sub Commander Rodgers failed us."

"No. President Lawrence shut down the planetary shielding from the rings to escape the planet and come to Nubia. He killed over 300 million people because of his action on Kush. We had to change our entire strategy. He cost the lives of some of my best friends because of his actions. I will not let that happen again. I will not use one missile to prevent you from dying. If you want to take a chance than you take that chance. If the people on the star die it is because of you and you alone. Land that vessel now."
"You will protect us. You are bluffing," said the President as the communication device was ripped from his hand.

"Hey baby. I know I told you to get hardcore but not with us. You are going to protect us, right? You are not going to let us die. From what I understand once we get into the black this thing goes stealth."

"No, it won't. They can track you in subspace. That craft is loud as hell in subspace. They will detect you no matter what you do. Only stealthstars can hid from subspace detection. You will get out of the atmosphere and then you die. You killed our children," said Masters in anger. Her demeanor changed and she got angry.

"No, if die you didn't protect your family. That is what people do. They protect their family. That is what you will do. You will protect your family. Now get ready to shoot the S2 or S7 or whatever he said."

"No."

"You can't be serious."

"I am very serious. How many times did I come to work with you and told you to vote a certain way? How many times has your uncle tried to cut my funding to give himself a tax break?"

"Okay, I see how it is. I was thinking about staying with you even after the stunt at the start of the conflict. If you can't protect me than I don't think we should renew our marriage when it expires. I think I need someone that will take care of me."

"Your best chance at survival now is for you to get as far as way from this planet as possible. I saw that you cleared the atmosphere. We will experience time delay on communication as soon as you accelerate."

"I don't want to talk to you anymore. Good by Malcom."

"Goodbye Layla. I love you," said Malcom as his son snatched the communication device. The man was just as large as his father and equally as muscular.

"Dad, what are you doing? We need your protection."

"Sorry. But if the Poveen want to kill you they will kill you."

"So you will let us die?"

"No. You are on a star with unaugmented humans. At best, you can accelerate at 2gs. It will take you a long time to reach the speed that we consider attack speed. Since our vessels can accelerate at 20gs our starships get to that speed quickly. That means we can support them with the S7 system because they are able to cover the distance between the satellites. You will be going to slow for us to help. Like I said the President killed you. You should know this," said Malcom as tears ran down his face. The emotion of the event was now overwhelming him.

"Why didn't you say that before?" yelled Layla in the background.

"I did tell you. I said if you go you die. Did you think I was joking? If you could get off the planet and be safe I would have gotten you off the planet before. Unless you turn around you are dead."

"Turn this thing around," yelled Layla. It was already too late. A Poveen cruiser blinked next to the starcarft and matched the acceleration of the craft. It fired the arched energy at the starship. It only took two shots from the main weapon to destroy the vessel that carried Masters' wife, two children, and six grandchildren. He stood from the machine that he monitored the battle plan and yelled as loud as he could.

The man dropped to his knees as tears ran from his eyes. He lost them.

PLUS 170 HOURS
COMMAND CORPS VICE COMMANDER PRIYANKA KAHN
HANNIBAL BATTLESTATION, CARTHAGE UNLOAD

Kahn was tossed from the comfort of her bed onto the floor. She hit the ground and ricocheted into the wall. Pain danced around her body before it settled on the left knee and right shoulder. The klaxon was deafening in her ear. Another jolt sent her across the room into the bed that she was tossed from. Constricted from the blanket Kahn struggled to free her body. Her vision returned shortly after the epic battle with the blanket was over.

Kahn scanned the room and found her exo-suit. Within seconds the suit was operating and the magnetics of the suit engaged to solve the bouncing off the wall issue. Next, she looked at the alerts that dominated her field of vision. First, the red alert notification was removed. The station was going back into battle mode. Hannibal Battle Station was under attack. Secondly, she connected to bridge command to find out the current situation of the station. Multiple hull breaches where reported. Not only were they under attack they took damage already.

Kahn stumbled to the bridge. The station took a beating. Kahn activated preset readouts on her HUD. Thirty seconds prior seven Poveen

Cruisers inbound from Kush blinked within a thousand meters of the station. Thousands of little pieces of the cruisers splintered and slammed into the station puncturing the hull. Shards reformed into breeching craft, assault craft, and troop carriers. Poveen soldiers and drones entered the station. The spherical and rear section of the craft moved closer to the hull of the battle station. Graviton waves slammed into the station forcing it to move, shake, and shimmy. The Poveen assault on Hannibal Battle Station had begun.

Kahn still had some questions. The Poveen cruisers just blinked three times father than any known blink on record. "Was this the real range of blink technology or was this a special variant of the cruiser?" she questioned. Next, how many damn squids are now on her station and did they have enough Comets and security personnel to repel borders. Kahn stopped her movement to the bridge and ran back to her room. She jumped into the battle armor that sat quiet since they arrived. Within seconds the armor closed and locked. The matte black armor covered her from head to toe. She grabbed the Dragon Spite Hand Cannon and stowed in on the hip of the armor.

Determination drove her to the command deck while the station shimmed and shook. Once on the bridge she watched as the white metallic cylinders hovered from the walls toward the officers on deck. They transformed and molded themselves into armor. It adjusted and readjusted until the fit on the officers was tight. The sleek white armor matched the walls and the exosuits that were once purple, the color of dress for the Orbital Guard, turned to white like a chameleon to match the new armor.

Station defenses erupted on the spherical sections of the Poveen Cruisers around the station. Kahn activated the S7 satellite systems that still contained the missiles from the region to fire. The Poveen craft were too close for the large caliber weapon systems of battle station to move toward. The battle station, now under motion, tried to move and arch to get the Poveen on a vector but they simply matched the spin.

The two carriers that survived the last attack but were too damaged to travel with Taskforce 1 moved into action. The last attack destroyed a lot of the assault craft but they launched what remained. Starfighter, interceptstars, star puppets, and starvettes raced to attack the shards of the cruisers around the station. The carriers themselves converted into a missile boat since the last battle. Instead of launching assault craft they filled the cargo holds with the ordinance Missiles were pushed out of cargo holds and launched out the side of the spacecraft.

Those missiles also burned toward Hannibal station with the intention of destroying the shards around the station. The Poveen spheres tried to intercept the missiles with arched energy but most of the missiles defeated the anti-missile fire. They smashed into the shards with anger. Poveen soldiers, drones, and machines spilled into the black of space. The battle raged and Kahn watched the Poveen Soldiers continuous infiltration of the station. Station security and the Comet force onboard began to move to secure vital areas as more and more Poveen entered the station.

Kahn reached out to Masters to give him an update and he answered her ping quickly.

"Vice Commander Kahn what is your status," asked her commanding officer.

"The Poveen have launched an attack that took us by surprise. The blink technology is three times better than the system most of the cruisers are using. They have landed soldiers on the station. It is hard to get an accurate number because they are still entering," said Kahn.

"We think that variant of the cruiser was designed to blink and land forces on the planetary ring system of Kush. They never had to use it during that battle because of President Lawrence and his foolishness. You should expect all those soldiers to be perfectly suited to engage you on the battle station. We have wondered why those cruisers hung back in previous battles but now we know why. They may have more so be ready for another wave.

"That makes since sir."

"What are your next steps Vice Commander?" asked Masters.

The moon base is preparing to receive our personnel. We are waiting for a window to get all the non-combat officers off the station. I don't know if we can hold the line when the rest of the Poveen force arrives. We will detonate the station and take as many of them as we can before we leave. It should destroy this entire boarding force and the Poveen cruisers in the process," said Kahn.

"No, you will not. You will defend that station to the last man. You have 2 of the 4 galactic level gates left in the system. If we ever find a way to breach the interdiction field, we will need that station. You will defend that station or you will die trying. Not even the last person alive on that station can destroy it. Is that clear?" responded Masters.

"Sir."

"You have 200 hundred thousand officers on that station and many more soldiers on the moon. Get them to the station. Defend the station," ordered Masters as he made his point extremely clear. She needed to hold the line.

"Sir, with all due respect for so many on this station it is a suicide mission," said Kahn.

"Quasar Might is burning toward the Poveen position in the deep black and Quasar Rodriguez will spear head the attack on Nubia. What do you think their chances are? Did they complain? Or are they doing their duty? Priyanka hold the fucking line," yelled Masters. Kahn was taken aback the normally calm and collected Masters broke from the calm. She was also startled that he called her by her first name.

"Okay, sir. I will hold the line," said Kahn.

"Do what you need to do to hold that station and defend those gates. We will need them shortly. Get those damn Poveen cruisers away from your hull and kill all the intruders. We are all counting on you. The entire system is counting on you," said Masters. Kahn took a deep breath and agreed. The direct contact with Nubia ended. Kahn begin to focus on the defense of the station and the movement of man and material from the moon base to the battle station in orbit.

Masters sent her command of more S7 missile batteries farther from Carthage. Kahn ordered those batteries to fire the missiles. It would take them roughly five hours to arrive at Hannibal Battle Station. The challenge that Vice Commander Kahn faced was twofold. First, she needed to remove all the Poveen off the station and defeat the advanced force of the Poveen. Secondly, she needed to prepare for the rest of the Poveen cruisers that travelled at speed toward the battle station from Kush.

She ordered 60 thousand of the 100 thousand comet corps forces from the moon to the station. Those soldiers would take off after the first wave of S7 missiles arrived. They are tasked with the fortification of weapon systems, shielding systems, and gate control. Drones and Comet Corps on the station already maneuvered down hallways and corridors to solidify the critical areas.

Emergency protocols forced crews to form fire teams of security forces. Once formed the teams were given tasks to help in the defense of the station. Unfortunately, those caught behind the lines were now being massacred by the alien forces on the station. The station was massive and contained three layered sections. The outer layer took most the damage from the early assault. Most vital systems were housed in the third layer. The second layer would be the layer that the humans used to defended the station.

The Poveen cruisers were devoid of the usually front nose section that provided 2 thirds of the offensive and defensive combat strength. Without out that section the cruisers could not provide an adequate defense. When the S7 missiles arrived at the battlefield the cruisers lacked the defensive capabilities to stop them. The missiles ripped into the spheres that hung just outside the battle station. The destruction of the of those vessels turned into a catch-22 situation. The collapsing graviton wave that destroyed so many Poveen cruisers when the singularity sphere on the craft was broken affected the space station due the proximity.

Thousands of breaches and damage occurred throughout the station. Kahn was even thrown from her feet and against the wall after a positive gravity wave was followed by a negative gravity wave. Causality reports flooded in across the damaged station. The gravity waves destabilized the defensive positions and caused damage in normally secure sections of the station. The missile attack, on the other hand, was a complete success. The seven cruisers that were hugged the hull of the station were all destroyed. That cleared the path for the thousands of transport starships to launch from the moon Hannibal to the space station in its orbit.

Kahn was stunned at what she saw next. The gravity damage opened major avenues into the third layer of the station. Poveen soldiers and drones moved to capitalize on the new avenue of approach. Command deck officers and crew had to get out of the section or they would be overrun with enemy soldiers. Kahn yelled at the Sergeant at Arms, SAA for short, and told him to get them all out. Crewmen fight or flight responses kicked in. The bullpup designed rifles that had been stowed were locked, loaded, and raised for combat. Officers moved to the doorway to look out and train the rifles down the hallways. Station personnel had extensive training and it was paying off in the conflict.

The new mission was to move to ER gate control to the south of the station and fortify the entrance to that section of layer 3. Movement to that section would take between 15 to 20 minutes without trouble but that was not likely. The Poveen drones and soldiers moved into the cracks and were already on the same deck as them. Kahn pulled up the rear with the Sargent at Arms after 30 seconds of arguing before she pulled rank. Vice Commanders should be protected the SAA yelled but Kahn knew what everyone knew. Her armor was the most powerful and her weapon was the more powerful than all the weapons they carried combined except for the SAA.

Thermite bombs were triggered on the command deck to destroy all the officer stations and wiring that lead to other areas of the station. Poveen teams would not move onto the command and be able to access the rest of the station. Throughout the region of the station officers and crew placed more thermite weapons on relays and other equipment. Lights flickered constantly in the white hallways.

Kahn back peddled down the hallways. The suit controlled the pace of movement which allowed Kahn to study the advance of the enemy and focus on command. After three turns they arrived at a long hallway that led into the other section of the station. Massive fortified gates opened to allow the officers into the more secure part of the station. Kahn stopped at the end of the hallway and relieved two officers ill equipped to repel any Poveen units.

They needed to hold the hallway until heavily armored Comet Corps forces secured the location. Kahn and the Sargent at Arms stayed at the corner and waited for the Poveen to arrive. He wore a comparable armor to that of the Vice Commander but it was in Comet Corps variant of heavy armor. Instead of a hand cannon he had a bullpup designed energy and projectile rifle. A set of officers bounced around the corner with fear in the eye, they knew the enemy was close. Gravity on the station was a thing of the past so to move with speed you had to propel yourself along the hand grips on the walls or with the use of air jets on the suits.

Kahn and the SAA moved to defend the T intersection. Kahn wrapped around the corner while the SAA exposed himself by walking across the hallway. Two Poveen drones turned the corner. The units were spherical in shape and grey in color. Behind the unit four long tentacles used to stabilize and push off the hand railed helped them around the corner. A gold circle indicated the front on the metallic drone. From the circle energy arched out of the drone at the two officers.

One officer moved to the wall of the hallway quickly to dodge the onslaught. White armor cracked and burned under the power of the drone. The charred body of the officer continued to float toward Kahn and the SAA. Gold particles flew off the drone as the cannon fire from Kahn and rifle fire from the SAA hit the drone. It turned lifeless with three direct shots. Kahn caught the burned body and stopped its movement. She handed the body to the fleeing officer and the two of them went into the more secure section of the station.

Over the next ten minutes 20 such drones rounded the corner and they all were put down by the two soldiers defending the T section. More officers also rounded the corners along the sides of the station. In all they saved over 30 more officers before the Comet Corps forces arrived.

Station Comet Corps forces looked more like roman legionaries than the other soldiers. They walked down the hallway in hard armor and shields that reached from the floor to the ceiling. The shield was built to clog hallways and to provide a stable firing platform in the defense of the station. The Poveen would find these forces formidable. Once Kahn was satisfied that they had enough forces at the gate to hold it she retreated to the ER gate command center.

Officers and commanders poured into the room. Makeshift stations and work areas were quickly constructed. The main functions of the command deck were slowly rerouted to the room. Kahn brought herself up to speed on the defense of the station and of the readiness of the gates. One gate took heavy damage while the other gate only took light damage from the assault and the gravity waves.

She prioritized the repair of the lightly damaged gate first. They need at least one to work when the time came. The estimated time to repair was two hours for the first gate and six hours for the second gate. Timing was going to be close. In the next six hours Quasar Might would reach the enemy force in the deep black of the system and Quasar Rodriguez would reach the force around Nubia. The station also had the Poveen space force from Kush barreling down on the station.

The next six to seven hours would determine the conflict. The war for the Nubian system was going to end one way or another. Vice Commander Kahn hoped that it ended in her favor. The forces of the station were holding the line inside the station but the enemy did make advances. Poveen drones and soldiers entered the station en masse and continued to do so. For the moment she could take stock of the situation an give commands. Her leadership could be the difference in this conflict and she was going to make sure she provided the best leadership that she could.

PLUS 171 HOURS
COMMAND CORPS SUB COMMANDER MIKE RODGERS
OKO STATION, OKO CITY, KUSH GUERILLAS

Sub-Commander Rodgers watched another city razed to the ground on the monitor that dominated the large command deck. The city of Kerma fell to the Poveen moments prior. The marine and airborne soldiers defended the city well. In the end they just didn't have enough fire power to stop the onslaught. He consulted with the planetary AI Thoth once again. The outcome remained the same. 0 percent chance of victory if they continue the current plan of action.

Rodgers didn't have any starships and a very small air force left. 2 hours prior the last resistance on the orbital ring went silent. The brave men and women of Orbital Guard fought to the last man and woman. His satellite network was in shambles. Lines of communication were intermittent at best. Supply lines have been gone for hours. The enemy took one city at a time and moved on to the next one. Rodgers didn't see a path to victory, only defeat.

The forces in the system fought hard and well but they could not seem to make a difference. They needed a change of strategy. The Poveen forces rapidly moved on to the two largest cities left on the planet. Oko City, his current location, was the major logistics hub of the planet and it held most of the food stores. The other location was the cultural hub and most populous city on the planet Napata. It was currently home to the second largest military group on the planet and his fiancée.

The tale of General Solis had become a battle cry among the Meteors formerly under his command. His selfless sacrifice to ensure the escape of the soldiers under command was the product of leadership that was hard wired into the man. Rodgers didn't know him well because he was a private man but from what he did know of him he liked. He was class. Rodgers hoped that when the Untied Planets of Humanity AI selected DNA for Protocol 5 humans they used a lot of him. An army of Solis's would reign chaos on the Poveen.

That thought provoked memories of Rodgers' two living children for some reason. Would they get siblings if he died? Would the UPH select his DNA to create thousands of soldiers? His fiancé was a P5 human. Laura Oban had mothers, fathers, sisters, and brothers that she never met and would never meet. How many more Laura's were under construction right now? A ping on his com system from Vice Commander Kahn jolted him from the line of thought he just traveled down.

"How are you holding up Mike? Lord Commander Masters told me that Buckhead is in trouble and Peachtree is gone," said Kahn probing in a way that hoped it wasn't as bad as she was being told.

"We are in trouble Vice Commander. A lot of trouble. I don't know if we can win this fight. Our soldiers are fighting hard and brave but…we cannot defeat these squids. They have more. They are better equipped. The commander here is aggressive. Extremely aggressive. Every time I try to prepare a battlefield that favors us they can maneuver out of it or somehow manage to get more forces at the point of attack," said Rodgers.

"Yeah. The Poveen cruisers meant to destroy your rings just attacked Hannibal Battle Station. The attack was bold and daring. That commander has taught the squids well I guess. We need to kill that bastard. We don't need to face fleets of highly aggressive Poveen like him. The rest of his cruisers will arrive shortly. I will show him who is boss when he gets her," said Kahn.

"Sorry about that. They should still be here fiddling around in space trying to poke holes in our shields. President Lawrence really fucked us good with that one. I am just at the end of the rope here. I need a new strategy," said Rodgers.

"Have you tried going to ground? Stop fighting the battle they want you to fight," said Kahn. Rodgers thought to himself for a moment. Maybe he did fight the fight they wanted. All his strategies were conventional. Of course, he was trying to win. The silence over the CU let Kahn know that she might have come off wrong so she spoke again.

"Sub Commander Rodgers, Mike, I am not here to criticize. What I am saying is the only strategy that has ever worked against a technologic superior force is to go to ground. Think barbarians verses Rome, Native Americans verses the Europeans, Vietnamese verses Americans, and Europa verses Mars. It is the only way. Bleed them to death," said Kahn. Rodgers understood the strategy and had contemplated it an hour ago but he could bring himself to give that type of order. To him it signaled defeat. He also remembered that Kahn's channel was still monitored by the Poveen.

"So, I have to face the fact that I lost the planet. I remember when Masters ordered me to Kush and you objected. I wish he would have sent you to Kush," Rodgers joked.

"I am glad he didn't because I would dead. I don't have the meteor kit in my variant armor. I would have been standing on the bridge of Oko Station the same as you. I would have burned up in orbit. Secondly, the battle of Kush was made for a knuckle dragger like you," joked Kahn in return. Rodgers laughed a little. That was the first giggle he had since he landed on the planet. It felt good.

"I am going to think about it. I still may just launch an all-out and attack and go out in a glorious battle. I will take your words to heart when I decide my strategy. Take care of yourself Priyanka. You have been a great commander and a good friend. I wish you luck. After we leave the city I won't be able to communicate until someone comes to get us," said Rodgers as if he was saying goodbye forever. That was a very real possibility after the events of the last week. Either one of them could die before the conflict was over.

"Good bye Mike. Take care of yourself," responded Kahn.

Rodgers waited a second and contacted Lord Commander Masters. A minute later Masters connected to him.

"Sir, we have a new plan of action for Kush. If we continue to engage with the Poveen in pitched battles we will not win the conflict. I believe the best and only solution to prolong the engagement and provide our forces with the ability to fight back is Guerrilla warfare campaign," said Rodgers to Masters.

"Damn. I am sorry Sub Commander Rodgers. I am sorry that I did not put you in a situation to win the ground war," said Masters.

"Sir, you are not to blame for this. When you have been around as long as I have you understand the difference between a shit assignment, shit commander, and fubar of war. This is fubar sir. We are still here because you acted with great speed when the conflict started. You didn't hide from your responsibility. You didn't make brass and dumb decisions. You acted like a great man and a great soldier. You have been dealt one of the shittiest hands ever and you are still in the game. No, sir. I won't let you take any blame for this. They will control Kush soon but they will not own Kush. We will go into the grass, wheat, mountains, lakes, and woods to regroup and then strike out one at a time. This battle is far from over," said Rodgers.

"Mike, good luck. Send an updated battle plan when you have it," said Masters.

Rodgers called an emergency meeting of what was left of the senior staff on the planet. For thirty minutes, they worked out the plan for dividing the forces. Each soldier will protect a family or a group of 5 to 8 civilians. Armored units will head to the massive forest to the south. Air units will head to the northern forested areas. Tactical Puppets would spread out and hid in barns and other structures.

Thoth, the planetary AI, provided a target location for every person and solider on the planet. The civilians still in their homes were ordered to stay and sent notification that one or two soldiers would come to join. Other civilians now homeless were attached to teams of soldiers. They would flee the cities and head into the country. Food and water would not be a problem for the resistance since Kush was agricultural plant and in the short term both resources were plentiful. The most important items for the people to take from the cities now were ammunition and battery replacements.

Thoth shut down the massive underground water network. The system would remain off for the next ten hours. Access to the massive tunnels would be available for soldiers and civilians to exit the cities. The deployment of had just started of civilians and the solider escorts began. The command deck bustled with activity. One soldier or officer after another left the command deck. In less than two hours the two major hubs of humanity that remained on the planet would be attacked and destroyed. Rodgers now raced against time to get as many people out of the cities as possible before the enemy arrived.

He walked into his ready room off the main command deck to make one more call before the network was destroyed. Rodgers was not the only Sub Commander on the ropes. The QEN on Kush was headquartered in Oko. When he left the city, they would destroy the network on the way out. This would be the last time he would be able to speak to Sub Command Yosef Amir until the conflict ended.

"Hello Sub Commander," said Amir as she grinned at the contact.

"I know you are a busy man so I will keep this short. I am about to lose my QEN. Before that happened I just wanted to wish you luck. I don't know which one us is fucked more but I think we will need all the luck we can receive in the hours to come. It has been a pleasure Sub Commander," said Rodgers.

"I wish you luck as well my friend. It has been a pleasure serving with you. If we get out of this. Drinks on you and I get to pick the spot," said Amir.

"How does that work?"

"You are old and you have money. That means drinks on you old man," said Amir. Rodgers laughed and Amir and smiled. Amir was not a good solider he was a great soldier. The service needed more like him thought Rodgers.

"Okay, drinks on me. Just don't have too many girls huddled around the table. Laura will get jealous," joked Rodgers. Amir laughed again. The two men traded banter for the better part of five minutes until the call ended. Rodgers put on his combat helmet and walked out of the ready room. It was time to start his preparation to move out of the city.

PLUS 171 HOURS 30 MINUTES
DRAGONS CORPS GENERAL
DESIGNATION: A1D7 NAME: LAURA OBAN
NAPATA CITY, KUSH
GET OUT

A1D7 gathered her team of officers together for the last time. The group of soldiers and officers were her family. They were all born in the same installation at the same time. They all lived the same life of the genetically engineered soldier. Most of them, like A1D7, had finally made a connection with the humanity that they protected. When the conversation started, it described tactics and methods of survival. A1D7 highlighted the terrain, the people, roads, bridges, and best methods of staying alive but the soldiers knew all of that.

When she ordered her fellow Protocol 5 humans to stay alive it changed the mood of the room. A1D7 removed the large black helmet shaped roughly like a mythical dragon. Orange skin, blue eyes, and short blue hair seemed to glow in the room. Soldiers and officers alike who watched and listened to A1D7, Laura Oban, removed helmets as well.

An array of colored faces highlighted the diversity of the corps. Orange, blue, purple, brown, white, and red skin tones reflected the various systems the DNA used to create these soldiers originated. The all-female Dragon Corps now free of the mechanical voices used by the helmets could speak freely. The once lifeless room suddenly had a soul. The women moved around saying goodbye to good friends. A1D7 walked over to E2D7, her best friend, Jamie Juelz. Short stubble blonde hair covered her head as her equally blue eyes looked locked. A1D7 pounded on the front of her shoulders and then leaned forward to touch her foreheads.

"Jamie, take care of yourself out there. Don't do anything stupid," said A1D7.

"Don't worry about me. I will be fine. But I must ask you something," responded Jamie Juelz.

"Sure, what is it."

"Laura, I do not have the clearance but I know you do. Is Solis still alive? The reports from that region of the battle are terrible. I need to know the truth. Please, tell me the truth," asked her friend.

"Jamie, Morris is dead," said A1D7 to her friend.

"That is what I heard. I heard from some Meteors that fled from Piye Station during the battle. I needed to know for sure. I will miss him. I need you to stay alive Laura. I can't lose everyone to them," said Jamie Juelz.

"I understand. I…I don't know what I will do if something happens to Mike. I…I…Jamie, take care of yourself out there. I expect to see you when this is over. Survive solider," said A1D7 as she fought back tears. Her friend Jamie Juelz was unable to speak and just nodded. Jamie Juelz wiped a tear from her eye and put on her helmet. The same discussion took place around the room and friends said goodbyes and wished comrades luck on the next stage of the battle.

Clicks, hisses, and pops echoed around the room as helmets locked into place. The current mission was to provide ground support to the withdrawal of the civilians of Napata City. The Poveen ground forces were almost at the outer perimeter of the city. The Kush regular army oversaw the evacuation of civilians out of the city and they would be assigned to accompany the civilians. Kush regulars were from the planet and the region. Army units had been broken down into small 2 and 3 man teams. The Kush regular army had been dismantled.

The Dragon Corps soldiers maintained the last fighting force in the city. They would continue to function as a fighting force until all civilians and soldiers had escaped. At that time, the Dragon Corps soldiers will disband and move to the designated outpost across the planet. That was the plan A1D7 was going to implement. She commanded that fighting force and the city was not going to fall under her watch.

Massive water distribution tunnels would be the avenue of retreat. It would allow the soldiers and civilians in the city to get of the city without the need to fight through the Poveen blockade. The Poveen seemed to be unaware that the massive tunnels were no longer filled with water and were now being used as escape tunnels. The Poveen will find out eventually but until that time it was the fasted way out of the cities and the safest. The tunnels stretched for hundreds of kilometers in all directions. One by one vehicles loaded with two to three soldiers and a family, group of friends, or a random selection of people hovered into the large tunnels and left the city.

A1D7 monitored the retreat of human forces while she simultaneously monitored the advance of Poveen. Hundreds of thousands of units raced to the city from all directions. She continued to press the soldiers and civilians to get out of the city faster but the retreat took much longer than they expected. The Dragon Corps would have to hold out for much longer. That meant more of her soldiers were going to die defending the city.

A1D7 stood at one of the forward operating stations at the edge of the city with the city center behind her. The matte black monstrous dragon armored soldiers checked her operating systems and weapons systems.

Once the checklist of items was completed she waited for the enemy to come. Sounds and sights of war could be heard and seen on the horizon. Automated weapons platforms meant to slow the Poveen advance were being silenced by the hoard of alien of invaders.

Automated anti-aircraft weapons erupted down the street from A1D7. The sound of the AA rattled around the glass and steal building amplifying the sound and volume of fire. That was when the panic began in the city. 60 percent had been evacuated but the other 40 percent now realized that the enemy was close. It started with a push and then a shove. The mass of civilians and regular soldiers moved with a greater sense of purpose. A1D7 called her units to the front. It was time for the battle of Napata City to begin.

A1D7 moved down the main street to a defensible position with the 100 soldiers of Alpha Company. Human drones took to the sky to battle the incoming Poveen aircraft. They raced and hissed skyward to challenge air superiority. A1D7 could feel the ground shake and rumble through the armored suit. The devilish wicked hum that accompanied the Poveen ground units grew louder by the second. A1D7 order one platoon of soldiers onto the roof of the five story buildings that dominated the intersection. The soldiers that remained took up positions on the ground of each corner. The enemy armor arrived.

The P5 human soldiers were the perfect response to a hostile universe. She was the byproduct of alien aggression and human engineering designed for this very mission. A1D7's entire life's purpose was to kill aliens and she would fulfill that purpose the best she could. An arched energy bolt slammed into the side of the one buildings. Glass and steel fell to the ground but the soldiers remained vigilant. Dust and debris limited visibility and the chaff fired by the human forces to confuse the alien sensors also confused the sensors of the Dragon Team. This fight would be an old-fashioned street fight.

A column of enemy armored units hovered down the main road in a single file line. Alpha Company fired on the armored units when they closed within 100 meters. The lead unit exploded shortly after the first barrage ended. The armored units burst into combat with sudden speed and agility. They bounced and darted over and around buildings to engage the dragon corps soldiers. The Dragons, unlike regular soldiers, could match the movements. To the surprise of the Poveen armored units they found themselves battling a swarm of angry equally equipped humans.

A1D7 watched as her soldiers fought to hold the line and it held. 10 armored units burned on the streets after three minutes of combat. Alpha Company sent a powerful message to the alien invaders. Napata City would be different. Her team reloaded quickly and waited for the second wave of aliens. A1D7's head set was flooded with reports of battles that occurred like her battle. The same battle took place around the city. The enemy would need to recalculate and that would take time. Time they needed because every second they delayed the advance of Poveen meant humans would safely get out of the city.

Poveen aircraft once occupied by drones and the anti-aircraft weapon systems swooped in on strafing runs. The first strafing run took the soldiers by surprise but the second didn't. Another combat education for the Poveen. The black dragon armor that all her soldiers wore was thick and heavy. The fire from the Poveen craft rippled and slammed into the dragon armor but it was mostly absorbed or deflected. The return fire, on the other hand, from the dragon's breath rounds fired from the massive rifles punched large holes in the Poveen craft.

The city of Napata would not fall quickly and the Poveen would understand that they would take heavy damage attacking it. If all the soldiers on the planet had her kit, training, and capability the Poveen would not stand a chance. Thought the cost and materials needed to make the kit uniform would probably bankrupt the system. Though, A1D7 imagined, aliens destroying the planets and moons was not good for the bottom line either.

Over the next hour her forces slowly decreased and she was forced to retreat closer to one of the exit tunnels. The city looked like a shadow of itself. Most of the buildings were now either on fire, frames of what was a great building, or a pile of rubble. The city of Napata would have to be completely rebuilt if it is rebuilt at all. A week ago the mighty city would have been rated in the top 5 of the human sphere for restaurant quality, scope, and culture. Now it was pile of steel and glass. The cost of war was not just measured in lives and property.

Loss of culture and history were equally as disturbing. She ate in the very square she stood in six months ago. Live instruments and reggae singers entertained as she sipped wine with her fiancée Mike Rodgers. Dancers would interrupt the singing with life and energy. Jazz musicians traded time with the reggae bands into the night. Freshly killed and cooked meats and grains were served. The well-seasoned and cooked food were the best she ate. Napata City was alive and vibrant when she visited. Now it was dead.

A1D7 received an update from the General of the Kush regular force that all the civilians were in the tunnels heading out of the city. The Dragon Corps could start to leave the carnage as well. Armored united moved down the street at greater number. Drones and automated units arrived en masse to support the armor. A1D7 dragged a member of Delta Company to a rear position of the line. Delta and Echo joined forces with Alpha. Together they only had roughly fifty soldiers left.

The Dragons completed the mission but the lines would soon break. A1D7 gave the command to her forces to retreat. She looked down at D3D7's smoking body. The soldier must have been hit as she dragged her to safety. A1D7 searched her kit for more ammo and resupplied as much as she could. The soldiers were running dangerously low on both ammo and power.

Escaping to the tunnel system was getting harder by the minute. More alien air units occupied the sky. They strafed any soldier that left cover. Enemy armor, the octo drones, and bio units pressed the attack around the perimeter. Even the shortest dip in the use of suppressing fire would lead to massive influx of enemy units. The enemy tried to bleed them of ammo of power with a full assault.

The satellite data she once enjoyed was gone. The Poveen space forces found the cloaked satellites in orbit. Communications were line of sight only. She sent the message to retreat but didn't receive many confirmations. Either more of her forces were gone or they did not hear the command. A1D7 had a choice to make. Either she would just broadcast the message to retreat and hope they all heard it or find higher ground to ensure that all her forces would make it.

For split second, she thought about ordering one of her soldiers to do it but she couldn't bring herself to. Sub Commander Mike Rodgers was all that she could think of next. This was a mission that was as close to a suicide mission as it got. This was the cost of leadership. Sometimes leaders had to eat last and in this case, she had to leave last. She turned to A2D7 and told him to lead Alpha company on the retreat in 10 minutes. A1D7 was going up into one of the last buildings that stood to transmit to the rest of the Dragon Division 7 spread out across the city.

A1D7 moved at speed to the tallest building not destroyed and ran into the lobby of the building. The once stunning lobby and courtroom were now covered in debris and dirt. All the massive windows were now destroyed and the ground now covered in a layer of ash. She ran to the elevator bank and found an elevator. Once inside she destroyed the ceiling of the elevator and flew up the passage to the roof under the power of her suit.

The 40-story climb took less than two minutes. She reached the subroof of the building. A1D7 ran to the window that faced the center of the city. The view was surreal. The once beautiful city was completely gone. Light from explosions and the sounds of war now owned Napata. Though it was mid-day the sun was muted by the sheer amount of smoke and debris now in the atmosphere.

She scanned the terrain for her force's transponders and then started to broadcast. One by one she received replies from the current company commanders with agreement. Once the last commander responded she turned to leave the building when she heard three distinct explosions beneath her. Three enemy aircraft flew through the building at speed ten floors down trying to collapse the building. It shimmied and shock but it held.

The sound of buckling metal highlighted her need to get out of the building. Outside the building ten enemy aircraft hovered on all sides waiting for whoever was sending messages to flee the building. A1D7 decided that she would go back the way she came even though the building could collapse at any second. It was still the safer option. She ran to elevator and jumped down shaft freefalling to the bottom.

Meters from the ground she kicked on the flight system and slowly landed. She rolled a small metal drone about the size and shape of a marble into the lobby. Outside the lobby armored units were taking up positions to destroy anything that came out. She cursed under her breath and then performed a quick check on her ammunition and power. While she scanned she saw the elevator pad had three buttons for basements listed.

A1D7 took out two grenades and armed them. Seconds later she dropped them to the floor of the elevator and counted. She stepped out the elevator and fired on the lead armor unit as the grenades exploded in the elevator and then jumped back into the shaft. The grenade ripped a hole in the floor that she jumped into. The freefall lasted a couple of brief seconds. When she reached the bottom, she kicked open the shaft door.

Her armor collapsed so she could fit down the normal sized hallway but this would prevent her from making any quick turns and would leave her back exposed. She tossed the last two grenades in the hallway behind her to collapse it as she continued to search for a way out of the building. A1D7 searched for a sewer entrance or the location for the water main. Both would lead to the massive tunnels that all the civilians and soldiers used to get out of the city. Above the building screeched and moaned. The building was going to collapse and she needed to get out.

Onboard sensors swept the area desperately looking for exit but the damage to the building and the sheer volume of rubble in the hallways made the reading confusing. Onboard AI struggled to locate the correct avenue of egress. The ground shook violently as the building begun to collapse. For the better part of a minute the ground shook and shimmed violently tossing her about. When it was over A1D7 lay in the hallway laughing. In almost the last second possible she found a subterranean hallway to the sister building that was destroyed earlier. She exited threw a maintenance tunnel.

She activated her active camouflage and stepped from the tunnel and made her way to the underground tunnel entrance. The retreat was surprisingly uneventful until she reached the exit. The battle raged between the dragon forces and armored spheres. A1D7 needed to move quickly if she was going to get out of the situation.

About 100 meters separated her and the front line of her retreating forces while 300 meters behind her more Poveen forces moved in for the kill. When the concentrated fire started to hit the armored units, she broke from her stealth and flew as fast as her armor could take her. Armored forces and air units were taken by surprise as if they didn't believe the readouts that an enemy soldier came from behind. Banking and dodging her suit made it past the enemy picket with minimal damage. Pleased that none of Dragon Corps soldiers shot her by mistake she quickly made her way to the exit area.

Dragon Corps soldiers filled the courtyard. The families assigned to the dragon team members had all left in panic with other forces. Though the civilians fled early the wounded Kush regular soldiers and Dragon Corps officers surrounded the exit. Combat medics quickly worked on the wounded and tried to find vehicles to support the exodus. Vehicles assigned for the dragons were converted to mobile hospitals and driven down the waterways.

Every healthy member took a wounded member after they were stabilized by the medics. Only three companies remained above. Alpha Company would hold the line until the other two companies were in ready to destroy the entrance to the waterway. Bravo Company contained a group of long-range snipers that held the Poveen at distance for the moment and supported Echo company who placed the demolition charges. They didn't want to be followed down the hole and they hoped that the time it took the Poveen to dig into the tunnels they would have escaped. The water network would turn on once they left the tunnels and if the Poveen followed at a later time they could be swept away in the torrent.

The word finally came that the explosives had been placed. Echo company took heavy losses during the fighting. A1D7 searched for E2D7, here friend Jamie Juelz, at the edge of the area that lead into the tunnel. Almost all the soldiers that arrived at the entrance to the tunnels were injured. That's when E12D7 landed next to the tunnel entrance holding E2D7. A1D7 walked over to the soldier and asked what happened. She was caught in a blast and was knocked out by the shockwave. The doctor said she would be okay shortly.

A1D7 told the soldier that she would take the soldier from here. She obeyed her commanding officer and placed her friend on the ground and picked up another wounded soldier and headed into the tunnel. Before moving away E12D7 spoke to A1D7.

"Take care of her," said the soldier.

A1D7 nodded in agreement and said out loud, "Her fate will be mine. This is my friend." A sense of relief came over the solider as E12D7 then moved out with another injured soldier. Members of Alpha Company poured into the tunnel. Each one gathered an injured member of another company and moved down the tunnel. The enemy made a massive push on the location. The last vehicle left in the tunnel signaled to A1D7 that all the injured soldiers were in the vehicle and that everyone could retreat. Though they would have to flee on foot they would have enough time to get hundreds of kilometers away from the city before the water returned.

It took less than 5 minutes for the rest of the soldiers that had performed guard duty to reach the entrance. Once inside they set off the first round of explosives. It collapsed the buildings around the entrance to the tunnel system and bought the soldiers that now ran down the tunnel at extreme speed more time. The second round of explosions destroyed the entrance to the tunnel system and the tunnel itself. It collapsed the tunnel on top of itself for a 5-kilometer radius around the previous entrance.

They made it out of the city in less than 10 minutes. Now A1D7 had to make it to the rally point hundreds of kilometers to the north to connect with Rodgers.

PLUS 175 HOURS
SPACE COMMAND QUASAR
VALERIE RODRIGUEZ
BATTLENOVA, PLANET KILLER, NUBIA
FIGHT ME

Planet Ender and Star Killer were reunited for the first time since their unit jumped into the Nubian system for repairs. Taskforce 1 formed in space an hour prior hurtling toward Nubia in preparation for Operation Avenger. Rodriguez, usually the most confident person in the room, felt doubt. The Nubian system was at the breaking point. This single conflict would determine the course of the conflict.

Rodriguez was helpless when the reports of the attack on Hannibal Battle Station flooded in. The collective military body of the system watched in anticipation for the outcome. Vice Commander Kahn won the battle and the station was currently holding. She equally felt helpless when reports of the total defeat of human forces on Kush. The United Planets of Humanity Armed Forces were forced to run and hide from the Poveen. They now engaged in guerrilla warfare against Poveen.

Rodriguez understood it was her turn to contribute to the war effort. The United Planets of Humanity Armed Forces lost Comet Corps Quasar

Tanaka on Peachtree when the entire moon's population was lost. Humanity lost System Logistics General Okafor at the Barca Staryards, System Meteor General Solis at Piye Station, and System Orbital Guard General Johnson on the Oya Battle Station. It wasn't clear if Sub Commander Rodgers and A1D7 were still alive on Kush. System Planetary commander Nasir was engaged in the largest land battle humans fought in over 100 years.

Her avatar stood on the beautiful computer generated bridge next to the tall Captain Reiner. The pale skinned man stood stoic with the gaze of power. Thirty officers sat behind them in regal white combat station. The bridge was reconfigured to accommodate the extra officers. All hands would be on deck for the battle. Systems were checked, rechecked, and then checked again. It was time.

Rodriguez turned to the bridge crew and yelled, "Here we go. Time to send these squids back to the hell they came from". Captain Reiner smiled and the started the starship's chant. The entire bridge crew erupted into the chant as they watched the first of the projectiles fired from Hannibal Battle Station struck the Poveen invasion force above Nubia.

The rain of the projectiles slammed into the Poveen formation. The Poveen cruisers were tightly packed into a large diamond formation. Overlapping shields absorbed most of the wave of projectiles. The larger rounds in the second barrage slammed into the Poveen cruisers. Those rounds seemed to create more damage on the Poveen.

One…two…three…four Poveen cruisers ripped apart under the tremendous power of the projectiles. At this range they could identify the 4 interdictor CIC cruisers. Every Poveen cruiser was identified by an orange triangle accept for the 4 CIC cruisers. These were highlighted with red on the massive tactic screen. Another wave of large projectiles ripped into the picket cruisers tearing them two of them to pieces.

The Poveen jumped into action after that attack. Heavy cruisers moved into position to block the path of the projectiles that remained inbound. The first salvo worked to expose the tactics of the enemy. The remaining salvos needed to destroy the enemy formation to allow for the destruction of the CIC cruisers. Rodriguez started to target the cruisers that needed to be destroyed for the attack force to pound the CIC cruisers. The S7 missiles that raced toward the planet Nubia from the surrounding local area now had targets. Captain Reiner began to pick out a firing solution of one for the CIC cruisers.

The second salvo of the first wave of fast-moving projectiles travelled toward the Poveen constellation 45 seconds ahead of the starship Task force. The second wave consisted of S7 Missiles fired from the Sentry 7 defenses system that now operated around the system. The once dominate system now launched weapons in anger to help the rest of the human forces in the system. The fourth wave consisted of thousands of assault craft from the Nubian Moon.

When the second salvo of the first wave was millimeters from the outer shielding of contact the entire Poveen formation blinked. They blinked 2 AU away from the planet of Nubia. Projectiles fired from the Hannibal Battle Station would travel for eternity in the deep black of space never to strike the target. The second wave of S7 missiles used the gravity of Nubia to sling shot toward the sun on the most optimal path to return to Nubia. Taskforce 1 quickly retargeted the front lines of the Poveen ground forces now exposed from orbit.

On the surface of the planet energy weapon fire burned through the atmosphere and decimated enemy forces. Due to the speed of the spacecraft they were only on station for two seconds but the orbital strafe caused tremendous damage. On the ground the explosions and impacts of thousands of space craft firing on the surface was clear. The Poveen ground forces suffered a major blow.

The fourth wave and the slowest moving wave of assault craft from Luna Nubia. Held back until this point they were now unleashed to the maximum of potential. The first group to enter the upper atmosphere. Unlike the SF-11 Tigers, the SAF-03 Wolverines, were fighter craft that could operate in the atmosphere and in the space. The dual usage made it extremely versatile in planetary defense and was the main reason why this fighter was exclusively stationed on the Nubia moon. The fighter craft shrugged off the frictions caused by reentry with a hard energy shield that absorbed the energy.

Next Rodriguez commanded the two hundred thousand craft spread out to attack the 3800-kilometer-long front line. They fired energy and kinetic weapons on the defenseless Poveen armies on the surface of the planet. One the attack run was over the Wolverines climbed into high orbit to travel around the planet and strike again. Starpuppets, also designed for use in space and atmosphere, raked the enemy lines next. Finally, were the starbombers. They inflicted tremendous damage with the sixty thousand pound kinetic missiles they rained down on the surface.

The waves of the assault craft didn't go unscathed in the conflict. Anti-starcraft weapons system fired on assault craft from the surface. The lower orbit and slower speed made the target much easier to fire upon. Poveen ground force units stopped the attacks on began to pull back from the front line. The space force broke many battle lines on the ground and Poveen moved to plug the widening gaps.

The blink of the alien formation was not by accident. Quasar Rodriguez studied the new deployment and the brilliance of the maneuver. S7 missiles travelled at relativistic speeds and lacked advanced maneuvering ability. If Taskforce 1 wanted to make the orbit around the sun with the S7 missiles they would have to accelerate to catch the missiles. When they accelerated, the taskforce would lose the ability to intercept the enemy formation and make the turn around the Nubian sun. Poveen heavy cruisers, on the other hand, would be able to rake both the missiles and the taskforce as they travelled past without the human force able to effectively return fire.

Rodriguez ordered the taskforce to accelerate to catch the S7 missile. The attack force would stick together for the moment. The battlefield was in motion. At times like this the commanding officers had to remain calm. Rodriguez and Reiner discussed the tactics of the enemy to search for the meaning behind the blink. Projections from the onboard AI projected that the Poveen formation would cause considerable damage when they travelled passed the formation but the taskforce would remain largely intact.

Reiner cursed before the soft-spoken Rodriguez. The Poveen taskforce that burned toward Hannibal Battle Station from Kush blinked as well. Due to the light delay it took over ten minutes for them to receive the data but that the maneuver was conducted. The second Poveen formation couldn't blink the entire distance but they would easily reach the intercept point of the formation that blinked from Nubia. With this one move the enemy could destroy the bulk of the human space force.

Rodriguez had three choices. The first choice would be to full stop all the missiles and spacecraft in the task force and burn back to the planet. This maneuver would eat up massive energy reserves and fuel. The second choice was to burn toward the Poveen Fleet instead of the current heading to use the sun as a slingshot. In this scenario, they would not be able to use the sun the sling shot but they would have engaged the enemy with offensive weapons if they decided to fight it out instead of using the blink technology. This scenario was the highest risk and reward mission. If it didn't work, they would be in the black for almost a day.

The third choice was to abandon the mission entirely. If the goal of the taskforce was to destroy the 4 CIC cruisers to open an ER gate out of the system to receive help from other systems to push back the enemy. If they discarded the current mission and took on the mission of destroying the massive Poveen ground mission then they would prevent the Poveen from occupying the planet. Rodriguez liked that plan the best and after a five-minute conversation with Lord Commander Masters he agreed.

The taskforce banked at the maximum allowed vector. The Space Command vessels and the human occupants moaned and creaked as the starships turned at 30 g back to Nubia. Once during the turn when the gravity spiked slightly over 30gs Rodriguez was ejected from the program and her consciousness was returned. She felt the full force of the maneuver on her body. Space Command officers usually were spared the pain of gravity maneuvers but not this time. The pain subsided shortly after and she was reinserted into the virtual environment.

Once she returned Rodriguez ordered The S7 missile to change vectors to intercept the force headed toward the previous intercept point. Now they would have to blink or fight the thousands of S7 missiles bound to sling shot around the sun. Masters granted her further access to more Sentry 7 satellites in deeper orbits around the system. S7 missiles fired from the Sentry 7 satellites and thousands more S7 missiles burned toward Nubia once again.

The full complement of starvettes, starbombers, one third of the starfighters, and one third of the starpuppet's force rounded Nubia and burned into deep space. The assault force would burn to intercept the Poveen formation that was previously in orbit around Nubia. This force was tasked with the harassment of the Poveen force. When the Poveen force blinked back to Nubia the assault craft would keep travelling until they reached Kush. At Kush, they would perform an orbital attack mission on the Poveen force that didn't have much space protection.

She was then pinged by System General Nasir. Rodriguez was not expecting the ping but welcomed it. "General what can I do for you?"

"You already did it. I don't know how you did it but thank you. You saved a lot of Nubian's today. At best, you turned the tide of battle at worst you gave us a chance to regroup and hold them to a stalemate. Either way I thank you. I owe you one," said Nasir. Rodriguez smiled at the notion. For the last thirty minutes, everything was so academic. The mental battles of leadership of Space Command but lives were on the line.

Rodriguez experienced war in the virtual environment, in contrast, war touched all five senses for Nasir. He saw the wounded. Heard the cries of the dying. Smelled the burned flesh. Touched the lifeless corpses. Tasted the ash in the air on the planet he called home. He could hide from the emotional responses the most basic sense would trigger. This compelled him to call in the middle of the battle. Rodriguez could only imagine the relief.

"No problem Nasir. We are not finished yet. We are on our way back. We are going to make another run before the enemy blinks back. If you want targets taken out send them to use. We will put them on the list," said Rodriguez.

"Take care of yourself Quasar," said Nasir as his avatar stared at Rodriguez in the vertical world. Rodriguez fell silent and the two just looked at each other.

"I am coming back that way now, get your drinks ready," joked Rodriguez. On the surface, they laughed for moment and then returned to the task at hand. Rodriguez moved back to the bridge of the Planet Ender and watched the countdown timer until the Poveen could blink safely again. Rodriguez and Reiner traded ideas on next steps and possible reactions to the maneuver they just pulled by the alien invaders.

Until this point in the battle Rodriguez wondered if Masters' decisions to hold the S7 missiles until this point in the conflict was wise. Rodriguez thought they should have been used sooner but their usage as a force multiplier to support a large space forces seemed to work. They allowed for the instant bolster of the fighting force. They presented a serious threat to lone or small formations of cruisers. The threat they posed took some options from the enemy. His plan worked so far and Rodriguez had to ensure that she held up her end of the bargain.

This force has already suffered massive damage but so has the enemy. They are close to the point in which they must have to choose to either call in the reinforcements from the outside or cancel the plan altogether. But two things would happen on the next pass of Nubia. Either Rodriguez would engage with the enemy in space or she would burn the ground troops into the fires of hell when they returned. In 2 hours that is what was going to happen.

45 minutes later and not one force deviated from the previous course of action. Rodriguez and her force burned to slow down to the enter orbit around Nubia and the moon in a figure 8 pattern. Taskforce 1 wouldn't have to slow down in this type of orbit but they wouldn't be able to linger on the station over the Poveen forces still on the planet. The assault starships force burned toward the Nubia invasion force and the S7 missiles from the original attack burned toward the Kush Invasion force between Nubia and the sun.

Quasar Rodriguez and Captain Reiner watched as new targeting information populated on the screen as one fire solution after another matched with the ground targets. The task force moved to engage land targets once again though this time they were travelling much slower than they were before. They would be able to fire down on the planet at least three times before they would move out of range.

As the first weapons fired the Poveen invasion force designed to attack Nubia blinked back into position. Rodriguez's task force was raked from higher orbit at point blank range by the alien invaders. The arching energy blast destroyed twenty percent of the force and damaged over 60 percent of the attacking force but Rodriguez's task force pummeled the Poveen ground forces. Three salvos of high energy, railgun, and missile ripped into the Poveen ground force.

Once again, the forces on the ground suffered horrendous losses from the orbital fire. The remaining space craft in the taskforce 1 rounded the planet and headed toward the moon. Every starship that could fly launched from the moon and moved to join the Taskforce. This would be the final assault on the Poveen formation.

Quasar Rodriguez yelled out loud on the bridge, "This ends now. Eject all nonessential personnel into the atmosphere above allied territory when we pass by Nubia. All remaining personnel prepare for hard ejection. We will ram the one, the other battlenova will ram the other CIC cruiser, and the rest of the force will take out the other two. The assault craft will clean up the mess we leave behind. Everyone got that?" The entire bridge was silent but within a couple of seconds the silence ended.

The Planet Ender took control of about 25 percent of the task force as the crew ejected into the Nubian atmosphere. Those starships would be used as the buffer between the 2 battlenovas and the Poveen force. The captain of the other nova performed the same maneuver. They would take out the four CIC cruisers on this pass or the task force would be destroyed. Masters sent her a message that merely said, "Good luck".

As the newly formed battering rams rounded the planet they fired the engines to maximum 30g burn toward the enemy. Masters ordered from the space station to move into vectors to expose themselves to enemy fire. Within minutes the stations started to fire on the Poveen formation. The energy beams reigned into the Poveen picket cruisers and heavy cruisers. The massive taskforce swung around the planet inbound for the Poveen force at high velocity.

One second she was on the bridge of the Planet Ender and a second later her pod tumbled in space. The horizon flipped and spun. Nubia and space flashed rapidly in all directions and spun wildly. The nanites franticly created a spacesuit for her in case the pod was damaged. Brilliant flashes of light could be seen all around the her but she could not pinpoint anything until the pod stopped its spin.

The pod righted itself after a thirty second tumble. Distress calls could be heard en masse. Escape pod beacons flashed by the thousands. The light from the antimatter explosions faded. Debris was everywhere in the orbit. Rodriguez could see large pieces of both human starships and Poveen cruisers falling into the Nubia's atmosphere with her. Assault craft whipped passed at least three times. Rodriguez saw another round of explosions before the heat from reentry denied her the ability to watch the battle. That was the second round of S7 missiles.

A projectile ripped into the pod. It vented nanites and air into space for a second before the hole closed itself. Two more projectiles ripped into the pod. Warning lights flashed on her HUD but Rodriguez knew what happened already. One of the projectiles ripped into her flesh. Her lower left leg was gone and half of the pod with it. The nanites corrected quickly but too much damage was done to the pod and to Rodriguez. The O2 leak exploded in the hot gas of reentry causing the pod to explode. Rodriguez's war was over and so was her life..

PLUS 177 HOURS
ASTRO CORPS QUASAR
NATASHA MIGHT
STEALTHSTAR, DEEP BLACK
BLINK

Natasha Might woke from her sleep in the crash bed. She performed a quick wipe of her blue eyes and turned on the light to a low setting. It was the first time she slept in forty hours. Six hours of sleep wasn't enough but it would have to do. They had roughly two and half hours until contact with the enemy. Might reached out with her CU to update her. Quasar Rodriguez was in one hell of fight around Nubia. In 30 minutes taskforce 1 would arrive around Nubia for the second time for another major battle.

The two-meter-tall woman stood from the bed and placed her pale feet against the black floor. She stood from the crash bed and stretched her hands but hit them on the ceiling. Returning to the crash bed she stretched her hands upward cracking her back and then stood again. She moved to the small shower in the commander quarters and turned on the hot water. It felt good to clean off the grim and grit of the previous standard days.

After five minutes, she exited the shower. Still wet she grabbed her exo-suit and quickly stepped inside. When she washed in the shower the suit ran a self-clean cycle to purge it of the impurities it absorbed over the past 40 hours. Something as small as a clean body and uniform performed wonders for the mind. Nervousness flooded Might as the reports of the battle at Nubia raged. If Quasar Rodriguez couldn't take out the 4 cruisers than what she was about to do was pointless.

She survived two engagements with the Poveen during the conflict already but the chances that she survived a third was slim. If she survived this conflict she would celebrate for days. Might would drink any drink, party at every party, and conquer any suitor worth conquering. A smiled dominated her face as she walked to the bridge of the stealthstar.

Quasar Might's constellation burned toward the last CIC interdictor cruiser in the deep black of the system. It was guarded by 97 Poveen Cruisers. The enemy placed it deep inside a diamond formation. The Quasar looked at the tactical readout as her forces crossed the 2-hour mark to contact. Her forces. That was laughable. She only had 107 starships in her group with only 31 being heavies. Normally they didn't stand a chance against a Poveen formation of that size.

The bridge of the stealthstar went silent as they watched Taskforce 1 round Nubia and eject life pods. Might smiled and yelled, "That crazy bitch is going to ram them."

Yells and woots overcame the bridge as they watched the battle like a major motion picture. Taskforce 1 dove into combat. Transponder beacons from the human starships blinked out all at once except for a couple. They watched as the assault craft and the S7 barraged hit next. The Poveen force over Nubia was decimated. The target craft were all gone after the assault. They did it, only one CIC cruiser was left and she was headed right for it.

The bridge went silent and the mood turned somber. They just lost the entire Taskforce in that mission and now the rest of mission would depend on them. Might didn't know how the enemy would react so she ordered the heavy starships to the outer front of the wedged shaped formation to ensure that they were ready for a blink counterattack. The remaining frigates and speedstars were still heavily damaged from the previous battle. Repair crews on the starships worked around the clock to get those starships ready for combat. Might had sixteen dreadstars mostly in good repair. That would be the backbone of her force. The heavy guns, maneuverability, and armor of the vessel will provide the punch that they would need to break the formation and fuck that asshole. Asshole remained the term the formation used to describe the CIC cruiser. After Masters' outburst, when he used the word asshole to describe one of the previous CIC cruisers. Might adopted the word and continued to use it, then her crew used it, and then the starship AI deduced its meaning and it used it. It stuck.

Her CU pinged. Lord Commander Masters was on the other end. Might surprisingly wasn't in the mood for a pep talk. She knew what had to be done but when your commanding officer calls you better answer. His dark brown skin and angular features filled her field of view.

"Quasar Might. I know we have asked a lot of you. We need one more thing from you. We need you to destroy or force the interdictor CIC cruiser to blink. That's it. Its destruction is ideal but if it jumps you completed the mission. Good luck, and by the way. Help is now on the way," said the Lord Commander as the communication ended. Well at least that was quick she thought but what help was he referring too.

Sensors on the bridge of the stealthstar went crazy with new contacts. A roar of cheers echoed on the bridge as the reality started to sink in. Masters activated the weapon systems of the Sentry 7 system. Thousands of missiles from the region burned to catch her formation at 90gs. As more time passed missile systems fired from locations closer to the projected combat location. Waves and waves of missiles now in formation burned on multiple vectors in various configurations.

Hours later Quasar Might's forces were only a couple of minutes away from reaching the target. The constellation rerouted to ensure S7 missiles wouldn't hit them when they performed advanced maneuvers. Space around the enemy formation was crowded with missiles and starships bent on destroying the last and final CIC interdictor cruiser in the system. The entire system was counting on her and Orunmila to guide the missiles, stars, and bullets into Asshole.

The Poveen formation fired on the incoming missiles. The first wave, on the other hand, were all kinetic missiles. It took much longer to burn them down to atoms and plasma but the Poveen forces were clearly ready for the attack. The first wave was largely unsuccessful but the second and third waves started to pound the outer shielding of the Poveen formation. Seventy-two vectors of approach made it extremely difficult for the enemy to intercept all the missiles. In all 3 thousand missiles approached at speeds ranging from ten percent the speed of light to one percent.

One after another Poveen cruisers who failed to intercept the missiles in time exploded or were ripped in two by the fast-moving projectiles. Might's starships burned into the maelstrom of debris and missiles. They smashed into the enemy at speed firing until they ran out ordinance. The human starships on the outside of the formations didn't last long as they were cut to pieces until they reached asshole. Every human starship that survived fired on Asshole. Poveen cruisers tried to get in between them and Might's taskforce but asshole was getting pounded…hard.

Finally, after ten minutes of pounding Asshole from every vector and angle the cruiser blinked and everything changed. The bridge of the stealthstar erupted in cheers but the battle wasn't finished yet. They were deep into a Poveen formation and the way out wouldn't be easy. The Poveen cruisers continued to fire on her forces. Over the open channel, she called for all units to break formation and vector to Cartage if they could. Together they would all die but alone some would make it out the fray.

The sudden breaking change in vector by the starships sent the Poveen into a frenzy. S7 missiles hammered the Poveen picket cruisers as another wave entered combat. The constellation was taking massive damage. One after one the heavily damaged Poveen cruisers blinked out of the region of space. The healthy cruisers began pursuit of the fleeing starships. "Fuck, they aren't going to stop until we are destroyed," said Natasha Might to herself. The stealthstar's ability to hide was compromised during the battle and its lack of armor left it extremely susceptible to death.

It was out of both rounds for its railguns and out of missiles. The energy weapons would not penetrate the hulls or shielding of the healthy Poveen cruisers that rapidly followed them. The ship was under 20g burn but the enemy cruisers moved at 50g rate. They were angry as hell for what they did to their Asshole. One of the officers on the ship grabbed her arm and told her it was time to go. They saw the writing on the wall just like she did.

The stealthstars cut the burn to 5 gravities and turned around to fire the main energy weapon at the cruisers though they knew it wouldn't penetrate the shields. This orientation, on the other hand, placed an exit away from the Poveen death squad that marched toward them. The shields held for the moment but the cruisers gained on the stealthstar and once they moved closer the shield would fail. She followed the officers down to a small cargo hold. Two stealth starvettes were clamped clammed down in the hull. Rear doors to the cargo hold were already open and it was in complete vacuum.

They ran into port starvette and clamped themselves into the crash couches on the bridge. Pilots ran into the cockpit of the craft and powered up the craft quickly. With more than half the seats of the craft unoccupied the starvette left the cargo bay and moved away from the parent craft. The stealthstar they left took heavy fire and the shields buckled.

It exploded but they were not out of the woods yet. The Poveen cruisers moved on the same vector they were heading toward Carthage. If they got close enough they would be able to detect the starvette. Quickly they vectored away from Carthage with maneuvering thrusters only to evade the Poveen cruisers. Ten minutes of silence on the bridge was warranted. The stealth craft was targeted 3 times and the cruisers barely missed the stealth craft.

Each time the Poveen cruiser was unable to reestablish a lock. The stealth held and when the last Poveen cruiser passed headed toward Carthage they breathed a sigh of relief. Two hours after the Poveen cruiser moved forward the stealth starship started to burn toward to Carthage. Might didn't have advanced information on the state of the system but she made the cruiser blink. The ER gates must be open, they had to be open, and if not this entire mission was for nothing. It would take hours for the light delay to reach her at her current location.

PLUS 180 HOURS
COMMAND CORP SUB COMMANDER YOSEF AMIR
BUCKHEAD STATION, BUCKHEAD, ATLANTA
ACTIVATE THE GATE

The officers on Buckhead didn't have much to cheer about. The Poveen force that destroyed Peachtree moved toward Atlanta. It appeared they planned to attack Buckhead the same way they attacked Peachtree. The cruisers blinked away to gather the cubes that were launched at them and then they blinked back into formation. Sub Commander Amir stood on the command deck of Buckhead Station and watched the force move on a vector to intercept Buckhead.

Buckhead was older than Peachtree and its defenses were more formidable but nothing could stop a hundred building sized cubes of heavy metal dropped on a city from it being destroyed. Twenty-five million people lived on the Mars sized moon and Amir was doing everything that he could to make sure they didn't share the same fate of the millions of people on Peachtree and his good friend Tanaka. Though they held out hope that some people survived the onslaught. Buckhead station sent thirty probes to the surface of Peachtree to look for survivors but all they found so far was glass.

Quasar Ryu Tanaka was killed when those bastards dropped a cube on his head. He didn't want to share the same fate as his friend but the likelihood that he survived was slim. Though this time he would have all the resources at his disposal. Masters granted him control of the Sentry 7 system near his area of operation that he didn't need to support Might's mission toward the enemy fleet in the deep black. Missiles from the outer reaches of the Sentry 7 system would arrive in as short as 30 minutes and some in a little over three hours. Though Amir was hopeful that the missiles could stop the fleet or at least damage a good number of cruisers he knew that if Might was unsuccessful those missiles would be redirected.

He would take it. They just needed Might to take care of business and hold out until the barrage entered the planetary system. That would be a task that he didn't know if he could do. They had at least 100 cubes and he only had about 50 of what they called the anti-cube measures. Buckhead was the main mining facility so they had access to the machines that split asteroids. These machines land on asteroids, insert nuclear devices, and crack open the cubes breaking them into smaller pieces. The smaller pieces cannot penetrate the surface. They have been fitted with extra engines from Lions and Hyena assault craft to increase survivability.

Amir hoped that after they destroyed the first couple of cubes the enemy will switch tactics before they launched them all but he couldn't rely on such hope. Luckily the planet had planetary weapon systems but they are suited to take on a pirate attack on one of the logistics stations. They aren't equipped to take on Poveen cruisers at standoff range. They would be cautious. They were not prepared for the cube attack and they don't know if we had any more of those cubes or the means to launch them into space.

They moved the ER Gate to low orbit. Buckhead's low gravity and lack of atmosphere made the maneuver very easy. This would make its destruction much harder for the Poveen would have to get closer to the planet's surface that contained planetary gun systems. These energy based weapon systems could stand off with the cruisers for some time before they would be overwhelmed. His plan was to hold off the enemy force long enough to open the gate after Might attacked the Poveen force in the deep black.

Amir stood ready to defend the moon and the gate. Quasar Might approached the enemy formation. Amir sent a quick word of encouragement to her and wished her luck. She would need it and he would need it too. The officers on the command deck stood focused but the mood was tense. Amir walked around the deck to inject confidence in the officers. Morale was not good but it wasn't lost yet. Hope was on the horizon. The last battle of Nubia felt like it changed the tide of the conflict to favor the humans but only time would tell.

Orbital Guard officers in gate control started the activation process. In fifteen minutes when Might's starship entered combat they would continuously attempt to open the ER gate to the Drake system. Two entire battle groups anticipated the gate opening. They were poised to burn through the gate and cause havoc on the Poveen force. A formal calculation by Orunmila and the SciTech government would be used to fix the time dilation effect the interdictor field caused in local space by the CIC interdictor cruisers of the Poveen. Only time would tell if that method would work or not.

Amir was confident in the plan and the people. He trusted Lord Commander Masters with his life. If he said the plan was going to work then it was going to work. That belief drove him to do the same with the people under his command. This plan would work and he pressed the officers on the deck to ensure that they believed it as well. It worked. By the time the enemy attacked the officers of the command deck were ready for the fight.

The Poveen cruisers moved closer and started to release the building sized cubes toward the planet. The planetary weapon systems fired on the Poveen cruisers that dared to approach the moon. This kept the cruisers in a high orbit and unable to attack the smaller starships that were sent to land on the cubes and destroy them. They needed them to stay far enough away so they couldn't intercept the anti-cube systems. Rockets from the planet sent the machines hurdling toward the cubes. The payloads landed on the target cubes and then inserted the nuclear devices and exploded.

It was working. The first 14 cubes exploded into thousands of pieces.

Some hit the surface at speed but without much mass. They caused minimal damage but far less damage than an intact cube would have. Some pieces were tossed back at the Poveen fleet or into orbit. The Poveen cruisers moved closer to intercept the rockets on the next attempt. The fire from the planet hit those cruisers but the shielding of the alien craft held. More Poveen cruisers moved closer to planet to aid those that went sooner. They overlapped shields to repel the powerful energy blasts from the planet.

The enemy launched the next wave of cubes. 21 building sized cubes barreled toward the gravity well as seven of the Poveen heavy cruisers fired on the launching locations of the anti-cube measures on the planet's surface. The installations fired before they were razed from orbit. Rockets burned out of the gravity well and then the second stage of the rocket fired the anti-cube devices. Nineteen of the cubes were destroyed but two made it through.

One city and one mining facility were destroyed. 3 million people died in the attack. 4 Poveen cruisers were destroyed as they attacked the rocket installation. 4 other cruisers spit and spewed atmosphere and they returned to high orbit. Amir cursed and awaited another wave of 21 cubes. Most of the launchers were gone and they only had the ability to send up 6 rockets. 2…10…20…30 new contacts appeared on the screen. The three closest Sentry 7 Satellites fired the full complement of projectiles toward Buckhead. The missiles accelerated bent on stopping the cubes if they could. The ballistic nature of the cubes made them easy targets for the intercepting missiles. S7 missiles burned at ten percent the speed of light when they slammed into the side of the cubes. Kinetic energy on kinetic energy created a brilliant light.

Lord Commander Masters gave them a fighting chance and Sub Commander Amir would keep up the fight until he died. Cruisers moved into low orbit and attacked the planetary gun installations. The maneuver also allowed them to hide from the S7 missiles. Amir had to divert the missiles from targeting the Poveen cruisers while they were so close to the surface because of the vector of approach. If he committed the missiles to strike at the cruisers and they blinked the missiles would slam into the surface of the moon. Over the next thirty minutes one by one the planetary gun installations were destroyed. The alien invaders took a lot of damage as well but the overwhelming attack from the Poveen took its toll.

The moon was now completely defenseless except for the S7 missiles that orbited the gas giant Atlanta. If need it would only take 5 minutes for those missiles to come on station. Amir ordered the gate into higher orbit. This would negate the Poveen's ability to attack the gate while using the moon as cover. It moved close to the Buckhead orbital station. The station wasn't military but it did have a powerful enough shield that it would survive until the missiles arrived.

Sub Commander Amir's eyes travelled back and forth from the two screens at the front of the command center. On the left part of the screen they watch the Poveen forces rake the planet with the arch energy weapons. The cities and major installations of the planet had shielding that could protect from the weapon systems but they would not last forever. On the right part of the screen they watched as Quasar Might's force attacked the Poveen in the deep black of the system.

For two agonizing minutes she battled the enemy until something wonderful happened. The ER gate in orbit sparked to life. The massive ER Gate shined with brilliant blue energy. The jump gate reached its entire size and then a second later it collapsed to the size of child's ball when CIC cruiser's blinked back into normal space. The gate struggled and pushed to stay open. The AI on the gate auto corrected the formula that it was given by the Orunmila and the SciTech government. The gate grew and grew over the next minute to 3 meters in length. It would take time to grow the wormhole but it was open.

"Open damnit," yelled Amir on the bridge as the situation got more tense by the second. Both sides of the ER Gate poured more and more energy into the rift to fight back against the push of the interdictor technology. The Poveen reacted almost instantly. When the gate opened every Poveen cruiser blinked to assault the station. Arched lighting like energy bolts slammed into the station shields. Sub Commander Amir responded by calling all the S7 missiles that burned around the planet of

Atlanta to intercept the enemy craft.

The missiles accelerated to intercept speed and the battle started. Ten of the Poveen cruisers turned to fire on the S7 missiles. They intercepted about half of the incoming missiles but not all. Poveen cruisers were struck by the missiles. Some were destroyed and other vented atmosphere but they were still in the fight. More and more energy arched into the shielding until it collapsed.

"Noooooooooo," yelled Amir. They were so close. The energy ripped into the station and the ER gates. The wormhole collapsed when the ring took too many hits from the cruisers. The station was destroyed moments after. Amir slammed his hand on the desk breaking it in two. The station was destroyed and he was left speechless.

He opened a channel to Nubia. He wanted to speak to the Lord Commander.

"Sir, I am sorry but I failed. We did not hold the gate open," said Amir.

"We are having trouble here as well. Don't worry our gate is open and Vice Commander Kahn has a gate open. We are going to win the day Amir," said Masters.

"Thank you for having confidence in me sir. Thank you. We don't have much time left here so tell everyone else I said goodbye," said Amir as the channel closed.

With the threat of the S7 missiles the Poveen went back into high orbit to the cubes that they left. Without any planetary guns and the rest of the S7 missiles over an hour out they had no more protection. The Poveen dropped all the cubes to the surface. Amir would share the same fate as Quasar Tanaka. The cubes hit the moon with such force that the shielding systems designed to protect the cities broke. The battle for Atlanta was over and Peachtree and Buckhead were now destroyed.

PLUS 182 HOURS
COMMAND CORPS VICE COMMANDER
PRIYANKA KAHN
HANNIBAL BATTLE STATION, CARTHAGE
HOLD THE LINE

When the final CIC cruiser blinked rather than face destruction at the hands of the super cluster commanded by Quasar Might the two massive ER gates attached to Hannibal Station sparked to life. At first, they sparked to full of glory but when the CIC cruiser reentered the state of reality from the blink the gates came crashing down. Energy poured into the gates from both ends trying to stabilize the bridge against the mighty interdictor technology of the Poveen.

The strain and forces were too much for the gate that was once heavily damaged. It collapsed, under the pressure of the unknown technology. Hidden forces from the quantum realm materialized into normal space to tear and rip the gate apart. The other gate fought to hold the gate open and it did. Though at first it was only a fraction of the size of the full gate. The 5-meter-wide diameter wasn't even large enough for a fighter to pass through. Over time as the AI on Hannibal station calculated and recalculated the best use of energy as it learned the new physics needed to fight the interdictor technology.

Kahn watched the ER Gate flash and buck until it grew. 6 meters…7 meters…8 meters the ER Gate was getting larger. Every 5 minutes the gate doubled in size. Her brown eyes widened almost in disbelieve. Help was on the way. She threw her hand in the sky and cheered. The rest of the officers packed into gate command following her lead. Every minute the gate was open was one more minute they had of winning this damn thing. Her smile only last a second or so before she saw the reaction of the Poveen. It was swift.

The ER gate around Luna Nubia also sparked to life. The remnants of the original Poveen assault force on Nubia and Kush blinked around the moon and they fired down on the base and gate without regard for losses. The force that was in the deep black that had not moved since they entered system now burned hard toward Carthage accelerating on a profile that they had never seen from a Poveen cruisers. The force from Atlanta was also on the way toward Carthage. The Poveen knew the battle just changed.

A small probe burst through the ER gate into the system. It was the first object to enter the system since the beginning of the conflict. Once the ER gate reached 12 meters in diameter the S7 missiles poured into the system one after another with only a meter or two separating them. Each missile dove for the mega Earth planet of Carthage. They would stay in high orbit until needed. The first communication link was established with the probe and Hannibal Battle Station and the force on the other side.

"Vice Commander Kahn, this is Galaxy Commander Sanchez of the 7th Galaxy. I understand you have an alien problem," said the angular purple faced man who clearly shared the same linage as Quasar Rodriguez.

"I do sir. We have some on the station too, would you be so kind and help us with that problem? So as soon as you can we need some support or this nice gate will close. An alien fleet is about an hour away and squids crawl all over the station. Get comets on this station as soon as you can. They have snaked through the station and it is on the verge of collapse. I don't care what protocols you must break. Protect this station or this system dies," said Kahn.

"Will do. Help is on the way. Stay tight we are going to purge this infection," said the Galaxy Commander as the line closed. Kahn nodded as the SAA pointed at the movement of the Poveen forces on the station. All attacks on other sections of the station stopped. The entire force moved toward the ER Gate and gate command. Some units moved along the outer hull and inside of the station toward the gate. The Poveen needed to shut down the gate and the humans needed to keep the gate open.

The commander of the Comet Corps on the station turned to Kahn in his stoic manner and told her he had to leave. The man placed the armored helmet on his head. His forces needed to move to defend all the new avenues of approach but without support they would not last a long time. The SAA walked to the door with all the security officers on the bridge. Those men and women were prepping the final defense of the embattled station. Kahn spent the last couple of hours focused on the gate and she didn't focus as much on the movements of the enemy. That was coordinated by the ranking member of the Comet Corps.

The missiles coming into the system stopped to be replaced thirty seconds later with assault craft. Comet Corps starfighters burned into the system with dropstars packed into the formations. The smaller dropstars entered the system engines first and once they cleared the gate they fired the engines and burned toward the station. The starfighters, interceptstars, and starpuppets, on the other hand, performed hi g maneuvers and began to strafe the enemy forces on the hull of the station.

Shards that pierced the station in the previous battle extracted from the hull and engaged the assault craft. For the first time in the combat human fighters and Poveen fighters engaged in small craft warfare. The starfighters and interceptstars broke to engage the Poveen fighters while the starpuppets quickly moved to protect the dropstars. Once again station defenses were left to stop the approach of the enemy Poveen but with every second more and more spacescraft poured through the ER Gate.

Half an hour later the gate was large enough to accommodate the Space Command, Meteor Corps, Astro Corps, and Comet Corps starfrigates, starvettes, and starbombers. The force was growing in scope and capability and was starting to overwhelm the smaller fighter craft. The heavier weapons of the starfrigates started to turn the tide of the local battle but if they didn't get heavier starships threw the gate then the force that raced toward them would destroy the station and the gate.

Kahn did the best she could to monitor the battle on Nubia. By all accounts it was not going well. The alien force pounded the shielding of the moon, attacked Ogun Station, and made a push on the ground. War was war but this was something else. Kahn felt like the galaxy was tearing itself apart. Why did the Poveen do this she thought to herself. The two races had disagreements but nothing like this before.

A ping on her HUD indicated that Lord Commander Masters wanted to speak. She quickly accepted the call. "Vice Commander Kahn it doesn't appear that we are going to be able to hold the ESHU ER gate on Luna Nubia. We are about to lose the moon and possibly Ogun station as well.

The combined fire power of the enemy is just too great without larger craft. We have stopped spacecraft from the 6th Galaxy from entering. To do so now would be a death sentence. They will continue to launch S7 missiles through until the gate is destroyed. The enemy is taking a beating but it will only be a matter of minutes before they breach the shield.

I must go. They landed troops here on Ogun station. I must go help with local defense. Attack patterns indicate they are coming for command and control. I may be out of contact. The remaining force of larger starships are currently jumping to the system the 7th is in. They will follow along side of the 7th. Be prepared to receive both. Keep holding, keep fighting, win the day. I believe in your leadership and so does everyone else. You are a fine soldier and officer. And Priyanka, hold the fucking line," said Masters with a smirk on his face. Kahn sucked her teeth into a smile.

"We will hold the line. My family owes a debt to this system. When no one would take in my grandparents the kind people of the Nubian system did. I plan to repay this system in full for that commitment," she said as the line closed. It was all up to her now. She then pinged Galaxy Commander Sanchez.

"I need you to hurry up and get some of the heavy's through. I know it is tight but the Poveen will be in the area soon and we need to be ready. Also, when Nubia Luna falls I have sinking feeling that a lot of those cruisers will redirect here. Prepare your commanders and your forces for a fight," said Kahn. Quasar Sanchez agreed and the channel closed.

For a moment it appeared as if the starships stopped coming through the gate. Kahn was puzzled until she looked at the visual sensors. Large darkspots appeared to move against the star field in the background. Stealthstars poured into the system. For the better part of five minutes the stealthstars came through the ER gate as the Poveen force was about to reach maximum blink range. 103 Poveen Cruisers blinked close to Carthage. In fifteen minutes at the current speed they would be in firing range. All the weapon systems of the station toggled to aim at the approaching force.

Suddenly a flash on the station she monitored caught her attention. The shields failed on Luna Nubia. The ER gate was destroyed. The battlestations around the moon and the military moon bases were also under fire. Time was running out on the system. The 120 steathstars under Quasar Sanchez's command were now in the system and taking up positions to strike the Poveen force that closed in on the ER Gate.

Kahn smiled broadly when the first Astro Corps sheildstars entered the system. The sheildstar, was usually the breach starship of the entire force. It was outfitted with shielding equivalent to ten times the strength of a normal starship of that size. These craft used the same hull construction as the dreadstar but were fitted with only shielding, interdictor weapons, jamming technology, and other countermeasures. One after another the space craft entered the system, moved from the approach lane, and then broke at full stop to overlap shielding with the station and the gate.

The station roared to life firing all the energy and projectile weapon systems that could be brought online at the Poveen Cruisers who approached at speed toward the station. Poveen Cruisers returned fire on the station from all the cruisers. Human assault craft that just finished destroying the last of the shards prepared to assault the Poveen cruisers that moved in on the location.

15 wolf packs of 8 steatlhstars moved in to intercept the force. The first volley of missiles from the stealthstars hit the Poveen cruisers same time. Ten Poveen Cruisers were hit by 24 stealth missiles destroying each of them. It wasn't until the second volley of 240 missiles slammed into another 10 cruisers did the Poveen react. Two massive blasts of graviton shock waves rippled from the cruisers as they changed targets from the station to the newly discovered steathstars. The gravity returns from the ripple provided the Poveen with a targeting solution. They fired on the weakly defensed stealthstars as the third volley of missiles heading towards the cruisers.

Another 6 cruisers exploded from the impact. Now discovered, the wolfpacks vectored apart from each other to make it hard for the Poveen force. Hannibal battlestation fired its guns to add to the soup of war that now grew around the station. By now the station unloaded energy and kinetic weapons at the Poveen cruisers whose formation changed dramatically when the fifty dreadstars entered the system. They came through the gate at speed and banked hard to flank the enemy force. The battle cluster of frigates from the various branches moved away from the station and started a missile attack to relieve the stealthstar who vectored away from the fray to regroup. Kahn smiled on the deck of gate control. Human forces rallied and were executing against the Poveen force. Every minute the human forces grew closer to space superiority around Carthage.

In an instant 224 Poveen cruisers blinked from Nubia to within 1 AU from Carthage at maximum speed toward Carthage. At the current speed they would reach Carthage in little under thirty minutes. Kahn hoped that the ER Gate would be large enough to accommodate the warstars and gunstars but it was unlikely as she looked at projections that it would be large enough for starcarriers and battlenovas. Kahn watched as more and more starfrigates poured through the gate followed by dreadstars and now starcruisers. Kahn could not remember in her life a time when she saw so many starfrigates in such a small area.

The steady stream of human starship began to fill up the space around the Hannibal space station. Comet Corps dropstars and soldiers landed on the station reinforcing the garrison while the puppets burned around the station picking off Poveen units on the surface of the station trying to destroy the gates. Astro Corps units took up positions around the station with the massive shieldstars and reinforced its ability to repel the arching energy of the Poveen Cruisers. Within that protective shell starfrigates and starcrusiers from the Astro corps launched long range volleys at the oncoming alien cruisers. Space command constellations poured through the gate forming larger forming clusters, super clusters, and battle clusters.

Kahn smiled wildly when the first Battlenova burst through the gate. The massive starship only had two to three inches of clearance when it charged through the ER Gate. I guess they didn't want to be late for the party. Kahn looked at the name of the starship and quickly understood why they would take that chance. The captain of the ship was from Nubia. She came from a strong and powerful linage. Her name was Samia Masters and she was the daughter of Lord Commander Masters.

The nightmare was coming to an end in space but on the station the nightmare approached gate command. Though the Comet Corps soldiers landed on the station to reinforce the garrison they found heavy resistance and boob ytraps on the way to reinforce the garrison. The Poveen ambushed them at every turn to slow the advance. Kahn wondered if by some chance of dumb luck they destroyed all of the Poveen craft that carried nuclear devices onto the station. 10 or 11 well placed devices could have crippled the station from the inside. 2 or 3 anti-matter bombs could also do the same but until now they didn't detonate any.

One after another the klaxons sounded to warn the soldiers and officers in the ER gate command room that the enemy was close. A blast door slammed shut behind the standard door to ER gate command. Kahn moved to the dragon armor she placed along the wall and jumped inside of it.

Kahn attempted to contact the both the SAA and the original Comet Corps commander but she didn't get a response. The internal sensors were partially down and they were only being provided information when a locked door was breached. Her helmet shut and she yelled for everyone to prepare themselves to repel borders. The officers on the bridge pulled out the side arms and readied the drones. The first blast hit the large door that protected the control center. Kahn walked forward in the power matte black dragon armor with her hand cannon pointed at the door in the middle of the room.

The rest of the officers took up positions behind her at their consoles waiting for the attack. Kahn quickly contacted Galaxy Commander Sanchez and informed him of the situation.

"Galaxy Commander Sanchez. The enemy is at the gate. Where the fuck is my support?" yelled Kahn.

"One of my best, Colonel Solomon Kincaid of the 115th Hailey's Helldivers, are on the way. ETA is five minutes. They are my best and they will make it," said the Galaxy Commander.

"Okay, tell them to hurry up. It's me and bunch of techs which means it is just me," said Kahn.

"Understood, I will light a fire under their asses," said Sanchez as Kahn dropped the line when the door turned from red to white under the heat of the Poveen weapons on the other side.

The station AI told Kahn that the door will give out in less 5 minutes. I am not dying today she thought to herself. Two explosions rocked the deck but they didn't originate from the direction of the large door. They erupted from the floor and ceiling. Kahn turned as tentacles reached up through the holes in the ceiling and the hole on the floor. They reached and grabbed the soldiers at the rear of the room and the least armed. Officers screamed and called for help in the small space. Panic spread in the room like a virus.

Kahn turned and ran toward the hole in the floor at fired down on the drones. They exploded on impact from her weapon. Two drones burst from under the remains of the falling comrades from the hole in the floor. She fired on those drones through the debris and smoke hitting both and killing them too. The damaged machines floated into the back wall. An arched energy blast hit her suit from the side. Kahn flew into the wall as her HUD erupted with blinking warning lights and other negative news from the armor. Before she could regain her awareness of her surroundings the suit moved her arm and fired at the drone that fired on her.

It continued to fire until she woke up and overrode the armor with her thoughts. One by one the officers in the room were killed by the drones that continued to pour into the room. Unlike Kahn, the officers on the deck couldn't absorb an energy blast. One by one the officers were struck and burned alive. She lay against the wall firing until she ran out of ammo for the hand cannon. She raised her arm and fired the energy weapon inside her gauntlet until she ran out of power. More and more drones entered the room. They moved toward her powerless and dead armor. Tentacles reached out to the chest armor pulling it hard. A drone picked up and lifted her armor and scanned it. Kahn hit the back escape and set the self-destruction device.

She held onto the back of the armor as it exploded outward like a claymore mine. The explosion tossed her body while it shredded the two drones in front of her and created a cloud of debris and smoke. The concussion from the blast knocked Kahn unconscious. The station AI took control of her suit and guided it into a panel on the floor and then sealed it. When the next round of drones entered the room the AI set off the thermite in the consoles and took control of the gates. The ER Gate would stay open and the enemy would not have any chance of taking the station controls from this location.

Kahn awoke shortly after the explosion inside the box. Drones circled above her scanning everything. They opened wall panels and connected to the systems of the station. Kahn moved but pain ran up her body. Two of the drones she could see started to fire energy weapons in the other direction. Kahn tried to stay awake but the pain and the concussion forced her unconscious.

PLUS 190 HOURS
ASTRO CORPS QUASAR
NATASHA MIGHT
HANNIBAL BATTLE STATION, CARTHAGE
THANK YOU

Quasar Natasha Might sat in the comically small chair asleep. The two-meter-tall woman somehow curled into a ball and fell asleep. The officer's medical bay contained two high ranking officers that were injured in the battle for Hannibal Battle Station. Might waited for her friend and commander Vice Commander Kahn to wake up from her injuries. The room was white and bright with the feel of over sterility.

Vice Commander Kahn awoke foggy in the medical bay. Her caramel eyelids opened slowly due to the light. Once she fought the light she looked around the all-white room. Machines hovered and worked on an officer next to her. When she turned her head to the left she saw Quasar Natasha Might. The giant redhead was folded in the chair like a pretzel sleeping. Kahn tried to gather her voice but her throat was too dry. She reached to the right-hand side of the bed and picked up the cup of water that was sitting on the white end table and drank it before she tried to speak again.

"Natasha…Natasha…wake the fuck up," Kahn said. The woman didn't budge so Kahn tossed the rest of the water on her. Natasha jumped from her seat as the cold water smacked her in the face. Kahn laughed at her.

"What was that for?" asked Might.

"I thought you liked that kind of stuff Natasha," joked Kahn.

"You know me so well Priyanka. I arrived at the station about two hours ago. You had a pretty bad concussion, neck injury, broken ribs, shoulder was dislocated, and some other minor things. They put you down for a couple of hours to heal. I heard the squids almost got you?"

"That is funny because I thought you were dead. When I saw you I thought I was dead too."

"They almost got me but they didn't," said Might as she flexed both her arms.

"Where are we?"

"You are on Hannibal Battle Station. The 7th and the 8th galaxies pushed the squids back. The battle lasted for about 4 hours or so. Little Masters led 9 battlenovas on a warpath of destruction. Did you hear. Masters lost his wife, son, and daughter in the fighting. Now Captain Samia Masters is trying to destroy everything in this system. She is just like her father. Right now the 8th is following what is left of the Poveen to Nubia. The 7th is protecting Carthage. The 3rd Galaxy is coming into the system right now. Oh yeah, and the 1st and 2nd Sci-Tech Galaxies are moving on Kush as we speak. The Poveen are in full retreat in the system.

The doctor says you should be okay in about an hour or so. The nanites are putting your little brown ass back together. We are still trying to figure out how you survived. You should be dead right now. Shit, I should be dead right now. Oh, don't think about trying to work or check any updates Masters put us both on leave for another 12 hours and blocked our access to the computer system to force us to stay on leave.

Check your fucking messages, I am tired of your fancy pants daughter sending me damn messages every hour. She is almost as annoying as you are. With this much time on our hands I say we Cinco Sierra this station," said Natasha Might as she stood from the chair stretching to her full 6 foot 6-inch height. Kahn smiled slightly and rolled her head as she tried to laugh at the officer but a pain in her ribs let her know that some things were still under repair.

The dark blue Comet Corps Colonel on the bed next to her turned over and spoke, "It is good to hear your voice. I thought I failed my mission."

Kahn turned to her right. A massive human being about the size of Sub Commander Rodgers lay on the bed. His blue skin and bulky frame highlighted his linage. The blue skin and bulky frame was the augmentation of the Atlas system. The same system her now dead friend, Morris Solis, was from.

"Who are you?" asked Kahn.

"He was the one that saved your brown ass from the squids. He dove on the body and took like three or four bolts to the ass. He should come with us on our Cinco Sierra run. I mean you owe him right?" asked Might.

"What is Cinco Sierra," asked the Kincaid.

"Shit, Shower, Shots, Sex, Sleep. In that order," joked Kahn in a raspy voice.

"The Meteor Corps started it. After combat or a tough situation is over they all used to yell Cinco Sierra. If you go into the head you would hear people yelling Sierra. When in the shower everyone would yell Sierra Sierra. When you were out you said Sierra, Sierra, Sierra at the bar. If you wanted sex with someone you said Sierra, Sierra, Sierra, Sierra and if they said all 4 back then you have sex. After sex, you say all 5 sierras as a cue for the other person to leave. If you said it 4 times then you are requested to stay and if they respond with 4 then they stay, if they respond with 5 then they are going to leave. The system allows for ease of communication," explained Might. Kincaid laughed as the man laughed hard to find out he also had injuries that also needed so work.

"What if you wanted to have sex before shots or shower?"

"For one you are nasty. Shower first you dirty blueberry. Follow the rules. But I guess you stand in the shower, take the shots, and then have sex. Why do you ask?" said Kahn.

"Well vice-commander, to be honest with you, I am a Comet. I have 10 hours before I have to report to duty again. This is not the end of the conflict but the beginning. There are a lot of Poveen cruisers floating around in this system that I know they will want us to take control of. If people are going to be drinking and fucking well I am going to need to know how to get to the fucking," joked the man.

"Oh, so you think it is that easy huh? You just walk up with your dark blue skin and all the woman fawn over you. Not going to happen," said Might.

"I am Comet Colonel Solomon Kincaid. I destroyed 145 drones and killed 3 Poveen assault soldiers on my way to rescue your ass. In 45 minutes these nanites will be finished repairing this wonderfully sculpted body. I am going to stand up and walk into that bathroom to take shit and then shower. Then I am going to walk back into this room ass naked and sit on this bed while I enjoy a couple of shots.

One of three things are going to happen. Either the tall redhead is going to get it, you are going to get it, or both of you are going to get. Your choice," said Kincaid with extreme confidence.

"I think they may have given you a hallucinogen or too many pain killers," said Kahn as Might laughed in the background.

"I like this one. We need to get him on the team," joked Might.

"You are a little old for my taste," said Kahn.

"You are a little too old for my taste too but I am willing to overlook it this time," joked the man. Might walked over to Kincaid and gave him a high five for being awesome. Next, she walked out the room because she had a mission to find some alcohol. This section of the station wasn't affected by the conflict. You would have thought nothing happened. She walked down the hallway out of the officer's section of the hospital ward and everything changed. Bodies of dead soldiers, officers, Poveen, and drones were ushered around the station to morgues and research facilities.

Human drones raced around the station. Might dodged the drones and the officers that darted around the station. Repairs have begun in full to the damaged areas of the station if the section could not self-repair. Some heavily damaged sections of the station have already been repaired and the structural damage from the gravity attack has been corrected. In ten hours or so the station will be fully repaired. Battle stations like this one were built to take a beating and keep going.

Quasar Might had become a hero of sorts around the station. The story about the mission that they performed in the deep black spread around the station. Might was stopped constantly as she walked around the station. This made her journey to find a bottle of alcohol tiresome. Finally, after an hour she returned to the hospital room. When Might entered the room both officers weren't in the beds. It seemed that the nanites and augments worked. Might could hear the shower in the bathroom.

Might entered the bathroom with the bottle in one hand and three shot glasses in the other hand. It seems that these two don't like to follow the rules. Grunts and moans of pleasure emanated from the shower. Might could barely see the small frame of Kahn behind the mountain of the blue man. Might marveled at the shredded back and firm muscular butt of the man. Might could only see Kahn's feet and legs as they tried to wrap around the waste of the Comet Corps Colonel.

Instead of making a joke or a scene Might walked back into the main room and poured three shots of the Nubian rum. For a second she debated whether to join in but she decided to let Kahn thank Kincaid for saving her. She went down the row and drank all three shots and then filled them up again. Might triggered one of her playlists in her CU and listened to the music as she waited. A song came on that triggered memories of the fallen soldiers.

She suddenly remembered the hallway shortly after the klaxon sounded. She remembered joking and carrying on with all the wonderful people. Quasar Johnson, Quasar Tanaka, Quasar Rodriguez, General Solis, General Okafor, and Sub Commander Amir were all dead. General Nasir and Lord Commander Masters were locked in the battle for Nubia with legions of Poveen. Sub Commander Rodgers and A1D7 were MIA and presumed dead. Lord Commander Masters lost his wife and two of his children. "What the hell just happened?" she thought. Some of her best friends were gone or missing.

The gravity of the conflict consumed her. Tears started to run from her eyes to the floor. She wiped them quickly and took another shot. With speed, they returned to her face but this time she didn't bother to wipe. All she could remember were the good times she had with those soldiers. The door opened and the two lust birds walked out of the bathroom to a crying Might. Kahn was startled and then she felt kind of ashamed.

"Um, Might, I am sorry we didn't wait for you. It was taking long and then he jumped in the shower and um," said Kahn.

"It's not that. Just thinking about the team. Not many of us left you know. Sorry, I don't mean to be the one that stops the fun. I could use a little fun right now. Get my mind off this stuff," she said as she stood from the chair and wiped her tears. She reached for the 3 full shots and passed them to the other officers.

"To Sub Commander Yosef Amir," said Kahn. The three of them drank.

"To Quasar Ryu Tanaka," said Might as she raised another shot for the trio to drink. The toast to the fallen went on for about 45 minutes. With most of the bottle gone the trio went to find a place to unwind. Some of the restaurants and bars had reopened shortly after the conflict ended. A lot soldiers would be recovering from the conflict and no doubt the station had an entire contingent at different phases of the Cinco Sierra. The trio was bent on finding that celebration because each one of them escaped death not too long ago.

Nine hours later Kahn awoke in her quarters. The officers' quarters level was spared from the damage on the station. She rolled over from her back to her right side pulling up the light grey blanket to her shoulder to cover her previous exposed naked body. She fought off the effects of the alcohol to piece together the events of the last nine hours. The nanites would remove the final traces of alcohol from her system shortly but she would have to drink water to get rid of the headache and brush her teeth to get the dead mouse from her mouth.

Kahn snuggled her head into the pillow while she bit her upper lip in remembrance of Comet Corps Colonel Solomon Kincaid. So, he was right. First, they had sex in the shower. Than in the bathroom of the bar called "Drink Hole" and lastly in her quarters. Well she really didn't do too much that time she mostly watched Solomon prove to Natasha Might that he could handle them both. Kahn wished she could give him a medal for his performance post conflict to match the accolades that he is going to receive for his bravery in combat.

Might's skinny pale freckled arm reached over her caramel skin. Her warm body rolled over and rubbed up against Kahn's back. She reached her long legs over Kahn to reach for the floor to slide over Kahn but remained under the covers to exit the bed. The tall angular perky low gravity built body walked over to her clothing with her tone freckled butt toward Kahn. Quickly she stepped into the body suit and closed it while turned to smile at

Kahn.

"That was awesome. I needed that. I heard stories about you but I didn't believe them. Usually you have that stick firmly up your ass. The next time Rodriguez and I... well…oh shit," said Might as tried to take back the comment. Kahn saw the pain Might was going through and stood from the bed and walked over to her and gave her a hug.

"Quasar Rodriguez was tough. That is one of the most stubborn women I have ever met. It was highlighted during this conflict. She disobeyed my orders and freelanced to the point of insubordination. I even spoke to Lord Commander about removing her from command because she thought commands were suggestions. That woman has fire in her stomach," said Kahn as Might perked up by the response.

"I imagine it must have been so hard for you to find out that Rodriguez was executing the real mission when you didn't know about it. I wonder how she convinced the captains of the starships to listen to her over listening to your commands," said Might as Kahn pushed back from the hug to look at the face of might as she moved back with her large brown eyes.

"What are you talking about? What was the real mission?"

"Did you not look at your messages?"

"What messages?"

"Shit Fuck Kahn. I thought you looked at it already and that was the reason why you drank so much. Masters was correct. He told me you were one of the most stubborn people in this system and he was not lying. Okay, since you won't check your own damn messages, this is what happened," said Might as she explained to Kahn what happened. With every minute and action that was taken Kahn went limper and limper until she was the one crying and squeezing.

It wasn't Rodriguez that got the people killed it was her. Kahn was the reason why some of the people died in those actions. If she could have coordinated better with Masters they would have provided a better defense. Was she wasn't contacted before Okafor died? Would she have made a different decision if that was not the case? She second and third guest herself for the next thirty minutes. All while being held by Quasar Might in the middle of her quarters.

Kahn accessed unread messages one by one from General Okafor, Quasar Rodriguez, and Lord Commander Masters. He apologized for his actions and hoped she would respond when she watched the videos. Kahn quickly understood. She scanned her memory of the previous week to find that everyone hinted that she check her military account, send messages, and contact loved ones but she was too busy to do that. It also creeped her out because she felt that doing so would be a signal that she was going to die.

"Natasha, I need you to leave. I don't need your pity any longer. That is why you are here right? That is why you spent the night right?"

"No, that is not the reason. Masters told me to keep an eye on you and to tell you what happened if you did not already know. The truth is that I was afraid of what I would do. On the way to the station, after we made the last asshole blink, we burned to this station. I lost Tanaka and Amir and the bulk of my force. I got low. Why was I alive when so many people died from my orders. I sat in the bathroom of the small craft and I put my sidearm in my mouth. In the silence of space with only thoughts in hand I walked myself down a path to kill myself. Why should I survive when I sent so many others to die I thought?

I left the bathroom then I sat on the cold floor of the ready room for two hours crying and sobbing before I finally pulled the gun out of my mouth. I was afraid yesterday that if I was left on my own I would finish the job I started on that stealthstar. I needed you last night. I needed your strength," said Might without one shred of sarcasm, sexual innuendo, or bravado. Kahn looked at the officer she served with for the better part of seven years and knew this was truth. If Kahn felt anything like Might she would need companionship soon. That was the reason Comet Corps Kincaid hung around too. Kahn remembered him talking about his soldiers that were decimated to rescue her. They traded all those lives for her life.

"Okay, here is the deal. You don't let me out of your sight and I don't let you out of my sight until we both feel that we are good. Agreed?" asked Kahn.

"Agreed. How could I let this nice brown ass out of my sight," said Might as she cupped Kahn's but with her long arms. Apparently, Natasha Might was only capable of completing a couple of sentences before she reverted to her braggadocios self. Kahn laughed slightly even though she hated the fact that she did and that was the reason why they needed each other now. Might needed someone to joke to and Kahn needed the jokes. Well for the moment Kahn thought.

They agreed to get something to eat and then go to the command deck to watch the assault on Kush by the SciTech forces. The Purge of the Nubian system was underway.

PLUS 200 HOURS
COMMAND CORPS SUB COMMANDER
MIKE RODGERS
SMALL FARM, KUSH
THE LAST STAND

Sub Commander Rodgers was 1 kilometer from the coordinates and hopefully his fiancée. It had been hours since he saw another human alive. The journey to the location was fraught with danger and destruction. Poveen patrols continuously flew overhead and on the ground other nightmares roamed. Ash fell like snow. It blanketed the terrain a muted grey with only patches of color exposed by the wind only to quickly be covered again. Thick clouds of smoke muted the sunlight. Plant life on the agricultural world fought to hang on to life but Rodgers knew that most of the plant and wildlife on the planet would not make it. The planet's average temperature already fell 3 Celsius since the planet entered combat.

He wanted to radio ahead but only line of sight communications would work now. The easily detectable radio signal would more than likely bring death and destruction from above. Rodgers had to remain patient. The flat terrain made it easy for him see and for his passive sensors to operate at a long distance. The mix of low light, distant fires, and silence created a death scape worthy of any science fiction holo-movie. Lighting from the highly-charged clouds struck the ground at regular intervals.

Rodgers hoped this wasn't the fate on Nubia. When the cities fell all the lines of communication fell as well. At that time the senior staff were all locked in mortal combat with the Poveen forces and unfortunately it didn't seem that anyone was winning the conflict they engaged in. Rodgers had faith though. About 4 hours ago a flurry of communications from starfights, starbombers, and starpuppets. They were assault craft from Luna Nubia. It was unclear where they came from or what the mission was but for a while the patrols ended and the Poveen seemed to be occupied.

Rodgers approached the farm house his fiancée was sent to defend. He could tell that the house was once white and yellow but now the grey ash now muted the once vibrate paint. Snow like drifts of ash built up along the sides of the home. Rodgers approached with his head slightly above the wheat crops scanning the area. The house looked empty but they would want it to if they were in it.

An hour prior he arrived at a home and was greeted by a massacre. It appeared that the family and the soldiers guarding it were torn apart by some sort of animal. The Poveen are known to have a large and vicious arsenal of bio-weapons that even in normal conditions can evade detection. No doubt these beasts roamed the country side now. Rodgers had only seen evidence of the them but he knew they would be around. The vicious bio weapons of war they use to terrorize civilizations. They are known to lie and wait for targets and then attack. He hoped he wouldn't walk into the house and see the same outcome.

Ten meters from the home he heard a scream. "Chaos." It was the prompt word of the armed forces to identify friend or foe. "Magic," yelled Rodgers. Two soldiers stood from the wheat with hand cannons pointed at him. They dressed in ranger field gear. The RK - 7 poncho was a combat wrap that protected the user from small arms fire. It also provided protection from heat, light, sound, and microwave detection.

The lack of light, the black hood, and black mask worn made the soldiers made them look like shadows. One solider was directly in front of him about ten meters out with a powerful hand cannon. To his left another soldier stood at about the same distance with another hand cannon pointed at him. The fact that the cannons still pointed at him gave him pause. Were the people and soldiers of the planet engaged in theft of resources? They also would not be able to identify his rank or person because his transponder was shut off and would stay off until he knew it didn't gave away his position.

"Settle down soldiers," he said as he eyes flashed to the right and left between the two soldiers that advanced on him with the hand cannons pointed at him. His dragon armor kit would be hard to recognize under the poncho. Maybe they were just as suspicious of him.

"Identify and get out of the armor sir. Sorry for the precaution but the last unit to come in was piloted by a Poveen imposter. We lost one person because of it. We must be sure. It's not personal," said the female soldier that approached. Rodgers lowered his gun. At this point it didn't matter. They had the jump on him and if they wanted to fire they would breach his armor before he could return fire.

"Will do. I just need one of you to remove your mask so I can identify. If I can do that I will get out so you can too. Agreed?" negotiated Rodgers.

The soldier in front of him looked to the other soldier and shrugged while the other soldier shrugged back. The soldier in front pulled up her mask while keeping the hand cannon pointed at him. Rodgers would know those blue eyes anywhere. Even in the darkness the blond hair and strong facial features stood out.

"Jamie. Jamie Juelz," said Rodgers as the armor opened and the large man ran out. Rodgers ran over and hugged her violently and picked her feet off the ground. It felt so good to see her. A familiar face was always welcomed. The fact that she was still alive and made it brought him so much joy. He was then violently tackled to ground by the other soldier.

She took off her mask as well. There she was. Her orange face and blue eyes peered down on him. She made it. She was here. His Laura. The two kissed for what seemed like an eternity. It was no longer about commanding armies and planetary leadership. The mission now was to keep themselves alive. For about 30 seconds they embraced and hugged. Jamie regained composure first and peaked her head above the wheat as she put on her mask once more.

Rodgers looked up as a third soldier stared down on them with his sniper rifle in hand. "Wow, I feel better I only grazed you now. I take it you all know each other. You may want to patch that up," said the tall soldier. Rodgers looked at his left shoulder as blood ran down from the top of his shoulder blade. In the excitement, no one heard the shot.

"All I saw was someone jump out of the armor and run at you. The only reason why the bullet didn't end up in his skull was because Laura said her fiancée was coming here at some time. I aimed to wound. If I aimed to kill he would be dead," said the man.

Laura mumbled, "and so would you". The man shrugged his shoulders but in the back of his mind he didn't think so. He was a professional scout sniper trained to shoot and kill xeno-terriost animals. The planet was constantly under attack by viscous animals unleashed by rival corporations and alien races.

Laura Oban and Jamie Juelz met him three hours ago outside of the farm with one of his partners. The group of four partnered up. The other sniper was killed when they encountered the Poveen human impostor. When they reached the farm, they found a family hiding inside the house. For protection Oban and Juelz moved the family to the barn at the rear of the home. Oban and Juelz placed the dragon armor units in sentry mode with one at the front of the barn and the other in the back of the barn.

Rodgers understood why. His armor only had seven percent energy. The bulk of the energy of the armor was used supported the human inside. With him inside he had about eight hours of use but once he stepped out of the armor it could last for two or three weeks. When they reached the front of the barn he left the armor and they activated sentry mode. From the compartment on the back, he took the survival pace from the machine. He had two of the RK – 07 Ponchos, flak jacket, three blankets, rations, combat dagger, and the Dragon Spit hand cannon with 100 mini dragon breath rounds.

The wooden barn was 20 meters deep and 15 meters wide. The empty stables were along the left side of the barn while work benches, wood stacks, and equipment were on the right side. The team moved the mattresses from inside the house into an alcove they created with the equipment and wood. Over the top of the encampment they hung the extra ponchos to cover the 4 members of the family inside the barn. This would shield them from overhead detection.

The mother and father huddled in the corner with one small bag of clothing and personal effects. Two boys, one 10, and other 13, watched a holo device of one their favorite movies. The father had a rifle slung over his back clearly ready to do what he could to defend his family if need be. A ladder on both sides led to the second floor. The second floor was only a walk way that ringed the edges of the barn close to the roof line. The beauty of this feature was the windows that faced in every direction on the second floor. Outside the barn the sentry mode armor moved 50 meters from the barn in three directions creating a triangle. They had complete 360-degree vision of all the angles of approach. On the ground floor, they had doors on every wall which meant that they could get in or out in any direction. That was the reason why he didn't detect any of them on approach.

Rodgers was exhausted from the trip and found the soldier's bunk separated by two wood piles from the family's bunk. The man collapsed on the mattress and passed out shortly after he entered the space. He woke up four hours later spooning his fiancé. Oban snuggled into his embrace as he slept. He dreamed of this moment for the last couple of hours and now it was finally upon him. Rodgers heard a noise and he moved his head to see the origin. When he turned, he saw the 13-year-old boy. His large brown eyes peered through his long dreadlocks coated in dust.

"I heard you are the Sub Commander of the system. They said it was your job to protect the planet. Is this all your fault? Did you fail?"

Rodgers stood from the mattress and looked down on the boy who held his ground to the mighty man standing in front of him. The people of Kush were some of the most serious people in human sphere and even the Kush children seemed to have the steel that was common among the people. "I was in charge when the planet when it was attack. We fought. We lost. Now we fight some more. Until we are all dead we did not lose. Every minute we stay on this planet our chances increase for victory," said Rodgers as he walked into the center of the barn.

Rodgers looked up to see the sniper looking out one direction of the second-floor window and Juelz looking out the adjacent window. The father of the two kids walked around the second floor looking out the two other windows at five minute intervals. This clearly was the rotation for the moment.

"My dad says that if you fail you should take responsibility for it. It is only a failure if you don't learn for it he says. What do you say?"

"I say he is right. Listen to that man."

"One more question. How did you all get so big? I have never seen anyone as big as you."

"Grow up on a low gravity planet. The lower gravity lets you grow taller. Then get pumped full of augments to fill yourself out. That's how the three of us are this tall. Though I think I would still would have been a tall guy in high gravity. Just not this tall," said Rodgers to the kid.

Rodgers looked toward the mother holding the other son as he leaned against her. The boy had the 1000-yard stare. He didn't even seem to look at Rodgers but he looked through him. It was chilling to Rodgers. He saw that face on too many soldiers too many times. Hopefully that kid was young enough to push these memories out of his mind before he reached adult hood. Either way he was going to need mental help after the war was over. If he was still alive Rodgers thought.

The last report he received on Poveen deployments on Kush before everything went dark was that the Poveen forces started to line up along the equator. One force moved north and another force moved south to counter the guerilla strategy. The strategy was a sound one for the Poveen but it would give Rodgers and the group of soldiers the edge in the small arms combat they would engage in.

A whistle from the second floor alerted him to danger. The sniper, pointed toward the south and the same direction he came from. Rodgers hoped that he wasn't followed to the location. Rodgers leaned down to Oban and woke her from her sleep. She quickly stood and readied her weapon. The father slid down the ladder to the ground floor as his family went into their zone of the protection under the hanging ponchos. The makeshift poncho tent secured the family from detection.

The mother wore a poncho with the 10-year-old tucked under her. The 13-year-old sat next to his mother and the father protected the group with his rifle. Rodgers moved to the front of the barn to the smaller door and looked out the window at the approaching group of Poveen soldiers. He received an information feed from the passive detection system on the armor kits outside. 7 Poveen soldiers moved to the location.

The suit of armor on the opposite side of barn from the enemy approach the barn and opened the door autonomously. It walked to the middle of the barn and stopped. Jamie Juelz jumped from the second floor to the ground and moved toward the armor without breaking stride. She quickly shed her poncho and dropped her hand cannon and got inside of the machine. Once again Jamie Juelz became E2D7 and walked toward the front of the barn. Rodgers moved to the east side of the barn toward the door.

Oban moved down the center of the barn and picked up the hand cannon and handed it to the father. The father then passed the rifle to his 13-year old son. She smiled and told them that she had to go outside now.

Oban gave them a smile to hide her fear and moved to the door behind the make shift shelter for the family. She readied her weapon and looked at the others.

The Poveen soldiers wore a layer of protective gear and armor. The Poveen evolved from an octopus like creature. It had an extremely large head body combination. It hunched over with its eyes and other sensory organs facing forward. Protruding from the top of the body cavity were two layers of long tentacles. At the end of each tentacle were a diamond shape claw that opened and closed like a flower with three digits.

Smaller t-rex like arms were under the body of the Poveen. Those smaller arms possessed seven fingers each with two thumbs and five digits. These arms performed the tasks that needed high motor skills and dexterity. Two powerful articulated legs pushed the mass forward. Each Poveen stood almost three meters in height. Thicker white armor protected the vital areas while a black exo-suit covered the rest of the body. They moved toward the house and the distant barn.

The Poveen moved in a long line about 15 meters apart. They crossed the road toward the house holding white spheres with a golden circle on the sphere that pointed forward. This was the primary weapon of the Poveen soldiers. It fired the same arched energy that all Poveen weapon systems fired. Unlike the large weapons systems on cruisers and in armor the energy in these weapons came from batteries.

The plan was to fire on the commanding officer and then move on the targets that remained. Rodgers and Oban would open the side doors and run down the side of the building toward the Poveen positions and then break for their armor. Juelz, E2D7, would open the front door and fire on the enemy positions causing them to scatter and take position while the sniper on the second floor would engage at will. They needed to hit the enemy fast and hard to even up the numbers. If they didn't the fight would not last very long.

Jamie Juelz kicked opened the door and fired onto the commanding officer of the Poveen. Poveen shields sparked to life but when the fire from

Jamie Juelz, Laura Oban, and Sub Commander Rodgers hit the enemy it was too much for the one soldier to handle and it was ripped apart. Rodgers and Oban emptied the magazine and broke for their dragon armor kits 50 meters to the east and west respectfully while they reloaded the hand cannons. The dormant armor sparked to life and fired on unsuspecting Poveen troops as the attack commenced.

They only enjoyed the upper hand for a couple of seconds before the enemy responded in kind. During that time, they killed the commanding officer and the soldier to his right but the other five moved quickly. The sphere weapons sparked to life and the arched energy weapon rippled at Juelz from three of the aliens. Her armor sparked and sizzled and then fell backward to the ground. Another beam of energy arched into the second-floor barn window. The wood exploded and sparked inside of the barn. The sniper fell from the second floor burned. His lifeless body hit the ground.

Oban fired on the enemy Poveen as the aliens raced to the house for cover. But it wasn't cover. That house was rigged to explode. Smaller homes on this planet are powered with the methane produced by the livestock. They rigged explosive devices on the massive methane containers in the house and then lined the outer wall with all the metal to create a claymore. Oban ordered her suit to turn toward her for cover. The armor moved at speed and once it reached her she detonated the home. Shrapnel flew in all directions and into the sky.

Rodgers ran toward his armor when the house exploded. He dove to the ground and took a quick look as the pieces of the house fall to the ground like snow. An arching energy beam hit his armor now only ten meters away. Three more bolts struck the armor and it slumped forward and stopped firing. Rodgers tried to look above the wheat at the enemy but he lost track of some of the soldiers. Fire from Jamie Juelz poured down on the Poveen around him. Rodgers stood and unloaded his hand cannon at the closet Poveen soldier. It fell to the ground dead.

Rodgers took a quick look at Oban's position and he didn't see her or her armor. He hoped she was okay but he didn't have time to wonder. He lost track of some of the Poveen soldiers. He ran back to the barn to regroup. Jamie Juelz slowly walked to Oban's position. When she arrived at Oban's position she was on the ground not moving. Her armor was out of energy. Low energy lights flashed inside of Jamie Juelz's armor. She popped open the of the armor and placed in back into sentry mode. Juelz picked up Oban's hand cannon and then grabbed the back of her uniform and pulled her through the wheat to the barn. Like Rodgers she had no idea how many of the Poveen were still alive and active. They needed to regroup at the barn.

Rodgers reached the barn first and he entered the door that he left a couple of seconds ago. Once inside the east entrance he heard a Poveen breaking through the rear of the barn. He fired on the Poveen as it entered. It fired the rippled energy beam toward him. Rodgers dove across the barn to save himself only to realize he landed way to close to hidden family. He jumped back into the line of fire to ensure an errant shot didn't hit the family as he fired the hand cannon. The father burst from under cover and fired the other hand cannon at the Poveen killing it.

The side of the barn exploded open and a tentacle reached into the barn and grabbed the father and yanked him out of the barn. The Alien tossed him with one motion. The man landed ten meters away to a chorus of broken bones. He didn't have the augmentations that the soldiers had to protect him from such violent impacts. Rodgers ran at the Poveen and jumped through the hole it made in the barn. He fired his hand cannon without mercy. Rodgers hit the armor of the beast and fell to the ground.

The two longer lower tentacles grabbed him and tossed him just like it had the father. The Poveen, this time, underestimated him. Rodgers righted himself in air and fired down on the Poveen from behind with the hand cannon. Juelz entered the fight with Oban's recovered hand cannon from the south of the barn as she exploded from the wheat. The Poveen turned to Jamie Juelz and fired the energy weapon. She screamed in pain as the energy struck her flesh and lifted her body off the ground into the wheat.

Rodgers landed ten meters from Poveen. He fired on the exposed alien with the cannon. It listed for a second and then fell to the ground. That was the last Poveen soldier. Rodgers moved to the father for assistance. The man had a dislocated shoulder and a broken collarbone. Rodgers pumped him full of medical nanites. They would numb the pain as Rodgers set the fracture. The bots would do the rest. In a couple of hours, he would be able move without pain and in a week or so it would be fully healed. Rodgers lifted the man and moved back to the barn.

When he got close he looked over to the location that Jamie Juelz should be. The high wheat made it hard to see from a distance but he got close he saw Laura Oban holding Jamie Juelz. Oban cried as she held her friend. Juelz was burned from head to toe. Her lifeless body fell to the floor. Rodgers paused as the two locked eyes. Juelz sacrificed herself to draw fire from Rodgers. He walked into the barn and placed the man on the ground without saying a spoken word.

Rodgers bounded up to the second floor and looked out each window to see if any other Poveen heard the noise and came running. He saw nothing but he knew that would not last long. That engagement cost them two soldiers and all three pieces of armor. If a similar force returned they would not be able to survive.

The first sonic boom startled him but the second and third made a trend. Rodgers scanned the sky of Poveen aircraft but he didn't see any yet. The low cloud cover and smoke prevented that. They must have called in the location to the rest of the Poveen in the area. Rodgers looked down at Laura Oban and pointed to the south so that she would look in that direction. Rodgers ran around the second floor to look to the north. At first, he had a hard time understanding what he saw but it was confirmed when his connection to a broader network began to flicker. He jumped down from the second level and walked out the back of barn to the south and looked upward. The design of the starfighters and starvettes were unfamiliar but they were human.

Rodgers looked to the east and to the west to see craft of all sorts flying south. The network flickered for about a minute. The network on the planet was reconnecting. Someone was in orbit. A cheek to cheek smiled was interrupted by a scream. Rodgers turned with his hand cannon pointed to the south at the source of the scream. The 13-year-old jumped up and down as he looked out the hole the Poveen made. Distant explosions popped on the horizon.

The mother stood up from the corner and walked to the celebrating child. Confused she asked what was happening and they told her to come look. The father also walked over to the door injured from the conflict but the sight of relief brought a smile to his face.

The connection finally pinged him. He connected to the new network. It was a Sci-tech network. Rodgers smiled and looked at Laura Oban whose network also came on. After 30 seconds of authentication it routed quickly through the UPHAF network. Suddenly he was pinged.

"Sub Commander Rodgers! Rodgers are you still alive. I knew you would still be alive you're a salty bastard. Somebody will be to you shortly to pick you up," yelled Masters.

"I never thought I would be so happy to hear your voice sir. What is the situation?"

"We have two gates open. Three galaxies have entered the system. The enemy is on the run."

"Great. How is everyone?"

"Vice Commander Kahn, Quasar Might, and General Nasir are still with us. Um…I tried to ping Laura. Is she still with us?" asked Masters. Rodgers noticed he told him who was with them and not who was lost. He processed that information.

"Yes, she is currently grieving. We just had a visit from seven Poveen soldiers. Took some hits but we won the engagement. One of those hits was Jamie Juelz. Tough loss. How is Nubia?" asked Rodgers.

"It is still sporty over here. We are not out of the woods yet. Get to safety Mike and I will see you back here soon when we finally exterminate this vermin problem we have," said Masters as the communication ended. Rodgers turned to the rest of the people in the barn and told them that a transport was on the way and that it would arrive in 5 minutes.

He moved to his fiancée and sat behind her as she held Jamie Juelz. He hugged her from behind and said to her, "we are going home. We are going home babe," and kissed her on the back of her neck.

PLUS 6 MONTHS
COMMAND CORPS LORD COMMANDER MALCOM MASTERS
OGUN STATION, NUBIA
DEBRIEF

Lord Commander Masters stood in his massive panoramic office that overlooked the repairs of Ogun Station. The man's perfect posture matched the perfectly groomed black dress uniform. Over the last couple of months he basically lived in the office. It was hard for him to go home and spend time in the apartment that once brought him so much joy. The man lost a wife, son, and daughter during the conflict. He knew that one day he would get over the loss or just find strength to move on but he hadn't reached that point yet. Time is the only things that can repair wounds like these.

Numerous people lost friends and family during the conflict and if you didn't you should consider yourself extremely lucky. So many of his officers fought bravely during the conflict to come home to find that they lost an entire family. The rate of suicide exploded after the Poveen were forced out of the system 72 days after they entered it. The rate slowed over the past month when they implemented new programs for the soldiers and civilians to help deal with the pain of the loss. With that said, the rate of the reenlistment of the system armed forces is at a record high. The people of the Nubian system are willing and able to protect the system that they call home.

A white coffee cup contrasted his chocolate skin as he sipped the warm coffee. Today was the first time the entire command staff that survived returned to the planet Nubia. Masters paced in the office ready to say his prepared remarks. The system remained on high alert. Though the conflict was over in this system it still raged in other systems. As of now, the Nubian system is the only system to have reopened ER gates since the attack.

In the Grant system, the planet of Grant Prime is still under the control of humans, but the rest of the system is in Poveen hands. The Siberian system has fallen but on multiple planets in the system a resistance fights the Poveen and conducts regular check ins. The Poveen forces in the system suffered massive losses and as of to date have not received any reinforcements. The UPHAF have not received any communication from the Indo System in three months and two months in the Sichuan System respectfully. Those systems are considered a total loss.

Many on Nubia feel that this conflict is over but Master knew the truth. This conflict has just begun. Humanity will not stand by while two systems destroyed and two systems have been taken. Masters couldn't believe the response from the rest of the human sphere. All the damaged battle stations have been repaired and the destroyed battle stations above Nubia have been replaced by donated space stations from other systems. Drones, repair bots, artificial human workers, and construction have been donated by over 2000 companies in the human sphere and has helped with the cleanup of the planet Nubia and Kush.

The SciTech government has taken it upon themselves to help rebuild the planetary logistical ring around Kush as a sign of cooperation. Almost 60% of the ring is operating at the levels before the attack and they feel that the entire ring system will be completed in less than 2 years. The machines once used to terraform Kush are almost finished removing the debris from the atmosphere and they are hopeful to begin planting again in about two months.

Atlanta took the most damage and lost almost its entire population. Mining has returned to both Peachtree and Buckhead. The old cities are a total loss and new ones are being built in new locations. A new galaxy class ER gate orbits Buckhead. Construction of a military base had also commenced on the moon of Kirkwood to ensure that Atlanta could defend itself it the Poveen return to the system.

Carthage is the only planetary system that has almost returned to normal. The population of Carthage suffered very little civilian deaths. The moon base on Hannibal took token damage. The massive Hannibal Battle Station has been fully repaired. Once again, the Barca Staryards is under construction. The production facilities on the moon Hamilcar wasn't damaged at all so the reconstruction of the base has moved along quickly. All eight construction births were donated by various staryards across the human sphere while two more births were under construction. All the materials are being fueled by the mining and enrichment facilities on Buckhead and Peachtree.

Masters sipped the freshly brewed coffee once again and looked out onto over the station and nodded his head. The army, his army, stood in defiance of an alien invasion and won. That was the second time he bested the Poveen and the United Planets of Humanity had taken notice. That was the reason why he called the meeting. He needed to speak with his command staff in person about the future of the system and the officer's careers.

The door to his office pinged and he turned from the window and faced the door. He commanded it to open. In walked the soldiers that remained of his command staff. They walked into the room and formed a line in the room and saluted him. He put down his mug and saluted them back. The man fought tears when he saw the faces of the people that had sacrificed everything for the good of the Nubian system. To fight tearing up he smiled wildly from cheek to cheek. The officers who also were trying to hold composure smiled wildly as well.

"I am so happy to see you all. I mean it, from the bottom of my heart, I am excited and happy to see all of you. I brought you back to Nubia today to discuss the future. Not only did you all need a break from the activities that consumed your day to day for last couple months, I felt that it was good for all of us to see each other in the flesh and bone. We have been through something together. We will never forget what happened in this system. In many respects, we are now defined by it. We stand as the beacon of human defiance against the alien races of the spiral arm.

The first thing I wanted to tell you is that I am staying in the United Planets of Humanity Armed Forces. I will remain on the planet for another three months or so but I am no longer the Lord Commander of this system. I have been promoted to Legion Commander. My new mission is classified but it deals with killing Poveen and sending them back to the swamps they came from. During my recruitment to this role, I made sure that all of you would land safely, in fact, my reenlistment demanded it. I would like to introduce the newly promoted Nubian System Lord Commander Priyanka Kahn," said Masters as the room erupted in celebration. Kahn's blushed cheeks could be seen through her caramel skin. The circles on her lapel suddenly adjusted to fit her rank with a black dot in the middle of the circle.

"System Astro Corps Quasar Natasha Might, though your vulgarity and personality has no equal, the UPHAF has decided to offer you a position in the Command Corps. If you accept the offer you must leave the system in the three days to begin with the next class. I can guarantee that if you join that class you can come back Nubia after the 24 months and serve as a Sub Commander under Kahn or join me in my new assignment. Your third option is to stay a simple System Astro Quasar yelling Sierra five times every chance you get," the room burst into laughter at the statement. Surprised that Master would make a joke Might laughed the hardest of all of them.

"I accept the offer under one condition. You will join us in celebration tonight as we yell Sierra, Sierra, Sierra, Sierra, Sierra," demanded Might. Masters smiled and shook his head in agreement not quite knowing what he just committed himself too. The next officer was the mighty Sub Commander Mike Rodgers.

"Sub Commander Rodgers the UPHAF has granted you the ability to leave the service early. That is after you finish your commitment as the new Vice Commander of the Nubian system. The over one hundred years of service forced them to grant you the life that you deserve to have. If you can wait 18 months you can retire at that benefit level with your years of service. You will not have to work again in this lifetime.

You are now reassigned back to Nubia," explained Masters as he shook his hand. Rodgers smiled from ear to ear. Rodgers worried that they would not grant him the early retirement since the conflict begun. He can now start planning his future with his fiancée.

"Laura Oban. Formerly known as A1D7. You have made my life a living hell. Not only did you break rules you did so with a senior officer. You are unfit to continue service in the Dragon Corps. You are now discharged from the service effectively immediately with a full honorable discharge. You will be given the full rights and privileges of a citizen of the Nubian System. You are now free to live your life in the pursuit of happiness. You are now free to marry Rodgers. He is all yours," joked Masters.

The relief in the face of Laura Oban was contagious. She turned to her fiancée and hugged him on the side and stood on her tippy toes to kiss him on the cheek. Rodgers blushed and pointed at Masters. Oban had to fight to control her emotions. For the first time in life she was free from war and conflict. That phase of her life was over. She could now be a woman, a wife, and hopefully a mother. Though it would be five years before her reproductive parts began to function.

"System General Nasir, we wanted to grant you a battlefield promotion to Sub Commander, but when I told them of your plans to run for System President that changed everything. The UPHAF will grant you an authorized leave of absence when you file your papers to run for president. If you win they will grant you an honorable discharge. I look forward to the day you become the President of this great system. You are a good man and I hope that when that day happens you and Lord Commander Kahn will get along," laughed Masters. Nasir smiled and shook his hand.

"Let's also not forget those on the command team that didn't make it. I have reached out to the families, those who still have families, to pay my respects. I think it would be wise if all of you did the same thing if you have not already. It is hard. Extremely hard for those of us that have lost but I need you to do it for the sake of the families and to honor the memories of those who fell in the service of the United Planets of Humanity Armed Forces. Let us not forget Sub Commander Amir, System General Solis, System Quasar Tanaka, System General Okafor, System Quasar Rodriguez and System Quasar Johnson. They all will be missed. Every one of them.

So now I believe we have a celebration or something. What is this Cinco Sierra shit that has spread across Carthage, Kush, and Nubia?" asked Masters. The now Command Corps Candidate Might went on to explain. Masters stood with a stone face as she explained the details and wondered if it was now possible to get out of his promise. He wasn't in the mood for that type of fun. It has been less than six months since his wife, daughter, and son were killed by the Poveen. Yet, it felt like yesterday to him. .

With chants and cheers they looked at Masters until he gave into the chant once and the team celebrated. His submission ensured that the team would have one more night together. Might than invited everyone to Masters apartment in Titun Legos in four hours to start celebration. This is what he needed to return to the world of the living. Layla took all her clothing and personal effects before trying to flee the planet. It was a wasteland of emotions but he needed to move on and this may help him. He agreed and the group cheered again. Once again Might lead Cinco Sierra chant.

Masters instructed all of them to leave so he could finish packing up the office. This would be his last day in the office and the next day it would be transferred to Kahn. The officers walked out of the room but the new Lord Commander stayed. Masters didn't know she stayed at first for he turned to look out the massive window once again. When he saw her reflection in the window he spoke.

"What is it Lord Commander?" asked Masters.

"Sir, I would like to apologize to you for…what happened…with the messages. If I wasn't so stubborn you would have been able to coordinate a better attack. I think I could have been of better service. I just don't know if this is the right choice. Surely there are people that have more experience," asked Kahn.

"There are more people with more experience but to be honest only a couple of humans have more experience fighting the Poveen than you. You fought them in space and on a station. You will do fine. I said the same thing to my commander when I was promoted. It is the normal reaction. Sleep on it. You will feel better in the morning. You are one fine officer Kahn. You have a bright future and I will keep an eye on your career with interest. With all serious, I need you to keep an eye on me tonight. I have only been back to that apartment once since the invasion. I have staying away for a reason. I think it is time to go back. You told me before you left for Carthage that if I ever needed someone to talk to or a shoulder to cry on you would be there for me. I think I may need you today. Would you go to the apartment with me before the others arrive?" asked Masters.

"Anything you need Malcom," said Kahn with a large smile on her face.

"The one thing this conflict has taught me is that life is short. You must live each day like it is your last because it might be. You must value friendships. You must trust those around you. Come one. Let's get out of here and relax a little."

"Sure. Hey, is it true that you and Might are dating. I thought you liked the young men?"

"Who told you that? Rumors, all rumors," responded Kahn as they joked in the room.

PLUS 2 YEARS AND 4 MONTHS
COMMAND CORPS LEGION COMMANDER MALCOM MASTERS
WAR STATION CALICO, VICTORY SYSTEM
FIGHT WITH ME

Masters sat in his office reviewing the latest updates and the construction of his 1st Special Operations Galaxy code named "Dark Spear". His small white office was a byproduct of the space restriction of space station life. The wall behind him projected a view of the planet below. His desk was made from Nubian Bamboo as an homage to his home planet. Masters sipped Nubian coffee from his cup. The flavors of hazelnut and chocolate colored his nostrils with. The mission was progressing just how he anticipated that it would.

The door pinged and Masters stopped work and closed the file. He leaned back in the white and bamboo chair and called for the officer to come in. The six-foot six-inch Sub-Commander Natasha Might walked into the room. The black uniform of the Command Corps fit snugly on her frame. Might gained more muscle mass since the last time he saw her and it was a byproduct of command level training. Fire red hair, deep blue eyes, and pale skin was the hallmark of Might. The newly minted Sub Commander saluted.

"Sub Commander Might, please sit down, we have a lot to discuss. How was the Academy?" asked Masters. He conducted small talk before that got to the real reason why she was in the office? Masters followed her progress and was interested in hearing her perspective on her experience.

"It was hard. I had a lot of growing up and learning to do. My commanders didn't like my personality the way you did. This one angry bastard almost kicked me out the program but I adjusted. In the end, I finished in the top ten of the class. Number one in battle simulation though. We all know that is where I shine," said Might.

"So are you going to join my unit, go back to Nubia, or have you found another mission you would like to pursue," asked Masters.

"Sir, you could have asked me that over holo. Why am I here? Why did you call me in? Did you just use this as an excuse to see my stunning beauty?" asked Might as she smirked. Master leaned back with a smile on his face. He folded his hands in front of him while placing his elbows on the desk.

"I see they haven't taken all the life out of you yet. I could not answer your questions over holo. But in here I can. In this secure facility, I can talk to you directly and answer directly without worry. I can't tell you the time or date but I can tell you the mission. If you would like to know more?" said Masters.

"When did you become the man of mystery? I know that in the Nubian System we will just sit in Ogun Station waiting for an invasion that may or may not come. I did that already. But you may get me killed do something stupid. I kind of like stupid. Tell me what you can?" said Might. Master smiled slightly as he realized that Might didn't lose all her snark yet.

"We have a plan to free the systems under squid control. We also have a plan to hurt those that hurt us. We are done being the doormat of the galaxy," said Masters.

Might leaned back in the chair with her hand on her chin. She attempted to speak twice before the words finally left her mouth.

"Sir, are we going to war?"

"We are already at war," said Masters. That response sent a chill down her back. The language he that he used was too deliberate.

"If I do not sign up for your mission, what are the chances I still fight Poveen in the future?"

"I can't say. But if you join my taskforce you will be at the forefront of what is to happen. Something will happen. You will either be running around a station yelling sierra all day or you will be on one of the greatest missions of human history. I need your type of crazy on this one," said Masters.

"I don't know if that was a compliment or if you just made fun of me Commander. You have always been fair to me and I owe you for that. You take my quips and quirks. Kahn told me you stuck your neck out to get me into the Command Corps when others wouldn't have accepted me. If you need me on this mission then I will go on the mission. I owe you that much," said Might.

"You don't owe me anything. It was the right thing to do. You are a great soldier with a special personality. I need to make sure you are doing this for the right reason. You will put your life on the line on this mission. We all will."

"I am in."

"Good you start in the morning."

"Great, now where can I get a good drink around here?"

"The entertainment deck has a couple of good options," said Masters. After roughly a minute of silence he looked up and Sub Commander Might who continued to sit in the chair. "Can I help you with something Sub

Commander?"

"What, you didn't think you were coming to? I don't start until the morning. Which means we can a drink tonight without you having a stick in your ass," said Might. She then made a very serious face and mimicked Masters, "Look at me. I am Legion Commander Masters the commanding officer. I cannot hang out with my officers. I cannot have any fun at all."

"I don't sound like that do I?"

"Sometimes. Come on. I didn't ask you to do cinco sierra. I just asked to join me in a beverage."

"Okay, Okay. Don't beg. Give me 15 minutes. Wait in the lobby."

ABOUT THE AUTHOR

M.Q. Abdullah grew up in Barnegat, New Jersey, at the Jersey Shore. He is the graduated from the University of Illinois for his undergraduate degree and the Pennsylvania State University Smeal School of Business for his graduate School degree. He currently lives in Morristown, New Jersey, with his wife and son.

Made in the USA
Middletown, DE
29 May 2017